THE LIFE OF RILEY

───•◆•───

BY

S. L. GAPE

*To Sarah & Nic,
I hope you enjoy reading & see some trendies, similarities & resemblances. So, you know this was the only copy I received. PRIVILEDGED! ☺ Take care love [illegible]*

Copyright © S. L. Gape 2016
This book is sold subject to the condition that it shall not, by way of trade or otherwise, be lent, resold, hired out, or otherwise circulated without the publisher's prior consent in any form of binding or cover other than that in which it is published and without a similar condition including this condition being imposed on the subsequent publisher.
The moral right of S. L. Gape has been asserted.
ISBN-13: 978-1523644537
ISBN-10: 1523644532

I would like to dedicate this book to Maureen, Margaret, and my Nan for being truly inspirational women in my life and wish they were still here to see this achievement.

This is a work of fiction. Names, characters, businesses, organizations, places, events and incidents either are the product of the author's imagination or are used fictitiously. Any resemblance to actual persons, living or dead, events, or locales is entirely coincidental.

CONTENTS

PART ONE 1

Chapter 1 .... *1*
Chapter 2 .... *9*
Chapter 3 .... *18*
Chapter 4 .... *24*
Chapter 5 .... *31*
Chapter 6 .... *39*
Chapter 7 .... *49*
Chapter 8 .... *59*
Chapter 9 .... *65*
Chapter 10 .... *71*
Chapter 11 .... *86*
Chapter 12 .... *98*
Chapter 13 .... *100*
Chapter 14 .... *110*
Chapter 15 .... *131*

PART TWO 138

Chapter 16 .... *138*
Chapter 17 .... *143*
Chapter 18 .... *146*
Chapter 19 .... *154*
Chapter 20 .... *159*
Chapter 21 .... *161*
Chapter 22 .... *164*
Chapter 23 .... *172*
Chapter 24 .... *178*
Chapter 25 .... *185*
Chapter 26 .... *197*

Chapter 27 .... *205*
Chapter 28 .... *210*
Chapter 29 .... *223*
Chapter 30 .... *228*
Chapter 31 .... *230*
Chapter 32 .... *237*
Chapter 33 .... *244*

PART THREE 246

Chapter 34 .... *246*
Chapter 35 .... *248*
Chapter 36 .... *252*
Chapter 37 .... *257*
Chapter 38 .... *266*
Chapter 39 .... *269*
Chapter 40 .... *274*
Chapter 41 .... *280*
Chapter 42 .... *284*
Chapter 43 .... *289*
Chapter 44 .... *292*
Chapter 45 .... *297*
Chapter 46 .... *301*
Chapter 47 .... *306*
Chapter 48 .... *310*
Chapter 49 .... *317*
Chapter 50 .... *325*
Chapter 51 .... *332*
Chapter 52 .... *337*
Chapter 53 .... *342*
Chapter 54 .... *347*
Chapter 55 .... *351*
Chapter 56 .... *354*
Chapter 57 .... *361*

Chapter 58 .... *365*
Chapter 59 .... *367*
Chapter 60 .... *371*
Chapter 61 .... *374*
Chapter 62 .... *377*
Chapter 63 .... *382*
Chapter 64 .... *385*
Chapter 65 .... *387*
Chapter 66 .... *390*
Chapter 67 .... *393*
Epilogue *397*

ACKNOWLEDGMENTS

I must thank first and foremost my family and friends for their help and support throughout this very surreal process; particularly Lisa Leigh, Jane and Ashleigh for being 'go-to proof readers'.

Lastly and by no means least a massive thank you to Jen, who I'm pretty sure was by no means disappointed to have regular 'hall passes' whilst I stayed at home writing, but thank you for being there to support me even if all I even got was 'That's really good babe!'

PART ONE

Chapter 1

Ba beh ba bom, ba beh ba bom put 'em high, push it high ba beh ba bomb ba beh ba bom put 'em high, and push it high...

"Arghhhhhhhh," Riley growled as she grabbed for her phone to knock her alarm off. She turned onto her side and threw her arm over her cover, drawing it closer into her until the realisation hit. "Shit." Her eyes flew open. "It's today!"

Riley pulled herself up into a sitting position as she focussed her mind; she could feel the tension mounting already. "Deep breaths, Ri, deep breaths." She reached over to her bedside table and took out the letter, reading it for the 360th time.

Riley had spent as long as she could remember wanting to work overseas. She had been on plenty of holidays, each time she was due to leave an additional part of her was chipping away; she didn't know what it was that captivated her but there was something there. Her parents said from the age of five she would repeatedly tell them that she wanted to 'work on holiday' – that's where her aspirations appeared to lie and today was the day that could potentially make these dreams come true.

Hightail Holidays were very well known and had different strands to the business; Riley didn't mind which area, just as long as she could achieve her goal of being a holiday rep.

"Riiiiiiiiiii-leeeeeeeccyyyyyyyy, are you up yet love?"

"Geez, Mum," Riley sighed. She rushed to her door, treading on the hard bristles of the brush she'd left on the floor. "Shit." *Bang.* "Ouch!"

"I keep telling you if you keep your room clean, you won't fall over on a daily basis, crash, bank and wallop. It's like a scene from a comic book every morning!" her mum shouted up the stairs.

Riley stood at the top of the stairs with her hands on her hips, salivating over the smell of the fresh bacon and coffee aromas coming from the kitchen and the frying pan in her mother's hands. "Mum, firstly, I'm twenty-four. You are aware of this, right?"

"Of course love, a little thing called thirty-seven hours of labour, darling," her mother said with a wink.

Riley smirked and said, "Secondly, you seriously need to realise I am not Adam, I do not have my music on loud enough for the street to hear, therefore, you do not need to scream like I am going deaf."

"It's your big day darling, this is what you have dreamed of for twenty years, and you have a long journey so I wanted you to eat before leaving."

"I'm fine, Mum. I don't need to eat." Riley

regretted the decision instantly as the smell caught in her nostrils again; her tummy growled and her mum began chuckling as she wandered off into the kitchen, humming along to the radio.

Riley checked herself in the mirror one last time. Whilst she mostly wore her hair down she pulled her long black locks into a tight high ponytail; she knew that the uniform requirements entailed hair up. She'd done her research, so she wanted to make sure that whilst she was only attending an interview, she looked the part. She rarely wore makeup, so was happy to complete her look with some mascara to her long, dark eyelashes and some light pink lip gloss covered her lips. Riley brushed down her skirt one last time and was happy she had found a jade green button-down blouse to finish her suit. Knowing this was the colour of the uniform with Hightail she was impressed it worked well with her olive skin and complimented her green eyes.

She smiled slightly and sighed. "Now or never I guess," she said into the mirror as she grabbed her bag and left her room.

As Riley reached the kitchen her mum handed her a large mug of coffee and placed a plate of bacon and toast in her hand. With a quick kiss to her cheek, she rushed back over to whatever she was doing. "Thanks, Mum," Riley said as she walked over to the dining table, and placed everything in her hands on the table. She pushed down the paper below her father's head, meeting his eyes. "Hey Pops." She smiled at him.

Her family had always been close but she was a total daddy's girl, not in a bratty way but there was just a bond between them, she enjoyed going golfing with him and to the pub and as a kid they'd spend their time just doing crossword puzzles together in the conservatory. Riley wasn't afraid to admit that whilst this was her dream she would miss her family like hell, and that scared her. She shook the thoughts away, saying the words 'positive, positive, positive' repeatedly in her head.

"Hey Princess," her dad said. "How's the nerves? Hope you're going to show them headline people what us Sharpes are made of, nobody's going to be a better rep than my daughter." Her father was her number one fan, as he said with the biggest grin on his face before lifting his paper once more and continuing to read.

"Dad, how many times? It's Hightail Holidays, not headline."

"Hmm, yeah of course," he grunted.

"Here's hoping," she mumbled before taking a couple of bites and returning the dishes to her mum with an apologetic smile.

Riley took one last breath, one last look in the entrance hall full-length mirror, and returned to the kitchen. "Here goes," she said, more to herself than her parents, before gathering the car keys and leaving.

"Good luck!" her parents shouted in unison as she left the house.

* * *

Riley had pre-bought her train ticket; as she rarely took the train anywhere she was unaware of the length of time parking the car, walking to the station and buying a ticket would take. But as always she was still early enough to watch the earlier train depart. She grabbed herself a coffee and picked up her phone. She scrolled through her texts. She smiled as she saw Cara's name. She clicked to open the last message and wrote, 'I feel sick' with a sick-looking smiley. She pressed send and immediately saw the grey dots appear to show Cara's immediate response. Riley smiled and waited patiently as in true Cara style, War and Peace would soon take over her screen.

'Don't be so daft, you soft ass git! You were made for this job and more importantly for getting me hot tanned Adonis's when I visit you. I'm reading the secret, it tells you to engage with the universe for what you want. I am sending my signals to the universe that I want you to have this job so I can get some hot ass tanned surfer.'

'C how many times I'm not going to Australia. Where has this surfer fetish come from?'

'I teach teenagers where do you think it's come from? I'm watching bloody Home and Away, god I need a life. FYI new head a bastard sure she is Mrs Trunchbull re-incarnated!!!'
She ended with a shocked smiley face.

Riley chuckled to herself, thinking if she got the job how much she would miss Cara and her over exaggerated behaviour. Once, at school, she had fell over playing rounders; before the final bell had even gone off her mum was there to pick her up and take her to hospital in a bid to save her only child from having to have her leg amputated. Needless to say her mum very nearly amputated it herself when she realised that Cara had nothing more than a scratch to her leg.

Riley replied, *'So teenagers now watch Matilda to I see ;)'*

'Piss off.'

'You love me really.'

'{sigh} I know I'll totes miss your sorry ass when you leave, don't go??? Correction, DO go just take me with you I'm only small.'

Riley laughed again before responding with, *'You know I would but, you would simply not cope with leaving teaching behind, as much as you say you hate it you secretly love it and just think 5 weeks of leave in summer to come visit. You could actually go out and shag someone without the fear that the next day it will be all over the school from the gossiping of living in the world's smallest town ;)'*

The dots again. *'This is why I love you, ever the optimist and this is true, you will have completely relinquished all best friend duties if you haven't set me up with at least one sexy Spaniard a week girly. Shit, bell, bleurgh, class, bleurgh, kids, double bleurgh!! Love you, good luck. Call me at lunch. Xxx'*

'Spaniard, what makes you think I'm going to Spain?'

'They all do at first.' Smiley face again.

Riley smiled at how much Cara pretended she hated school when in fact she was the same when they actually attended high school. Cara would act cool around the other kids, pretending to be a 'Hater' when in fact she would rush home to complete her homework just to ensure she could get into the best college and university to study teaching and follow in her parents' footsteps, then she wanted to come back home to teach. Riley had always been so jealous yet so proud of her love and ambition in her choice of career, and hoped that today would be a chance for her to discover what that felt like; whilst she liked numbers and was happy she followed her dad's route, it wasn't her. She wasn't passionate the same way Cara was. In simple terms Riley had only managed to have half of the 'Love/Hate' relationship with her accountancy career and that was entirely the latter.

Riley wasn't unhappy with her life, until her accountancy degree had given her a 'back up' and of course stopped her parents worrying that she was going to disappear off overseas at eighteen and end up claiming benefits instead of having a career like they'd had. She'd been very lucky and in her final year was picked for a graduate programme in Manchester City Centre; it was slightly further afield but was doable. For the last two and a bit years she had worked hard alongside the Finance Director before the company went into liquidation last year and she decided it was now or never. She figured she wouldn't get another chance to be a rep and was very lucky in that she had the exposure and degree behind her for when she wanted to return.

The train finally arrived and Riley boarded; she found her seat, removed her suit jacket, and retrieved all items from her bag that she required to keep her busy for the next couple of hours. Riley placed the buds in her ears and put on her rock playlist; she looked over her cue cards again, and thought about her presentation. She'd done it more than 100 times and sat back, considering thoughtfully the day ahead. She shook her head in a bid to shake away the thoughts, she had trained her mind to not think about it, as in typical Riley style she had a tendency to overthink everything and that would just cock it all up, she was sure. She picked up her Kindle and started to read her book instead.

Riley sighed as she realised she'd read the same line over and over. She placed her Kindle back down on the pulled-out table and looked around, giggling once more as she eyed the 'Candy Crush domination'.

With a growl and a dirty look from the elderly gentleman sat next to her from, *god forbid,* laughing in the quiet section, she was once again drawn to the variety of people playing that bloody game. She suspiciously eyed the kids, parents, grandparents, suits, builders; she was stunned at the realisation that it wasn't only her parents who were addicted to it.

Chapter 2

As the train pulled into London, Riley grabbed her belongings and shuffled off, being herded around Euston station with all the commuters. As she finally found her way outside, she shivered, and was glad of the choice of tights this morning. Riley made her way to the cab and gave him the address of the head office.

As Riley pulled up she was in instant awe of the head office building, being brought back to reality when the cab driver did a low whistle, saying, "That's a bloody good bit of architecture there, love," in an accent fitting for a member of the EastEnders cast.

"Hmm hmm," was all she managed. She threw the money, mumbling to keep the change and stepped out of the cab, unable to look away from the building. "You have a good day, love. Miserable bloody northerners," tutted the cab driver as he pulled away.

Riley walked through the revolving doors and advised the receptionist that she was here to attend an interview with Hightail, issuing the smiley blonde girl with her letter.

"Please take a seat, Miss Sharpe. Georgina will be down shortly to collect you, good luck for today." She smiled politely, showing off teeth that were clearly something out of a Colgate advert.

Riley smiled back, saying, "Thanks," and did as she was told.

Ten minutes later Riley was met by Georgina, who introduced herself as head of recruitment; she insisted on being called George, and told Riley all about her experience as a rep which had now landed her in this job. George was really likeable and could see that she would easily be able to calm the nerves of the many participants of today's group interview. The letter had stated there were to be fifteen interviewees and with each stage of the day a break would happen and anyone who wasn't successful in the previous stage would be sent home. Riley recalled reading it and remembered the fear, thinking how harsh it was and how devastated she would feel if that happened. *STOP. Positive, positive, positive*, she once again reminded herself over and over in her head, so as not to lose the plot at this stage.

The bell dinged at the 9th floor, as George led her into an open-plan room with three sets of tables and five chairs around each. There were two long tables with four seats at the front. Riley smiled as she saw the front tables lined up with jugs of water and four individually placed Hightail glasses – it was like American Idol only without the famous people and blurred advertising.

* * *

As the next half an hour passed more people were being escorted into the room and each of them were having conversations of how excited they were, how desperate they wanted to get away, the clichéd 'my boyfriend ran off with my best friend so I want to run away to another country' sagas. It was surreal to just be here and as the last person, a boy of about eighteen with matching diamond studs, perfectly preened and not a hair out of place, with a three-piece suit on, entered the room and sat down, it hit her – this was it. Everyone went silent as the collective realisation registered to each of them.

* * *

Shortly after, George arrived back in the room with another girl, Kate, and two guys, Paul and Jeff. Each person was either a manager overseas or worked in the recruitment department, and all formed part of the interviewing panel. They confirmed the content of the day, stating it would be an introduction to each other with one secret and one funny story about yourself; then a break, an English test followed by a break, a math test followed by a break, an 'ice breaker', lunch, and then the afternoon would be filled with the presentation you had to prepare for, a break, and then the results of the day.

Riley was suddenly feeling as though she was about to have a panic attack at any given moment and was slowly trying to calm herself when she looked up at a good-looking guy sat across from her, who gave her a shy, knowing half-smile.

Riley remembered thinking what beautiful blue eyes he had and couldn't help but smirk as she considered Cara's words if she was facing this 'toned god' in front of her.

The next hour passed quickly; there were stories of horror, disbelief, fear, fun, and sheer humiliation. She was grateful that the panel had decided to start with 'cute guy', who did in fact have a name, and Scott actually seemed genuinely nice and down to earth, with natural good looks and a sophistication that age brings, yet he was probably only around Riley's age. She had spent the break with him and he had been working with another company for the last four years, until he reached his goal of working in long haul and found his island manager girlfriend was sleeping with a Mexican guy behind his back. Scott wanted to remain overseas but it was too difficult being there, plus she sounded like a royal bitch to him when he found out, so he came home and applied to work for Hightail. Riley cautioned herself to not get involved with anyone overseas, she'd waited too long to do this and if she got the chance she wasn't going to risk jeopardising it. Of course she had made friends with reps and watched the TV shows so knew what they were all about, but no relationships!

After coming back from the break two people had gone. She didn't know their names and wondered if maybe that was part of the reason. The tests were issued to each individual with twenty minutes to undertake it; one person was removed to do it separately due to him having dyslexia, which he mentioned to us all, and therefore he was able to do it in a separate room with additional time. Once finished we were advised to go to the breakout area to wait for the tests to be marked. This would be the case for the math test immediately after, and then when they had spoken to the individuals, they would just go to lunch and to return at 1pm.

Riley had finished with a little time to spare, which in reality she had expected, being a math geek after all. She returned her paper, smiled politely, and then left the room quietly. She walked to the vending machine and got a Coke Zero out as she waited for someone to come out.

Over the next twenty minutes each of the eleven remaining people came out before they were split into three groups. Riley was told to go with Kate; she was disappointed that Scott wasn't in her group. It's interesting how shows like the X Factor take over normal working practices in these situations as it was apparent this was how they measured their interviewing styles; each break they had lost some more people and now it was looking as Scott or her were going to go too.

"Shit," Riley whispered as she took on board the fact that this may be it. Scott had worked overseas for a competitor for the last four years; he was good enough to even get long haul, so there is no way he wasn't going to get in. Riley suddenly felt subdued and disheartened but was soon taken out of it as Kate stood in front of the three people before her.

"So guys, how are we all feeling after the morning?" said Kate. There were some quiet mumblings between them all and she heard Kate start to laugh. "Ok, ok I'll put you out of your misery, guys. Congratulations, you are through to the final stage. DON'T get complacent though, seriously the presentation is the hardest part and it's all about the delivery. You need to remember that this is what you will be doing from anything from one to ten times per week, and from three people to 500 people, so BE prepared. You might be wondering why we leave this until the last part of the day considering it's so important to the role. Well, what you *will* find is that presentations, for those of you not used to them, are far more difficult and stressful when you are doing it in front of peers, so here at Hightail we like to make sure you have got to know each other, become friends, more so when you get 'tighter' with each break return and see more have disappeared." She stopped and smiled, letting it settle in so far. "So, given that in resort you will be presenting your welcome meetings in front of your colleagues, friends, and managers, we like to prepare you as much as possible in case you are successful. Understood?"

All three recruits nodded and Kate smiled once more, nodding to the door, showing that we were done and to go have lunch.

As Riley walked through the door to the breakout room for lunch, talking with the others, she looked up at the food area and saw Scott; he moved out of line and she rushed over to him. "Hey, you're here," she said excitedly.

"Yup, you too I see." He smiled and hugged her.

"You smell, hot boy." Riley hit his arm as she grabbed the tray and winked to him. "Save me a seat."

When the lunch was over and the remaining eight people went back into the room, they were all told about the next part, which was the presentation. Each of them was issued with the details prior to the interview and would each have ten minutes to discuss their favourite holiday, the highlights and lowlights.

Riley was the first to raise her hand when they were asked who wanted to present first out of the group. She had always been a firm believer that the longer you waited the more stress it caused, and for that reason she was always ready to get things over and done with.

Her presentation was on her holiday last year where she and Cara had spent two weeks in a gorgeous hotel in Cancun; much more importantly, they visited over spring break.

Cara was the absolute epitome of a child in Candy Land, as she spent days amongst American college kids 'hunked up to the max', in her own words, as she constantly questioned why the boys at school didn't look like that. We drank cocktails, jet skied the crystal clear waters, partied like we were on the streets of Ibiza, and pretty much had all the fun we could manage in the time there. Her presentation seemed to go down well, Scott nodding and laughing, obviously aware of exactly what she was talking about, having left there not so long ago.

By the end of her presentation, she had got a round of applause and was happy that she'd maintained eye contact throughout. Riley knew this was important from friends she'd spoken to over Facebook, who had highlighted it.

Everyone waited patiently, listening and laughing as the group all gave their various tales; they were all watching in amusement, how everyone sold their destinations, friends, tours, and comical stories. All in all, it was a fun afternoon. When Scott began his presentation, looking and smirking at Riley, she was thrilled when he began and was talking about Cancun, talking about when he worked there for a season as opposed to a holiday experience.

George called Riley back into a room an hour later.

"Hey, hey come on in, Riley," she said, gesturing for the girl to sit down.

"So, how do you think today went?" George asked.

Contemplating her response, she slowly answered, "Well, it's difficult to say I guess. I've loved it, met some cool people and stuff; but I guess the issue is you listen and speak to people who seem to fit perfectly and then return from lunch and they're gone! Sorry." She smiled shyly, thinking she was over-speaking.

George laughed and touched her arm. "Riley, you did great, we all loved you. We had a really great group today. Believe it or not when we do these so regularly we don't normally have this many people that go through on the day – we were really impressed and I genuinely feel you'll make a great rep. Hell, I'd have taken you on my team any day."

Riley was looking up at her questioningly; she apologised, embarrassed due to the fact she had missed what the girl was saying, whilst she was in a complete day dream. Riley, was stuck on the fact that George had told her 'we all loved you'. Her head was spinning. Looking back up to George's blue eyes, she asked, "So, does that mean I have the job?"

George laughed again. "Yes, Riley you have the job."

Hearing a scream, she was unsure what the sound was exactly, but she didn't really care at this point, jumping up and hugging George in a tight embrace, completely overjoyed by the news. "So what happens now?"

George confirmed that in the coming week, letters would be sent by way of confirmation on details of dates and hotel that would be the commencement of the training course. Following that, on the final day she would receive her destination details and would be flying out within the next forty-eight hours, most likely.

Riley was dumbfounded with all the information she was trying to register. "Riley, Riley," George said.

"Yeah, sorry," Riley said.

"So you need to be pretty much ready to go in the next two weeks, right?"

"Yeah, yup. Allllll ready, I'm ready, I can be ready, and nope, I'll be ready," she said with a dopey grin on her face.

Chapter 3

Riley didn't really remember much about the journey home, the screams of Cara when she was on the train, the night in the pub jumping up and down every ten minutes, and the tears as the realisation hit. In fact she didn't really remember a great deal about anything else over the last two weeks either. Now though, as she made her way down to Nottingham to a hotel for her first day of training, she was completely brought back to life. The last couple of weeks were a whirlwind; the company sent a letter as George said they would, followed by a call from the recruitment team advising that she could be flying as soon as that night, so she needed to make sure her season luggage was packed and ready to go from the moment she arrived home. *This is mental*, she thought. *How the hell has this happened?*

Riley checked herself in the mirror as she arrived and wiped her tired eyes. She hated long-distance drives, especially when so sleep deprived. She nodded knowingly at the realisation that she was never really going to have been able to sleep the night before training. Riley picked up her luggage, locked the door, and went on the hunt. She checked in and was given her room key. As she walked down the hall as she heard, "About bloody time, bird." She smiled, instantly recognising the voice. She turned around and was already in Scott's arms and kissing him on the cheek. "Hello gorgeous," he said. "We're two pints on you, what the hell's taken you so long?"

"Awesome, get me a bottle of Corona and lime, I'll dump my bags and come join you!" she squealed with excitement to him, and ran off as Scott chuckled, walking back to the bar to get Riley a drink.

As she pushed open the door to room 552 she could hear water running. She saw the bed closest to the door had been taken and so dumped her bag on top of the other bed, opening it and removing the clothes to hang up quickly – the rest she could sort later, she thought. As Riley heard the shower stop running she thought she best speak up in case the girl came out unaware and she startled her.

"Hey, I'm Riley, your roomie through training. I just wanted to say hi?"

The door clicked unlocked and a short ball of blonde hair pulled on top walked out. She was only about 5 foot 2 with a crooked front tooth. "Hey, I'm Sally," said the strongest Scottish accent Riley had ever heard. "I was wrecked, long-ass journey and all that, I just needed a shower. So it's Riley, ehy?"

"Yes, yes, and tell me about it; and for that reason I NEED a beer," she said to Sally, raising her eyebrow in question.

"You don't have to ask a Scot twice, I'll just get dressed and be right with you."

Riley left the room allowing Sally to get ready, and wandered back down to the bar. Sally seemed nice and Riley was getting a good feeling about this week already.

* * *

Throughout the course of the day about twenty to thirty people arrived. Riley was unsure exactly how many. She had had far too many drinks and was starting to feel like already she was living the dream. Amongst all the people who'd arrived there were also the two trainers – they were two resort supervisors – Glen worked in Alcudia in Majorca and Keri worked in Lindos in Rhodes. They were like walking adverts of Hightail, sun tanned, gorgeous, confident, and energetic. Riley was stoked in anticipation of the training starting in the morning.

We had been drinking for nigh on six hours, and she was suddenly aware that whilst everyone appeared to be in high spirits we were slowly taking over the whole hotel bar. She had become very conscious of this fact and whilst she drank, like most 24 year olds did, in a small village where everyone knew everyone else she wasn't really used to being in big groups of drunken people taking over areas. Well, other than at uni. She felt Scott nudge her, when she looked up into his swaying eyes concern danced around in them. Smiling, Riley touched his arm gently. "I'm fine, just a little drunk and overwhelmed by it all I guess, I'll be right back," she said, and kissed his cheek. She heard a few ooohss and wit woos as she tried standing up before losing her footing completely and tripping over her stool. Before Riley knew it she was laid on the floor with her legs in the resting absent her stool, with a number of faces looking down over her in hysterical laughter. Riley looked up, giggling with them all, and mumbled something about needing some water.

Scott grabbed her hand and pulled her up. "You

ok?" he asked.

"Yeah, buddy. I'm fine, just need water and then another beer." She winked.

She stood up carefully this time and walked over to the bar, requesting a bottle of water from the barmaid. She had smiling eyes and pretty sure that she had recently had a box office viewing to the entertainment she had just provided. Inwardly cringing, Riley rubbed her eyes.

"Don't be so embarrassed, it happens. You didn't hurt yourself did you?" said Keri.

Riley wanted the ground to swallow her whole. "Hey, ummm I don't normally do that. I can normally hold my drink, I uh, just kinda lost my footing, I guess," said Riley. She was suddenly feeling completely sober as the reality set in that she could have just royally fucked her chances before she'd even begun. Riley kicked herself for not eating and doing this in front of the trainers. "I should have ate, it's the, um..." she mumbled, embarrassed. Riley looked up and smiled at the waitress as she handed over a fiver for the water.

"It's the adrenaline, the fear, the excitement, the new friends, the ummmmm... hot guys." Keri pointed her eyes back to Scott; she had a weird look about her that Riley couldn't place. "Nothing's going on with Scott and me," she said.

"I know we said don't screw the crew, Ri, but seriously everyone does it, especially on training," Keri said as she smiled and walked back to the table. "As long as you don't do it in resort, what goes on tour stays on tour on training week." She winked behind her.

She knew my name, thought Riley. *Shit, I'm already under the radar.* Riley rested her head on the bar and sighed.

She heard a voice whisper close to her ear. "As cute as you are, I don't think you're selling our hotel bar that well." Riley lifted her head slowly and was looking into the big brown eyes of the waitress grinning like someone who had just won the lottery. "Tough day, huh?" said the girl, whose name was Jo according to her name tag.

"Really?!" said Riley. "You've sat and watched me drink for the last God knows how many hours with a load of other pissheads. Can I really get away with tough day?"

Jo laughed. "No, you're right, just trying to make you feel better," she said as she walked off to serve another customer.

* * *

Shortly after, they all went down for dinner. Keri and Glen told everyone to have an early night due to an 8am start the following morning all the way through to 7pm. That apparently would be the same throughout the week.

Riley said her goodbyes to the remaining stragglers; it was now a little after 9 and she had been drinking since 1pm, no wonder she felt shit! Riley had left Sally majorly flirting with Glen. She couldn't quite work out if he was into her or not but just hoped she wouldn't be woken too late, she needed her beauty sleep before tomorrow began.

She got into her room and took a quick shower before slipping into a pair of CK shorts and a Hard

Rock Café Cancun vest. She switched the TV on and watched a rerun of Friends.

Picking up her phone and opening the message to Cara, she typed, *'Hey you, how goes it? I'm pretty sure I have screwed up on day one.'*

'PMSL, you are so melodramatic Riley, what have you done? I promise it's not as bad as you think! Any talent?'

'Worse, C!! Got drunk, no food, adrenaline took over, fell off my stool, upside down, everyone saw, everyone laughed! :(<sigh>. Even the trainers, they know my name, I'm on the radar! They told us to not fuck up or were out!'

'Oh and the bar staff saw too, and even took the piss.'

Riley sighed out loud as she watched Monica walk in from the Caribbean humidity with outrageous hair. She smiled slightly.

'You are a goof! Why are you so hard on yourself? Babes, you are totally fine, every holiday we have gone on the reps are the biggest piss cans about, why are you worried? They probably thought it was hilarious! I know I would :), ever think maybe they know your name as you're super-hot?'

'Piss off.' Riley smiled as she knew only her best friend could ever make happen.

'Just saying ;) get sleep and go kick their asses tomorrow and don't sweat it, you'll do fine Ri. Good night, love you XXX'

'Love you too X'

Riley switched the TV off and checked her alarm on her phone. Sorted, she rolled over and gently fell to sleep.

Chapter 4

Ba beh ba bom, ba beh ba bom put 'em high, push it high ba ba beh ba bomb ba ba beh ba bom put 'em high, push it high...

Riley rolled over and switched her alarm off. She noticed Sally wasn't in her bed and it didn't look to have been slept in at all. Riley got up and went to the bathroom to shower and get ready.

The letter had outlined that as you would receive your uniform on the first day to start wearing from the following day that on day one you could wear your own clothes. They had stated however, to take into consideration this was a nice hotel so hoodies, trainers, and tracksuits were not acceptable.

Riley put on her favourite pair of Levis, some brown pumps, a white shirt with the buttons opened down to her cleavage and a navy jacket over the top. She checked herself out and was happy that she didn't look too casual or too smart. "Happy medium," Riley said, and grabbed her bag.

As she opened the door she crashed into Sally, who seemed shocked and severely hungover. Riley looked at her with a questioning smirk.

"Don't ask," said Sally. "Please get me a coffee and

save me a seat. I'll be ten, I promise, I just won't wash my hair." She looked upset.

Riley grabbed Sally's arm. "Don't worry, I got it. In my bag on the table I have some dry shampoo, if you need it."

"I love you!" Sally shouted, and ran in past her, leaving nothing but a cloud of smoke in her midst. Riley giggled to herself as she made her way to breakfast.

When she entered the dining area she found the Hightail area had been cordoned off, thinking to herself it was a shame they didn't do that last night. She wandered over to the gang and dropped her bag at the bottom of the table where there were quite a few seats free.

"Smell, do we Riley? Or just feeling the effects of the little trip you took last night, babe?" shouted James, getting a lot of giggles and smirks from the gang.

"Funny James, funny! No, just saving some seats is all," she said to the class clown.

"Ahhhh of course, the next Posh and Becks, how could we forget?" James said, rolling his eyes.

"Huh." She caught Keri's eye again. *Shit, she looks pissed at me. Great!*

"As much as I'm not blind and this girl is hot, I told you all last night, Riley and I are just friends," Scott said with his hands on her shoulders.

Riley sighed, unable to get involved in this right now. Why could nothing ever just go simple for her? Everything was always a constant story or mission. Riley grabbed herself a bowl of cereal and a cherry yogurt. She felt a hug from behind and looked up to see Sally, looking somewhat better with appreciative eyes.

"Thanks, I'm so sorry," she said in her broad Scottish accent.

"For what?"

"I would never normally do that, I don't know what came over me, but if you fancy it we could order a pizza in tonight and catch up," said Sally.

"Sure, I'm all into hearing all the goss," Riley said, laughing.

"Touché, misses," she quipped with a wink, and walked off to get her breakfast. Confused once more, Riley walked back to the table and sat eating quietly.

* * *

The day was a blur. It was hard going and a lot to take in – they went from sales techniques to customer service training, roleplays, team building, 'get to know you's', amongst a whole other host of things. They were sized up for the uniforms and eventually were allowed to leave. Riley was completely trashed and happy that Sally and her had made their own plans tonight.

A few of the guys were arranging to go and have a few beers after dinner and she'd told them that they were going to grab a pizza and stay in the room with shit TV and to do the 'homework' they'd been assigned for the night. There were a couple of sarcastic remarks made about her being the 'entertainment for the evening'. As she looked up, rolling her eyes, she saw Keri smirking and was glad she seemed to be impressed with her output today, thinking that maybe Riley was no longer on the radar. She sighed, relieved, and looked up to see Scott who was walking towards her. Dejected. She caught his eye, questioning him, and he just shook his head and walked off.

"Lovers' tiff ehy Riley?" James shouted across the room, laughing. She looked up to him, annoyed. Unfortunately, as she caught their boss's eye, she clearly had put her back on the radar. Riley shook my head, pissed off, and ran after Scott. She located him in the bar, head in his hands. He looked bad. Riley was now getting worried over what was going on.

Riley went to the bar and ordered ten bottles of Corona and asked if she could buy a lime.

"Yesterday wasn't enough beer for you?" Riley heard as she looked up into the deep brown eyes of the barmaid, Jo.

"Hey. Apparently not," she smirked, and she nodded her head back over to Scott.

"Yeah, he doesn't seem as happy as yesterday to say the least," Jo said.

"Here's the beer, the lime's on me, hope your boyfriend is feeling better soon," and handed Riley her change. She inwardly sighed as she looked up and just smiled; as she turned around she was stood in front of Keri and Glen. Deflated once more, Riley just picked up her head and walked directly past them, telling Scott to come with her right now.

Scott followed Riley out of the bar and took the bucket of beers from her hands; she was throwing the lime in the air before getting to the room and unlocking the door.

"Hey, just in the shower real quick. You forgot your uniform in your rush out, silly; I grabbed it for you and hung it in the wardrobe. What pizza do you want? I have the JustEat app on my phone so we can choose!" Sally shouted from the bathroom.

Riley shouted back, "Ok, thanks, I'm easy. I'll wait until you get out and we can decide."

Riley got two beers and realised she didn't have a knife for the lime! "Bollocks." She opened two bottles and handed one to Scott. "Improvisation, good looking! Whilst we have no knife, there's no lime! When we collect the pizzas we'll run into the restaurant and grab one. So hit me, what's going on?"

Riley and Scott looked up as Sally walked out of the bathroom.

"Oh, I'm sorry, I didn't realise we had company," said Sally.

"Sorry," said Scott, "I'll leave."

"No, you need some friends. We have a bucket and a half full of beer and were ordering in. Sal, I'm sorry. Scott is having a bad time and I thought it would be ok that the three of us bitch, drink, eat, and put the world to rights together."

Sally nodded and grabbed herself a beer. "Gimme five," she said, before taking her clothes into the bathroom and returning in a pair of joggers and an oversized t-shirt.

* * *

"So she actually said that? What a fucking bitch," said Sally. I looked up at Scott, smirking at how much broader her accent got when A) she was drunk, and

B) she was angry.

"I know, waste of fucking three years of my life. I wouldn't mind, I loved Mexico, ya know?" said Ben sadly. "Anyways, to friends," he said as he took another slice of pizza and chomped away, wiping his mouth and swigging his beer. "Anyways, enough about me, as Riles and I here are hiding your sorry ass in the love stakes, what's going on with you and Glen?" asked Scott.

Sally seemed to get very embarrassed before responding that she liked him, and unless he was a bloody good actor he appeared to like her too. Sally told us about them taking it easy because they would be disappearing off to different destinations again in a few days, but for now she was having a great time with him. Sally had also sworn us both to secrecy as he was technically the boss on the course and they didn't want anybody knowing about it.

Riley looked up, asking the others if they wanted more beers; they had only had three each, so agreed, and she ran to the bar with her yoga pants and her favourite Knicks basketball jersey on. She ordered another ten beers. She figured she could chuck them in the fridge if they didn't get drank this evening.

Keri stood beside Riley.

"Hey," she said. "Everything ok?"

"Hey," Riley said back. "Yeah, just chilling with some friends watching movies and bitching, as you do. Requiring additional supplies," she said to Keri, raising her eyebrows.

She looked as though she was about to say something but instead just smiled. "Enjoy your night

Riley, you did good today."

Riley was happy that she hadn't been reprimanded again for the whole 'Scott and Riley' saga. She was also glad that today's efforts seemed to be keeping the trainers off her back somewhat.

Riley got back in and handed them each a beer, climbing onto the bed and taking another slice of pizza. She had always had a passionate affair with cold pizza; most people thought it was gross, she thought it was heavenly.

A while later Sally's phone beeped and she looked to each of them in turn sheepishly. Sally gently brushed her blonde curls behind her ear and with almost only a whisper, said, "So, uhhhmmm, would you guys mind if I left you to it?"

Scott and Riley laughed at the same time, knowing exactly where she was going.

"No, knock yourself out," Scott said. "And hey Sal, thanks for tonight and letting me crash, that was really cool."

Sally walked over to Scott, hugged him tightly and moved back, hitting his bottle with hers. "Here's to the bitch and the biggest regret of her life." She winked at him.

Scott smiled sadly, nodding, and Sally was gone.

"One for the road, gorgeous?" Riley said to Scott.

"Sure, why not!" he replied.

Chapter 5

The alarm went off and Riley rolled over, feeling far better than yesterday morning. She saw Scott lying next to her and smiled. "Hey, sleeping beauty, what you doing in my bed?" She laughed and hit him playfully.

"Oh, if only, Riles," he laughed. "You do realise we'll be the talk of the town," said Scott.

Riley sighed. "Aren't we already?"

She made her way to the bathroom, shouting to Scott to let himself out. She noticed once more that Sally had still not slept in her bed.

Riley was glad of the fact that at least the colours of her uniform complimented her skin colouring, as it really wasn't the most flattering of clothing. She put her shoes on to complete the outfit and left her room.

As she walked into the dining room she went to the Hightail area and dumped her belongings.

"Ahhhh here's half of love's young dream," James laughed. Riley was disappointed to recall that Scott and motor mouth James were sharing; Scott was right, everyone would know they spent the night together now.

"James, maybe if you spend a little less time on other people's love lives and more on your own maybe you wouldn't be sat gossiping and enjoying some action yourself," Riley laughed as she walked to get her breakfast.

There were lots of oooohhhhs and cheers as she left the table.

The following day, much like the day before, had been a whirlwind. They were informed throughout, that on the Thursday night they would have a little award ceremony in a private room in the hotel with free-flowing beers and wine and a three-course meal. Then Friday morning would be spent finding out their destinations and flight details, with the close of the course around 12pm.

Riley realised it was already Tuesday night and was starting to feel sad that it would soon be done. She shook herself out of it and continued to dry her hair. She had her hair down tonight and straightened it quickly. Looking in the mirror, taking in her jeans, white vest and shirt over the top left open, she nodded in approval and grabbed her key card, cash and phone, stuffed them in her pockets and walked down to the bar area.

Everyone appeared to be there already, she knew this would be due to the overly long conversation she and Cara were having whilst getting ready. Even Sally had dumped her beer and given up on Riley, signalling she would meet her downstairs.

Scott raised a beer to Riley which she took and sat down; she looked up at the barmaid, Jo, who waved to her and danced a bottle of water on the bar at Riley and winked.

Riley rolled her eyes and mouthed 'haha' to the

pretty dark-haired girl. She realised that the fitted black uniform perfectly accentuated the barmaid's figure. Riley turned back around to face the crowd to join in with the conversation.

* * *

She needed the bathroom; they were so right what they said about peeing and drinking. "Like Pringles, once you pop you can't stop." She giggled to herself as she managed to hold on to every surface like she had a broken limb. "No more being tonight's source of entertainment, Sharpey," she said, giggling at her new nickname. Riley thought back to earlier in the evening when the 'week 20-3 team' had gave each other nicknames and apparently Riley's surname was quite fitting from the 'sharpness' of her tongue and how 'sharp' she looked in the mornings despite the previous evening's antics.

Returning from the bathroom, Scott beckoned her over to the bar. "Come on Riles, we're doing shots," he said.

"Waheyyyyyyy!" A group of cheers surrounded her. Suddenly feeling somewhat nauseous, Riley looked up and smiled; suddenly a shot was thrust under her face and she was unsure what to do with it. Looking around at '20-3' team, as they had called themselves due to the training being on the week of the 20th of March, Riley shrugged it off and took one for the team. As the warm liquid slid down her throat she was completely convinced she was about to throw up and tried to concentrate on the situation around her.

"This is Glen." Sally smiled sheepishly to Riley. She smiled wide and laughed at Sally, making it known that he was also the tutor, trainer, manager, boss, whatever the fuck he was. She had only known Sally a short while but they appeared to be smitten with one another. The only concern was that it wasn't just a 'rep' game, another tick in the box or score on the scoresheet. Riley wasn't stupid; she had watched the movies, read the books and spoken to enough reps about the lifestyle they led. Whilst Riley didn't allow that to faze her she didn't want Sally to get hurt. On the flip side though, surely Sally would know the likelihood of her getting placed on the same island and same resort was very slim, and like she said last night, for now it was just about some fun together.

Riley could feel she was getting progressively drunker, and knew she was in for a killer headache in the morning.

* * *

Riley woke the next morning as the sun was shining in her eyes; she cursed as she realised that she'd obviously gone to sleep without shutting the curtains. "Ohhhhhh I think I'm dying," she said aloud and groaned. Riley heard a laugh and knew it had come from a girl; she clearly hadn't had a pyjama party with Scott again. As Riley slowly opened one eye, trying not to blind herself from the light, she was face to face with those big brown eyes again. Instantly squeezing her eyes shut again, Riley threw her arm over her face and groaned.

"Charming. You weren't saying that last night, and if memory serves me it was a very different groan," a laughing Jo the barmaid said.

Riley slowly opened her eyes again. "I'm sorry, I

didn't mean to be rude," cringed Riley as she said it. "I don't have a whole lot of memory left from last night, it appears. I didn't mean to make you feel shit." Riley caught sight of the long dark hair encompassing the whole pillow. Jo was really cute and as the thick white duvet was pulled around her she could see just enough skin peeking over the quilt. It looked incredibly soft and had Riley not felt like a camel had shit in her mouth right about now, she would totally be all over that.

Jo was lying smirking in front of Riley. "Hey, can I help you?" she said quietly.

"So guess you were right about your roomie not returning." Jo pointed her eyes to Sally's bed.

Fuck, how had she ended up in this situation! "Rarely wrong, me," Riley said and smiled.

"So, um, how's the head?" said Jo.

"As expected, sore, painful, devastated at the prospect of training for the next twelve hours," said Riley. Jo smiled and gently ran her finger down the side of Riley's face, stopping as she reached her lips. "So, I'm kinda shocked about you, I'm not going to lie. To be honest we have a fairly big gay scene here you know, but I totally thought you were hooking up with the cute guy you're always with," said Jo.

Riley couldn't help but be drawn into those big brown eyes. She recalled the beginning of the night as she thought back to seeing Jo in her uniform. She recalled the perfectly fitting black skirt and shirt, and then her black apron around her waist. Jo had the first three or four buttons undone on her work shirt which showed just the perfect amount of flesh off. As she looked back now she was showing even more of that perfect flesh off lying in her bed, seemingly naked. Riley suddenly had a flashback to last night when she was having a shot with the team and recalled Jo bending down in front of her. As Riley reflected, she could see Jo bending down to get the glasses for the shots and seeing down her shirt; she remembered seeing the black lace bra with an electric pink outline. *Shit.* She remembered being caught out by Jo, and cringed as the thoughts came back to her.

"You ok? Or regretting it already?" Jo laughed uncomfortably.

Riley didn't do this often, living in a tiny village and all that, but she didn't want to make Jo feel shitty by any means.

Riley moved closer to Jo, and gently stroked the backs of her fingers across her cheek. "Of course I'm not, silly," she told Jo.

Jo smiled and kissed Riley's forehead; she moved the cover back and changed into her clothes. "Don't sweat it, Riley," Jo said happily. "I work here, I see this every other week and I'm not expecting commitment or anything else for that matter. I know you guys are going to fly off to the hot destinations which will bring you to all sorts of, ummm, experiences," she said with a wink. "I am not naïve enough to think we'll be walking off into the sunset, it was one night of pure adult fun, just you and me, and well, a good night." Riley went to speak as Jo stopped her with her finger to her lips. "It's fine. We're young and single and this is what life is all about," Jo said. "You will have those young lads flocking around you, as they become aware that you're one of the hottest lesbians with Hightail." She smirked.

"One of?" Riley questioned Jo, trying to find out more information from her.

Laughing loudly, Jo said, "As I said, I see this week in week out pre-summer. There's quite a few of you with this company these days." She winked at her as she picked up her messenger bag and threw it over her shoulder.

Riley really liked Jo; she didn't know why or what it was about her. Well, other than the fact she was gorgeous, but she genuinely felt shit that she couldn't remember a great deal, kicking herself at the lack of memory of sleeping with such a sexy woman.

Riley moved over a little to let a fully clothed Jo sit on the bed next to her; Jo was looking at her intently. Jo shook her head softly. "Anyways, I'm glad for last night," Jo said quietly. "More importantly, I'm super glad of that tattoo you got down below last night and let me share in it," she giggled quietly.

Riley felt all of the blood drain out of her face and quickly swiped the cover back over her body, lifting up and searching her lower body. She stopped, looking at Jo questioningly. Jo leant down to Riley and kissed her lips softly. "Just needed to see that hot-ass body one last time." Jo winked and pulled the cover back over Riley; she kissed her lightly and said, "Goodbye Riley." Suddenly she knew it was the last time she would see her.

Riley sighed as she recalled the jigsaw puzzle of the night before, but she was completely unable to bring it all together. She threw her head back and smothered her face with a pillow. Riley couldn't remove the Cheshire grin from her face, let's face it, Jo was super-hot!

* * *

Riley had struggled the entire day; she was knocking back pills on the second of every fourth hour to try and clear her head.

Luckily Glen and Keri has said to them all that this always happened; as such they always made sure that Wednesdays were the easiest and shortest days of the training course.

As it happened, the day was fairly fun-filled and light-hearted, with the most part dedicated to the training and practicing of the 'transfer spiels'. This was the speeches they would be conducting when picking up the guests and transporting them to and from the airport. As we each took turns, sitting with our backs to the team at the front of the class, we had to read out from the transcript over and over and where possible put our own spin on them. There was lots of laughter as people were filling in gaps in a bid to wash over their own fears and embarrassment of the task.

At the end of the day they each went and changed and met shortly after for dinner. Riley had never been so happy in her life, as she was when she noticed that the dining room sign said Wednesday night as 'Roast Night'. She was still feeling the effects of last night and a big roast and pint of Diet Coke was her way to a happy ending, she was sure of it.

Chapter 6

After a long, drawn-out dinner they all went back to the bar. Riley wasn't drinking tonight, she was happy to stick with her Coke but she didn't know how she felt about seeing Jo again; the memories hadn't really come back to her and she felt bad for that. She liked her, she was fun and cute but in reality she was right. Even if she wasn't leaving the UK they were nowhere near each other. Riley laughed inwardly at the realisation of being a total lesbian, and the joke of second dates with lesbians involving moving trucks. She'd never been one for sleeping around and whilst she didn't feel ashamed of the one night per se, it was more about the lack of memory that was making her feel shit and guilty on Jo. Riley didn't want to come across as the type that was just typically looking for a few points on the score sheet.

The after-dinner drinks were a lot more reserved than the previous evening with most of them opting for soft drinks and alluding to the fact that an early night was on the cards. As many of them were now fully acquainted in more ways than one, Glen had said that following on from the interview they should each go round the table and share our 'secret' which had formed part of that interview process, only a mere few weeks back. As they went around the table, they heard different stories being told and secrets being publicised from each of them. Next was Scott. Riley didn't know if he would share something so personal to him. Riley waited anxiously as to what he was about to share and he began his story. Everyone knew he had worked overseas before, but they were all yet to find out the reason he left.

Scott confessed to the team how he had decided on asking Angela to marry him. He had picked up his bonus, for achieving the best sales results for the winter season, and had gone to one of the many malls in Cancun; he had spotted the perfect ring and bought it there and then.

Scott was sharing more than he had shared with Sally and her the other night and was distant whilst speaking. She just wanted to grab him and embrace the guy who had become her very best friend throughout this experience. He continued with his story, sharing with everyone all that as all of the hotels were offering New Year's Eve functions for the guests, one of the five star hotels he worked in had a beautiful private beach dining area, saved for honeymooners or weddings. Scott had gone to the hotel manager, fully aware that the likelihood of it being used on the function night was slim and bared all to him, before asking if he would be able to use it that night. The manager was thrilled and Scott had a slight smile on his face as he shared his tale of the Mexican man.

"Latin in love," Scott elaborated, rolling his eyes. But it was all set, he'd even organised to use the kitchen so he could cook Angela her favourite dish, his mum's lasagne recipe which she frequently craved. When they had eaten their dinner the manager had arranged for one of his chefs to carve 'Marry Me' into a watermelon, which they would bring out with an assortment of desserts for them.

Scott had it all planned out, and to him there was nothing more perfect for his perfect girl. Scott stood and put his hands in his jeans pocket and retrieved a silver necklace with a diamond ring dangling from it. As he listened to the gasps, he laid it carefully on the table and watched as all eyes danced over the sheer beauty of the ring. He noticed Gemma, one of the girls from the course, staring intently at him with what appeared to be watery eyes. "So what happened next?" she asked concernedly. Scott smiled shyly, before continuing to tell them that whilst he was trying to arrange the NYE proposal, he shouldn't have actually been there at that time and as he was driving back, he caught her kissing one of the suppliers. He went home later that night and confronted her and Angela had admitted she had been having an affair with 'Jesus' for the past six months and she felt her future lay with him and not Scott.

There was a lull in the conversation as everyone was digesting Scott's revelations; it was one of those moments in movies when someone shouts 'Psyche!' or 'Gotcha!' and laughter erupts. Sadly, this wasn't one of those moments.

It was evident Scott was still deeply hurt and as he lifted his bottle to us all, he smiled sardonically to everyone and said, "So, whilst I'm not going to deny this here is a fucking hot bit of stuff, I'm not really into getting caught up with anyone else just yet." He laughed, took a swig of his beer and said, "Not that she would if I was ready though." He winked over to her.

Riley loved Scott. He was one of the very few genuine guys she had ever met, and she was sad to see him hurting this way. Riley was glad that 'Angela' remained in long haul – there's no way a new rep would get sent to long haul, which was a good thing. Riley thought she'd end up punching her square in the face for what she did to her buddy.

"So Riles, we're all anxiously waiting now. You guys, it seems, have been very IN-appropriately nicknamed Posh and Becks on the course as we all sat back and watched the relationship unfold around us, and apparently we were all wrong," said James.

Gemma looked at Riley. "Unless she's just waiting in the wings, being the caring friend waiting for him to make her move, only to swoop in on him."

Riley couldn't help but smirk. "Not really my thing, Gemma; but I'm glad someone else is equally as fond and protective of my Hightail bestie," she said sincerely.

Scott looked at Riley with compassionate eyes; she knew he was letting her know it was ok either way. Whether she told or didn't, he was going to have her back. She really did love this guy and was genuinely upset at not sharing their adventures together.

"Well, my story is, I love this guy! Simple as! We went to interview together, and within that process I remember at the start, this guy," she poked him in the ribs, "looked up and caught my eye, with a kind hearted, 'don't panic' smile. I remember instantly feeling relaxed. Then when it came to the introductions, I maintained eye contact to calm myself and when I shared my secret, his reaction didn't change, he still looked deeply into my eyes, calming me through the moment. At that moment I knew he would be in my life forever!" said Riley.

"So what was your secret then?" asked Keri. Everyone looked from Keri back to Riley intently.

"I'm a lesbian," she said.

"You don't look like a lesbian," said James.

Only him. She laughed thoughtfully and rolled her eyes

"Enlighten me James, what does a lesbian look like? For the record, it's stupid-ass comments like that which will make your career in tourism very short lived," snapped Keri.

Riley was taken aback by Keri's response; she didn't really need anybody sticking up for her. Riley had realised she was gay from being eleven, when she started high school. As clichéd as it sounded, the gay PE teacher had occupied her thoughts for five long years thereafter.

Riley had always hated confrontation and wanted to lighten the mood; it appeared to have gotten a little too intense. "It's ok, James. It's all very stereotypical these days. We're in 2015 and therefore, there isn't a specific look anymore." She winked at him.

As she walked to the bar she laid her hands on James shoulders and as he looked up, she smirked. "So how many points do you think Scott will get after not coming home the other night?" and everyone laughed including James, starting to relax again, giving her a sheepish smile.

* * *

Michelle from the course had been, for want of a better word, in a different group or clique to the people she had been hanging with. She had not spoken to her since the first day of training but she spoke confidently and jovially. "I think I have been duped by your secret, Riley," she said, grinning. "See I knew you were gay after the lip locking I witnessed between you and the barmaid last night," she said.

There was raucous laughter amongst the group as she could feel herself going red; Riley wasn't bothered, she knew they had become a tight-knit group even if there were different subgroups among us. She laughed along with them and raised an eyebrow to the crowd, lifting her Diet Coke up before saying, "What can I say? I'm a woman who loves beautiful women! On that note, I'm getting off, I need my beauty sleep before tomorrow's antics."

Scott stood up and said to Riley and the group, "Don't think so, lady. You spout all this bullshit that I'm your best mate and I don't know shit about this, one more Coke for you. I am living my depressing state of a life through you, I want gossip!"

"Ermmmm me too," smirked Sally.

Riley looked at her group and couldn't help but laugh. "Get me a beer. JUST ONE!" she shouted. "I need the bathroom."

As Riley walked into the bathroom she saw Keri stood at the basin; she was unsure when she had left the group to come here. Keri was leaning over with water dripping from her face.

"Hey, are you ok?" Riley touched Keri's arm.

Keri snatched her arm away, glaring at Riley. "I'm fine, I'm fine!" she snapped.

Riley was shocked, what had she done? "It's not contagious you know, and just because I'm a lesbian doesn't mean I fancy every girl on the planet!" she snapped back.

Keri wiped the water from her face with a tissue and leaned her head back against the wall, the front of her shoulder-length blonde hair slightly curling where the water had hit it. She sighed. "Why didn't you tell me? Why did you let me think you were with Scott, Riley?" The words were softer this time; she closed her eyes tight.

Riley moved forward again, cautious after the last time she attempted to touch Keri. "What's going on Keri, what did I do? I'm lost! Did I do something to offend you? If so I can only apologise, but I don't think I deserved to be treated that way before," she said.

"I'm sorry, you haven't offended me. I was disa... ummmm, oh don't worry, it's fine. Ignore me, I'm just tired," said Keri.

"No, something is clearly bothering you. Tell me what it is," Riley said as she put her hands on her upper arms. Riley couldn't help but notice the sadness in Keri's blue eyes, she hadn't realised the clearness of them, and they were like ice.

Before she knew it Keri's lips were on her own; she felt the softness of them, and then it stopped. Keri pulled back and looked like a rabbit caught in headlights. "Fuck," she said, and moved past Riley. Her hands were in her hair as she was shaking her head torturously. "Fuck, fuck," she condemned herself again.

Before she could stop herself, Riley had pushed Keri against the cubicle door, kissing her passionately, intensely. She pushed her into the cubicle and locked the door behind them, pushing Keri firmly against the wall and pinning her there with her own lips. Riley couldn't decipher whose breaths belonged to whom, as they were blending into one. Riley lifted one hand to Keri's face, lacing her fingers through her soft hair and pulling her further into the kiss. With her other hand she pushed Keri's arm above her head, pinning it to the wall as she gripped her wrist with passionate force.

Riley felt Keri's tongue slip inside her mouth and was soon exploring and actively seeking her own. As their tongues danced and their lips pressed firmly to the other's, they were forced to stop when they heard the bathroom door open. They were stuck; eyes caught wide, hardly any space between them, each feeling the quickened, heavy breathing on the other's skin.

"Keri, you in here?" they heard.

Riley quickly put her finger to Keri's mouth to quieten her, fully aware that she had told them all she needed the bathroom, and acutely aware that Keri had not made any such disclosure. Keri giggled lightly, looking quizzically into Riley's eyes.

"Riley, are you in here?" they heard this time.

"Yes, I'm here," Riley responded. Keri raised her eyebrow to Riley and they tried to stop themselves from giving it away and laughing.

"Are you ok?" she heard next.

Riley sighed heavily. "Yes, I'm fine, just weren't really sure how I felt about outing myself," she heard herself saying with a lopsided grin on her face. "Just give me a minute please, I'll be out in a sec," she said.

Keri was looking at her with her eyebrow raised so high now it was almost in her hairline. Keri looked like some kind of caricature at this moment in time; Riley was struggling once more to not giggle loudly.

"If you're sure," she heard, and then the door closed again.

Keri went to speak and Riley hushed her again, keeping her hand pinned still and with her other hand pulling the door back slightly to check they were alone again. As she closed it and locked it again she moved her finger from Keri's lips and they both burst into fits of laughter.

"So, the whole 'woe is me' works for you then, huh?" Keri laughed, shaking her head at Riley.

Riley let go of the arm she had been pinning against the wall and stepped back against the opposite cubicle wall and smiled, holding her hands up. "Busted," she said.

They laughed again and Keri said, "We should probably get going, before we really do get busted! Don't want you getting any more of a hussy rep, do we?"

Riley stopped and turned back to her, looking facetious. "Charming," she said. As she became more serious she looked into those icy blue eyes again. "On the contrary, I wouldn't normally do this."

"What, make out in the toilet cubicles?" Keri teased.

"Make out? What are you, a fourteen-year-old American now?" said Riley playfully. She quickly and ever so softly placed her lips on Keri's and grabbed her hand, pulling her out of the cubicle.

Chapter 7

Riley straightened herself up before leaving the bathrooms and walked back to the table, taking her beer from Scott. She took a swig, whilst looking over at Keri with a small grin forming on her lips.

"So, come on then," James said. "We've all been waiting to find out what happened last night?"

Riley cringed inwardly as she recalled the conversation before she went to the bathroom. The gang wanted all the dirt on last night. *Shit, this isn't good*, she thought.

Riley couldn't recall the time when Keri went to bathroom, but she was in there when Riley had arrived. What if she didn't know about Jo? Fuck, she would be seriously pissed. Riley recalled Keri passing a comment about her being a hussy; she was sure she knew about Jo.

Scott nudged Riley back to reality. "Come on, you are the only one that has had any action on this course so far, we're all waiting," he said.

Keri snorted her drink through her nose, and mumbled her apologies to everyone.

Riley didn't like to lie. Whilst she knew she would likely never see Keri again after this week, she didn't like the prospect of being surrounded by lies and being too afraid to speak for fear of getting into more problems.

With that being said she also didn't feel comfortable with everyone knowing Jo's business, being that they still had another couple of days here.

Riley knew what she had to do. "We met outside at the back of the bar. I was really drunk and was getting some air, we flirted, and we kissed. No big deal," she said. "We kissed some more around the hotel, end of!"

Luckily the guys had been so overcome with the talk of two girls kissing they bought it.

A bit later, she was met by Scott and Sally when the three of them were alone.

"Come on then, the real story?" said Scott.

"What do you mean?" she scoffed.

They weren't letting this go, she could tell.

She shrugged. "Simply put, I have another secret, I'm a shit drinker! I remember thinking she was cute, checking her out at the bar when I had a shot, and Brownie's promise or swear, whatever they say," she smiled, "I don't remember another thing until I woke this morning and she was in my bed," Riley said awkwardly.

"You slept with her?" Scott smirked.

"Apparently so! Listen, it's not my proudest moment. She is cute, and I wish I could remember, but, the fact of the matter is I can't!" Riley said.

* * *

Riley was laid in bed, recalling the toilet scene in

her head. She'd not really got the opportunity to talk to Keri again, so, looking back it was all very surreal.

Riley liked Keri, she hadn't really thought of her in that way until now. Keri was undeniably beautiful, for want of a better word she was like a poster child for Hightail Holidays. But after tonight she was completely thrown off balance by it all.

Riley picked up her phone. It was only 8.30, she knew that Cara would no doubt be sat in the dining room listening to their rock playlist they'd created last summer with a large glass of Pinot, marking assignments and reports.

She heard the dial out tone and it was answered on the second ring. "Hey, I was just thinking of you," said Cara as she answered the phone.

"Procrastinating again, I see."

"Seriously it's not even slightly funny, I'm pretty sure these kids are gonna end up making more money than I am on that sodding Benefits in Britain TV show," she said. "Ri, it's not even funny, they'te thick as pig shit!"

"C, I'm pretty sure you can't say that! On another note we have an interlude for you now, should you wish to accept."

Riley heard the pen smash down. "Riley Laura Sharpe, you have information! I can hear it in your quietness."

"I'm pretty sure there's no such thing."

"Hmmmm, you do have something to tell, you are at the avoidance stage. Ooohhhh do tell, excited muchly."

Riley laughed at Cara, she always did get overexcited for any form of gossip; Riley filled Cara in on the gossip of the last twenty-four hours. There were plenty of oooohhs and ahhhhs, with giggles and remarks about Riley being a floozy.

Cara was unable to stop herself from laughing as the story came to a close. "I can't actually believe you! You didn't even behave in this manner at uni, what on earth has come over you?" said Cara.

"It isn't that bad, C. I just don't remember how last night happened."

"But you certainly remember tonight though," she laughed. "So do you like her then?"

"Well it's kind of unimportant really isn't it? I'll never see her again after Friday so what's it matter?"

"Great, that's even better," Cara said.

"How so?"

"Well you can screw her and do one." She laughed.

"Ms Johnson, if your mother could hear you now." Riley laughed.

"Piss off, you know I hate 'Ms'. You can't be a Ms until you've been married at least once, therefore I'm still a Miss, thank you very much. Plus, don't threaten my mum, I'll tell her you've been straying away and that's both of us sent to Mass for 500 Hail Marys and 600 Our Fathers." They laughed.

"So, seriously, what are you going to do? Do you like her? Would you want anything else to happen?" said Cara.

"Hmmmm... she's gorgeous, C. I mean, I'm not

kidding, I couldn't control myself in the toilets until we were caught out," she said.

"So, do you...?"

Knock knock.

"Hold up a sec, someone's knocking."

"Ohhhhh maybe it's her." Cara was laughing.

Riley opened the door and was standing face to face with Keri; she looked Riley up and down in her vest and CK shorts; she met Riley's eyes again and looked serious.

"Keri, hi. Uhmmm, you ok?!"

Keri looked down at the quiet laughter coming from Riley's hand.

"I'll call you back," Riley said, hanging up before Cara had a chance to say anything else.

"What's up?"

"I'm sorry to call so late." Riley looked confused at her watch, checking how long she'd been on the phone to Cara it still wasn't even 9pm.

"Is Glen here?" Keri said pointedly.

"Ermmm no, sorry."

"Look, I know you and Sally are friends, but I know about her and Glen, and it's kind of important," she said.

"I have no reason to lie to you Keri, they aren't here. Last I saw them was when I left the bar," she confirmed again.

Keri sighed loudly, rubbing her eyes. "I'm sorry, I don't mean to be an ass, it's just really important I find him."

"Stupid question but have you tried calling him?" Riley said.

"Hmm hmmm, do you have Sally's number maybe?" Keri said, hopeful.

"Yeah sure, come in, we'll try her." She smiled and opened the door for Keri to walk in.

She looked down as her phone started vibrating; she saw the incoming message from Cara. *'Don't do anything I wouldn't do, you tramp,'* the message read.

Riley shook her head and scrolled to Sally's number. "It's ringing," Riley said, hopeful.

"Hey you, everything ok?" said Sally into the phone.

"Hey, listen, Keri is here. She urgently needs to speak to Glen; I'll pass you over, ok?"

"Sure thing, I'll hand it to him now," said Sally.

Keri was there in a flash with her hand out for the phone. "Hey, I'm so sorry to bother you, I have been trying to call you. Ah right, no worries. Anyways, HR has been in contact. The resort team have contacted me as they couldn't get hold of you, one of your team were involved in a crash. One's seriously injured and in ICU, Glen. They have the resort team manager with them and along with the kiddy supervisor, so they've said there's no point in returning. Yeah, it's Mike Castle and Lucy Parrott; it's Mike that's been admitted, Lucy has just broken her arm and has already been released. Hmmm, yeah. Yeah, yeah, of course. Well as I said they don't want you returning as they won't be able to get a filler for the last couple of days so they have just said it's all sorted and they'll see you Saturday. I've said when I speak to you I will call them back so if you get your phone charged at least that way they can contact you. I'll explain to them about the phone situation and give my number, that way they have a backup. Ok bud, see you soon and for fuck's sake put her down for two minutes," Keri said, laughing.

"Thanks for that, Ri. I'm sorry to intrude on your evening. I'll let you go back to your call." She pointed her eyes to Riley's iphone as she handed it back.

"It's ok, it was just my best friend Cara, she was entertaining me with stories of how her students will be making their appearance on Benefits in Britain. I daren't tell her it's maybe her teaching." She smirked. "Anyhow, I'll call her back tomorrow. You look stressed, do you want a beer?" Riley said.

"As much as I'd love that... I don't really fancy seeing them all to be honest. I hope you don't mind?"

"Well I don't mind at all as I had no intention of seeing the team in my 'ever so sexy' PJs, I meant here!" Riles said as she opened her fridge filled with Coronas.

Keri smiled with what looked like a sigh of relief. "Oh my god, yes. Thanks," said Keri as she took a bottle from her. Keri pulled her Converse off and sat back on the seat, resting her head back and putting her feet up on the corner of Riley's bed. She relaxed and sighed as she took a large gulp of her beer.

"Sorry I was an ass before," said Keri, "and for the record I'm glad you weren't planning on sharing those sexy PJs with the rest of the team!" She smiled lazily.

Riley threw a pillow over at her, calling her cheeky.

There was silence for a while, she didn't want to push Keri; it didn't feel awkward, and seemingly she was enjoying the stolen glances on her part. Criminal Minds was on the TV and Riley cringed at the thought of having Keri in her room and she had managed to put the most gruesome show on Earth on.

"What you thinking?" Keri said with her eyebrow raised.

"Oh, um, nothing."

"Clearly! I got that when you started looking horrified! Do you want me to leave?" Keri was looking expressionlessly at Riley; she would love to know what she was thinking right now.

"No, I really don't. I was just a teeny bit embarrassed," she said, closing her finger and thumb into a small pinch. "I was suddenly aware of the fact that after this afternoon, you are here and I've got Criminal Minds on; I mean don't get me wrong, I love this show, it's one of my favourites but it's, ummmm, not really the most romantic of shows, is it?" Riley was horrified. *Shit!* "Ermmm, I don't mean that I am trying to be romantic," she said, blushing. She looked up to Keri smirking with her eyebrow raised.

"Not really helping am I?" She sighed.

"You're pretty shit at this, aren't you?" Keri said as she walked around to the bed, sitting on the edge.

Riley frowned looking at her, disappointed.

"Hey, I'm kidding. I meant because you're supposed to be cheering me up and you then go and get all sorry for *yourself*." She touched Riley's arm softly. "Chill, Riley."

"Oh right! I'm sorry, I didn't mean…"

"Shut up, Riley!" was all she heard before she realised her lips were on hers. The tables were turned and Keri was taking control.

It was different this time, there wasn't that forcefulness and urge to rush. The passion was still there but it was slightly slower. Once again Keri's tongue was in her mouth, chasing her own. Riley wanted to feel her, she wanted her hands slowly running over her body but she couldn't look past last night. She didn't do this ever; whilst she knew they wouldn't see each other again she couldn't risk her finding out from somebody else. Riley pushed Keri back and rolled her onto her side, following suit and turning in to face her.

"What's wrong? Is everything ok?" she said.

Slowly shaking her head and covering her eyes, Riley said, "Keri, I don't want to lie to you. There's this total passion here which I was unaware of and now it has taken over me. I don't want you to hear this from anybody else because it is unfair on you and spineless of me to just keep going without making you aware!" She sighed. "About last night, I didn't only kiss Jo. I'm not trying to justify or defend my actions by saying I don't remember what happened, and I know that may seem worse but it's the truth."

"Jo?" Keri questioned.

"The barmaid! I woke up this morning in bed with her, I don't remember it and I am not saying that in defence because actually it made… correction, *makes* me feel even more shitty about the whole situation; but the fact of the matter is I slept with her last night. I like you, but, I can't for reasons that are both morally and ethically wrong to me, do anything with you tonight. I am not that person and I respect you and myself more than that."

"Oh."

OH? Oh is never great. "Keri, please talk to me."

"Listen it's been a really long day, I'm gonna... I'll go. Thanks for the beer, Riley, and letting me chill here for a bit."

Before Riley had even digested the words Keri was gone.

Chapter 8

No matter what Riley did she couldn't make herself look or feel any better. Having had approximately one hour's sleep, she had let the frustrations take total control. She understood that Keri was shocked; she had had a pretty shitty day, she got that, but angry at her!? Really! Riley had only found out she liked her a couple of hours previously, hell, she didn't even know she was gay. Geez, she still didn't!

On top of that she really liked Keri, she knew they wouldn't see each other again after tomorrow; but she'd come to enjoy her wit, sarcasm, and sense of humour throughout the training. Keri had an ability to maintain authority and superiority as well as being friends with the team too. Riley stopped herself from putting another layer of foundation under her eyes; she never wore makeup and if she continued she would be giving a clown a run for their money. She resigned herself to the fact that she looked and felt shit and was going to have to just deal with it.

Riley had decided against breakfast this morning, she wasn't really feeling it and didn't feel very sociable. She grabbed her bag and slipped her feet into the mandatory court shoes that were a prerequisite with the uniform, and headed directly to the training centre.

Riley walked in not, looking up along the way. She spotted Sally's questioning eyes and sat down next to her. Sally had pretty much moved in with Glen, and in terms of the room, Sally was never back at their place anymore. It hadn't bothered Riley so much until last night, when she was seriously debating calling her and getting her back. She thought better following the news that Keri had given Glen and knew he would need her.

"What's up? Are you ok?" Sally asked Riley as she sat down.

"Fine," said Riley without looking up.

Luckily the class began immediately so she didn't have to face the inquisition from Sally. She loved Sally, who had become a good friend in such a short time, but she just didn't really feel up to talking right now.

* * *

The last morning of training was group work and group presentations, which made it go quickly. Riley kept her head down in her work and other than when Glen and Keri came round to assist the teams on their group work, she had managed to stay out of Keri's way.

When it came to the presentations Riley was the last person to speak; she was pissed at herself for letting something so trivial burden her. It was affecting her nerves and causing her to worry over letting her team down. As she waited patiently, she couldn't stop herself from replaying the events of last night over in her mind. How had this happened? She didn't know how she'd got herself into this mess and was stressing that she didn't know what to do. She hated games, confrontation, and deliberately hurting people but she didn't feel like she had in this case; yet it appeared she had.

Riley was brought back to reality as she felt the nudge of an elbow in her ribs. Shit, she couldn't remember her part. What she was supposed to be saying or doing? She looked down at her cue cards, shaking the fear and nerves off. Riley had waited forever and a day for this opportunity – she wasn't going to screw it up over some girl.

Riley pulled it around; she literally picked it up like she had always been ready for this moment. She was confident, maintained eye contact, *with everyone but Keri, obviously*, and well and truly smashed it. Even the rest of the team said the same thing and she was glad that it was finally over.

Riley went to her room to check her phone at lunchtime, after sending an abundance of texts to Cara last night and this morning. She typed a quick reply to her best friend and then left her room to go back down to lunch. As she pulled the door behind her she looked up to see Keri letting herself into a room which Riley assumed must be hers just a few doors down.

Riley stopped, tempted to turn around. It was too late, Keri had spotted her; she gave Riley a sombre smile. Keri turned to Riley just as she had opened her door. She went to speak and couldn't; she looked sad, Riley thought. "Are you ok?" asked Riley.

"Not really, no. I just wanted to say well done today," said Keri.

"Oh… thanks," Riley responded, disappointed. As she turned to walk away, she felt Keri's hand on her arm. As Riley looked down she noticed a sandwich in her hand and looked up questioningly.

Keri looked intently at Riley. "I, um I didn't really feel like I wanted to be at lunch today so figured I would just grab a sandwich and eat it here, I don't have much of an appetite anyway," said Keri.

"Why? Why are you doing that? You need to eat properly and if you feel shit you need to be around the team!" said Riley sharply.

"I'm sorry, Riley."

"Why? Just come and eat with me, I don't feel great but we can mingle with them all, get caught up with all the dramas and forget it all," said Riley.

"No, I'm sorry for last night." Riley noticed how sad Keri looked and she was sure she was welling up. "I just needed to tell you that, you should go back to lunch with the guys. I'll see you back in class," said Keri.

Riley pushed past Keri. "No Keri, I'm not doing this. I've felt shit all day, I've not slept, and I'm confused to fuck! I don't know if you are gay, if you're not gay I didn't know you liked me until yesterday, that's if you even do. I was fucked on Tuesday night as you are well aware, I felt shit yesterday morning after waking up with someone whom I didn't recall going to bed with, then I felt shit about having to tell you when in reality I wished I could have just taken it all back… Honestly speaking I wouldn't have slept with you last night regardless of the Jo situation. Simply put, I am not normally that person. I like you and yesterday was… WOW, it was hot, it was more than hot. It was amazing. But I don't know how I have got the blame for this. I don't know why I have been made to feel so shit. As previously stated this is not me, so the guilt from my conscience is bad enough without getting it elsewhere." Riley didn't know at what point Keri had moved to sit on the bed, but when she looked over, the girl looked small and helpless as she sat on her legs and covered her head with her hands.

Riley rushed to her side, putting her arm around her, pulling her close and letting Keri relax into her. After a few minutes, Keri's breathing evened and she looked up to her. "You think I'm insane, I think I am insane," she sniffled.

"Keri, you don't know me. Please don't assume you do. Talk to me; tell me what's going on. What have I done to you?"

"You haven't done anything at all. I had a shit day and that's no excuse. I really enjoyed the whole bar, toilet thing, and I just wanted to see you. I was so relaxed being with you, chilling, watching shit TV after everything and I just got caught up in the moment as you would expect. I had no intention of sleeping with you, like you I don't tend to do this. I have come out of a fairly shitty relationship not so long ago and… well you're the first person I have been near since we split. Yes I'm gay, and I was with my girlfriend for two years. I don't know, I guess… I got engrossed in it all and when you stopped and told me that, it just hit me… hard. I just got blindsided, I suppose. I don't know if that's the right term. I know I have nothing on you and you are right, we haven't done anything or spoke, I mean, I only found out you were gay less than twenty-four hours ago, but I suppose the only way to describe it is that all the pain and bad feelings came flooding back. I was an ass, Riley. Completely unprofessional and I would totally understand if you wanted to send that feedback back to HR." Keri sighed heavily.

"Trade for a trade," Riley said back to Keri, who was looking back at her quizzically. "I won't dob you in to HR, if you don't kick me off the course? It's the only thing I've ever wanted to do and I can't go back to my life in finance whilst I'm this close," she said.

Keri smiled lightly. "You're the best rep on the course, Ri. Glen and I have already fed back and are fighting to take you to our own destinations."

Riley raised an eyebrow. "Well that could be dangerous, yet considerably fun," she said, laughing.

Riley stood up; she held out her hand for Keri to take. When she took it, Riley pulled her up, and kissed her lips softly. "Come on, we have twenty-four hours left, let's make the most of it." Riley squeezed her hand. Walking backwards to the door, she winked and kissed her lips once more before they left the room and went to the dining hall.

Chapter 9

Riley had the radio playing loudly through the TV whilst she was getting ready. She was just packing the last few things into her suitcase, ready to check out and dump her bags before the last couple of hours tomorrow. She was enjoying the freedom of the room allowing her to dance around in just her underwear, it was fun but she was saddened at the prospect of leaving the team, the antics, and the friends she had made.

The invite had confirmed the requirement for one smart outfit throughout the course, as she opened her wardrobe she pulled out the two choices she had brought with her. She'd tried on the black and cream shirt dress and even though her heels dressed it up, she wasn't feeling it. She packed it away in her suitcase and pulled on the sleeveless and backless black jumpsuit. She put on a long silver dress necklace with matching earrings and put her cream high stilettos on. With flats, Riley was 5 foot 7, so with her favourite Kurt Geiger shoes they easily made her over 6 foot.

Riley had applied her make-up, grabbed her clutch bag, and checked herself in the mirror one last time. She rarely dressed up, ever opting for jeans, but when she did, it always gave her a boost of confidence.

Riley knocked on Scott's door, they'd arranged to go down together and as he opened the door he whistled long and slow. "Blimey, Ri, you scrub up well," he said.

"Funny, come on." Riley smiled, pulling Scott from his room.

As they walked in, Sally ran over and hugged Riley and Scott. "Hey you, who are you trying to impress? Is Jo waiting tonight? You look incredible." She smirked.

Riley chose to ignore the comment. "You look fabulous too," she said, pulling Sally and Scott towards the bar. "So where's Glen?"

"Trying to be inconspicuous." She rolled her eyes.

They were stood at the bar talking, drinking, and laughing; she'd miss this, the fun, the experience, her friends. Riley wondered if it was like this overseas, if, when they got overseas this is what it would be like. She'd wished she could go with Sally and Scott, it would be perfect, but she knew the chances were slim to nothing.

As Riley looked up, she saw Keri walk in with Glen; Riley had to catch her breath as she took in the sheer beauty of the woman. Keri was wearing a red dress with her hair up, which Riley acknowledged was the first time she had seen it anything other than down. As Keri turned slightly to greet someone, Riley noticed there was no back to the dress. It dipped, wow, *all* the way down to the small of her back with a sharp V.

As Keri began walking towards the bar Riley noticed a slit all the way up to her thigh. She looked incredible, and as Riley's eyes returned from the thorough exploration of her body, she paused, catching sight of her breasts; they looked amazing in the outfit, and it had certainly wakened her senses. As Riley continued looking, she met Keri's eyes, and noticed her smirk. Fuck, busted again.

Scott nudged Riley. "You getting a good look there, ya little tart," he laughed.

Riley could feel herself going the same shade as Keri's dress as she had seemingly been caught out again. "Can't blame a girl for looking, she looks freaking amazing."

"Is she gay?" asked Sally.

"Noooooo. Well, not that I'm aware of."

"She got pretty shitty with James last night when he said about the whole 'stereotypical' gay thing, maybe she is and don't want to come out," said Scott.

* * *

The dinner was lovely; the company and hotel really had gone all out. There was free-flowing beer and wine throughout. The alcohol had clearly kicked in now, and as the last of the plates were cleared and the beer and wine replenished, the awards ceremony began.

Riley had never been to an awards ceremony before; the closest she had got was her graduation. Keri and Glen stood up and thanked everyone for the commitment on the course; they explained that it was nice that they hadn't kicked anybody off from this course, whilst making jokes about 'James' nearly coming close, which got a laugh from everyone.

They had said that the awards were like no other, with a grandioso build up, when they lifted a wholesale box of Haribos, and again, got a laugh from everybody.

There were a number of different awards. 'Class clown' went to James; Scott got the award for 'most lovable' which got a cheer from everyone, with the embarrassment clear on his face.

"The next award," said Keri, "is for the best kept secret. And of course it goes to our very own 'don't look like a gay girl, gay girl.'" She smirked over at James, who was now standing and bowing to the room as they erupted in laughter. Riley was mortified, she didn't like being the centre of attention at the best of times but it was worse now. She looked back to Scott and Sally, who were pushing her to go up to collect her 'award'.

I walked up as quickly as I could. As I took the bag of sweets, following suit, I leaned in and hugged her. She smelt incredible. As I pulled away I felt the softest breath against my ear as I heard, "Don't drink too much tonight, I want you to remember." As I pulled back and looked at her, checking if I'd heard right, her smile confirmed everything. This woman was a tease, but God did she know exactly how to cause a stir in my body.

The remaining last few awards were given out, including the final one for best achiever on training which went to Michelle, someone who had kept her head down on the course and kept herself to herself.

All in all it was a great evening; the drinks were flowing, spirits were high, everyone was dancing and mixing with one another. And the entire night she was unable to keep her eyes off Keri. She looked phenomenal and the more inebriated she was getting the more impossible it seemed to be.

Riley was just about to leave the dancefloor when 'Never Forget' came on; she felt someone grab her arm and saw Keri smiling back at her. Riley was pulled back into the circle that everyone had started forming. With their arms around each other's shoulders the chorus came on and the group were all singing at the top of their voices. It was a sad moment; the realisation kicked in that this time tomorrow they would no longer all be together. In fact, she could actually be on her way to the airport. Riley felt saddened at the prospect of the course coming to an end, her body must have reflected that as she felt Keri pull tighter, singing loudly with everyone and giving her a quick wink.

At the end of the night, everyone said their goodbyes. Scott was at the bar, laughing with Gemma. She liked Gemma; she was nice from what she had spoken to her, and seemingly was majorly crushing on Scott.

Riley said her goodbyes to Scott, warning Gemma to look after him; she found Sally and Glen, who were stood with Keri. She gave Sally a kiss and a hug, and did the same with Glen, saying her goodbyes and thanks for the awards as she lifted her bag of sweets. She was apprehensive with Keri, nobody knew what had been going on with her but she'd also been caught out earlier by Sally, checking Keri out. She decided it would look odder not doing anything, so thanked Keri for the experience she and Glen had provided on the course and gave her a quick hug and kiss on the cheek. God, she smelt divine. Riley could smell the coconut from her shampoo and the faint scent left from her perfume; she pulled herself away and said she was going to bed and she'd see them all in the morning.

Riley felt disappointed as she'd walked away from Keri; she looked back and saw her engrossed in a conversation with Glen. She heard the ding of the lift arriving and rested her head against the back wall as she waited for the doors to close. Riley heard, "Wait!" and hands appeared between the doors; she hit the button to reopen the doors and saw Michelle.

"Hey," Riley said, smiling to the quiet girl. "Good night, huh?"

Michelle looked like she had enjoyed her evening and had a somewhat goofy grin on her face. "Yeah, it really was." They had a bit of small talk on the ride up, with Riley congratulating the girl on her best training achiever, before the lift came to a stop and the doors opened on their floor.

"I'm this way." Michelle pointed in the opposite direction to Riley and stumbled off to her room. Riley stopped and leaned against the wall; she needed to take her shoes off. She couldn't remember a time she had been on them so much. She grabbed them and continued the walk to her room. As she turned the corner, reaching into her clutch for her room key, she looked up as she heard the tut-tutting sounds.

Chapter 10

Riley looked from Keri, back to the lifts, and back to the pretty girl standing in front of her door again. "How the...? What...? Have you got some kind of superpower you failed to mention?" said Riley.

Keri raised her eyebrow, smirking at Riley. "No, I just run along the beach every morning overseas, so when I saw you leave I said my goodbyes to Glen, just reaffirming tomorrow's decisions, and ran up the stairs in a bid to arrive before you did." She giggled. "So are you going to let me in or are we going to wait for the course to come to bed so we have another big secret to share with them, Miss Sharpe?" She winked.

Moving past her, looking questioningly into her eyes, she opened the door, extending it for Keri to pass.

Keri walked past her and into the room. "So I'm disappointed to see you have removed those shoes, very sexy," she said to Riley.

"I'm glad you approve," Riley said, smirking. She threw the shoes into the corner and walked around her bed to where Keri was standing. Slowly interlacing her fingers in Keri's, she looked up at her, considerably smaller now her heels had been removed. "You look incredible tonight," she said to Keri. "You completely took my breath away when you walked in, and I've been unable to take my eyes off you all night."

Keri smiled bashfully. She lifted up Riley's right hand and kissed the back of it slowly, she lowered it before repeating the gesture with her left hand.

Riley was elated she had controlled the consumption of her alcohol this evening; she couldn't remember the last time she felt this entranced by a woman.

* * *

Riley wasn't like other twenty-four year olds. She hadn't really ever been in a real relationship, and whilst she wasn't exactly shy of sexual relations, she also never felt the need to sleep around. She loved women, there was no doubt about it, and loved the closeness and intimacy of being with a woman, but aside from Jo, whom she still couldn't remember the details of, it had actually been a while.

Keri was beautiful and Riley was desperate to appreciate every inch of her body tonight.

"What are you thinking?" Keri asked, as she slipped out of her heels and followed Riley's lead, throwing them over into the corner.

Riley was at eye level with Keri now, and as she looked into those icy blue eyes once more, she could feel the butterflies in her stomach. "That you're beautiful, and suddenly… I'm nervous," she said with a small smile.

Riley didn't know what it was about Keri; she couldn't remember the last time she felt this nervous about being with a woman. In fact it was probably the first time she had slept with a woman, but there was just something that Keri brought to the table that had Riley completely unnerved, yet somehow left her in a completely euphoric state all at the same time.

Keri smiled slightly, and kissed Riley's lips softly. She pulled her down to sit on the bed. "I don't know what it is about you, Ri. I'm completely drawn to you; I was the first night I met you, and... Well that just isn't me. As I said, I came out of a bad relationship which made me swear myself off relationships, and as a result of that I just shied away from any type of interaction with a woman, in a bid to protect myself. I like you as an individual and apparently I'm very attracted to you, but I think maybe the tequila before I came down tonight may have gave me a bit of Dutch courage when it came to what I said to you at the awards. I wouldn't normally say anything like that," she said, looking embarrassed.

Seemingly that was all Riley needed; before she had a chance to think about anything else, she was pushing Keri back onto the bed, straddling her, and was kissing her softly.

Riley wanted her so desperately in this moment, but she was definitely not going to rush it. The kiss yesterday was fuelled by passion and excitement, and tonight wasn't going to be about that, it was more meaningful – slower, softer, more sensual. Tonight, it was just them, in the here and now.

The kiss deepened; Keri had her hands rested on Riley's thighs that were straddling her own body. Their movements were slow and steady, their tongues exploring. Riley couldn't control the need to softly run her nails up and down Keri's bare back. Keri felt amazing and it was taking everything for Riley to maintain control.

Keri pulled back slowly, resting her head against Riley's. "Wow," she said. "Are you sure about this Riley? There isn't any pressure to do anything."

"Are you kidding right now? Were you actually here for that kiss?" she said, laughing.

Keri was smirking with a glint in her eye, Riley was turned on to hell as she had no idea what the look meant or what Keri was planning; but in this moment she was oozing confidence. "Good," she said, as she pushed Riley off her and back onto the bed.

Keri got up off the bed, standing before Riley, who lifted herself up onto her arms to get a clearer view. "You're making this incredibly difficult, laying there all sexy and shit," she said.

"I don't know what you mean," Riley said, smirking.

Keri rolled her eyes. She stood confidently, quietly. "Payback's a bitch, Riles," she said, liking the way in which she said her name. It simply rolled off her tongue with such appeal.

Keri pulled the clip from her hair and let it fall to her shoulders; a gasping Riley took in the unbelievably sexy woman in front of her. She lifted her finger to one of the shoulders of her dress, gently placing it underneath the strap, pulling it ever so slightly down, whilst looking at Riley questioningly.

Riley started to move up towards Keri. "Uh, uh," she said, as she stepped backward and pulled her strap back to its starting position.

"You're loving this, aren't you?" Riley questioned.

"You have NO idea," she said, putting extra emphasis on the 'no', and smirking the whole time. She had her, she completely knew it as well; Riley was losing all control and couldn't help but just let go.

She got back into her previous position and lay back on the bed again. "Continue," Riley said, winking.

Keri looked down at her shoulder, looking back over at Riley without moving her head; she looked so sexy and confident in this moment. She slowly pulled down the strap over her shoulder – very slowly. The anticipation was killing Riley in this moment, but she didn't want to forget it; Riley was well aware that this was the craziest sexy woman she had ever been around and she was blowing her mind right about now.

She reached over and this time was even slower in pulling down the strap of her dress.

Riley leaned back and lifted a pillow over her face, screaming into it, "You're killing me!" She didn't stop looking for long though. She was desperate to see what was beneath that red dress. She had an incredible body and Riley couldn't wait to catch sight of every part of it.

Keri knew what she was doing and could tell Riley was craving her; this led her to prolong the agony even further. It felt like ten minutes had passed before she did anything. In reality it wasn't, but Riley felt like a participant in one of those reality shows where the presenter waits forever, or announces a break.

* * *

In the blink of an eye, she had released her grip on the dress and it had fallen to a heap on the floor. Riley gasped as she took in the beautiful woman stood in front of her in nothing but black lace French knickers; she noticed a small silver heart detail at the front connected by a red tie. Riley couldn't look away, in her opinion her body was perfect, she had curves in all the right places, and her breasts were alert to attention. Riley could see she had a tattoo on the left side of her body, words inscribed there, but Riley couldn't see what they said right now. Every part of Riley was suddenly alive and her body was reactive and responsive to her sensuality.

Looking deep into her eyes longingly, Riley wanted her. In fact Riley was mentally aware she was desperate for her, knowing Keri was reading her like a book; she stepped forward and stood before her. In between Riley's legs she gently stroked her fingers against the still-dressed girl's thighs before leaning down and kissing her purposefully.

Keri maintained the kiss as she slowly pushed her down and climbed on top of her; she pushed her thigh between her legs and deepened their kiss, leaving Riley with nothing but hunger for her. Riley wanted her on every level at this moment and was longing to taste her and feel her.

Riley couldn't control herself any longer and needed to take the control back, she wanted to ensure they were comparable. Slowing the kiss right down, Keri looked down, perplexed; Riley gently stroked her cheek with her thumb. Pushing her blonde hair back, she lifted up and kissed just close to her ear, whispering to her how beautiful she was. Riley rolled her over; kneeling above her, she unclasped her jumpsuit.

Undoing the belt and removing that, she unzipped the back of the outfit. Riley leaned over her, hands both sides of her head, and kissed her slowly. She stood up before removing her arms from the pantsuit and letting it fall to the floor, revealing the matching hot pink underwear set. Moving back onto the bed, she straddled Keri once more and allowed her hair to fall over her face.

Keri reached up and softly grazed the girl's face, whispering about how sexy she was finding her in this moment. Riley sat upright, straddling her, unable to keep her eyes off of her, staring at her shoulders and gently running her nails all the way from Keri's shoulders to her breasts. Cupping each breast, feeling them come to life under her thumbs, they seemed to fit perfectly in Riley's hands. She reached up and put her hands on Riley's bra, sighing heavily, smirking at her. "Told you payback was a bitch," she whispered.

Reaching down, Riley took each of Keri's hands, lifting them above her head to keep them in place, taking her other hand and gently stroking her face once more. Riley leant down and kissed her softly; moving her hair out of the way, she gently kissed her ear lobe before sucking it between her teeth. Riley moved down to her neck, softly sucking it, making sure not to leave a mark, and kissing it gently. Riley continued to do so until she reached her jawline, gently nibbling here, and hearing her soft groans.

Sitting back up, she moved her hand up to meet the other one, lightly running her nails down over her wrists, inner arms, and sides; resting her hands around her waist, slowly and gently massaging the sides of her tummy, there was something about her that was making her not want to rush the night. Riley stopped and took in her tattoo – it was incredibly sexy on her body. Twisting slightly, she stroked the area and read the words: *'Dream as if you'll live forever. Live as if you'll die tomorrow.'* Treasuring the words on her body, it was just something else to add to her perfection.

As Riley slowly moved her hands further down, she gripped the edge of the lace, looking at Keri, wanting to make sure that she was ok with this; her eyes confirmed everything Riley needed to know. She softly pulled her knickers down, in awe of how bare and soft her skin was. Riley's breathing quickened and she realised she had no control over it any longer. Quickly making her way up to her lips, she immersed herself in their kiss… in her. She kissed her softly, moving her hands up to her face, and stayed this way for a long moment.

Moving Keri further up the bed, Riley knew she needed to begin her exploration of the beautiful woman's body. She moved her way down Keri's jawline, taking her time along the way and relishing in every moment. Slowly scraping her nails down her sides, kissing down her right side at first, before moving up to the left and working down that side. She moved her fingers around to the front of Keri's body, slowing, softly scraping her nails down her tummy, feeling her arching into the graze in a sign of acceptance, making Riley want and need her even more powerful.

Riley moved her lips to her heart, softly kissing her skin there; she slowly worked her way down her tummy, gently nibbling each part as she moved downwards. Keri's body was building up as she got closer to her centre. Moving herself further down the bed as her mouth had reached Keri's tan line, Riley again slowly grazed her nails around the middle where her knicker line would be. Moving slower, downward, she could feel the frustration beginning to build; she could tell she was ready for her to take her but Riley wasn't quite ready for that yet, and was enjoying getting to know every part of the girl's body. She kissed her appealingly soft skin, fully appreciative in this moment. As she moved down a little more she heard her groans become louder. God, she wanted her so bad right now but was desperate to hold out. Completely uncertain she would be able to contain herself, Riley pushed Keri's leg out slightly further, allowing herself easier access to where she needed to be. As she did, she could hear Keri's sighs; it was almost with relief, but Riley still wasn't ready just yet.

Riley stopped close to her lips, taking in her scent. She smelled divine and it took every component in her to not stop and delight in the woman. She craved time to indulge and explore her, letting her quiet breathing gently fall upon her inner thigh. She waited until she was succumbing to desire, before leaving her hanging once more. Riley felt her hand in her hair with a sense of urgency, ignoring the emotional instruction and continuing down, lifting her foot in her hand, gently kissing her foot, moving up her inner calf, stopping and gently biting and sucking the back of her knee. Riley slowly moved up her inner thigh, slowing down her pace immensely. Feeling and hearing her breath quickening, Riley was so captivated by the enticement she knew she couldn't resist the urgency to taste and feel Keri any longer.

Riley wanted to repeat the action on the other leg but she knew she didn't have the willpower, slowly running her tongue between her lips, stopping and introducing pressure where she needed it. Riley bent Keri's legs up, moving her arms underneath and reaching around to lock their fingers together. She then continued to put pressure where she knew Keri needed it. Riley slowly manoeuvred her tongue, making circles around her pressure point and tightening her grip on Keri's fingers. Keri was pushing herself further into Riley, gripping tightly, and she could tell she was getting close; she moved her tongue very slowly down from where it was, before reaching her parted lips, appreciating her scent and taste. Slowly inserting her tongue deep inside Keri, she was taking absolute pleasure in the act, as she could feel and taste her readiness. Keri gasped before her breathing quickened rapidly. She moved her head back against the pillow, biting her lip; she looked incredibly sexy in this moment and Riley was desperate to feel the anticipation come to an end around her.

Riley released one of her hands from the grip of Keri's and slowly ran her nails down her stomach once more, lifting her right leg over her shoulder, allowing her to deepen where she wanted and needed to be. Moving her thumb, rubbing firmly over her pressure point, she pushed her tongue inside her further, basking in her warmth and readiness. Riley slowly began to rock into Keri and could feel her tightening around her. She could tell she was on the edge as she felt her leg tighten over her shoulder and her hand move to the back of Riley's head, thrusting her into her further. Riley couldn't ever remember having ever experienced such intensity with a woman and realised she was not the only one on the verge; she was close behind her, she could already feel it. She felt her grip on her hand tighten as she rocked faster allowing her once more to go deeper with each movement. Riley heard her cry out in pleasure as the release washed over her. The waves continued to ripple through her body as she moved her thumb but slowly kept her tongue moving in slow circles, indulging in her sweet taste. In doing so she couldn't stop groans of her own pleasure being released.

* * *

Keri looked totally spent, but seemingly that wasn't going to stop her. In one fast movement she had moved Riley off of her and was now straddling her; God she was hot, she thought. She'd pulled one side of Riley's bra down, before softly biting her nipple; it was a complete contrast of pleasure and pain, causing her to acknowledge she wouldn't last very long, at all. Keri leaned back up; with one hand she began caressing Riley's hardened nipple and with the other leaned backwards before moving her fingers inside the damp underwear, slowly sliding two fingers inside Riley's wetness. The feeling of Keri taking control was an amazing feeling, Riley thought. She looked up, observing Keri as her back arched, her pert breasts moving as her body slowly rocked against Riley's middle section and her fingers were pushing deeper and faster with each movement. Riley had no control over her body, it was suddenly unbalanced to her command and as she quickened her pace, her body was working against her and had buckled, releasing the total pleasure she had bestowed upon Riley.

Keri softly removed her fingers from inside her and collapsed onto her body, laying her head between Riley's breasts. Each rested their hands around the other. Softly stroking hair, they laid, silently, enveloped in each other's bodies as they collected themselves.

After a while, Keri looked up at her with a lopsided grin. She could see the fire in her eyes and whilst Riley was knackered, she couldn't deny her body's longing to be with the woman again. She was slowly crawling up Riley's body, stopping to face her, smiling back down before kissing her softly. She slowly ran her tongue over her bottom lip before gently taking it between hers and sucking it gently, groaning loudly into the kiss. Keri pulled away, looking back intently. "You have an advantage over me, Riley Sharpe. Whilst you look fucking incredible in that underwear set, it's simply not fair play when I am lying here naked," she whispered into her ear. God, she knew how to drive her crazy, and nobody had ever had the ability to do that before; she put those thoughts away, thinking she would analyse that information later.

Working her way slowly down her body, she softly bit Riley's shoulder; whilst doing so she lifted her back slightly and unclasped her bra. Slowly and gently, she laid her back down and returned to kissing and biting slowly down Riley's shoulder and down over the top of her breast. She was very carefully working the bra strap down with her fingertips. Moving a strap from the other woman's body, before slowly releasing her breast, she kissed slowly and moved towards her hardened nipple. Riley had always had incredibly sensitive nipples and at the moment she was craving her lips there, aching for her over her unhurried actions before she finally reached her destination. She rolled her tongue in tiny circles, before catching it between her teeth, gently pulling and sucking. She began to flick her tongue hard and fast over Riley's nipple and she couldn't help the cries of pleasure as she did it. "I can't cope, please, I am going to come right now if you continue this," she said to her.

Keri looked up, surprised and grinning. "Interesting, but I'm not ready for that just yet, so I'll save that for later." She smirked.

She removed the remainder of her bra, throwing it to the floor before finding her way again and kissing slowly down her abdomen. She worked her way from side to side, biting down Riley's sides whilst scraping her nails down the other side at the same time. How the hell this woman knew exactly what she loved, she had no idea. Riley knew she was paying her back for the lengthy exploration she'd earlier bestowed upon her.

She reached her knicker line and looked up into her eyes expectantly. She couldn't say for sure, but she was pretty sure she'd stopped breathing in that moment. She kissed over the top of her underwear and softly scraped her finger down her lower tummy. She ever so slightly pulled the central rim of Riley's knickers a tiny amount. Gasping, she didn't know if she had the self-control; she could feel herself bubbling once more, ready to explode in pure ecstasy at this incredible woman tantalising her. Keri moved her hands up to her breasts, giving each nipple a slight squeeze before moving around to her sides and scraping her nails not so softly downwards; she was actually killing her right now and she didn't know how much longer she could hold on.

She moved her hands past her knickers and slowly lifted her fingers back under them; she pulled out and slowly moved them down Riley's legs. She seemed captivated as she looked down at her bare skin. She stroked the area softly and moved up, allowing their bodies to come together. Breathless at the contact of them here in this moment, Keri kissed her again before continuing her descent. Kissing softly all the way down the centre of Riley's body, she stopped and grazed the backs of her fingers over her soft skin below her waist. She kissed downward, pressing her tongue to Riley's clitoris. This caused her to buckle against the touch; she pulled the hardened area in, sucking it gently between her teeth. Once more she was making her lose all self-control. Keri took her nipple between her thumb and forefinger, gently caressing it and with the other hand, reached down and slowly pushed her index finger inside Riley.

She heard Keri groan loudly, and assumed it was the welcome as she softly entered and pushed inside of her. She curved her finger, touching exactly where she needed to be touched. There were so many varying levels of sensation bubbling inside at this moment, trying her damnedest to concentrate as she struggled to focus on the different elements of pleasure within her body.

It was only a matter of moments before her body

was taken over with complete euphoria; Keri moved to meet her lips with her own as wave after wave came over her. Riley had never had bad sex per se, but in this moment she felt like this is what it was about, coming together, and becoming one. As her body tightened around the fingers, her legs tightened around Keri's body; she was completely absorbed in their kiss and this wholeness between them.

Chapter 11

They lay half under the covers, the TV on in the background with a chick flick playing that they were seldom watching. Keri was snuggled into Riley, tracing shapes on her tummy. She sighed blissfully. "I didn't think I could have seen a better sight than last night in your CK boxers and vest; then this evening in your jumpsuit. Fuck, you blew me away; but now, here, wow, you are incredibly beautiful. I could look at your body all day long," she said.

Looking down at her, Riley was scrunching her nose up. "Touché, gorgeous. You can tell you run along a beach every morning." She smiled. "I love this." Riley traced her fingers over the side of her body with the words inscribed there.

"Ohhhh, we could have matching and you could get the same." She smirked, tickling Riley's sides. She was squealing like hell, which amused her immensely at the realisation that the girl was incredibly ticklish. She managed to trap her hands, in a bid to stop what she was doing.

Getting up, she went to the fridge, feeling her eyes on her naked body; opening two bottles of Corona and inserting a slice of lime in each of them; she picked up her bag of 'award' Haribos and walked back, handing Keri a beer. "Bit late, isn't it?" She laughed. It was, she knew it was.

Ripping off the corner of the sweet bag with her teeth, she nodded soberly. "Yup, pretty much, but at the risk of uttering the most ridiculous words on a one night stand, I don't want it to end. Not yet!" she said. "So... one of two choices for you really. Go to sleep and get your rest for the last day and returning overseas, *or* not think about that for the time being, and just enjoy ourselves while we still can."

Riley had no idea what came over her, and she could feel the heat rising. Luckily before it reached her head, Keri was looking over at her sincerely. She smiled shyly and downed half of her beer in one go, laughing. In that moment she knew she wasn't alone. One of her favourite things about her was her ability to maintain a situation's importance, yet alleviate the negative feelings attached to it.

Riley laughed at her goofy-ass grin; not wanting to dampen the mood, she followed suit. "Great." She jumped on the bed, spilling her beer slightly on the cover. "Oops, sorry! Anyways, good choice, because I have been waiting all night to do this." She winked.

Searching the Haribos seriously, she collected three rings from the bag. She moved down to her foot, lifting it and placing a ring on her second toe, slowly creeping up with a sweetie ring on two of her fingers. Smirking, she came face to face and kissed her softly, placing another in between her lips. She went to speak and was immediately shushed, moving her own finger to her lips, raising an eyebrow. Riley moved backwards slightly, leaning down and flicking her nipple with her tongue. She watched as it sprang into action, placing the ring over it and looking very pleased with herself, making the other girl laugh.

Riley reached over and grabbed her beer, taking a mouthful; she swallowed some, relishing the cold liquid as it slipped down her throat, before leaning down to her other nipple and slowly dropping a little bit of the beer over the area. Keri gasped and grabbed the sheets as the cold hit a sensitive part of her body. Slowly licking the dribbles of liquid around her nipple, Riley sucked it into her mouth not so gently.

Riley looked up at Keri, laughing as she lay there with a ring in between her lips. She tried to suck it in, before she thought better when she was glared at seriously and raised her hands in defeat.

As Riley lowered herself to the bottom of the bed, she kissed the sole of her foot in small bursts before reaching the ring, using her teeth to move it up over her toe, into her mouth and enjoying the sweet. She moved further up her body, kissing all the way up, slowly, softly, until reaching the ring around her nipple which Riley gently sucked and pulled off, continuing to enjoy the sweetie. As she continued the remainder of her journey up to Keri's mouth, she put her lips on Keri's. Holding her body up with one arm and using the other to hold her head, gently massaging the back of it with her own fingers, Riley looked squarely at Keri, smiling, knowing it had reached all the way to her eyes. She sucked the ring from her lips and into her mouth before beginning to chew the sweet, rolling over beside her, sighing and drinking the beer.

"Oh my fucking god, you actually just 'bloked' me," she said incredulously.

Riley was unable to control her laughter, causing her to spit her beer out. *Attractive, Riley*, she thought. She was desperately trying to contain herself. Finally, when she was able to she rolled over, facing the woman, and asked her, "I whatted you?" Still giggling.

"You 'bloked' me, you actually just... you..." She pushed her in the chest lightly with her finger. "Had your fun, rolled over, ignored me and went back to your beer. YOU... bloked me," she said, scoffing. Riley could tell it was killing her, trying to contain the smile desperately peeking through Keri's lips. "I mean seriously you literally only need to reach down and scratch your balls and you have actually mastered it," she said, shaking her head in mock disbelief.

Gasping loudly, putting on her best worried look, Riley looked under the covers for a long time, before falling back on the bed forcibly, lifting the back of her hand to her forehead, feigning bewilderment. "No, we're good, no balls down there!" She smirked.

Keri punched her in the arm teasingly, shaking her head and rolling her eyes.

Riley lay down on the bed, still facing Keri. She pulled the cover up over herself and picked up the beer, taking a swig before resting it on the bed in her hand.

"Why so serious, beautiful?" said Keri as she leaned down and kissed the tip of the girl's nose before copying the actions.

Unable to work out what was going on in her head, it must be the drink, she pondered. Shaking her head, both to Keri and the thoughts, she lay there looking at her, examining the trainer in her bed.

Riley could get totally lost in those eyes, she thought. She traced her fingers over the words on her side. "I really do love this tattoo, I've never really been a fan of them but, for some reason I love this." She smiled at Keri. "It's incredibly sexy, I must say," she said once more. She could just imagine her in resort, on the beach in a bikini with that on show. Riley was almost glad she wouldn't be with her. I'm pretty sure she wouldn't be able to control herself in that situation, which clearly wouldn't be appropriate!

"Tel..." She stopped herself and took a sip of her beer instead.

Keri lifted her chin with her fingers, forcing their eyes to meet. "Stop this, be open with me, Riles. Be you. You're forgetting something very important; I was the one that made the first move! I... ME." She pointed. "I was the one that pointed out there was something about you that intrigued me on day one! Stop second guessing what this is, what you're feeling, and why you're feeling it. Let's just make the most of tonight and each other, ok?"

After everything she'd told her about the bad breakup with her ex-girlfriend and her removal of all women or intimacy in her life, something clicked in that moment with her. She was right, Riley needed to stop wasting time. It was stupidly late, she knew it, and daren't look at the time, for some reason she just didn't want this to be over.

"I'm good, sorry, just the drink I guess! Rightly or wrongly I want to know more about you, just in this moment, so let's just talk? I mean don't get me wrong there's no way I'm not gonna go back to this awesome bod before we go to sleep tonight," she said, winking. "But right now, you ok to just chat?" she said to her seriously.

Keri looked shocked, but in that same moment she looked apprehensive too. She could feel her demeanour and breathing relax after a moment or two. "Yeah, I can do that." She smiled nervously.

Taking the last of her beer, she held it up to her, asking if she would like another. She downed the remainder of hers and handed the empty bottle over. She walked back to the fridge feeling her eyes on her, this time looking over, squinting her eyes, letting Keri know she'd been caught out. It was the first time she'd seen it but she got embarrassed and it was totally sexy on her. Avoiding her uncomfortableness, Riley said, "Ten questions?"

"Ok, you first?" she said, sitting up a little.

"Full name?"

Keri eyed her questioningly, she clearly thought it was a waste of a question, but Riley didn't care, she wanted to know as much as she could about her.

"Kerianne Lottie Sarah Johnson."

"Hmmmm, Kerianne." She nodded in appreciation of this newfound information.

"No," she said sternly. "You call me Kerianne, I can guarantee, you'll never touch me or be touched again, and *that* is a promise," she said, with extra emphasis on the 'that'.

"Ok, ok," said Riley, holding her hands up in mock defeat.

"You?"

"Riley Laura Sharpe."

"Pretty."

"Your turn," Riley said.

"Age?"

"Twenty-four. You?"

"Twenty-eight. Next?" Keri said.

"Where are you from?" asked Riley.

"Brighton, you?"

"A little village in Cheshire."

"Oooh, posh girl," she mocked.

"Hardly, next!"

"Siblings?"

"One... brother... Adam Christopher Sharpe." Riley laughed. "You?"

"Three brothers, one sister."

"Wow, close?" Riley questioned, getting caught up in more than one question at a time.

"Question five?" She smirked.

"Fucker."

"Oooohhhh you swore. Punishment, punishment!" she said.

"Huh? What are you on about now?" She laughed.

"COME ON? Seriously? You must know this, no swearing in the game – it calls for punishment, to be chosen by the opponent." Keri was taking this very seriously.

"So, um, can I ask what said punishment is?"

asked Riley, smiling at the girl.

"I'll go with a long, slow, soft kiss, Riley."

She loved how she said her name. She was more than happy to accommodate on this occasion. As they finished the kiss, Riley pulled away slowly. "You totally made that rule up didn't you?" she asked Keri, laughing.

"Yup, pretty much. Needed a kiss! What can I say?"

This girl was seriously too much.

"Anyways, your bonus question. Yes, we are an incredibly close family. I miss it a lot, being around the family and the kids and stuff. I'm the only one not close by, and it's hard." She suddenly seemed very vulnerable and normal; Riley was desperate to wrap her up in her own arms and hold her tight.

"How about you?"

Smiling, she answered, "Yeah, same, real close. Adam and I are so alike yet so different; we are a close family for sure. Ad's at uni at the moment. He's three years younger than me and training to be a barrister."

"Wow, intelligence as well as good looks." She giggled. "Next?"

"Hmmmm, what got you into repping?"

She sighed. "Wow, toughie. I have a normal family, a big family, one of the youngest, all happily married, kids, Catholic. We were expected to be straight. I tried it, I hated it. I did the whole boyfriend, engagement, but..." She stopped and pondered on her words for a moment. "Have you ever been to Brighton?"

"No, never."

"Brighton's hard to be straight, if you have an eye for the girls. Wow, Temptation Island, let me tell you. I tore myself up from one day to the next; I wasn't like my sister and brothers. Hell, I wasn't like anyone in my opinion. I fought and fought, before I ended up in a state of depression. I went to therapy for a while to overcome my guilt of disappointing my folks and the fear of coming out." She stopped again. After a few moments, continuing, she had a faint smile on her face which was catching. Riley looked back, smiling, waiting for her response.

"So, I had a couple months of this group therapy thing, came home, and we had a huge Christmas dinner a few weeks later. My sister-in-law, Kimmy, who FYI I LOVE."

I raised my eyebrow in question.

"Not like that, silly, she's ace, we get on so well. Well anyways, she stood and said she'd missed out on the 'youth' games, and as the kids were upstairs playing she wanted to relive her youth. It's weird, Kimmy is an in-law but she's kinda the one that binds us all together, she has always been like a big sister to me. Anyways she said she wanted to play 'I have never', allegedly due to falling pregnant so young with Jason, my eldest nephew," she said, gleaming. It was a new look on her. "So, she spouted this entire BS. We went around the houses and in the end my brother Jason said, 'I have never slept with anyone of the same sex.' Everyone went silent and I could feel myself blushing and knew it was now or never, and at that moment, Justin, the baby of the family, downed his drink. Everyone was completely stunned; he's in no way camp and you really wouldn't have expected it. The table fell silent and I could see Justin getting concerned over it all. At that time my father stood up and said, 'We've all been waiting so bloody long for Kerianne to come out, we missed that Justin was in the same camp.'" She wandered off for a moment, before looking at Riley. "Have you ever had one of those defining moments in your life, Riley?"

Riley loved her family, they were so close and they had had so many defining moments, but nothing like she was explaining now. She was a little jealous, shaking her head slowly. "I don't think so, no."

"In that moment, I knew no matter what, my family were proud of me and loved me regardless of me being gay, and would do anything they could to stop any pain their children would ever feel. Kimmy feigned shock and said something about getting with the wrong sibling, and we all rolled about laughing for the rest of the day."

Riley felt touched that she had shared such a story with her, and leaned in, kissing her softly. "You're the most incredible person I have ever met, Keri." She smiled, drinking more beer.

"So how about you?"

"What do you mean?"

"What made you want to do this job?"

"Ahhh!! From as long as I can remember it's all I've ever wanted to do. I don't know what drew me to it, but, I've always had this hidden passion there. Call me stupid for not having bigger ambitions. My folks were hoping it was a phase; my dad was an accountant, mum a teacher. I followed in his footsteps. I'm a daddy's girl," she blushed, "and have worked in finance for the last few years, just slowly losing my dreams, I guess. Anyways, on a plus, bad times at work caused me to rent my house out to my best mate Cara, move in with my folks and concentrate on the application and interview process of life as a holiday rep, so that I could either do it or at least say I tried."

Keri was staring at her intently; she rested her head on Riley's arm and they just lay there silently, looking at each other.

"You ok?" Riley asked her.

"Why couldn't you have been a new rep in my resort?" she asked sadly.

The realisation was suddenly kicking in; she reluctantly picked up her phone, and shut her eyes sadly.

"Do we need to go to sleep, Riley?" she asked like a small child. It completely tore her up in that moment.

"As much as I don't want to baby, I think we should."

As much as she'd spent all night looking to appreciate her body more throughout the night, it was not what she wanted anymore; she just wanted to lay and cuddle the girl.

"I need to brush my teeth," she said to Keri.

"Mine's not here." Keri looked to the door.

God, she wanted to hold her so bad. As much as she'd always had a thing about people using her toothbrush, she didn't seem to care in this moment.

"Don't go, use mine?"

"Riley, a bomb or a fire is the only thing that is going to remove me from your arms tonight," she said with a small smile.

"Bit extreme," she said, pulling her up.

They brushed their teeth and Riley handed over her toothbrush whilst she cleansed and toned her face; Keri couldn't help but look in the reflection of her perfect body. She was simply stunning!

They went to bed, shutting the curtains to the already creeping-in sun.

Keri held open her arms to Riley; they kissed a long, silent kiss together before she leaned into her and they fell asleep on each other, staying that way throughout the remainder of the night, or morning as it were.

Chapter 12

Riley wasn't in the mood for the alarm to be going off in her ear this morning. Turning to face Keri after silencing the alarm, she took in the girl's beauty, her blonde shoulder-length hair fanned out over her arm and pillow. She seemed to have such an impact on her.

"Stop looking at me in that lustful way, Riley Laura Sharpe."

She laughed instantaneously.

"I dunno what you mean," leaning in to kiss her.

"I have morning breath," she said.

"I don't care, I need a kiss before we have to get up and get ready; I'll effectively never see you again after a few hours," she said sadly.

"Well there's a nice positive and uplifting way to wake up," Keri said, shaking her head. "This time tomorrow I'll be a distant memory, Riles. You will be in resort living the dream without a second thought of me!" she said.

"Wait, I'll be there tomorrow? You know when I'm going and where?" she said, smirking. Her demeanour changed slightly. "But, if you're 'alleging' I'm going to forget about you, then guess I'm not going to Rhodes," she said sombrely.

"You wouldn't want to come where I was, you need to go off and experience it first-hand." Keri touched her face.

"For the record Keri, I've known you 'intimately' for about thirty-six hours and that's all, but I'm well aware that I have never had this reaction or connection with any other woman I have been with, so I can assure you, you won't be a distant memory. I'm pretty sure I'll remember last night forever." She smiled a little.

Gently stroking her fingers over Riley's cheek, Keri leaned down and kissed her entirely.

They lay with their bodies immersed for a short while; Keri moved first, getting up and pulling Riley with her. She wrapped her arms around Riley's neck, holding her tightly. "As much as I'd love to stay and do this all day, we should get a move on," she said softly.

Smirking slightly, Riley kissed her passionately, taking her hand and leading her into the shower for one last moment together.

Chapter 13

Riley put her case in the car, and walked back to the hotel to finish checking out. She'd had a great week and if this last week was a fraction of what life overseas would be like then she knew she was going to have a ball.

She couldn't help wondering where she was going, and was apparently feeling a little disappointed that she wouldn't be going with Keri; she was probably right though, things would be different. Maybe one day they would cross paths again, if Riley enjoyed the job and lasted, that was.

As the group came together, Keri and Glen went through the highs and the lows of the course. They thanked everyone for their hard work, before telling them they thought they would each be a credit to the teams they were going to, even James, which caused everybody to laugh. They explained that they would each be taken by either Keri or Glen. At that point they would give feedback based on the work throughout the course that they thought would aid them in the future overseas; after that they would be told which resort they were going to and given their flight details.

Riley was feeling anxious, uncertain about where she would be going and what the people would be like there. She'd been told that people either start in Spain or in Greece and they then have a tendency to stay in those places rather than moving between the two. She wanted to explore, learn, travel these places, and didn't want to stick to the same place the whole time; it would defeat the purpose of doing it, she thought.

Riley spent the first hour and a half chatting with Sally and Scott; she was really hoping that she would be sent with one of them so she had a friend to go with. They had all agreed that when they were done they would wait for each other so they could share all the details.

The hours had passed and there were only a few people left in the room to find out; Riley was sure Keri was doing it on purpose to prolong the agony. Scott was called up next; both Sally and Riley gave him a hug for good luck and off he went.

Glen came out then and called for Sally; she hugged her friend and told her she would be at the carpark when Riley was done so she could say bye to Glen. Riley sat alone in the room staring at the clock, she thought about the training on the welcome meeting speeches and how they had been told to concentrate on a clock on the back wall if there was one so as not to lose yourself and get caught up in the nerves.

Scott appeared at the doorway. "The hottie's waiting for you," he laughed.

She ran over to him, punching his arm. "Jerk. Well, what happened? Where you going?" she asked.

"Well, I had a chat with them both at the

beginning of the week and explained I had spent a year and a half in Tenerife, and whilst I don't really want to be reminded of Angela, I kinda felt like I wanted to go back there; dunno, call it unfinished business. They had some space and basically I'm going back to where I started," he said.

"That's amazing, so you're stoked right?" she asked him.

"Yeah, Riles I'm stoked!" He grinned sheepishly. "Listen, she's waiting for you, I'm gonna wait for Sally and then head off. I fly tonight." He winked. "I am gonna email you as soon as I land with my new number and I want a weekly catch-up with you; you, me, and Sal. The dream team and my two new best friends." He smiled genuinely.

She hugged him hard. "Buddy I love you, and I seriously hope you meet a wonderful girl who'll treat you exactly as you deserve to be treated." She squeezed again and then kissed him before leaving him, in reality she didn't know until when.

She knocked on the door to room 3, where she had been directed, and walked in to find Keri sat writing some paperwork; Riley noticed that she was wearing her glasses and had forgotten how sexy and intelligent she looked in them.

Keri looked up at Riley, smirking. "Well Miss Sharpe, please take a seat," said Keri. Riley sat down, mumbling her thanks.

"You ok Riley? Don't think I've known you to be so quiet," she said.

"Yeah, I'm good." She smiled.

"Ok, well let's start then, I guess. So, you have been an exceptional student throughout the week and the content, drive, and enthusiasm was second to none. We have thoroughly," she coughed, "ummm, thoroughly enjoyed being with you this week." Riley could see Keri's cheeks flushing. "You have picked up everything we have said and utilised those tools immediately after us giving them to you. In terms of negative there isn't too much, luckily." Riley looked up as Keri placed her hand over hers. "I would say you need to work on that eye contact, I know you *can* do it. I know this first-hand, remember? But that will come with experience and your confidence will grow. Your confidence in the job respect, I meant." Riley couldn't help but laugh as Keri was the colour of a tomato following her words. "Ermmm, sorry, I didn't mean that, I wasn't meant to say that," she said as she pulled her glasses off and rubbed her eyes. "Long day, I'm sorry!"

Riley turned her hand over and laced her fingers through Keri's. "Forget it, it's fine. For the record you're incredibly cute when you're embarrassed." Riley laughed, squeezing her hand.

"Hmmmm. So... that was really, the only constructive criticism we had for you, you were an incredible participant this week and both myself and Glen feel very privileged to say we were your trainers. Anyways, without further ado, the most important part of your week. You will be going to..." Keri said, before leaving the room deathly silent.

"You're kidding me, right? Are you trying to give Ant and Dec a run for their money? Just tell me already?" Riley sighed, giggling.

"You're going to Kos. You will be flying out at 3.30am tomorrow morning so will need to be at Manchester airport for 1.30am. Here are your tickets and a letter to inform the ticket agent you are resort staff so the allowance is set at 50kg for you." She smiled. "Congratulations Riley, you did awesome."

Riley was lost for words, trying to assemble all the words that were rushing around in her mind at that moment. "Thank you Keri, for what has been the most amazing week of my life; the most *amazing night* of my life," she said quietly. "For the record this isn't the most important part of the week for me; it was, it would have been, and maybe it should be, but all that changed because of you last night," Riley said.

They stood up and Keri pulled Riley into an embrace. She grabbed Riley's chin with her thumb and forefinger before lifting it up to meet her. "Stop looking like a little lost puppy, you're killing me right now," Keri said.

"Snap!"

They laughed and Keri pulled her chin closer so that their lips met for one last slow kiss. It was the most breath-taking kiss Riley had ever had, causing her to sigh into it. They moved back and rested their foreheads together.

"To meeting in another time and another place," Keri said.

"Most definitely," said Riley.

"Come on we need to go, Glen will be waiting for me to go the station," Keri said.

Riley turned her around and pushed her up against

the wall, kissing her with utter force and passion. She pulled away, smiling at Keri.

"Fuck, I love how you do that," Keri said.

"I know, you told me, remember? I wanted to make sure you didn't forget this week." Riley said to her.

"I can assure you that won't ever happen, Riles," she said, kissing the tip of Riley's nose. They opened the door and made their way to the carpark in the search for Sally and Glen.

* * *

As they approached the carpark they saw Glen and Sally in an embrace; they were leaning up against her car, Sally with her arms around Glen's neck. As Riley and Keri arrived at the car, Sally squealed, running to her friend. "Where are you going? Where are you going?" Sally was like a four-year-old jumping up and down.

"Kos, how about you?" Riley asked.

Sally looked back at Glen, who looked over to Keri; they were all smiling at each other. Sally looked sheepish. "Majorca."

"Wow, you guys are going together?" she said, disappointed.

"Well actually no, I'm going to Palma Nova, the opposite end of the island really, compared to Glen," she said.

"At least you guys can see each other," Riley said back to Sally. She took her friend into a hug. "I'm made up for you, honestly, that's so cool."

"Thanks, Riley. So are you super excited about going to Kos? I've been there on a girls' holidays, it's so good; I love the place," she said.

"Yeah, I'm stoked," she said.

Riley felt Keri looking at her; she looked up and away again, she didn't want her to see the disappointment in Riley's eyes.

"So Keri, I was kinda hoping for a favour?" said Glen.

"Huh?" She looked away from Riley and up to Sally and Glen, who were now back in each other's arms.

"Well, we aren't on the same flight; this one has a weekend of spoiling before she arrives in resort, so she's asked if she can drive me to the airport. Allegedly, Manchester is on the way to Scotland!" He rolled his eyes.

"Oh, ummm yeah, that's fine, I'll just grab the train up, the flight's before mine anyhow isn't it? So it's no big deal," Keri said, dejected.

Riley couldn't stop herself from feeling pissed that Sally and Glen were going to be together, and she had no reason to be. She was made up her friends had a shot. In the grand scheme of things they had been together all week, whereas Keri and Riley had only got it on last night.

"You ok?" said Sally, looking at Riley.

"Yeah, I'm fine." She smiled softly.

"Ermmm, I guess I'm going to go back and order my taxi to the station. I may see you at the airport tonight then, ehy?" Keri said, looking to Glen.

"You sure you're ok with this Kel? If you'd rather me not go with Sal it's fine, I won't," he said to his friend.

"It's fine, honestly." She smiled and grabbed her suitcase handle.

"Where are you flying from?" Riley turned to Keri.

"Sorry, what?"

"Where are you flying from? And when?"

Glen answered Riley. "We're flying from Manchester, middle of the night flights unfortunately, but we have train tickets booked from here to Manchester in an hour and then we were just going to chill there together until we flew," he said. "Hey Riley, are you not flying tonight from Manchester?" he said expectantly.

"You're from Manchester, Riles. You could take her, couldn't you? So she's not alone?" said Sally.

Riley couldn't help herself, she wanted them to know this was not their idea; she'd started this. She wanted to make them know about her and Keri too, she didn't know why, and didn't know how Keri would react, but honestly she didn't care.

The silence killed Keri, she felt unbelievably awkward. "Ermm, it's ok, honestly it's fine. I'm a big girl, I have stuff to do. It's fine you guys, honestly."

"Go on a date with me?" Riley blurted out, looking at Keri.

Keri looked stunned, and it made Riley immediately regret it.

"What?" Sally and Glen chorused, aghast.

"Ermm, why? We can't, we have to go to resort; I'm confused, what are you asking me?" said Keri.

She didn't want her, thought Riley. She looked up sadly at Keri, aware that Sally and Glen were confused and looking between the pair of them.

"Why?" said Keri again. "Why, Riley?" she said, sterner this time.

There was something in her eyes, she could see it. *It's now or never*, she thought.

Riley dropped her bag on the floor and walked over to Keri. "Come with me, I'll drive you to Manchester but I want to take you out along the way. You are incredible, intelligent, beautiful, and oh my god have a body to die for; and for that reason and a million other reasons that I can't quite work out, I want to have another day with you. I don't want it to end now after last night. I want to take you out on a proper date, ride with you, finding out more about… Kimmy, the kids, Brighton and everything else I am able to find out about you. Come with me, Keri? in typical lesbian style, you are gonna have to kinda come home with me and meet my parents whilst I grab my cases but I promise I'll give you a date to remember." She was holding Keri's hands now, looking into her eyes with hope.

A slow smile spread across Keri's lips. "You sure?" she said questioningly.

"Rightly or wrongly, I've never been surer of anything in my life," said Riley, leaning and kissing the girl.

"Seriously, you didn't think to tell me this?" said Sally.

Riley had totally forgotten about the others; she turned around, still holding Keri's hand. Looking at Sally, she took in the girl rested in Glen's arms. She hoped they worked out, they seemed so right for each other.

"Ermmm, when exactly? You haven't come up for air in the last week for me to tell you." She laughed. "Anyways, selfishly, I am going to politely leave yous off now so I can take this incredibly beautiful woman on the date of her life. Nothing like setting yourself up for a fall." She laughed before kissing and hugging them both goodbye. Riley grabbed Keri's suitcase and held her hand out for the woman to take; she followed suit, saying her goodbyes, and then took Riley's hand, walking to the car.

Chapter 14

"You're kind of insane, you know that?" Keri said, smiling.

"Ok, new rule... no more repeating; seriously I'm starting to think you left your vocab back there." Riley grabbed her hand, squeezing slightly. "Ok, ok. I'm crazy, I'm insane, and I've lost the plot. I get it and for the record I do apologise for outing you that way," she said, concentrating on the road.

"Riley, you can't 'out' me, when I'm already out. I don't hide who I am; I just don't broadcast it to, what technically are students that I'm training. I have no care that they found out I was gay, nor do I have any issue with them finding out we've been. Well... been. God, that we had sex last night," she said, and looked out of the window, shaking her head.

Riley liked it when she got tongue tied; as the silence crept over her, she thought how much she also liked what she did with her tongue. Shaking her head to get the images out of her head, today wasn't about that, she thought.

"And FYI, Glen and I had a chat at the bar over shots on the first night of anyone we liked; I said there was someone I had my eye on. We just never got as far as me telling him it was you," she said quietly.

They sat in silence for a short while after that. Eventually Riley broke the silence. "Shall we stop for a sandwich or McDonalds shortly?"

"Yeah, that'll be nice." Keri turned to her, smiley, and taking her hand again.

"So, you know we didn't finish off ten questions, and I vaguely remember something along the lines of you 'alleging' you wanted to find out my life history." She leaned over and kissed her cheek.

"Watch it lady, you'll kill us both doing daft things like that. Fine, you start?" said Riley.

"Favourite singer?" Keri said.

"I don't really have a favourite, I guess it depends what mood I'm in. I'm pretty much into anything within reason, but I must say I am a massive boy band girl, I love One Direction. I went to watch the boyband reunion last year, and it was so cool," she said.

"Shut up!" Keri said, laughing almost hysterically.

"Don't laugh at me," she said sadly.

"Shit, I'm sorry, I thought you were winding me up. I would never laugh at you, Riley. I didn't…" Keri stopped as she realised that Riley was now the one laughing hysterically. "You bitch, I can't believe you just done that to me," Keri said.

"I'm sorry, it was payback for torturing me with kisses whilst driving," Riley said, pulling into the service station.

"Ohhh, ok. I'll remember that next time you want a kiss, you won't get one."

"Hmmm, on the contrary; it's nothing to do with not wanting your kisses, it's more about doing that whilst I'm driving, making me want more, and being fully aware I can't have more," she laughed.

"You are a funny one, Riley Sharpe!"

"I know. Just think how different your life would have been without having ever met me? Come on, gorgeous; I do believe I've promised the date of your life, so Maccy D's is awaiting," she said animatedly, kissing her quickly.

"Hamm, forgot what I signed up for, huh?"

Riley grabbed her hand and they walked into the service station together, it all felt so natural. Riley was shocked about how things had changed in her life this last couple of weeks.

"Ok, so we'll be going for dinner properly this evening, just so you know. I, ummm, don't mean that to sound like I'm being tight or saying that you can't eat a lot. I'm sorry, I'm not used to this," Riley said doubtfully.

"You're doing just fine, beautiful; I'll make sure I just have a Happy Meal so I can enjoy a beautiful meal with a beautiful girl this evening, that cool?" Keri said to Riley.

Riley smiled shyly. "Thank you."

"Let me buy you lunch, you have taken me back and are driving me about, so please?" said Keri.

"No way, and it's not open for discussion," she said seriously. "What do you want?"

Riley ordered their lunches and walked to a table for them to sit at. It felt weird to her; they hadn't had done this, it felt so normal, yet so strange. Riley was getting too comfortable and she knew it wasn't good but she didn't seem able to stop herself for some reason.

Riley opened her Happy Meal and pulled the toy out, handing it to Keri. "Don't say I don't know how to treat a woman." She winked.

"So, how do you feel about your placement?" said Keri.

"Ermm, yeah I guess. It's all very surreal if I'm honest, and not really how I kind of anticipated it."

"What do you mean?"

"I don't know really, I can't explain it. I guess you just get to know all these amazing people and you want to continue the ride; that probably makes no sense," she said, putting a French fry in her mouth, deep in thought.

Keri placed her hand on Riley's. "It does completely, and so you know, everyone feels this way. You get friendly with everyone, you have the same wants, desires, so it's not unreasonable or surprising that you want to continue that journey with them; more so because of the fact that irrespective of whether people have wanted this forever or for a month, it's still kinda scary shit, ya know. Ultimately, you are moving to a different country, living within different cultures and leaving all you've ever known."

She did know. She knew exactly what she meant. She nodded, taking in Keri's words.

"I just want to go to the bathroom before we leave," Riley said.

"No worries, I'll grab us some waters and a magazine for me to read whilst you're driving."

Riley met Keri at the front door. She noticed the bag. "You bought the entire store, I see." She bumped her shoulder.

Keri rolled her eyes, dumping the bag in the boot but removing the magazine, newspaper, and drinks.

* * *

After a while of silence, Keri looked up from her magazine, turning to the side. "Continuation of the game?" She looked at Riley expectantly.

"Sure? Hit me baby." She laughed.

"My word you're grim," Keri said, shaking her head and rolling her eyes at Riley.

"See that sign there?" Keri looked over to see a 'hard shoulder in half a mile' sign looking at her; she looked at Riley questioningly.

"You'll be left there, you keep the backchat," she said, seemingly pleased with herself.

"Do you want kids?" Keri asked quietly.

"Wow that was... deep."

"I'm sorry, took the game too far. I was struggling with questions."

"It's fine, stop apologising for this. I'm loving this journey, us. I know I'll regret that but for now let's please both of us stop overthinking it, right?" Riley said.

Keri looked up through her eyelashes, and gave a lop-sided grin.

Riley sighed. "Honestly, it's a difficult one. I would have always said no. I love kids, don't get me wrong, but actually love giving them back more. My life has always been the dream of this job. I may last a day, a week, a month, or forever, I honestly don't know. I have never had a proper relationship, really. So I guess until I meet that one person I want to spend the rest of my life with then I wouldn't like to say. I'm sorry, I copped out of that answer completely. You?" Riley said.

"Yeah, I think so. I have the typical 'American' family. Massive, close, holidays and celebrations all together, I don't think I would like the thought of one day just being me, or me and my partner being the only ones without kids at shindigs," she said.

Riley was nodding her head to the girl. "Ideal marriage?" she said.

"Wow, these *are* getting deep," Keri said.

"You started it."

"True, true. Well as much as I love my family and we are big and close, I'm kinda private, so for me I'd much prefer something small, private, and intimate if I'm honest. How about you?" she said, turning in her seat to face Riley, resting the side of her face on the seat once more.

"I don't think I can concentrate with you sat looking all cute like that, I'll be pulling off into a hotel for a quickie." Riley laughed.

"Charming, and they say romance is dead. I'm not moving so stop playing avoidance and answer."

"Ok, ok. So demanding." She rolled her eyes. "I'm

pretty much on the same page really. I am very private, so whilst I wouldn't want to upset my family, I would have to do something with them, but I guess I like the idea of eloping. Going somewhere really cool where gay marriage is legal. I'd love it on a beach, fairly casual, but both perfectly private and perfectly meaningful; sounds shit I guess, but I suppose that's just how I've pictured it if it ever happened."

"I don't think it sounds shit, I think it sounds perfect," said Keri. "So where are your top three destinations?"

"For marriage?" Riley asked, looking at the girl.

"No, no. Off the subject of marriage. Just in general, where are three places you would give anything to visit?" she confirmed.

"Bora Bora, Chicago, and Rio de Janeiro," Riley said.

"Wow… that easy. And, trust you to want to go to the world's most expensive destinations," she laughed.

"Whatever," Riley said, laughing. "What about you? Where are your top three?"

"Ermmm, well I've always quite fancied the UAE so I would definitely love to do Dubai. And… as clichéd as it probably sounds, I've always wanted to go to New York so that would be number two, and lastly, I love cities as I love to learn about the history and culture, so probably somewhere in Italy; I've never been and imagine it to be so romantic yet so culturally fulfilling and historical. Not quite as exciting as yours, I'm afraid," she said.

"Achievable though, we could skip out on Hightail and just go visit your three places." Riley smiled.

Riley pulled off the motorway; she was happy they had made it before the rush hour started. "So, we're like fifteen minutes away. My folks are going to beg us to go out for a final supper just so you know. I will explain that we need to go out and do some bits and then will be back and ask for a lift to the airport. I don't like lying but I will bend the truth a little. They know I'm gay, but, ummm, I hope you don't mind…"

"Riles, we slept together last night, you're giving me a ride to the airport. You do not need to take me to your family and declare your undying love for me. It's ok, I'm cool, and I'm your friend you offered to give a ride as we're flying at similar times. I'm looking forward to meeting them." She smiled, squeezing Riley's knee.

* * *

Shortly after, Riley pulled the car into the drive; she grabbed her suitcase from the boot and winked to Keri, as she could hear the door opening. Her mum was squealing down the drive to her daughter. "You're back! Oh Riley, It's so good to have you home. Please say you have some time at home before you leave," she said, holding her daughter's face in her hands.

Riley felt awful, but she had warned her mum that this may be happening. "Sorry Ma, I fly tonight." She looked over to Keri.

She looked disappointed, but in a mum's true fashion, shrugged it off and got on with it. "Hmmm, yes. I noticed a pretty lady with you, is this?" She looked back at her daughter.

"No Ma, this is my friend Keri. We're flying the same time so I said rather than going on the train up here alone and then spending twelve hours alone at the airport, she could ride up and we could go together; you know, some moral support for me?" She winked at her mum.

"Well, I can hope one day my only daughter will bring home a beautiful woman to settle down with," she said, putting her arm through Keri's and pulling her down the drive, asking fifty questions without letting up for air. Keri looked over her shoulder at Riley, smirking.

She could feel that this was going to be trouble already. "Don't mind me, I'm ok, I'll manage… alone!" she shouted to them.

Riley walked into the kitchen where her mum and Keri were completely engrossed; she saw her father and watched as he was weighing up the random girl in his kitchen that apparently had the same ability to speak a thousand words a minute with no let-up of air.

She laughed as she bent down to embrace her father.

"She with you?" he whispered, eyeing both his daughter and the woman inquisitively.

"Yup, a friend from training, Keri. We're flying roughly the same time, so thought I'd do my good deed for the day and travel together so she weren't alone on a train and airport all day," she said.

"Ooohhhh my ever so generous daughter." He smirked, returning to his paper.

"Don't get ideas, mister! She's only a friend. Anyways, I'm pretty sure I left you here, have you actually moved since I left a week ago?" She laughed, checking the date on the paper for clarity.

"I'm hiding, pretending to busy myself from your mother," her father said back.

"Pops, you are aware that only a four-year-old actually believes you can hide behind a paper, right?" She laughed.

He feigned shock horror as he inspected the paper all around.

"What are you two whispering about?" Her mother turned around to look at them.

Before she could answer she heard the door open.

"Piles, how the hell are you, ugly?" Adam said as he came in.

"Adam Christopher Sharpe, watch your mouth, we have guests," her mother reprimanded her little brother, causing her to giggle.

"Oh, hey. I'm Adam, the better looking one obviously. Nice to meet you," he said, waiting for an introduction.

"Hey, I'm Keri, a friend of your sister's, and yes, would have to agree you are most definitely the better looking one." She laughed, getting a scowl from Riley.

"I like her already, Piles," Adam said.

"Stop with the name you little runt, how come you're here?" she said.

He looked over to his mother; looking at her sheepish grin she knew her mother had made him return.

"Mum, why did you drag Ads home? He should be studying and partying, not being pulled home to see his sister for fifteen minutes," she said.

"Well you have to have dinner, I've got lamb in. I was going to do a roast dinner as your last meal," her mother said sadly.

"Ma, we can't. I'm sorry but seriously we have to do a few things before we leave and we'll be back late and then we'll need to get off. I'm sorry but I did tell you this," she said, feeling horrible.

"Come on Ma, we don't want Piles with us for dinner, surely you would rather a night out with your favourite child. Come on, the intelligent, good-looking one," Adam said, pointing to himself, trying to lighten their mother's mood. "I was going to tell you about the placement offer I have in a top worldwide law firm and the new dating interest I have?" Adam said.

Her mum looked saddened, and you could see she was trying her best. "Ok, that sounds good, new girlfriend and new job, that's great Ads." She looked up at her only son proudly. She walked away from her family to the fridge.

"I love you," Riley mouthed to her brother, giving him a wink.

"Ok, I'll not be long, Keri. You wanna come up or you ok here?" Riley said.

"It's ok Piles, I'm going to keep your mum company." She winked.

"Good-looking and sense of humour. I like her already," Ads said.

"Nice one, idiot." She punched her brother playfully before running up the stairs to her room.

* * *

She walked into her room, dropping her case on the floor and resting her head against the door. She eyed her room carefully; this was really happening, she thought.

Lifting her suitcase onto the bed, opening it and removing the items, she stopped and picked up the family photo on the side of her bed. She ran her finger over the picture containing the four of them hugging and smiling into the camera. She remembered the day a couple of years ago at a family christening, it was just before Adam left for uni. She lifted the picture and wiped away the one fallen tear. *Come on Riles, you can do this*, she pushed herself.

She lifted her main suitcase and transferred a couple of bits from the training course into it. She lifted the bag of all her new stationary. There was a list of what was required for arrival in resort but she went overboard and made sure she had everything that would quite possibly keep WHSmiths in stock for the year. She paused, thinking for a moment before smiling softly. She opened her notebook and biro, before she began writing.

She stopped writing when she heard a knock on her door she shoved it under the suitcase. "Come in?"

"Hey, you ok?" Keri said, shutting the door behind her.

"Oh hey, you ok?"

"Yeah, your family are fab; I don't want to

interrupt. I know it's hard, going packing to leave your family, more so when it's the first time. I was just, well, I was wondering what we were doing tonight and when we would be leaving and returning?" she asked questioningly.

"Is everything ok?" Riley asked her, concerned.

"Yeah, totally."

"Well ok; I guess as soon as it's done! I don't want to tell you where I'm taking you, it's about half an hour away. Do what we have to do for about half an hour and then go for dinner and come back, we'll be back around 10ish, I guess. Maybe earlier, is that ok? Will that be enough time for you?" Riley asked.

"Yeah, that's fine," she said distantly. She walked past Riley and picked up the picture on her bed. "This is lovely," Keri said. "You really are beautiful. And you have an incredible family," she said, scanning the picture.

"I know they're fab. I don't know if I can do it, Keri," she said. "I feel so sad. I feel awful about upsetting my mum, I just don't know if I have the courage to go and leave behind what I know and love."

"Everyone goes through this Riley, I promise you. It will be hard at first, it'll be new, but you'll either love it or hate it; if you hate it you come home. Nobody will force you to stay, the company will book a flight. Kos is really popular. The longest you will have to wait will be a couple of days MAX. But, I can assure you, every one of you on the course will be sat thinking exactly the same now, with the exception of Scott. I felt like it too, and like you, hated leaving my family due to our closeness, but I love the life. I love my job and my family come out at least twice through a season," Keri said, finding the woman's sad eyes.

"Thanks."

Keri pushed Riley up against the wall, kissing her hard; she put her fingers through her hair, pulling a little, and heard Riley groan into the kiss. She deepened the kiss and allowed her tongue to find Riley's. They stayed this way for a few minutes, getting caught up in the moment, the kiss and the passion that accompanied it.

Keri pulled away and they stayed staring at each other, allowing their breathing to subside. "You stole my trick?" Riley said, holding Keri's hands.

"I know." She lifted her eyebrows. "I've wanted to do it all day; plus I figured you needed it. Worrying any less?" She smiled.

"Well, I'm no longer worrying about leaving; now I'm just worrying about how ready I am to throw you on my bed and do all sorts of things to you, which really wouldn't be very appropriate. Plus, we need to go shortly so we don't miss it." She laughed.

Keri squinted her eyes in wonderment of what Riley's plans were. "Ok, I'll leave you be. Most disappointed that I won't get to BE with you one last time." She looked back over her shoulder, smirking.

Riley sat down on her bed, laying back harshly. "Arghhhhhh, what's this girl doing to me?" she said out loud, feeling incredibly turned on.

Sitting up and pulling the notebook from under the case, she continued writing; when finished she pulled the page out and pushed it in her back pocket, smiling. Following the writing she felt like she had just had a surge of energy and finished transferring the last few bits from her training case to both her main case and her cabin case. She put in her laptop and placed the photo on top before shutting it closed and taking one last look around her room. Sighing, she took in the surroundings and left.

* * *

She could hear the laughing from the landing. Intrigued by the noise and commotion, she wandered back downstairs. She walked through the kitchen to the conservatory and saw the four of them sat on the sofas, laughing naturally. She noticed the almost empty bottle of wine on the side. "You guys been busy I see." She directed her eyes to the empty bottle and came in, sitting on the arm next to Ads.

"You ok love?" her mum said.

"Yeah, all done and dusted. Hey Ads, do me a favour? Will you bring my cases down for me? I don't want to have to go back up there," she said seriously to her brother.

His earnest expression, taking over the previous amused and laughter-filled look meant everything to her. "Sure thing, sis." He patted her back softly and winked at his big sister.

They had always been close even as kids, but as much as they pranked and tortured each other they were always there for one another regardless of anything else.

"So I guess you are leaving now, to go... SORT your things out?" her mum said.

Riley felt terrible. "Um, yeah we do, I'm sorry Ma."

"Hey Riles, I was wondering. I mean, if it's ok with you and if your parents don't mind eating late, but, you said we should be done in about an hour and a half to two hours, with travelling time, right? Well, if that's ok and they don't mind me crashing their family night, we could forget dinner and go out with your family instead?" said Keri.

She looked at her mum, who had tears in her eyes. In that moment she knew she was royally screwed when it came to Keri. "You sure you're ok with that?" Riley said to Keri.

"Surer than sure can be, as long as your folks are ok?" she said.

"Oh, just ignore the gorgeous intelligent brother and our private special meal, don't worry, I'm used to it." He sniffed. They all laughed and before Keri could say anything Riley's mum was hugging her tightly. Riley watched the embrace and thought she would never forget that imprint on her mind.

"Come on then, we need to get a move on, the sooner we go the sooner we're back," she said to Keri.

"How about instead of eating out I still do that roast lamb dinner, I'll even make banana splits for desert?" she said excitedly.

Riley looked questioningly at Keri.

"Oh my god I would LOVE a home cooked roast, and lamb is my total favourite," she said.

"Great, see you soon. Adam, run to the store and get me whipped cream and flakes please," she said, dashing off to the kitchen.

"Nice one, idiot." He playfully punched Keri and winked at her.

Her dad sat in his armchair, legs crossed, tapping his fingers on his paper, nodding his appreciation to the women as they left the room.

* * *

The journey only took around twenty-five minutes; for a Friday night the roads were fairly quiet, everyone must have left early to embrace their weekends, she thought. She wouldn't tell Keri where they were going each time she asked, which was amusing her immensely.

They parked up on a side street; there was a chill in the air and Riley grabbed their coats off the back seats and handed Keri hers. She looked at Riley, confused. "Where are we?" she asked.

Riley grabbed her hand, smiling. "West Kirby," she said.

Keri obviously had no clue and the response still left her confused; she continued hand in hand and following Riley.

As they reached the end of the street, they turned the corner and Keri smiled as she stopped and saw a beach with the sun beginning its descent. It looked beautiful already as it was starting to turn the sky a wonderful shade of pinks and oranges. "You brought me to watch the sunset?" said Keri thoughtfully, but more as a question.

"I know it's kind of lame, and I know it won't be a patch on what you experience on a daily basis in

Greece, I'm sure. But, well, we used to come here as kids and then watch the sunset and it's one of my favourite places, so I just wanted to share it with you," she said.

"It isn't lame, why do you always doubt everything? You are the most beautiful, sincere, sweet woman I have ever met. You have given me the best last day ever, I love it. Thank you so much for sharing this with me," she said truthfully.

They sat down closely next to each other in silence, just watching and appreciating Mother Nature at her finest. Keri kept pushing closer to Riley, not taking her eyes off the picturesque scene; she reached for Riley's hand, taking it in her own and intertwining their fingers.

As the sky was illuminated with various shades now, the sun was getting lower quite quickly and she knew she'd been right to bring her here. She leaned into Keri, "Turn around," she whispered.

Keri turned to face her. "Yeah?"

"No, that way." She pointed behind her.

"But we won't be able to see it," she pointed out to Riley.

"Just for a few moments." Keri did as she was told and Riley mirrored the movements; she reached into her back pocket of her jeans and pulled out her phone. Going onto the camera on her iPhone she leaned her head in closer to Keri and set it so she could get them both in the picture with the sun setting in the background. They both smiled into the shot; Riley turned and kissed Keri and snapped a couple more shots. She pulled away, smiling. "Go on, you can turn back now." She smiled at Keri.

They watched the last of the sun setting over the beach in silence; Riley couldn't help but feel disappointed that she wouldn't be able to do this with Keri more often overseas like Glen and Sally would be able to do on occasion. She shook the thought from her head. Seriously, what was wrong with her? She had only really known her forty-eight hours. Yeah, she had liked her prior to that but where was all this coming from? This wasn't Riley, and it was pissing her off that it was impacting her so much and occupying her thoughts continuously.

"You ready?" she said to Keri when the sun was completely set and it was mostly dark.

Keri sighed. "Not really, no, but do I have a choice?" she said.

"Nope, but my mum's roast lamb and banana split will hopefully make up for it." She smiled, pulling the girl to her feet.

"Hmmmmmm, oh yeah. Come on, let's hit the road," she said, running, dragging her along, laughing.

They got back to the car and Riley sat there a few moments before she started it up. "Do you work with the girl that hurt you?" Riley regretted it as soon as she asked.

Keri rested her head back on the rest. "Yes, but luckily she isn't in my area so I rarely see her. I am going through my management plan, otherwise I would have requested a transfer, but my mentor is fantastic and they reckon I will be promoted for next season."

"Right," Riley said, and started the car.

They drove the entire journey in silence. As they pulled back onto the drive, Riley asked, "Are you ok to do this? If you'd prefer I can make excuses for you and get you a taxi to the airport?" she said.

"Do you not want me here? If that's the case I'll order a taxi."

"Of course not, I completely do. I just... You were just, quiet all the way back. I thought I'd pissed you off is all," Riley said.

"It took me by surprise, Riley. I'm over her. I hate that I have to see her at all because it reminds me that I wasted my life and that what I thought we had wasn't real. However, I need to concentrate on this last season; the manager has moved her to the opposite end of the island. I wasn't quiet for that reason, you didn't offend or upset me; on the contrary you made me realise for the first time in a long time, well, since it happened I suppose, I didn't feel anything when I spoke about it. I haven't spoken about it to anyone through not being able to; I guess I was just trying to analyse what that meant and I guess how exactly that's happened, when exactly that happened," she said, sighing.

"Ok, if you're sure," she said quietly.

"I don't think you could ever upset me if you tried, Riley." She looked to the house. "Quick, nobody's looking," she said, and pulled Riley in for a quick kiss.

* * *

They walked in the house and heard her mum singing in the kitchen to the radio which was blaring.

Keri looked questioningly at her.

"Welcome to my world," she said, mouthing 'E-very-day,' to her.

Adam came out of the kitchen with a lighter and cutlery in his hands. "Golden child's back!" he shouted.

They walked into the kitchen and her mum was a walking advert for a Stepford wife at this moment in time. "Ermmm, you ok Mum?" she said, smirking.

"You were quick; dinner's almost done." She kissed Riley's cheek and handed them both a glass of pink fizz.

Riley looked at her father reading the paper again. "Still hiding, Pops?" she said, kissing his cheek.

"She's insane, she's lost the bloody plot this time," he said, rolling his eyes and lifting the paper again.

"Be quiet you, ignore your father. I have my beautiful children home and I don't know when, if ever, I'll get this again. Go and get seated into the dining room please," her mother said.

* * *

The meal was amazing; she was glad she had done this and more so that she'd got a final homemade roast before heading off. The drink was flowing freely, more so than probably should have been. In fact, so much so, that they had had to order a taxi to take them to the airport as everyone was clearly far too intoxicated.

Chapter 15

Riley was arguing with her mum about her whole family coming to the airport with them, which she wouldn't have had an issue with had they been driving but now they were having to grab a cab it seemed ridiculous.

Her father finally stepped in and her mother reluctantly agreed to say goodbye there; they got the bags out of the back of the car and transferred them over to the cab, saying their goodbyes. Her mother pulled her in for one final hug. "Don't give up on what's meant to be, Riley," her mother said.

"I know Ma, I promise. No matter how hard it gets, no matter how homesick I get, I promise I will not give up on this."

Her mother sighed, shaking her head. "I saw the way you looked at her, Riley. Don't fight what's meant to be; love's not meant to be easy all the time, and the difficulties only make things even more special. Just don't fight it, baby." She kissed her daughter, silencing her before she had a chance to speak. "Go, Riley, and leave before you see my tears." Riley walked backwards, trying to make sense of her mother's words; she stepped in the cab, blew kisses, and waved excessively to her family as they pulled out of her close.

* * *

Pulling into the airport terminal, they found their checking-in desks; they checked in and finalised everything before walking through to the departure lounges. They had worked it out so they could have an hour together; they were in a huge open-plan airport so it wasn't like they were going to be able to do anything but they would have some time all the same.

They wandered around a store or two, talking and laughing at each other. The familiarity and normalness was so natural, Riley thought.

"Anywhere else you need to go?" Keri said to Riley.

"Yeah, I want to just go to WHSmiths to get some magazines and goodies for the flight and to see if they have a CD I'm after, then I'm all yours. Well, as much as I can be in the middle of Manchester Airport. We could go and share a bottle before we go?" She winked.

"You are aware you won't be able to drink this way overseas, you'll literally kill yourself." She laughed at Riley. "That sounds good. So what music you getting?" she asked.

"There's an album from a band I like. Unfortunately, they're not big here in the UK but I want to see if I can find it as I love one of their songs," Riley said.

"Oh right, who are they?"

"They're called Gloriana; they are an American country band."

"Are you fucking with me again?" She laughed, pushing Riley.

"Actually no, sit here a moment. I heard this song and I loved it, hence the reason I wanted to buy the album," she said to her. She pulled out her iPhone and ear buds, giving one to Keri and putting the other in her own ear. She googled, 'Kissed You, Goodnight' by Gloriana and brought up the song on YouTube for Keri to hear.

The first words hit Keri hard. Riley could see that in her eyes as the song began and the first lines, where the words said, 'Dropping someone off, just after midnight'. She noticed Keri look at her watch and could see the sadness in her eyes.

She allowed Keri to listen to the words and got lost in her features; she was incredibly beautiful, Riley thought. The song came to an end and Keri looked over at Riley. "You know when you said to me it was country, I really thought you were winding me up again; then when you said you were serious, I thought, wow first thing about this girl that I've not, well, not liked, I guess, for want of a better term. But after hearing that song, those words, it's incredible. Who'd have thought I'd like country?" she said, laughing. She grabbed Riley's hand and pulled her. "Come on, let's go see if we can get you that album," she said to her.

Riley picked herself some magazines out for the flight and some crisps and chocolate; she lifted a copy of Diva up to Keri. "Do you read it?" she said, smirking, and then looked at the goodies, looking back to Keri. "A must."

Keri laughed at Riley. "Guilty pleasures, ehy? And yes I read it, actually I have a subscription so it gets sent over." She smiled.

"Shut up! Really? Oh this is awesome, I made my mum promise that she had to get it each month and send it to me," said Riley.

"Yes really, you can subscribe and it can be sent which is good, and all very discreet." She laughed.

They looked through all the Gs in the music section of the store and were disappointed that it wasn't there; she knew it would be a longshot but there was nothing she could do. She noticed that Keri looked more disappointed than her, which she found odd. She paid for the things she had bought and they went to the pub. Riley went and got a table which she purposely found hidden away in a corner, and Keri went to the bar. They didn't have too long left now so when Keri returned with a bottle of pink prosecco she smirked, shaking her head at the girl.

"You do realise we only have like, half an hour, right?" she said, laughing.

"I know, but I wanted to say thanks and just enjoy the last bit of time together really," she said honestly. They opened the bottle and clinked their glasses, mumbling cheers to each other. "Riley, I just wanted to say I don't know what's been going on with us, and whilst I'm conscious of the fact that I'm trying not to overanalyse, or Jesus, not analyse it all, I do feel that something has, was, building. I have had an incredible few days with you; today was simply perfect in my opinion. The ride was great, your family are wonderful and a true reflection of you and the amazing person you are. Tonight at the sunset, well I was truly touched that you went to all that trouble to think of something so beautiful, but also want to share such a big memory and family experience with me; actually on that, I want you to send me that photo please. Anyways, I wanted to say thanks and I really wish we could have met at a different time or under different circumstances because you truly are the most incredible, beautiful, sexy, funny, intelligent, witty…"

"Alright already, my head won't get on the plane at this rate," Riley said, laughing.

"Yeah sorry, but you truly are amazing in my opinion and I wanted to thank you from the bottom of my heart for what you have opened me up to, and shared with me these last few days," she said.

Riley could feel herself blushing. "Thank you, I do feel the same you know; so many times today I have questioned everything I'm doing but I just can't turn my back on something I've wanted so badly. I've never had a true relationship and that's not because I'm not into it or a player, regardless of the impression I may have gave this week; but I guess I've just never found someone I wanted more than some fun with. I know it would have been entirely different if I'd met you in a different time and place, but as they say 'what will be, will be', I guess. That's whether that fits with my wants and desires or not. Thank you also for an incredible couple of days and thanks for everything you have taught me this week. I know I'll do well simply because I have been taught by the best. End of. And like you, I would have to agree, you truly are something special, and I feel privileged to have met you. So what's your number, babe?" She smiled.

"Well, we like to do things backwards it seems, normally you do this before everything else," she winked.

Riley took Keri's number and sent her the photo of them smiling with the sunset behind them. Keri opened the photo and smiled wide. "I love it, it's so good Riles. I don't know what else to say other than I actually love it," she said shyly.

Riley sat up. "So I need to give you something. It's kind of stupid so please don't laugh, but I wrote you something." She pulled out the paper from her back pocket and handed it to Keri. She paused as Keri was due to take it. "Keri, promise me you won't open it until after I've gone. At least when you're on the plane. Promise me?"

"Of course, I promise. I won't look at it until I get on the plane; I also have something and in the same fashion would appreciate it if you also left it until we're, well, we're apart." Keri reached for the carrier bag from the service station earlier today and handed it to Riley. "I suggest you put it straight in the case until the flight," Keri informed her. "One last thing, can I have your phone?" she asked Riley questionably.

"Why? You have my number."

"I know, I know. But I need to do something," she said, holding out her hand.

Riley handed her phone over to Keri and watched as the girl was doing something on it. Keri pulled her purse from her bag, and opened it out, pulling a bank card out. She spent a few minutes, occasionally looking up at Riley and hiding what she was doing from her, before finishing putting her card and purse back and handing Riley's phone back to her.

Riley looked at it. "What have you done?" she said, looking through and not noticing anything different.

"I'll tell you later," said Keri.

"When? You have to leave in ten minutes."

"Later, be patient." Keri leaned in and kissed Riley softly, covering her hand with her own and squeezing it gently.

They continued drinking the bottle, until they heard the call for Keri's flight. They looked up to each other sadly, knowing it was time to say goodbye. Riley noticed there were tears in Keri's eyes, and pulled her in close. "Please don't get upset, please," she whispered in her ear.

"I'm sorry I'm being ridiculous, I must be due on," she said back to Riley, squeezing her tight.

Riley pulled back, taking Keri's face in her hands, looking at her intently. "You are incredible, and I won't ever forget you and the time we spent together," she said, kissing her long and hard. They spent a moment looking at each other. The silence spoke volumes and in that moment there was no need for any words; they were speaking unspoken words.

Riley watched as the girl walked out of her life forever and in that moment she felt pain like she couldn't ever remember ever having felt before. She felt the tears fall from her face. She wiped them away and downed the last of her drink, leaving the seat that she and Keri had shared, before making her way to the departure gate.

PART TWO

Chapter 16

Keri

Seriously, what the hell is up with you? She scolded herself, as she thought back to saying goodbye to Riley and getting upset. She stepped onto the plane, trying to locate her seat. She got her phone, earphones, and purse from her case and then put it in the overhead locker. She sat in her seat, grateful that she had gotten a window seat, and stared distantly out.

She plugged her headphones into her phone and found what she was looking for; she hit play and smiled as she rested her head against the seat.

Pulling out the piece of paper from her pocket, she held it tightly in her hand and sighed. She was terrified of reading it, uncertain of what it would say but more concerned over making more of a tit of herself and crying further, this time on a full aircraft.

"Ladies and gentlemen, the cabin staff will now be closing the cabin doors…" she heard over the tannoy. She heard the words advising the passengers to ensure all electronic devices were now switched off or onto airplane mode. Keri quickly opened her phone, smiling at the new screen saver she had uploaded of her and Riley at the beach. She opened her messages and found Riley's name – she began typing the message.

'Hey you, sorry I was an idiot and got upset :(. Thanks for the lift, and the meal. I don't think I'll ever forget that roast lamb and banana split dinner, hmmmm!! I hope you have an awesome flight. I am just about to take off and I have just picked up your letter to start reading when I'm in the air. Ps look in your music ;) Keri xxx'

She listened to the words of the song, and watched Manchester and the UK disappear once more, only this time it was different. This time she was watching Riley disappear from her life too.

* * *

Keri pulled down her tray, accepting the beers from the cabin crew. She lifted her legs underneath her, getting comfortable, and opened the letter from Riley; she sighed uncertainly, before she began reading the words before her.

Dear Keri,

Well this is the surrealist thing I think I have ever done; I mean I am so not the letter writing type of girl. But as I sit on my bed in my room taking everything in and packing my last bits up, I keep being awoken with the laughter from you, coming from downstairs. Downstairs in MY house, with MY mum and MY family and I'm not sure how we've got here in two days and I don't know why I'm liking being, well 'here'!! I've been unable to stop myself from thinking about if things were different and if I'd met you at a different time in our lives, and honestly, it's killing me, because honestly I think we'd have had the happy ending. Maybe I'm being childish and ridiculous, and I guess you could argue that I'm too inexperienced to know what I'm talking about having never had a relationship, but I was brought up to be open and honest and not lie. So whilst you're probably flying high on your way back to your life, your friends, your job, home – well everything in Rhodes, I can only imagine you're thanking your lucky stars you had a lucky break from the weirdo girl who's practically fessing her undying love to a girl she slept with only two days ago. {Sigh} (FYI, I do the whole 'sigh' thing quite a lot just so you know!!) Anyways, I'll stop digressing, the point is I don't know how or why this has happened but I'm glad it did, and I'm gutted it's ended. Simple as!

WOW, WOW, WOW. You have just come up to see me, weirdly to ask about where we're going later, but fuck you turn me on. Nobody has opened up my senses like you do. I'm completely unimpressed you just stole my own weapon and used it on me, but hell you're a turn on when you take control, pushing me up against the wall and kissing me like was genuinely the BEST thing ever :).

Honestly I think I could waffle forever but as I am now on page two, I guess I should really get to the point which is that, I wanted to thank you wholeheartedly for coming into my life, for being the best, and boy do I mean more than ;) trainer/teacher, honestly, I am never ever going to be able to call you a teacher again, it's got me imagining all sorts. I'll put that away, maybe in my 'wank bank' for a later date. OMG I can't believe this letter probably started so nice, appealing, loving even and now I'm talking about wanking; geez, I really am shit at this! Anyways, I guess I wanted to let you know that if the time and the place was different you would be the girl of my dreams and I'd jump all over... behave, dirty mind :). I'd jump all over the prospect of you being my first and last girlfriend.

I'm sorry if this is/was too much, but I wanted to let you know how I was feeling. You truly are the most incredibly wonderful woman I have EVER met. I have never met anyone so beautiful, intelligent, sexy, funny, witty, and gorgeous; seriously my list is endless but I just wanted you to know you are... truly perfect to me, Keri.

I hope that one day our paths cross, but I will caveat that with, if we do we are both single and not in the same position we are in now.

I wish you the very best for the future, for your career and hope more than anything that you meet someone who will treat you the way you should be treated and not the way that stupid bitch of an ex (I'm sorry I shouldn't have said that), treated you.

Anyways I hope I have made your flight somewhat more amusing and I hope I haven't scared you off entirely, you never know you could be my manager next season, if I last that is.

Take care Keri, I hope to speak to you soon and I genuinely hope you like my surprise as much as I want you to. All my love, now and always. Riley XOXOXOXOXOXOXOXO

Keri sighed heavily, taking the last sip of her first can of Bud. She could feel the tears in her eyes. She never knew what to expect when reading the letter. Keri was so negative when it came to women, she had been so screwed over by Emma that she couldn't do anything other than expect the worst and that's what she genuinely thought the content of Riley's letter would contain. But it didn't, she seemingly was on the same page as her. Fuck, now what did she do?

Keri was brought back to it when she heard the album she had on loop, replay the song she had got to know and love. She nodded her head in tune with the music as the first words played over. 'I dropped you off, just a little after midnight...' She smiled and let her head fall back into the seat, not letting go of the letter and letting her eyes relax.

Chapter 17

Riley

Riley sat down on the seat facing the doors where the ticketing agents were now preparing to let the passengers onto the aircraft. She relaxed and took in a deep breath, trying to control her emotions. As she sat and waited patiently she felt her phone vibrate in her pocket. She picked it up, looking at the picture of a smiling Keri illuminating the screen, notifying her of a text. She opened the message.

'Hey you, sorry I was an idiot and got upset :(. Thanks for the lift, and the meal. I don't think I'll ever forget that roast lamb and banana split dinner, hmmmm!! I hope you have an awesome flight. I am just about to take off and I have just picked up your letter to start reading when I'm in the air. Ps look in your music ;) Keri xxx'

"You weren't an idiot. You weren't," she whispered to herself. She read the message over and over, taking in the words. She did as Keri had asked of her and went to her music, as she opened on the front screen she noticed the recently added. There it was, when she was on her phone she had obviously bought her the album she was looking for in WHSmith. She looked over in wonderment the Gloriana, A Thousand Miles Left Behind album. She went to track 4 and got lost in the words that the last time she heard, she was sharing a moment with Keri.

Riley boarded the plane, putting her case above; she sat in her seat, throwing the blanket over her. She had the album playing in her ear, listening to songs she'd never heard before but was instantaneously falling in love with. She picked up her phone and grazed her thumb over the screen photo of her and Keri kissing in front of the beautifully illuminated sunset behind them. She opened her messages and started a response to Keri.

'Hey good looking, you really are fastly becoming my perfect woman, thank you so much, I love it, and now it's always going to remind me of you. I'm going to listen to it throughout my journey. I have never met anybody who has done anything so thoughtful and considerate in my entire life. I am just on the plane and waiting to taxi. I kinda wish we were here together, but you can't change what's meant to be I suppose. You are completely more than welcome for the lift. What can I say? It was the second best 'ride of my life' ;) the first was Thursday night after the awards obviously. Anyways for the record, my ma taught me everything she knows, I promise you one day I will cook you that meal, but even better. I hope you liked my letter and didn't think I was too much of a knob. I miss you already, Riles. Xxx PS. Just remembered my gift, I'm going to get it now thanks so much for being you and meeting me. :) xxxx'

Riley stood up, thankful that she had an aisle seat so as not to disturb the people in her row. She pulled out the carrier bag from her case and looked inside, seeing a Me to You bear. She lifted it out and looked at the medium-size bear with a sweater saying 'I miss you already'. She sighed deeply before seeing the mug inside, duplicating the bear and the words. She couldn't help the tears this time and leaned back, listening to her new favourite album.

Chapter 18

Keri

As the doors to the plane finally opened Keri sighed, happy to be home. It was a long-ass week irrespective of how amazing it had actually been. She breathed, taking in the heat and the smell of plane fumes. It was still only early and the sun was just rising. She felt rough as hell, she thought, but they had drunk shitloads yesterday. "Bleurgh," she said to herself, shaking her head at the thought.

Keri collected her luggage and went through to the Hightail office. She saw a couple of her team waiting for the guests at the entrance of the arrivals area. "Hey boss, good week?" Jack said to her.

"Pretty good mate, yeah." She smiled and walked over to the company office. "Hey," she said, smiling at the airport manager Karen.

"Ahhhhhh, you're back. How are you? Were they nightmares? Have we got any coming here? God it's so good to have you back, love," said the woman in one breath.

Keri was laughing. "Ohhh, how I've missed you." She loved Karen; she was probably around her mum's age and frequently took on the role of her adoptive mother. She had lived here for years and was now happily married to a lovely guy with two adorable kids. She saw Emma walking up to the office with Dan, their manager, and enter the office. Dan stopped and kissed Keri, and Emma just smiled and nodded. She hated seeing her. Before she left it was real hard, now though, now it felt different.

"How you doing, gorgeous?" said Dan.

"That's what I've just asked, she was just telling me," said Karen.

"That I was. Yes, it was good, the class were actually fantastic. Unfortunately no newbies coming here, which is a shame as there were some awesome characters," she said thoughtfully, thinking back to her class and Riley, smiling slightly.

"You met someone," said Karen, matter-of-factly.

She felt Emma's head snap up and look at Keri. She ignored her ex and focussed on the eyes of Karen and Dan that were now intently on her.

"What? What do you mean? Where did that come from?" said Keri.

"Avoidance, Kaz, she's trying to put us off scent." Dan said, smirking.

"You did, I can tell. YOU, are glowing, and I've known you a long time and when you left here you didn't look like that. Spill, NOW," Karen said.

Keri could feel her face redden. "I don't know what you mean." She laughed.

"You dirty dog," Dan said to the girl, winking and punching her arm.

Keri's phone bleeped in her hand, notifying her that her battery was dying. "Shit, do you have a charger in the car?" she said to Dan, who had come to pick her up.

He grabbed her phone out of her hand and smirked at the photo. "You're definitely a dirty dog," he said handing the phone to a jumping and shouting Karen, desperate to get a peek. "Where are you? There weren't any beaches near Nottingham last time I was there." He was laughing now.

Keri was still trying to retrieve her phone from the playful pair.

"OH MY GOD, Keri she's gorgeous. Was she one of the newbies? Was she good?"

"That's what I wanted to ask," said Dan, laughing.

"You're terrible; I'm still unsure how you got to be the level you are at," Karen said, laughing and rolling her eyes at the area manager of the island.

"Good looks and charm failed me so I slept my way to the top; I've told you this enough," he said, laughing.

Keri was still laughing, finally getting her phone back with a serious and expectant Karen waiting for her response.

"Yes, she was a newbie. I know, I know I wouldn't have normally but I was drawn to her from day one. She was fantastic to be fair. ON the course, Dan. And no, no beaches. We were in West Kirby. She took me to watch the sunset last night," said Keri.

"Why ain't she here then?" said Dan.

"Just better suited elsewhere I guess," Keri said sombrely.

"Keri, she's stunning. You are glowing and I haven't ever seen you so happy," Karen said, with extra emphasis on the 'ever'. Purposely done, Karen had to be polite to Emma but she had made it clear that she was unhappy about the way Keri had been treated. Clearly doing her damnedest to make a point, her words had the desired effect as Emma got up and left the office, telling Dan she would call him later.

"You shouldn't do that," said Keri.

"What? I don't know what you mean. I didn't lie, that girl is beautiful and she has warm eyes and a warm smile, and as I said you are glowing and I haven't seen you so happy in a very, very long time, Keri. So I am just speaking the truth," said the woman, smirking. "It's not my fault if she took it all so personally, I mean it's not like I was having a personal dig," she said, laughing. "Anyways, the angry mob are on their way, so do you fancy dinner tomorrow night? Yiannis is at the restaurant so we can have a barbecue, cocktails after the kids have gone to bed, and you can tell me all about the mystery woman," said Karen.

"Great, I'll call you tomorrow." She leaned her head into the office window and kissed Karen on the cheek.

"Come on then, you look like you need your bed," Dan said as he took Keri's suitcase and walked back to the car.

When they got in the car, she lifted her phone up to him. "Charger?" she said expectantly.

"Blimey, she has won you over, hasn't she?" He handed her the charger. "Anyways, on a different note. How are things? Really? You are doing an awesome job, girl, you know that, but how's things on the Emma front? I know Karen's... well Karen, and we all love her, but that just there, is that normal? I can't have anyone feeling intimidated or bullied. We don't want to be under the HR spotlight, ya know?" he said to her.

"I know, yeah. No, it's the same, Dan. We're polite and courteous to each other and we keep out of each other's way. That's the first time I've actually seen her in a while. And you know what Dan, Karen can't help herself, she's my friend and looks out for me, but she didn't do anything other than say I look happy," she said to her boss. She liked the guy a lot; he was close to her age, at thirty-one. He was a loveable rogue and completely suited his East London accent. He was also her mentor on her management development programme. They got on well and regularly spent time together; because of their close relationship they could speak openly to each other also.

"Calm down, I'm just checking. You know what the UK are like though; HR will be on the first flight investigating potential bullying claims. I totally get where Karen's coming from but we do all have to work together, and more importantly I don't want anything to affect the promotion. You are doing wicked mate, and I'd like to give you more responsibility this season so we can guarantee you get something next season," he said.

"Yeah I know, I'll tell Karen to rein it in a little tomorrow night; I'll explain to her that she could risk my promotion and she'll ease off of Emma," Keri said.

"So who's the hottie then? What's her name? Good lay?" He winked as he floored his car upon leaving the airport.

"You're such a bloke, ya know that? Her name's Riley, she was shit hot on the course. Me and Glen were both pretty desperate for her."

"Oh I bet." He smirked at her again.

"Piss off. Nah she was good, she'll go far with the company, and I can assure you of that!"

"So, seriously, why didn't we bring her here if she's that good?"

"Dan, I've got one psycho ex here that publically humiliated me in front of everyone last season; honestly I don't know why she's back here, but she is. I wouldn't want Riley to be here and be a part of that. She wouldn't be able to work under me which would mean she would ultimately be under Emma. Can you imagine? Really! Then she'd basically spilled on the course that she had always wanted to do this since being a kid, so in reality it would have been a bad idea. It would have affected my MDP work and her experience of the job. So it made more sense," she said, looking out the window.

"I see what you mean. I get it and you've made the right choice. But, you're regretting it already, ain't ya?"

She sighed heavily. "Why can't anything ever be simple?"

"So where did you send her?" he said to Keri.

"Kos, Glen's mate is a manager over there and they had some issues last year with people burning out. She has this incredible passion and drive, I think she'll cut it," she said.

They chatted rubbish for the rest of the journey before he pulled into her apartment complex and dropped her off at home.

* * *

She got into her apartment and got a bottle of water from the fridge; she needed to unpack but she needed to sleep. She had a couple of hours before she needed to go to work. She would sleep for an hour then unpack, she thought.

Opening her case so she could get her charger, she went to her bedroom and plugged her phone in. She was disappointed she hadn't received a text from Riley; she thought when she had landed she would have got a message from her.

She opened her messages, re-reading the message she'd sent to Riley, smiling slightly. She noticed the small aeroplane on the top left hand corner of her phone. *Shit* – it was still on airplane mode. She swiped up and took it off, and watched as Vodafone Greece appeared.

Her phone bleeped a load of times; picking it up she saw she had a text from her mum, Kimmy, and Riley. She went to Riley's first, reading what she had to say. She smiled at the thought that they had both been listening to the album. She hoped Riley had liked the bear she felt a little silly for doing it now.

She pressed reply on her phone, typing a response to Riley.

'Hey you, you're more than welcome. :) I hope you liked it. I must say on the flight home I have become an avid country

enthusiast and track 9 'turn my world around' is my new favourite song! Well, I'm home now, just in bed as I'm wrecked and rough as hell thanks to you and your family of alky's ha-ha. Thank you so much for the letter, I didn't think you were silly, I thought it was beautiful, nearly as beautiful as you are! Soppy tart I know! I hope your first week of training is great; it's the best time with all the excursions you get to do and people you'll meet. Have fun Riley and take care. Keri XXX'

She opened the message from her sister-in-law and remembered the conversation she had had with her the night in the toilet when she'd kissed Riley. The barbecue allowed them to speak; they had not actually spoken to her since then. She made a mental note to call her later to fill her in.

Chapter 19

Riley

Riley retrieved all of her luggage and headed through the arrivals door. She saw some girls in the jade green uniform holding their clipboards and headed towards them.

"You must be Riley," the girl whose name badge read 'Clare' said to her.

"Erm, yes," she said, surprised. "How, how did you know?" said Riley.

"Luggage," she laughed. "We knew to look out for you on this flight and even workers don't have this much luggage due to the cost. I'm Clare by the way, come with me and I'll take you over to Katie. She's our manager and is going to take you to your apartment. There's a bar at the top of your road on the corner, we'll all be out tonight from around 9ish if you fancy it?" she said, smiling. "Ben, your roommate, will be out anyhow so if you come up with him, you'll know where the team hang. Hey Katie, this is Riley, our newest member. Bye then, I'll see you tonight," said Clare.

Riley liked Clare, she seemed nice and Riley was hoping that she would be in the same resort as her;

she'd made an effort to invite her out so she'd be someone Riley could hopefully become friends with.

"Hi Riley, how was your flight? Tiring I guess, rubbish flights here unfortunately," said Katie.

"Hey. Yeah, little bit tiring but the excitement's outweighing the tiredness luckily," she said, smiling at her new manager.

"Good job; it's going to be a long week for you. You ready? I'll take you to your home for the next six months," she said, smiling.

As they got into the car, Katie handed a folder over to Riley. "Welcome to Kos," she said, smiling. "Here's all the details of the week you have planned. You will be starting straight away, I'm afraid. You will have a couple of hours at home and then I have set up for Jason to come and pick you up. He works between resorts so he has a car, nobody else really does but he has a big welcome meeting at 11.30 so he's going to pick you up and you can shadow him. I'd suggest you take a pen and pad with you to take notes on the content, layout, as well as the information on the island and resorts, ya know?" Katie rested her arm on Riley's. "Sinking in now?" She smiled.

They arrived at Riley's new home. "And here we are," she said, getting out of the car, taking all the luggage inside. "Right, this will be your room," she said. "I've told Ben to make sure the place was clean so apologies if this is as good as it gets. He's a good guy, major player, with the looks to go with it. I'll put money on the fact he'll be trying to get in your pants before the night's out," she smiled.

"Well, he'll have a hard job on achieving that one!" Riley said.

"Boyfriend?"

"No, lesbian." She smiled.

"Ahhhhhh, I can't wait to watch this one play out then. Do me a favour will you?"

"Sure, if I can?"

"Don't tell anyone until next week."

"I'm gay? Why?" Riley asked seriously.

Katie started laughing. "He is a fab guy but as I said, a major player. We have bets on how long it would take him to conquer you. My guess was a week, which was the longest. I guess you could say I had a feeling about you," she said. "I will owe you one, dinner on me with the winnings?" she laughed.

"I knew I'd like you, I love this evil streak." She smiled over to her manager.

"Ok, then I'm off. You have about two hours, you may wanna crash, or you may want to go to the store and get a chip for your phone. At the end of the road, turn left. The majority of us are on Vodafone Greece as it's cheaper and free to call each other however, Cosmote normally have better deals. Your call really," Katie said.

Riley pulled her phone out. Katie saw the notifications of messages and smiled. "Cute pic, but you may wanna change it until we've won the bet." She winked and left her home.

She liked Katie, she thought. She was concerned she'd have a bitch of a manager but she seemed pretty cool. It was looking ok so far, she thought. She was riding high on the adrenaline so ignored the tiredness and decided she would unpack her stuff and then go and buy a SIM.

She sat on her bed and opened her messages first. She knew her mum would be desperately waiting for news of her safe arrival, so she opened that first.

She responded to her mum's message asking if she had arrived safely and if the flight was ok, letting her know it was all good and she was fine.

She saw a message from Cara and Adam too, checking her whereabouts and informing her of the shitty weather, amusing her immensely at the intensity of the heat in her apartment.

She opened the next message and smiled, lying on her bed as she read the words from Keri and replied:

'Hey gorgeous. Well I have just landed in my new home for the next 6 months. Met my boss who's actually pretty cool, and she's got a wickedly evil streak asking me to not 'out' myself for a week as my roomie is apparently going to try to shag me. Haha. I'm loving that I've converted you to a country fanatic, I have just put my phone on to that song, I'm loving it already and the words are perfectly fitting. It's not fair play telling me things like you're in bed; I am now wishing I was laid next to you kissing your beautiful body. And FYI you held your own with my "alky" family lady ;). Glad you liked the letter and you didn't think I was too much of a nerd, it felt right at the time. Well I'm hoping that the first week is as good as you say as I have literally got like an hour and half and then I am being thrown straight in and going with some guy to his welcome meeting and then shadowing him. I met a girl at the airport who invited me out tonight to so I will meet some more people

hopefully. Oh hey, do you have WhatsApp? Also, what network are you with? Apparently Vodafone Greece is big with my team and you can get free calls, I thought you may like to sometimes stay in contact, uhmmm if you want to, and if so I will go to the provider you are with. Well, now it's me being the soppy tart, so I will let you get some beauty sleep, not that you need it, and I will hopefully speak to you soon. Sweet dreams beautiful Riles XXX'

She watched the message send and smiled over the War and Peace that Keri was going to wake up to. She quickly changed the current pic of her and Keri kissing on her phone to the one of them both smiling.

She hit repeat on the song that Keri recommended and turned it up loud as she started the chore of unpacking her stuff.

Chapter 20

Keri

Keri stirred as her phone started bleeping; she made a mental note to make some ring tones later. She picked up her phone, it was a little after 9. Yawning loudly, she sat up, taking a big glug of water. She opened the phone to Riley's message, wiping her eyes to try and clear her vision.

She smiled, seeing the world's longest text message, and began reading the words. She felt a twang of jealousy at the details of her boss and how well they were getting along. She shook herself out of it. "It's nothing to do with you, Keri," she said to herself. As she continued reading the message she felt a stir through her body at the thought of Riley's lips being on her own, the thought of her fingers and lips all over her body. Keri tried to resist the urge, but was unable to ignore the call of her body right now. She moved her fingers downwards and imagined Riley was there with her now. She came quickly as her body released in pleasure; she sighed in contentment and picked up her phone, shaking her head amusedly.

'Hey good looking. How you doing? Glad you got there ok. What's the apt like hun? Arrived and saw Emma at airport and then got a little bit of dressing down from my AM. But my

'Honorary Rodos Mom' (long story) is protecting me and I'm going to hers for dinner tomorrow. This all probably sounds a lot worse than it is though :) I have a tendency to over exaggerate lol. Aside from that all good; oh apart from the fact we need a new rule. NO MORE BED talk. I was going to tell you but I don't think I can, I can assure you though, BED talk makes me naughty!!!! NO more bed talk, Riley Laura Sharpe!! Anyways I'm glad all good that end, PS hope your new boss has two heads, 8 fingers and a super gross wart with pus coming out on the end of her nose. I do have WhatsApp yeah, and I'm on Vodafone Greece also, so actually would kinda really like to speak to you some more. Enjoy sexy girl, speak soon K XXXXXX'

"Come on Keri, you need to get your ass into gear," she said to nobody; she knew she would end up getting herself into serious trouble if she stayed where she was and let her thoughts continue heading in the direction they had been. She forced herself out of bed and started unpacking her suitcases.

Keri put her first wash load on and then had a shower. God, she needed that, she thought. She dried her hair and put on her black city shorts, a sleeveless powder blue blouse and some black sandals. She styled her blonde hair and put a loose clip at the front, holding it back from her face. Grabbing her car keys, she threw her phone and purse in her Hightail messenger bag and left her apartment.

Chapter 21

Riley

Riley finished the last part of her unpacking with some time to spare. She pulled out the bear that Keri gave her and placed it on her bedside table behind the photo of her family. She decided to get a quick shower so she could go grab a SIM card and then it would pretty much be time to leave.

She threw on a black pencil skirt and pink vest and was checking herself over in the mirror when she saw her screen light up with an incoming message from Keri. She leaned against her bed, smiling like the cat that got the cream; god she was a geek, she thought, as she started reading the message. Reading about Emma made her feel weird. She didn't like it, but she couldn't control or think about that; worst still was that she appeared to be in trouble with her boss because of that bitch! She continued reading as her eyes widened; she re-read the words as she put her hand out on the bed to sit down. She wasn't sure for certain, but was Keri implying she had got horny and done stuff to herself? She sat down, reading again before realising that she was at the wrong side of her bed and completely missed it and fell off the bed. She was lying on the floor. "Fuck," she said, rubbing her head, "it truly is a talent you have excelled at, this falling on the sodding floor," she said to herself.

"Hey Riley, glad to ermmm, meet your acquaintance. Must say it normally takes more on my part before I get to see a beautiful girl's knickers," said Ben.

"Arghhhhh nooooooo. Ben, right?" she groaned, covering her eyes.

"Yup, pleasure to meet you," he said standing over her, smirking and holding out his hand. He pulled her back to her feet. "So, do that often I see?"

"Normally around once a week," she said, flustered. "Nice to officially meet you, I didn't think you were due back until later?" she said to him.

"Yeah that's right but I forgot my ticket book, so I've had to come back in between meetings to get it, and I'm kinda glad I did," he laughed. "Seriously though, I'm Ben, nice to meet you." He held out his hand seriously this time.

"Nice to meet you, I'm Riley, officially." She smiled lopsidedly.

"Right, I do really have to go. Clare said you were gonna come out tonight, right? I'll be home around 8ish, do you fancy getting a bite to eat first and then going on to meet the rest? There's a great little taverna down the road and they look after the reps here so we can go; get to know each other if we have to live with each other and then get, well, fucked up?" He smiled.

"Sounds, uhmmm, romantic. Why not?" She winked.

"Yeah, I DON'T do romance, this is all about getting to know each other, nothing else," he said to her.

"Awesome, a first date," she smiled, touching his arm gently.

"Stop fucking with me Riley, payback's a bitch." He smiled an incredible smile with gorgeous dimples at either end of his grin.

She could see how he managed to bed as many girls as she'd heard; he must just smile them into bed. Ben seemed like a lot of fun, and she was sure after she'd played the game and hid her 'secret' for a week they were totally gonna get on like a house on fire. *Shit, phone*, she thought. She put her pumps on and then ran to the store that Katie had directed her to.

Chapter 22

Keri

Keri's phone rang, and as she pulled it out of her bag, she didn't recognise the number. She hated not knowing who it was; it always ended up being an hotelier that was calling to give some form of devastating news. She sighed heavily and pressed answer. "Good morning, Hightail Holidays, Keri speaking, how may I help you?" she said.

"Well, you could start by telling me you didn't actually DIY without calling me for a helping hand, Kerianne?" She heard Riley's voice and smiled.

"Hey, you got a SIM. When I arrive at work I will save it. How are you? It's so great to hear your voice. FYI, I told you what would happen if you called me Kerianne!" she said, laughing

"Well, in reality what the hell can you do? You've already shown your 'selfish' side. I mean how rude," Riley said, laughing. "Seriously, did you really do that? Is that what you were actually implying?" she said seriously.

"Ok, ok. I need you to stop talking about it now; I feel weird and getting embarrassed, I've never done that and I've certainly never told anyone," she said.

"You've never masturbated? Really?" Riley said incredulously.

"Noooo, dumbass. I've never felt the need after reading a text and then told someone of the need to do it. Anyways I really am getting ridiculously embarrassed now, so subject change please. How's you? Are you on the way to work now?" she said to Riley. "I like hearing your voice, I kinda miss you."

"I know, right." She heard a heavy sigh down the phone. "For the record, I like that my text did that to you, and FYI I will be sending more if that's the reaction it gets. I like hearing your voice too. I'm glad I got a phone; I may have had another student loan to contend with if I'd gone to that Cosmote network. I am just waiting to be picked up now, he should be here any minute so I will have to go when he arrives and call you back later if that's ok?" Riley said.

"Yeah of course, thanks for calling," she said.

"No worries, I can't wait to speak to you again," she said sombrely. "Oh and Keri, make sure if you feel the need to DYI again, you call me first. I'm sure I could give a helping hand. No pun intended," she said, laughing.

"Shut up, and stop making fun of me."

"On the contrary, I want to make sure I can be there to lend a hand. Ok he's here, I'll call you later," she said, saying bye.

Keri hung up and felt a complete mixture of emotions, but Riley had this incredible ability to pick her up, and regardless of the sad feeling inside of her, she couldn't help but laugh at the beautiful woman's voice and words.

* * *

Keri pulled up to the hotel, and took the phone from her seat; she saved the number and saved the edited picture of Riley's smiling face as the screensaver, changing the ringtone and text tone, so she knew when it was Riley calling. She opened up her messages and typed a message to her new number.

'Thanks for the call, the tiredness is having a negative effect on me and you just completely brightened my day. Well, after the thoughts of you kissing and touching me of course. Think I may have to try that instead of counting sheep in future. Well I'm just about to go and have a meeting with one of my staff :(enjoy your first welcome meeting and I will speak to you soon. Don't get too drunk tonight; the first week of excursions is normally pretty hard going. K xxx'

She was practically skipping into the hotel as she stopped to speak to the hotel owner and his daughter. She walked into the bar area and found Julie writing tickets with a group of six boys; she was twirling her hair between her fingers and giggling. She was a nice girl, but geez she was doing Keri's head in at the moment. Keri asked for a bottle of water and waited until the girl was finished. Once the group of lads had left, she walked over to Julie and sat down opposite her. "Sorry I'm late," Keri said.

"No worries, probably good, I've just made some more sales," she said indignantly.

"Julie, I'm not accepting this tone, I'm your manager and whether you like that or not, I've now had three separate conversations with you. You go out and get pissed, turn in for work late most days, you're not devoting time to all of your guests, seemingly it's only the boys. This IS your final warning, I don't have the time to dedicate to just one person and we're coming up to summer properly where I need all my staff on the ball. I have been more than lenient and then to come back to find out that you walked out on a bar crawl to hit up some guy, AND when a fight broke out? Seriously, what would you have done if Jack needed you? We can't have people like that on the team. You got it?" she said to Julie.

"I think you're being completely out of order, I'm twenty-one. This is what this job is all about. You've been a bitch since Emma cheated on you, it's not your team's fault Keri, and you should maybe bear that in mind and maintain some professionalism. I've spoken to Emma last week when you were gone and she's going to have a word with Dan about me moving up there; my experience will be more suited to the youth side and then I'm sure I won't get bollocked for flirting with guys to make the company and island some money!" She said it with such venom as she stomped off. Keri sat there, stunned; when the incredulity subsided she was seething, she was fucking boiling and knew she needed to calm down, because she was about to blow.

Keri was brought away from her thoughts when Maria came over with a clear liquid in a short glass. "You look like you need this, no?" the elderly woman said to her. Keri just stared incredulously, completely unsure what had happened and more importantly why the fuck people were talking about her when she was gone. She downed the drink. *Fuck, that was strong*, she thought, swallowing with difficulty. "Efharisto," she said, pulling her purse out.

The woman put her hand to Keri's face. "No, no," she said, and followed it with something in Greek. She always spoke to Keri in Greek and most of the time she just nodded and smiled, this time she gave the woman a kiss on the cheek and shouted, "Yassas!" before running out of the hotel.

* * *

Keri rested her head on the back of the chair and counted to ten; she felt like shit and didn't know what to do. She debated going to see another of her team but thought better of it, worried that they were all talking about her and would slate her like Julie just had. She started the engine and drove the thirty-minute journey to the office; she plugged her phone into the cigarette lighter and hit play on the Gloriana album. She went to track 9 and pressed play; she wished she could speak to Riley.

When Keri finally arrived at the office she was more relaxed; that was until she saw Emma's car in the parking lot. "Fucking great," she sighed loudly, hitting the steering wheel with her hand. Picking up her bag, phone, and keys, she walked into the office, desperate to not let anyone else rile her today – she needed to get a grip.

Stopping at the door, she forced herself to think of this morning and the thoughts of Riley; she smiled to herself. Lifting her phone, she went to Google and found a black and white image of two woman sensually kissing on a bed. She looked closely, making sure it had the desired effect and didn't look like some form of teenage boy's fantasy. It looked loving, yet sexy, she thought. She opened WhatsApp and sent the picture to Riley. *"Wish this was us; shit day :(Xxx"* and pressed send.

She had done right, she thought; she could already feel her troubles release a little. She pulled open the door and walked into the office, keeping a tight grip on her phone. She walked past Emma, not even acknowledging her, and sat at her desk opposite Karen. "Hey Momma." She smiled sincerely. "How goes it?"

"Well apparently not as good as you," she said, smiling and putting down her pen, smirking at Keri. "Sooooooo, how's you?"

"I'm ermmm, pretty good, I guess," she said, smiling. She kept her head down and opened her computer, purposely placing it so she was able to turn her back entirely to Emma.

"Hmmmm apparently so, Little Miss Happy. Would it be something to do with the gorgeous girl?" Karen was smirking.

They spent a short while in silence before Keri heard the ruffles behind her; she looked up to Karen, who was watching the girl seemingly pack up. "Going," she mouthed to Keri.

Emma walked past Keri and Karen and knocked on Dan's door which was closed. "I'm heading out, ermmm, assuming you are going to take care of the issue in hand?"

She heard Keri saying, "Great well let me know when the deed is done, I don't want no more issues occurring," she said, and slammed the door, walking out of the office.

"Ignorant little madam," Karen said to her, tutting.

"Keri, a word?" she heard Dan say.

She looked over to Karen who was looking at her questioningly; she rolled her eyes thinking this would be her bad mood coming back!

"Hey," she said, walking into Dan's office. "You wanted me?" she said pointedly. "I know what it's about, Dan, and I don't want to put you in a shitty position, so just give me it."

"Ok, so here it is. Apparently they have been getting close, I don't know in what context and don't really want to, considering how Julie slags it about with the lads. Honestly, I think it's the right thing." He sighed. "I'm going to send her up with Emma, let her take the fall for her and deal with all the issues you've had last season and this one," he said, rubbing his temples and looking totally stressed out.

"Wow," she said solemnly. "So basically, we're rewarding her for fucking up; anywhere else they would have sacked her ass, Dan, you know this. So she goes fucking crying to my ex with the sob story; the pair of them are fucking laughing at me, making out I'm some 'jilted bride' overcome with jealously and depression, so that she can come to you and make out I'm no longer competent or capable? Is that what this is? Really? Unbelievable!" she said. *So much for keeping control*, she thought.

"Keri, calm down! Seriously, I know you're pissed, but here's the alternative. You sack her, she's gonna go to HR. You don't sack her and keep trying to manage her and she's gonna go to me or to HR and say you're bullying her. She's a decent seller, but unfortunately, she's a royal pain in the ass. As unprofessional as this may sound right now, even Emma's starting to become the same. They will become as thick as thieves and soon after, either Emma's gonna go elsewhere, Julie's ass will be gone if she fucks up again, or they will screw each other over in one form or another. I know you don't think this is ideal and I get that," he sighed and leaned back in his chair, "but, stop being reactive and think logically. You don't need this shit. All eyes are on you, babes, and this girl has been nothing but a pain in your ass since day one. If she starts piping up she's gonna fuck this up for ya. Let her go Kel, let her go. Let Emma manage her and keep out of it. I'm saying this as your manager, your mentor, and your mate, Kel. Please, do this for me?"

Keri couldn't do this, she could feel herself getting upset. She didn't want Dan to see her like this, it wasn't fair. Knowing this would be killing him caused her to feel bad but she couldn't be here, not right now. She shook her head soberly and left his office, just nodding at him. She grabbed her belongings and walked out the office, seeing Dan resting his head in his hands out of the corner of her eye.

Chapter 23

Riley

Riley saw the red opal Corsa pull up at her apartment. She walked over to the open window and saw an overweight guy with glasses on. He smiled at her. "Riley, I guess?"

"Hey, you must be Jason, thanks for the lift. I'm excited about seeing your welcome meeting."

He laughed loudly. "Blimey, you're keen. You do a couple of these and the novelty soon wears off, I can assure you."

They had a bit of small talk through the journey, but Riley was hardly listening and instead thinking back to the call she'd made this morning. She couldn't help but question the decision she was making to keep up contact; she couldn't seem to control herself though. The car pulled into the large hotel and brought her out of her daydream.

"If you would mind sitting at the back for me, there's a post, I wouldn't mind you going there? I know it's pretty lame but no matter how many and boring these things become, everyone hates being watched by their peers or managers." He smiled at her.

"Sure thing, buddy," she said to him, getting a bottle of water and getting comfortable in the hidden seat as requested.

The meeting was good. Katie was right, he was a good person to shadow and she'd made loads of notes. She was just waiting for him to finish with the guests when she heard her phone report an incoming message from Keri, much to her delight. She read the message with concern about the bad day but loved the picture. She started typing a response.

'Hey you, thanks for the message, you make me smile. :) You also make me incredibly mad, I am literally going to have to fly my ass over there on my day off if you continue to talk dirtily, and you're actually killing me. Hope you're ok? You said you were having a shit day? I'll be home at 5 for a couple hours before my roomie lands, you wanna chat? Ps wish that pic was us too, I miss you, and I don't feel like I can let myself enjoy it. {Sigh}. Hope you are ok. Speak soon gorgeous. R xxxx'

Riley spent the next couple of hours shadowing Jason and finding out everything that she could from him; she liked him, he was a nice guy. He said that he'd been working for Hightail for the last six years and loved Greece; he had no interest in becoming a manager or moving on, he loved his resorts and as his knowledge grew he was given more responsibility but not too much, was given a car, and some good hotels following the relationships he'd built up with his hoteliers.

He was a nice guy – she could easily see why they continued to keep him. She found it strange that someone would want that from this job but I guess it was each to their own, she thought.

"So fancy having some lunch and a friend to assist with your resort ramble?" he said to her when they were driving back. He had told her that Katie had said when they'd finished Keri would have a few hours to spare, and had given him an envelope of places to find in the resort. "I'll tell you now, I'm not doing it for you, and I'm merely accompanying you and giving some assistance where necessary."

"I'd love that, thanks," she said, "but, if you insist on wasting your time to help me then I insist on buying lunch."

"You have a lot to learn, Riley." He smiled widely at her.

They drove down and parked by her apartment. He locked his car up and handed Riley the envelope. They walked down the road and came to a little English bar, appropriately named the White Lion. "Really? You're taking me to an English bar?" she said, confused.

"Firstly, you'll see why; secondly, you come to relish and relax in these places, and thirdly, I believe you have already got a date in a Greek tonight. I didn't want to ruin the moment by it not being your first experience in a traditional Greek restaurant," he smiled.

"So what length did you have?" she said to him.

Laughing, he walked through the door and 'arm hugged' a guy she was introduced to as Tony. "And this is Riley, she's our newest recruit, and I think gonna be one to watch," he said.

Tony handed them both a beer. "Nice to meet you Riley, I'm sure I'll be seeing a lot of you." He smiled warmly. "So what do you want?" asked Tony.

"Same as usual for me mate; they do the best pie, chips, and gravy here. It's like home from home, 'specially with some bread and butter on the side."

Riley picked up the menu and read through. "Steak and onion ciabatta please." She looked to Jason, holding up the beer in question.

"Welcome to life overseas, come with me!" he summoned.

She followed him out the back of the pub onto a terrace; there was a side entrance gate saying 'employees only' which he was walking towards. "Ermmm, is this the right place? Should we be going this way?" she said, worrying.

He held the gate open for her, which she reluctantly walked into. She walked around the corner and saw lots of people, most of which were in tour operator's uniforms. There were people in the pool drinking and people scattered about eating. There was a little kiosk style bar in the corner where they were serving drinks and shouting the orders of food up to the customers.

"Get it now?" he said to her, smiling. "This is our 'secret hideaway'." He laughed, directing her into a corner under some shade.

She opened the envelope and studied the map that was there. She took in the list of things she needed to find. They dug into their food and Riley was already marking off parts that she spotted when she hit the store this morning for her SIM and the walk to the

Lion. The resort didn't look too big and she thought that with a little assistance from Jason she should be able to do it easy enough.

"Great food and I get what you mean now," she said, looking around the joint. "Anyways, you didn't answer; how long did you have me down for?" she said, smirking.

"Dunno what you mean." He took a bite of his chip and pie sandwich and laughed.

"Hmmmm, yeah, of course not."

They finished their food, and Tony was insistent that as it was her first day it was on the house. "Remember to send your guests here!" he shouted as they walked down the road; she turned back around, saluting him and waving back.

* * *

Riley walked into her apartment, throwing her bag on the floor of her room. She was wrecked. A mixture of the little mini bar crawl Jason had insisted on whilst doing the resort ramble, along with the sun, had wiped her out. She had only had three beers – she had never felt like this after three beers but she knew it was the daytime and sunshine drinking. She looked at the time – 4.17pm. "Just like being back home," she said, laughing to herself. She sighed and switched on the air conditioning unit. She got undressed and headed into the shower. In her experience, she didn't really know of a powerful shower overseas, but this one certainly did hit the spot despite the whole flooding issue she had to contend with. Despite that, she'd kill for a bath right now, thinking as she allowed the pressured droplets to fall over her head and body.

She dried herself down and wrapped a towel around her hair and went back to her room. Opening her laptop that was still on from this morning, she put her new album on and lay on her bed, slowly drifting off.

Chapter 24

Keri

She arrived home and poured a glass of wine; after a long run on the beach and a long, large swig she was finally seeing the logic in what Dan was saying. She removed the bottle of JD from the carrier bag on her dining table and placed it next to her bag.

She checked the time – 4.30. *Shower, phone call, and then grovelling*, she thought, looking to the bottle.

She allowed the shower to burn over her skin, thinking she needed exactly that. She spent a long while in there, just letting the day's stresses wash over her. She looked up to the shower head and closed her eyes, relishing of the effects it was having on her body and mind.

Finally departing the shower, she dried herself off and put a CD on; she threw her running gear in the laundry bin and lay on her bed with her phone. She didn't know if she should just call or whether she should check Riley's availability by sending a message first.

"Come on, Keri," she said aloud. "What the hell's up with you?" She knew the answer. She liked Riley, and she liked her a lot. However, she didn't want to;

firstly, because how could it work? They lived on different islands. Secondly, she didn't even know if Riley wanted this. It was her first season and there was so much to explore and experience. Why would she want to be tied down? Plus, she couldn't get over the pain, the wasted years of her life, for someone to realise she wasn't the girl for them and screw her over royally. *Seriously, you are overthinking all of this. You haven't even known the girl a week!*

She picked up her phone and pressed call; after a couple of rings it was answered by a sleepy Riley.

"Hey sexy," she said sleepily. "How are you? What's happened today?" She yawned.

"Oh, sorry. You said you'd be free around five. I'll um, I'll let you go back to sleep, you have a busy night," she said awkwardly, scolding herself for being a dick.

"No, no please don't. I was just lying on my bed waiting for five so I could call you, I don't even know your hours and when you can and can't speak so I just wanted to wait and then just dozed. I have wanted to speak to you since this morning. Well, unless you have somewhere to be," she sighed.

"Were kinda shit at this aren't we?"

"Yeah... why do you think that is?"

"Honestly Riles, I think it's because we're both trying to lead normal lives, ignore whatever's here, this, us. Honestly, I don't think that's possible."

"Do you want me to stop contacting you?"

"I would love to say yes, Riles, but I can't. I don't know why because I'm absolutely petrified, but I loved spending time with you. Now your face appears when you call, I smile; I think of you, I smile; you text, I smile; I listen to 'our' album, and I smile. The common denominator, well clearly that's you. You are the one that makes me smile and I want to keep smiling."

Keri sat there listening to the silence on the phone.

"I thought it was just me. I can't stop thinking about you and although I enjoyed today it wasn't right not being with you to share it with. But I'm not going to lie, I'm scared too, Keri."

"Me too, baby. Do you want to stop talking or continue?" she said, taking control.

Her voice was childlike and quiet. "Continue."

Keri sighed with relief. "Ok, in that case, let's stop overanalysing and set some ground rules. We will call and text whenever we want to. If we are busy we will call or text when we can. We will play it by ear and continue with our friendship, agreed?"

"Agreed, so fill me on what's happened today then?"

They spoke for ages. Riley was listening intently and offering her advice; she'd made her see where Dan was coming from and Keri knew they were both right. She apologised for being so self-absorbed and asked to hear all about Riley's day. They chatted light-heartedly, laughing and teasing, it felt like they were just normal. The reality was, she didn't know what normal was.

"So, when you off out then?" Riley asked Keri.

"When we get done, I just need to get dressed and

that's it, how about you?"

"Woahhhh, REWIND. What do you mean you need to get dressed? You telling me you been talking to me for nigh on an hour naked?" Riley said to her.

"Riley Laura Sharpe, you are the biggest pervert I have ever met," she said.

"You can't hold me personally responsible. I have seen that incredible body, those words sexily inscribed on your body, your amazing breasts that come to life at the simplest of touches. I can't help it if that picture, those moments, are imprinted on my brain. I can't help but get turned on and imagine what I'd do to you if I were there when I know you're laid on your bed naked."

"We can't do this, you know that right?"

"I don't know what you mean," she whispered.

"Don't use that tone with me Riles, I can't take it."

"What tone are you talking about?" she purred .

Keri couldn't help herself, she lowered her hand. She could feel she was ready. "You are so naughty," she sighed.

"How so? We're both adults."

"So tell me, what you would do to me then if you were here?" she whispered to Riley.

Riley illustrated in great detail, explicit detail, of how she would worship and appreciate her body, taking great pleasure along the way by kissing, caressing, and loving her.

"Are you doing it too?" Keri said, feeling somewhat exposed.

"I am; I'm so… ready, imagining you and your body and how much I want to be there," she whispered.

Keri was breathless as she and Riley released together; they were silent for a short while.

"Are you ok?" Riley asked her.

Suddenly she felt a complete mixture of emotions. She could feel it beginning, she was losing control and she didn't know if she could take it.

"Yep, I'm fine, are you?" she asked.

"I dunno, I didn't feel like I was doing something wrong, but I don't know, I can't help myself with you. It's taking me by surprise and I've never been this way before," she said.

Keri broke the silence, speaking first. "I miss you," she whispered.

"I know, me too."

They sighed in unison.

They had a little more chit-chat, and Riley had talked about her weeks' worth of planned activities. She said she was looking forward to the booze cruise as the team had been put on it too, and also the traditional Greek night with plate smashing and authentic food. She laughed about her 'date' this evening and she spoke of her disappointment of the trip to Turkey next week where they couldn't get anyone to go with her, however, they had caveated it with the fact she'd have her hotel by then, so if she could get some guests on it for that day she wouldn't be alone.

Eventually they admitted defeat and finally said

their goodbyes, with promises of texts later on.

* * *

Keri pulled up in front of the big villa before her; she lifted her bag off the seat and locked the car up. She pressed the doorbell and waited for the door to open; as it did, Dan looked tired. She was pissed at herself for being the cause of that stress. "Peace offering?" She smiled, holding up the bottle of Jack to him.

"You're a soppy tart but I love ya," he said, pulling her into a hug.

"I'm sorry, I was an arse today! I know that! I was just really pissed about the whole thing. The way she spoke to me, the audacity, and the thought of them all talking and laughing behind my back. But, ya know what, more than anything else, the fact that they thought it was me being heartbroken over that stupid bitch! But there was some truth in it because before I left that was completely right, I was heartbroken over how she'd behaved but that has never ever, not once impacted my job and how I have done my job," she said seriously.

"Kel, you are shit hot and she ain't a patch on you babes, I promise you. Don't let them bring you down though; you've come back a completely different person and you need to be away from this aggro now, cause if you don't babe, they'll fuck it for ya, I'm telling ya right now," he said, handing her a drink.

"I know, that's what Riley said. I'm sorry I was a jerk, I promise I'll pick my game up and I promise I'll keep out of their way. Now, what do you want to eat?" she said to her friend and manager.

"What makes you think I ain…"

"Dan, you're a bigger girl than me; when you're stressed you starve yourself." She laughed. "Go light the barbecue, I'll make us something."

"Yes boss." He saluted her and kissed her cheek.

Keri opened the bottle of wine, and made a carafe of lime water. She made some mixed kebabs, foiled some jacket potatoes, and threw some salad into a bowl; she took the kebabs out and put them on the barbie.

The friends lay on the sun loungers together, drinking, talking about women and the delights of Emma and the problems of the team. They enjoyed the food, conversation, and quality time together, and it was exactly what she needed.

Chapter 25

Riley

Riley felt great after her conversation with Keri, but she was annoyed about all the rubbish with Emma and that jumped-up rep. It wasn't her place to be pissed but she was struggling. She'd not seen this side of Keri yet, and she seemed so deflated and down; she wished she could have just been there to give her a hug. She knew she had held it together well by not slagging the girls off, and just listening, empathising, and advising where she could. From what Keri had said about her boss he was a good guy and she knew that her going to him tonight would be the best thing.

She was thinking about the conversation about them and then what they had done. Riley had never done it before, but it felt right. She knew she was getting in deep and didn't know how to stop it, more importantly, if she wanted to. After all, this was her, she hadn't even held down a normal relationship let alone a long-distance one, and could just tell it was going to end badly. But despite all else, she genuinely liked this girl as an individual and wouldn't want to lose that friendship. Fuck, how had she got into this situation! She had only wanted this job, not a relationship, and certainly not with a cloud over it.

Riley was thinking back to her mum's words. 'Don't fight it, love isn't always easy, not always hearts and flowers.' That's what she said, or words to that effect. *She knew, she knew this was going to happen*, she thought.

"You ready, pretty lady?" said Ben, dipping his head into her room.

Riley shook herself out of it, making a conscious effort to park that away to analyse later. "Ahhhhh, my 'non-date' date with the infamous Ben." She smiled and held her hand out. "Purely so I can let all those swooning girls know you're mine." She smirked

"Fuck you," he laughed.

"To protect you from the all those broken hearts?" She smiled, still holding out her hand.

"You and me are gonna smash it this summer, mate," he said, taking her hand and leaving the house.

* * *

Ben was awesome, they got on like a house on fire and had done exactly what he'd said; they basically got to know one another. He was twenty-three, an ex-personal trainer from the Midlands, the youngest of four boys, which he used as his 'pulling' card with women. They had lost their father young, and his mum had never met anyone else; she normally visited him at least three times a year and despite 'avoiding' relationships at all costs, it appeared through fear. He was totally in awe and devoted to his mother and despite loving the job more than life itself, he would totally give it all up if his mum needed him, it was clear in his eyes; this surprised her completely.

Ben reminded Riley of Scott; she smiled, remembering she had not texted him in her new number text frenzy today. She excused herself to the bathroom and quickly texted Scott's number.

'Hey good looking, it's your fave lesbian, this is my new number. Hope all well so far. In case you have spoken to Sal already sorry for not filling you in. If you haven't, goss sesh required ASAP. Send me your availability; on the piss tonight :) love you, Riley xxx'

Riley returned to the table and Ben got the waiter's attention. He came over and ordered a carafe of red and their food, opting for a Greek platter following the mouth-watering description that Ben had presented her with.

"So what's so great about this job then?" she asked him seriously.

"Honestly, it's just wicked. In summer we get involved with the youth crowd which is loads of fun but still have normal guests, ya know, and in most part due to the three Ps," he said, smirking.

"Why do I feel like I don't want to hear this?" She was reluctant to say too much in order to not give it away; plus, she was already feeling bad about lying to him, having to fill him in on a 'cheating boyfriend' that caused her to run away, but it would only be for a week, she thought.

"Well the three Ps *are* what make it and they are," he drum rolled on the table for extra effect, getting an extra laugh from Riley.

"Go on, oh mighty one, share thy wisdom."

"Easy! Plenty of booze, plenty of fanny, and plenty of money to be made." She spat her drink out, laughing, alarming the customers surrounding her in the process.

"You are wrong, on so many levels. You know that right?" She laughed, picking up her phone that had just notified her of an incoming message.

"Love interest?" Ben questioned, pouring them both a little more wine, pointing his eyes to the phone.

"Friend from training," she said, lifting up a stuffed vine leaf from the platter and reading the message coming through.

'My beautiful girl, how goes it? Thanks for the number and yeah spoke to Sal earlier, was a bit surprised, you dirty dawg, you. ;) Defo need a catch up, call me tomorrow anytime, I am on a day trip shopping so be able to speak whenever. Love you gorge. Xxx'

Putting the phone back down, she could feel Ben watching her. "Yeeees?" she said, drawing the single word out, still continuing to analyse the platter before her instead of looking at him.

"Nothing! So you looking forward to meeting the team? This is the best; here, look. Take some of the flatbread, some tzatziki, and some lamb souvlaki. Taste," he said, handing it over to her.

* * *

Riley was confused about Ben. He was awesome, she really, really enjoyed his company, and he seemed like a genuinely nice guy. She didn't know if this was his way of getting girls but he appeared almost gentlemanly, and this surprised her. She couldn't quite gauge him; she felt totally comfortable with him, like he was a really good friend, but this wasn't the person she was warned of, so she was having difficulty relaxing at present.

Ben insisted on paying the bill, which the owner had given them 50% off, they left the restaurant and Riley could already feel the effects of the wine; seemingly it was just a top-up of today. They wandered down the street, taking in the bars setting up for the big nights ahead of them. They headed towards the beach; the picture was perfect, with the sun setting low creating a mixture of colours, and the cool warm air was perfect, she thought. She wished Keri was here to appreciate this moment.

She wanted to speak to her and pulled out her phone from her shorts, noticing there was a message already waiting for her.

"You really are Little Miss Popular aren't you?" Ben said, nudging her as they walked side by side.

"And you are incredibly nosey, or jealous?" she said, raising an eyebrow.

"Nah you're not my type love, plus don't screw the crew and all that," he said, laughing.

"You have no way not shagged any of the reps, that's bullshit," she said, laughing. "Ok serious though, this is my bestie." She showed the picture of Cara on her phone to him. "She's seemingly just booked a flight today after a shit day at work and is gonna be here on the May school holiday, so you my friend, go near her, try to bang her, I'll bang a fucking nail through your cock!" she said, laughing and replying to Cara of her sheer excitement over her impending 'piss party'.

"Ouch, I can't quite determine whether this is 'serious' cock blocking, jealousy, or whether I should be offended that you don't think that you and I would be hooking up in three weeks?" he said, smiling a lopsided grin.

And there it is, she thought. "Baby, you couldn't handle me; we'll be no more than friends, I can guarantee that!" She punched him.

"Hmmm, I like a challenge," he said, laughing loudly and pulling her into the bar.

How had he just changed so drastically? she thought, smiling to herself. "So this is your pulling tactic, ehy? You wine, dine, and play the perfect gentlemen and then go in hard with the flirting?" she said, laughing at him. She quickly opened her messages, and typed:

'Hey beautiful, how is it going with Dan? Miss you, can't wait to speak to you like we did tonight again ;) PS my date went well; he's now hitting on me R xxx'

Ben walked to the bar, ordering a beer for them both; he had also ordered a shot for them both and handed it to Riley.

"No way, I am already feeling the effects from today, I can't drink that," she said.

"You won't last unless you grow a pair," he said, downing the Sambuca.

This was not a good idea, she thought. She downed the shot and then turned to him. "No more, seriously," she said to him intently.

"Told you I love a challenge." He smirked and did that gorgeous 'win me over' smile; she couldn't help but laugh at him. She was now finding it easier in denying him the truth about her, but at last was happy to settle and relax with him too.

"Stop bullying my new staff, Cassie." She turned and saw Katie.

"Hey, how was your first day?" she said, smiling.

"Cassie? Yeah it was awesome, thanks. I learned a lot, ate some awesome food, and just got forced into my first shot and I am so not a shots girl," she said to her boss.

"My surname, there's no story in it," Ben said, and left the two of them at the bar.

"So what do you think of 'the hunk of the week'? He is a good and likable guy but God he's obsessive with women," Katie said, laughing to her.

"He is super cute. I've warned him off my friend that's gonna be here in three weeks, or I'll chop it off," she said, laughing and swigging back her beer.

"Your 'friend' is coming?" she said questioningly.

"Yes, I didn't think that was a problem. We both know I'll be working; she'll crash by the pool," she said, concerned at the fact that Cara had already booked her flight.

Katie looked at her, amused. "Stop freaking out, I have no worry about you having people coming over. I will caveat that with, for future reference you are supposed to let your boss know; I really don't give a shit, but for future seasons you'll know. The reason I was questioning was about it being your 'friend'," she said in inverted commas. "Is this a 'friend' or what? Is Ben going to go all out to set up a hidden camera to watch two beautiful women make love?" she said, laughing.

"Oh my god he wouldn't?" she said, startled. "And for the record, no, it is actually my bestie." Sighing, she said, "Keri wouldn't be coming out for a holiday here, she wouldn't get the time off work. And thanks for the heads up, I am sorry, my best mate Cara is a teacher and although loves it, will die trying to convince all otherwise. I texted her my number today; she texted me half hour ago that she'd booked something." She laughed. "I wouldn't mind, I haven't even told her which resort I'm in yet," she said.

Riley's phone signalled a message coming in. She grinned widely as she saw Keri's name.

"Must be love," Katie said, laughing. "I'll leave you to it. Come over when you're ready and meet the team."

"Oh no, no, it isn't. Ermm. Were just friends," she said, stuffing the phone back in her pocket.

"Righto." Katie smirked.

"No, no really. I mean seriously, we're just friends," she said, running alongside Katie, in a scene which must have a looked like a little puppy chasing its owner for attention. She was so lame at times!

They reached the team and Katie introduced Riley to everyone, there were about twelve people. Ben, was mingling amongst the boys and she could only imagine that the conversations were about the current bets. She met Clare again and they chatted freely, getting to know each other with a couple of other girls.

A while later Riley could feel that she was clearly intoxicated. She had been pushed into another two shots and these people all appeared to just live for drinking shots. *Mental note, do NOT tell Mother about this*, she thought. Shots weren't really her thing and at this rate, she literally wouldn't be getting up tomorrow. She excused herself from the table and went to the bathroom. God, she felt rubbish

She pulled out her phone and saw the three messages from Cara, Scott, and Keri. She opened Keri's first as she knew she'd had it for a couple hours now and didn't want to seem like she didn't have time for the girl.

'Hey you, I'm great, Dan's great, were both great. I can't wait for you to meet him. He thinks you're hot, so you know :) and he thinks your, wait let me think, ermmm "super intelligent" because you said the same to me as he did re the 'psycho bitches' that's what we've called them. 'Psycho, psycho bitches' hehe. I'm good, I miss you, and I'm drunk. I'm gonna regret texting you tomorrow I KNOW it. But we been on wine and half through the bottle of Jack I bought, not good. I have a long ass day tomorrow its liquidation, bleurgh. Anyways, tell the boy he needs to back off because he ain't a girl and YOU like girls. FACT. I like girls, I like you. His asking me what I'm texting and if its war and peace or I telling you I love you. I need to go before I got myself into more problems. His right its war and peace I'm sorry. Ps whenever you want another "phone call" brings it on. Pps I miss you A L O T. just saying. Bye Riley enjoy your night. K xxxxxxxxxxxxxxx'

She laughed at the message. "Meet him," she said, resting her head on the cubicle door. "She wants me to meet him."

"Hey, are you done? We're desperate out here."

She heard bangs on the door.

"Sorry, just coming." She smiled to herself; she felt the same, she wanted to try this. Riley felt like a kid in a candy store. "Yes." She thumped the door, laughing as she walked out of cubicle, apologising to the girl waiting.

She opened her phone and pressed respond to Keri.

'You have no idea how much you turn me on, you have no idea how much I like you. I love war and peace Keri, I love getting messages from you, and I can't wait for our next 'phone call'. Miss you baby girl xxx'

"So this is where you're hiding? I was worried you were being sick. You looked a bit, erm, peaky. But instead you're sexting your girlfriend," Katie said, smirking.

"I told you… ya know what, it don't matter, I'm fine, very drunk, so I'm gonna leave. I have an early start in the morning and had zero sleep last night," she said, trying to hold herself upright.

"I'll take you home, you look like you might struggle at the best of times, but I don't hold out much hope you finding your way home A) in the dark and B) on your first night."

"No, no, no," she said, waving her arm around. Hell, how had she got this drunk?

"The alternative is Ben is going to offer to be the gentleman and in this state I'm concerned you may wake up in bed with him," she said, laughing.

"He'll force me," she said soberly.

"Nooooooo, you idiot. But you're that fucked I

don't know that you'll be able to resist his charms or hide your sexuality."

"Ohhhh, you're protecting your interests," Riley said, laughing and pointing to her boss.

* * *

They had stopped to get a slice of pizza on the way home. Katie was insistent that she needed more food or she would be paying for it tomorrow. Riley eventually admitted defeat and asked for a slice of Hawaiian. They were walking down the road; it wasn't far but, it was long enough with her in this state.

"So do you think you'll last?" Katie asked her seriously.

"As long as I control myself. I can't do this, I mean I drink, too much in my mum's opinion, but I'm a normal twenty-four year old girl I suppose. I can drink, but NOT shots. Shots and me, nah, were not mates. We have a 'love-hate' relationship, they love hurting me and I simply hate them love hurting me," she stated matter-of-factly, looking at Katie who was looking amusedly at her. Choosing to ignore it, she continued, "But yeah, I will cause it's all I've ever wanted," she said before taking another bite of pizza. "Are you gay?" she said to Katie.

"Wow, that was out of the blue. Why do you ask me that?"

"Just get the feeling."

"Why?"

"I don't know, I just do, and maybe it's my 'gaydar' reacting, maybe I'm completely off scent but I don't know, just wouldn't surprise me I guess."

"Yes I am."

"Oh right."

"Is it a problem?"

"Nope, why would it be?"

They arrived at Riley's apartment. "Put your alarm on now whilst I'm here or you'll sleep in tomorrow," Katie said.

She did as she was told and then went in. She leaned against the door. "Thanks for today and tonight, you're a good boss. I think we're gonna get on," she said, smiling. "I need sleep, see you when I see you," she said and shut the door, walking to her bedroom. She fell onto the bed frontwards and fell asleep that way.

Chapter 26

Keri

"Seriously, if you look again, I'm gonna push you in the facking pool," Dan said, evil-eyeing her.

"You were right, I put too much. It was like War and Peace, or because I said you said I was in love, or because. Oh shit, why? Why did YOU let me text? You know what I'm like. I can't believe I did it. I'm a tit, an actual tit. I'm a tit on a stick. She'll be running a mile thinking fuck this shit, that's what she'll be doing. I mean I may have just gone all out and said to her 'I love you,' or 'Wanna marry me?' in true lesbian style," she said, putting her head in her hands.

"You dykes are fucking mental, you do realise that don't ya?" he said, handing her another shot.

"I can't, I can't possibly drink any more. I'll text again, I'll have no self-control, and maybe we should go to bed. Actually, no, scrap that I do need it, calm my nerves," she said, again downing half the tumbler of JD.

"There's me thinking I'd finally get my wicked way with you," he said, laughing at her.

"Piss off, you are the most loved up I've ever seen. You're all 'old' and shit, don't go out, sit at home drinking big boy drinks, with your slippers and fire on. You'll be getting a woolly cardi from me for Crimbo," she said, laughing at herself.

"Buddy, it's thirty-eight degrees at night. I can assure you I don't have slippers and a fire on," he said, laughing.

BEEP BEEP; BEEP BEEP, they heard.

She dived across the table and lifted her phone. "It's her." She smiled at him and the phone. "She doesn't hate me, she likes it, we're good," she sighed, slipping down into the seat, relaxing.

"So, you know you're in deep, right?" Dan said, coming and sitting next to her and putting his arm around her gently.

"I know, and I'm terrified. I am not this person, I don't know how to be this person, Dan. What do I do?" she said, lifting her feet up, snuggling into him and resting her head on his shoulder.

"What do you want, Kel? Do you want her? Do you want to try and make it work? I mean it won't be easy, it's fucking hard, mate," he sighed, taking a sip of his drink and resting his head on hers. "But babes, if you want her then you're gonna have to fight for her! Simples, but do you know she wants the same?"

"I don't know, I think she might, but I genuinely don't know."

"Is this you talking, or the insecurities from silly bollocks?" he said.

She laughed softly. "I do love you; you're the most kind, caring, unprofessional manager I have ever had."

"Says the fucking girl who got sent to be a trainer and was slagging it about," he said, laughing down to her.

"Ohhhh don't," shaking her head and cringing at his words. "What am I gonna do, seriously?" she said.

"Honestly? If you want my view, fight for her babes. She seems normal, she's fit, she's just starting out so she won't be fighting for manager or long haul or shit, so you'll easily get placed together if you last the season and make it work. It'll cost a bit but there's ways and means if it's meant to be; she can come here, you can go there every day off if yous wanted that. But I think you're majorly into this one, maybe more and I ain't gonna lie, babes, I ain't never seen ya like this. Do it, what you got to lose? She says no, at least you know either way," he said sincerely.

"What if it works for a while and then she changes her mind? There'll be a load of temptation, she could do the…"

"Babes she ain't Em, alright, so stop talking like that. You can't be scared off forever because of one silly cow, don't let her impact the rest of your life choices. Ok I've got a plan, pass me my phone?"

She looked at him questioningly. "Just do it," he pushed.

She passed his phone and watched him messing about on his phone. "Right, I've got a plan," he said, smiling, seemingly pleased with himself. "Ready?" he said sheepishly.

"You are the best friend, ya know that? And a massive softy now that you all loved up," she said to him. "Sorry, crack on."

"So, Tuesday you work."

"That's my da…"

"Hold up, let me finish! So you WORK Tuesday, you change your day off to Thursday instead. You 'unofficially' find out what time she's getting to Bodrum that day, on one of your calls, and book a ferry to go too. You arrive half an hour before she gets there, you find out where it's docking, and wait for her to get off. You said that she was going alone; you can spend the day together. If it all feels the same as it did last night then say to her you wanna make a go of it. Bob's your uncle, Fanny's your aunt, and I'm a fucking genius," he said proudly.

She was dumbfounded, his plan had silenced her. Could it work or was she actually that pissed? She thought. Her gut told her that Riley would love it; she didn't know if she could go the whole hog and attempt the whole commitment thing, but she had some time to think about it which was pretty good, and like Dan rightly said, they would just play it by ear.

"I love it," she said. "Thanks, you sure you don't mind?"

"Not at all babes, I'll make sure I can help you any way I can," he said, pulling her back into him and hugging her tightly.

Now she just needed to make sure she didn't let slip. She picked up her phone and saw it was nearly 2am. She replied to her message.

'Hope you having a wonderful night beautiful; I miss you too and like you a lot also. Be careful, sweet dreams Riley. Speak to you soon Keri xxx'

She pressed send before kissing Dan on the lips and heading off to bed.

* * *

She woke with the biggest headache. "Oh, why do you do it?" she said to nobody, reaching down for her bag, her eyes still closed, moving about to find the well-placed ibuprofen. She grabbed her water off the side and downed the tablets. "Shit." She sat up, spitting the neat Jack Daniels out that she had just downed. "For fuck's sake, why did you feel the need to take your drink to bed!" she scolded herself.

She walked downstairs and grabbed a pint of water, picking up the letter for her. He'd written to her:

Gone to work, let yaself out and I'll see ya later, made you a choccie croissant hope heads ok.

She took a bite out of the croissant and downed another pint of water. Heading back upstairs with her third pint, she lay back down, picking up her phone and checking the damage she'd done the night before.

"Ooooohhhh," she cringed whilst reading the message. She saw the typos, the complete nonsense, and the waffling. She was an idiot. Just as she was reading she noticed the grey dots appear to show that Riley was now typing a message to her.

She sat up, smiling, and awaited the message.

'Feel poorly sick, need a beautiful girl here stroking my hair and making me feel better :(xxxx'

'Me too baby, Real bad!! I wish I was there stroking your hair, tickling your back and cuddling up to you ☹'

'Now I feel worse... {sigh} me too. Wouldn't that just be perfect? Ps where's my kisses {sniff sniff} xxx'

'Sorry gorgeous, all my kisses are for you. xxxxxxxxx it would be more than perfect (pretty sure there isn't such a thing) I'm so rough. How was your night? Xxx'

'Yeah ok, too much to drink, too many shots, people seem cool, not as cool as you ;) oh and my boss is gay, she walked me home xxx'

'Oh, right.... well you liked her so that's good. X'

Shit, she seemed off, she was being an arsehole. *Silence speaks volumes*, she thought.

'I'm not interested in her, she didn't walk me home like that, I was pissed. I guessed she was gay, but she don't seem to have any interest in me. Maybe because she kept taking the piss about me being 'loved up with my gf'!! xxx'

'GF??? Xxx'

'Girlfriend! xxx'

'Ahhhhh with you. You failed to mention you had a "GF" :(xxx'

'YOU, dopey, she kept saying you were my gf and I was loved up!! Xxx'

'Flirting, sounds like your lucks in! xxx'

'I don't want her, and I really genuinely don't think she has any interest in me and I'm really not just saying that. Even if she did I don't care, I don't want her, I don't want nobody here xxx'

'I know, I'm sorry, I'm hanging and being an idiot because I don't feel well. I shouldn't take it out on you, I know you're not into relationships and stuff and I know how important the job is to you xxx forgive me??? Xxxx'

'{sigh} this is so hard for me. I'll always forgive you, you'll never be able to do anything to me that would cause me not to. I want you, that's why I have no interest here, I want you, I want you now, here with me, I just want you xxx'

'Ohhhh xxx'

'Really?????????? Ohhhhh??? :(Xxx'

'Sorry, shit, I'm so sorry I just wasn't expecting that is all xxx'

'Clearly! Well I am getting picked up soon, I need to get ready I will call you later Keri x'

"Shit! NO Keri, sort this now!" She pressed call straight away.

"Hey." Riley sounded small and sad.

"I want you too," she blurted out.

There was a long silence

"Really? Do you mean that?" asked Riley.

"Yes I do. I spent all night pining over you with Dan and even he said the same thing."

"He did?"

"He did!"

"So what does that mean?"

"It means let's not overanalyse and fuck this up. Let's be adults about it; you have to get off, as do I. Let's go and do what we gotta do today and arrange a proper phone call this evening. We could even FaceTime if you like, I'm missing that sexy smile; then we can digest these new revelations over the course of the day and can reconvene tonight and discuss at length. What do you say?" she said.

"Honestly. I'm imagining you in a hot pink underwear set, saying those words with your glasses on in front of me right now; I think I'd have to get my first disciplinary if you were actually here like that because I am that unbelievably turned on!!"

"You are odd, Riley Sharpe, but I love your 'oddness' and you are a pervert." She laughed.

"It's your fault, not mine. Ok, really gotta go, I'll defo get to speak to you tonight?" she said pleadingly.

"Yes baby, enjoy today."

Chapter 27

Riley

Riley didn't know what had come over her but she felt relieved that she had got it off her chest. She didn't allow herself to worry about the results and whether it would mess up everything both personally and professionally; she couldn't help it, she needed to tell her, she thought.

She picked up her bag and left the empty apartment. Walking down to the hotel where she was getting picked up, she could already feel the heat on her skin. She got her phone out and went to the phonebook. She found what she was looking for and pressed call.

"Hello gorgeous," said Scott.

"Hey, what's happening?" she said to him, interested in how her good friend was.

"I'm good babes, apparently not as good as you like," he said, laughing. "So you spoke to Sal?"

"Nope, she's next on my list. Is she still loved up?"

"Worse, she don't fly till Monday, I think she said. She sounds like a broken-hearted teenager," he laughed.

"Oh geez."

They chatted for a little while about his hotel, which was already allocated due to him knowing the region and resort. He sounded so happy. She filled him in with what had happed with Keri on training and since then. He seemed happy and was making fun of her and the 'perving' he and Sally had witnessed at the awards, but ultimately, he was genuinely happy for her.

They had arranged to have a weekly 'siesta' Skype session when Sal had arrived to resort, so got her timetable details. They wanted to make sure they all maintained contact regardless of anything else.

She said bye to her friend and jumped onto the coach, handing in her ticket to the transfer rep. They were off to Kos town for the day to do some shopping. She was looking forward to it, and seeing what the capital was like.

* * *

Riley wandered the historical town; it was incredibly beautiful and she could have spent all day getting lost in the ancient archaeological heritage scattered about. She was in complete awe of the beautiful place and knew she would have to bring her parents here when they came to visit. *They would love it here*, she thought.

She found a little Greek taverna down by the harbour. She ordered an espresso, a half carafe of red, and a chicken pitta. She already loved the food, the flavours were incredible and the simplicity of it all was perfect. She took some pictures on her phone and sent them to Cara, her mum, and Keri, telling them she wished they were there.

After finishing her lunch she continued to explore the area; she went into a few stores and got some local gifts to put in her room. She also bought a brown leather friendship bracelet with 'αγαπώ' on it; which meant 'love'. She didn't want to think why she was drawn to it, but she kept it in the pretty pouch and tucked it away in her bag. Checking the time, she realised it was time to start heading back to the pickup spot to head home. Meeting the transfer rep and some of the other guests, they got back onto the bus, finding a seat towards the back, where she closed her eyes and slept for the duration of the journey.

When she got back she was wrecked; she had a fair bit of time before Ben would be home and was thinking she may just chill with a movie tonight due to the intensity of the following day. She knew this was going to be a hard sell too, as everyone was on day off tomorrow. But she didn't feel like going out, not tonight. She'd be fine when she was working and not training still, she thought. She would be fresh tomorrow and was kind of looking forward to having a phone date with Keri.

She opened her phone and texted her to tell her she was home and would be available all night, so for Keri to let her know when was best.

Keri typed straight back, confirming it was ok and that she couldn't stop thinking about Riley and couldn't concentrate. She'd said that she would call when she was done.

Riley showered and put her laptop on; she was desperate to watch a chick flick, but knew she couldn't put any lesbian movies on in case Ben came in. She opened her documents folder and went to the romance folder; she saw The Wedding Date and smiled. Pressing play on that, she got herself comfortable with a bowl of crisps and a virtually frozen bottle of water, and lay on the bed as she watched the drama unfold for Debra Messing, pretending to be dating an escort to make her ex jealous.

* * *

When she heard the words of the song they'd shared at the airport, from the ringtone she'd made specifically for Keri, she smiled. The words including, 'I shoulda kissed you, I shoulda pushed you up the wall, I shoulda kissed you, like I wasn't scared at all,' lifted her mood whenever she heard them.

"Hey you," Riley said.

"Hey, how's today been? You ok? God, I missed you today," said Keri.

"Me too, Kos town is incredible and everywhere I turned just stunned me. I so wished you were with me so we could have shared it together, ya know?"

"I do, we'll do it together one day, I promise. I hear it's got lots of ruins and is beautiful?"

"It totally is, Keri. I can't wait to show you it!" she made it clear this was more a statement of fact, than a question.

"Well you know Rhodes is similar and they have ruins in Rhodes town, so I will take you there too. We can visit them both together?"

They chatted for over an hour, talking about their days, what they were up to that evening, the next couple of days of Riley's schedule, her conversation with Scott, and everything else in between.

They both sounded disappointed at the fact they had to end the call due to Keri going to her friend Karen's house. They didn't really touch on the morning's conversation, but they both agreed that they didn't necessarily need to and they would just see how the next week or so panned out, speaking regularly and just enjoying doing what they were doing. Then, potentially, look at maybe one of them visiting the other in a month's time when everything had settled down.

They said their goodbyes and Riley suddenly felt the loneliest she had ever experienced. She rested her head on her pillow and took the teddy bear from the side table and hugged it close to her. She lay there thinking about the night they'd spent together on training, getting lost in the memories.

Chapter 28

Keri

Keri felt great after her conversation; she was still feeling the effects of apparently ¾ of a bottle of Jack, but Riles had totally picked her up and now she needed to sort the day over at Bodrum to surprise her.

She wrote on the letter, 'I love you, always.' Pinching a takeaway coffee mug filled with black coffee and the half-eaten croissant, she left for work.

She threw her overnight bag in the boot and stuffed the croissant between her teeth whilst she started the engine, put her belt on, and safely cradled her coffee in the cup holder. She took another bite and then reversed out of the drive, making her way down to her team meeting. She would only have Julie for this meeting, and that was something to be positive for, she thought.

As she got there Jack, Tegan, and Sarah had already arrived and were laughing and joking.

"Hello boys and girls," she said with a clear spring in her step.

"Miss got laid last night. Hope she was hot." Jack winked.

"Unfortunately not, I had a date with a guy friend so nothing to report, just feeling good is all," she said, and as if by some movement in the universe, she noticed Julie arriving as she finished the sentence. She couldn't help but giggle at the truth in the statement.

Claire asked if everyone wanted something to eat and a drink. Keri most definitely needed something, she was seriously not feeling the love of the effects of the booze from last night. Combined with missing her morning run, which had always impacted on her healing process, she jumped at the chance to order, shuddering at the thought and brought herself away. "Hi Julie," she said happily.

"Ermm, hi," she said, looking her boss up and down.

Breathe, two, three, four, five, she thought inwardly, still maintaining a huge smile, which realistically wasn't false – it was merely because she was getting rid of her once and for all.

Jack and Tegan had worked alongside Keri for a number of years and whilst she had normally had a tight-knit team and they all got on well, even they were looking at their friend Julie, annoyed.

The waiter took their orders and Keri, who was writing some notes in her pad, was brought to the attention of Julie, telling them all that Emma had driven down last night and helped her move in and then they stayed up all night and she was 'dying' now. Keri couldn't help but feel a twinge of hurt; she knew it wasn't jealously, she knew she was out of that a long time ago. But she was human after all, and couldn't help but feel pain that she knew they would have been sat up all night laughing and joking about her. Or, maybe they're shagging, she thought. She shuddered at the thought. "Ewwww."

"You alright, boss?" Tegan said.

"Yes, sorry, had a nasty thought in my mind," Keri said.

"Oh yeah? You didn't shag that bloke last night and now you're feeling grossed out? If you want to give a bloke a try, I told you we can have an interlude in our boss-bum relationship and I can assist you?" Jack said, laughing wholly, causing the team to laugh along. Well, with the exception of Julie.

"Jackie boy, you will always be the first I'd call if ever I felt the need to go the dark side, I promise; anyways come on, let's get on it," she said.

Their food arrived and they ate and worked; she collected the tickets and money from the team in preparation for the office liquidation day tomorrow. She said a polite, almost humble goodbye to Julie on behalf of the team, and she said professional and friendly goodbyes to everyone bar her. With the promise to them all that they could come up and stay with her anytime, as they'd all LOVE it, which caused Keri to smirk. She lifted her phone out of her bag and just looked over the messages this morning. She sighed, stroking her phone, smiling.

"You are totally fucking with us, boss. You got a hot bitch, look at your face!" Jack shouted, interrupting Julie's little speech, much to her obvious annoyance.

Keri went red, which really didn't help matters. "There's nobody guys, you would be the first to

THE LIFE OF RILEY

know, I promise," she said.

They all sat back down with their boss and Julie just stomped out; all in all not a bad outcome. *Karma really is a bitch*, she thought.

* * *

She pulled into the office and walked in, waving at Dan and sitting at her desk.

"Hmmmm, well I don't think I've ever seen this look on you," said Karen.

"What's that?"

"Death, yet happiness?" she laughed to Keri.

Rolling her eyes, Keri said, "You are funny, Mama. I'm ok, had a little too much to drink."

"But then you spent all night having phone sex with the beautiful stranger and whispering sweet nothings in her ear and now you look happy as well as death." She laughed hysterically at her own wit.

"You are insane, you know that?" she said, hearing smashing about behind her, making her flinch as she looked around and saw Emma, who she'd missed when walking in.

"Well I can tell you now shorty, you will be filling me in tonight at my house, and I need a girlie night, so you have the next twelve hours to get over the hangover!" she said pointedly.

"Shorty? You are aware I'm like three feet taller than you and hardly short?" she said quizzically.

"Oh, the restaurant had a group of kids in last night drinking. They requested a TV show where they were all calling each other shorty and I like it, I think it suits me," she said like the cat that got the cream.

"I'm pretty sure, it's like, a name for your partner, or, when you're a pimp or something? At least I think so," she said, laughing hard, more so when Karen was looking constipated as she was clearly recollecting the shows and the form in which they were constituting the nickname 'shorty'.

"You two look like you are having some fun. Coffee anyone?" Dan came out of his office.

"Yes, apparently I am a lesbian or a pimp, it appears," Karen said matter-of-factly, and still confused.

"Do I actually even wanna know?" Dan said to the women.

"Nope," said the chorus.

"So you told her yet Kel?"

"What?" he heard both women say to him.

"Keri, is going on a mission to surprise the new love interest in Bodrum on Tuesday when she will be there and fess up her undying love and ask her in true lesbian fashion to marry her and have babies!!" Dan said, gleaming.

"You're a dick," she said to her friend and boss.

"Oh, lady, you have so much to fill in on tonight. How is it that the boss knows this but not your mama? Me and you are seriously through, unless you tell me every morsel of information," Karen said.

"Thanks, big mouth."

"I'm done, I'll see you tomorrow." Emma stomped out.

Keri dropped her head onto the desk. "Seriously, you really need to keep making things harder for me," she said to them from the desk.

"Leave her be, she's become a right attitude on legs recently. Well, more so than usual," Karen said.

Dan laughed, walking to the kitchen and making them all a drink.

* * *

She pulled up to Karen's house, reliving the conversation with Riley on the way over. She wished she could have stayed on the phone longer, or been there, laying watching movies with her. She sighed, getting out of her car and retrieving her nomad bag; it was literally difficult to think of it any other way due to the amount she stayed out.

"Thia Keri, Thia Keri!" She heard the screams from her two gorgeous protégés calling her auntie. She saw them jumping up and down at the gate.

"Yasoo, ti kanis?" she said, the greeting which was the very few words she knew, walking inside, hugging them both tightly.

"Did you bring us a present?" she heard the excited children shout, climbing into her bag.

"Eleni, Nikos, do NOT be so rude. You do not speak that way." Karen came out, reprimanding her children.

"Sorry Mama," they said in unison, walking off dejectedly.

"You're so mean," Keri mouthed.

"I am not, I don't want these brattish children with

no manners," she said, kissing her colleague on both cheeks. "So if I could give you the best news of the night what would it be? Removing, that your love interest is here or Emma is leaving from the equation?" she said animatedly.

"You didn't?" she said, eyeing Karen intently. She started sniffing the air. "Noooo?"

"Of course I did, anything for my honorary daughter," she said, laughing.

Keri ran off to her back garden and saw the slow-roasted lamb on the spit in front of her. She was a major fan of two things, roast dinners and lamb; roast lamb was the best thing on the planet. Next to Greek roast lamb. Nobody made a better joint of lamb than a Greek, and then a Greek spit lamb, it was heaven, and there was no other way to describe it. Oh, this was just sheer perfection; she was stood in front of the spit just watching it go round and round.

"What are you looking at, Thia Keri?" asked Nikos, interested.

Karen said something in Greek to Nikos which got the two children laughing hysterically. Keri had no idea what she had said but they were clearly amused at her.

"No fair, when I don't speak Greek," she said to them all.

"I'll teach you some Greek, Thia Keri," said Eleni, coming and sitting on her lap. "Would you like to come play in the pool? Mama said no because we need to go to bed soon, but I'm sure if I play in the pool a little, it would make me and Nikos a lot tired and will sleep much better." She smiled widely, wrapping her arms around her 'adopted' thia, or Aunt Keri.

"Momma?" Keri said to Karen pleadingly.

"Thirty minutes only, that's it," she said seriously.

Keri practically threw Eleni on the floor as she jumped up and removed her board shorts and vest, down to her bikini.

"Geez, you're like Superwoman," Karen said. Without even finishing the sentence Keri was diving headfirst onto the lilo in the pool.

"Yay, super girl, super girl," the kids were singing and jumping excitedly into the pool.

* * *

The kids were now tucked in bed, after arguments over getting out, which luckily Keri was able to resolve by blackmailing the children out with the Kinder Eggs she'd brought over for her niece and nephew. After the most delicious lamb she changed into her sweats and relaxed on the lounger with her wine.

"So you ok, really?" Karen asked.

"Yeah I am, just trying to keep my head down really and get through my MDP. Once I've done that and achieved everything I have been working towards then, great. But it's been hard, I won't lie; and all the shit with Julie, well it hurt me, ya know? But I don't want people to think that I'm jealous or pining; I'm not, Karen, honestly," she said sincerely.

"Baby girl, the day you returned and walked over to my office, you were different. I have never seen you like that, you were oozing happiness. You were glowing, and if you'd ever stopped to think why things were so bad with you and Emma, well that's why," she said.

"What do you mean? We know why Emma's the way she is?" she said inquisitively, like she was missing something.

"Look, Dan and I were discussing this at lunch today. Actually he said he was coming tonight; anyways, think back to before you left. If I remember correctly, you had agreed to meet at the positive, professional, and polite 'pub' shall we say? Agree to disagree, I think you said. Keri, you were talking, albeit awkwardly, but when you left you were talking."

She was right; as awful as it was, they WERE talking. *What had happened?* she thought. She felt ashamed.

"Why are you looking like that?" Karen asked.

"Because you're right, I have been a bitch and I'm not that person, Karen. I'm not," she said, feeling shit.

Karen moved onto her sun lounger. "Lovely, you still aren't. This is what I'm saying, you made it professional and normal, you put your hurt feelings aside, and you were the bigger person. And the minute you got home looking happier than anyone's ever seen you looking, she became a difficult bitch and caused issues with others. Keri, this is our point, this isn't you, darling girl. This isn't you at all. You have always been the bigger person. Dan and I knew you two weren't right for each other, but whilst neither of us have met Riley, Keri we have never seen you like this. Emma likes control, she was ever so controlling of you, and you allowed her to be, so I'll defend her on that front. But don't you get it? She's lost that, because she still even had it when you split up, because YOU went and requested a truce from her being difficult. Now you have come back a different person, you have come back relaxed, happy, and she doesn't have that control any longer. She wasn't the one that made you flutter, so she's annoyed she's lost the control. See?"

Keri was struggling to take in everything she was being told, but as she was thinking on, she could see the sense and truth in what Karen was saying. She lay back on the chair and digested the words.

Solemnly, she asked Karen to pass her phone. "Do you mind if I call her?" she said.

"Emma?" she said, shocked.

"Nooooo, Riley," she said shyly.

Karen looked at her with an unreadable expression. "Yes sure. I'll clean up, while you do."

She grabbed Karen's arm. "No, please don't, I want you to, speak with her, please." She knew she sounded childlike and hoped Karen wouldn't feel put out. Her eyes told her otherwise. "Thank you, you're the best momma and best friend ever," she said.

"Well as long as the drunken party girl isn't going to start speaking dirty, I can't deal with all of that," she said to Keri, nudging her gently.

"She's at home. She wanted to stay in for tomorrow and so we could speak tonight," Keri said shyly. She pressed speaker and called, waiting for the dialling tone to begin.

"Hey beautiful," Riley answered.

"Hey you. So in true Davina style, you are live on Channel 4, so please do not swear," she said, laughing.

"Righhhhhttt. That sounds ominous, and you sound like you are being led astray," she laughed.

"Excuse me, she's leading my lovely children astray!" Karen shouted in the background.

"Oi oi!" Dan shouted in the background.

"Dan, shut your bloody big mouth, I've just got those children down!" Karen shouted.

They were all laughing at the big boss getting told off, including Riley. Dan sat down on Karen's lounger opposite the women, becoming aware of the phone on speaker in front of him. "Hey Riley, I'm Dan, the unfortunate task master of these two mentalists," he said, laughing.

"Daniel, you're so rude. Excuse him Riley, no manners. I'm Karen."

"Ouch, what you doing that for?" he said rubbing his arm from where Karen hit him hard. "I just arrived, I didn't know that you hadn't all been here on the phone for ages."

"Nope, the fun's just beginning, Daniel." Riley laughed at them.

"No, no Daniel. It's Dan," he said sternly.

"So who's there?" asked Riley.

"Just Karen, me, and Dan who is now eating the leftover lamb. You ok?" Keri said to her.

"I'm fine, kinda like listening to you all," she said.

"Hey Riles, I'm Dan, and contrary to popular

belief I'm the one that keeps her in check."

"And I'm Karen, I'm her momma. How are you, sweet girl? You are my new favourite person so why do you sound so sad?"

"Hey Dan, nice to meet you. Karen, how can I sound sad, you haven't spoken to me?" she said interestedly.

"Well there's a reason this beautiful girl I'm looking at right now calls me her 'adoptive' momma. I've been there, I came here, and started where you are. I'm not saying it's the job, or missing home, or even my beautiful baby girl Keri that's getting you down, but let's just say I can hear it in your voice," she said softly.

"You ok, Ri?" Keri said, concerned.

There was silence for a while. "I'm fine, tired and maybe missing home and my family somewhat. I hope I get to meet you guys sometime, you seem pretty awesome and Keri is really lucky to have you with her, especially with all the shit going on," she said.

"We've sorted that tonight, didn't we lovely girl?" Karen said, stroking Keri's arm. "Riley, from what I've heard, and I'm normally a good judge of character, you seem like a good one, and our girl over here is ever so happy, so I hope something comes of this friendship."

It went silent for a while.

"Thanks, you guys. It's been good talking to you all. I was feeling pretty homesick. Probably lying in bed in PJ's watching chick flicks didn't help matters on my second night," she said, giggling.

Saying their goodbyes, they ended the conversation for the night. Keri felt uncomfortable. Something wasn't right with Riley; she didn't know if it was homesickness, the forced call to her friends, or maybe something else. Keri was worried but she couldn't quite establish if it was for Riley or herself anymore.

Chapter 29

Riley

Riley put her laptop away and put her phone onto the love playlist. She turned over, hugging the bear tighter; she was feeling really low, and didn't know how to get herself out of it. It was her choice to stay in tonight and now she felt so much worse. Riley knew it would be a hard week, and luckily it was only today and Bodrum that she would be alone. She needed to make an effort with the team and get herself out there, she'd always been outgoing and easily made friends. In reality, she had done yesterday; but she had a good excuse for tonight because of tomorrow's back to back excursions, then starting working with another rep on Tuesday, before her first welcome meeting Wednesday. Things would be different then, she thought.

She picked up her phone and started typing a message.

'Sorry if I came across rude, I'm wrecked and missing you, home my family. Please send my apologies to your friends I don't want them to think badly of me :(. I'm gonna crash now; I made a playlist, a love one (I'm a dick I know)! I'm just listening to it now, your number 9 Gloriana song is on :), I love it. Good Night Keri, speak soon. Xxx'

'Hey, you didn't come across rude at all; I'm worried about you gorgeous. I hope you sleep well, sweet dreams beautiful. I hope to speak to you tomorrow? Xxx'

'Honestly, I don't know if I will get a chance I am back to back excursions tomorrow and apparently there isn't really any chance, plus I'm with people all day. :(I'm sorry xxx'

'Oh, ok. Well have a good day, I'll speak to you when you are next free I guess. Night x'

'Please don't be mad at me, I feel so shit, already. I just don't think I'll get a chance to talk tomorrow, I hate not talking to you, and it's horrible the prospect of going a whole day without speaking to you. But the alternative would be 2am when I get home, if I get any opportunity of course I'm gonna call. I hate this, I feel like I need you. I feel lost and shit and all I want is you to be here holding me tight telling me it's going to be ok, instead of the teddy you gave me, in your absence. R xxx'

'Ohhhh baby, I'm sorry, I thought you were being weird, I thought it was me and you were backing off. It's so hard so far away and doing everything in text :(. I wish I was there too; I like your cuddling my teddy though. I was worried you would find it lame! If I was there I would pull you in close to me, wrap my arms around you, play with your hair softly, kiss your temple, tell you to close your eyes and think back to West Kirby sunset, and think about all the future sunsets that we will watch together, with your love playlist playing 'our song' in the background. Good night, beautiful girl. K xxx'

'That made me cry :(that sounds perfect. I wish we could have that!!! I guess I should crash. {sigh} xxx'

'We will have that, baby. Somehow! One day we will. Xxx'

'Do you really think that? Xxx'

'Most definitely, I genuinely do Riley. We were brought together for a reason, and when things are meant to be then they work, they aren't always easy, but that's what makes it perfect. Xxx'

'My mum said something like that about you, when we left for the airport xxx'

'She did? Why, what did she say? Xxx'

'Don't fight it, love isn't always hearts and flowers, if it's meant to be you need to fight for it and work at it, roughly put :/ xxx'

'Right. Xxx Riley, do you want to… ummm… fight is probably the wrong word, but do you want to see if we can do something then? Xxx'

'Honestly, I don't know.'

Keri's heart sank as she read the first words and laid her phone down, taking a deep breath to try and calm her racing heart. She picked it up again.

'I have never done this and I didn't think that my first relationship would be long distance, I hate not seeing you and that's what concerns me, that I won't be able to cope without seeing you often. If we were together, there would be no doubt in my mind, but I'm just so scared. I want this with you here with me. But in the same respect, I wouldn't be able to continue talking to you if I didn't, and that breaks my heart, because, well {sigh}, if I'm honest, somehow, I've developed feelings for you. I'm sorry to throw that out there, I shouldn't I know! But I believe in being honest, both options come with pain and I don't want to hurt. {sigh} xxx I'm sorry it all got very deep! :('

'I know exactly what you mean, I didn't want any of this, I wanted to just come home and continue my life, maybe we

shouldn't have carried on speaking when we got back. I'm sorry I've caused you this stress, it shouldn't be like this for you :(xxx'

'There's no part of this that's your fault please don't think that, and I wouldn't change meeting you, spending the night with you, taking you to my parents, the airport or even speaking to you since arriving. What are you thinking? Xxx'

'Honestly?'

'Yes, irrespective of my feelings, I'd rather you be honest? Xx'

'Right, well I was thinking I'd give anything to be there now holding you and making love to you to our song, and your playlist xxx'

'Haha. You tit, all this seriousness and you're thinking about sex, typical lol. Thanks for making me feel better. You amaze me more every day. Xxx'

'I'm worried I will get hurt again, but.... {sigh} I have developed feelings too, and it's terrifying me. :(xxx'

'You stole {sigh} haha xxx'

'{smiles} xxx'

'You can't start making new {} up; we have to deliberate on such decisions, tut tut. Haha xxx'

'I'm sorry chief executive of the {}; I thought you were going to put me in a position of authority to be able to make such executive decisions {double sigh} xxx'

'Hahahaha thanks for making me feel better xxx'

'I hope you are, I always would try to make you feel better, you should sleep, and it's late. Sweet dreams xxx'

'I'll dream of us xxx'

'Good xxxxxxx'

'Do you want an us? Xxx'

'SLEEP xxx'

'Ok, ok xxxx'

Riley lay there silently, staring at the light from the street lamp outside illuminating her ceiling. She was trying to digest and explore the meaning of their conversation. Keri hadn't put any pressure on her; smiling softly, she turned over and went to sleep.

* * *

Riley returned home that night after an amazing day's worth of excursions. It was just what she needed, she thought. She'd managed to text Keri a few times through the day, and more so through the night when she had been drinking, and had seemingly lost her cares of being with the team at the traditional Greek night.

Getting undressed, and packing her bag for work the next morning, feeling the excitement and nervousness as she was quickly approaching her first ever welcome meeting, she'd need to do it tomorrow on siesta, she thought, and finish it in the evening.

She looked at the time – 1.54am. She wished she could have spoken to Keri today. She opened her phone and wrote one last message.

'Glad I got to message you some today, hope you had a good day. I did, but have missed you incredibly. Good night my sexy girl. Riley xxx'

She hit send and went to sleep.

Chapter 30

Keri

Keri felt sad from the texts that Riley hadn't said, she now knew she wanted to fight for a 'them', but she didn't want to push Riley. If she had never had a relationship she would be feeling the fear of the pain more than anybody, she thought.

Though feeling happy she'd managed to relax and cheer her up a little, she was so worried about her tonight on the phone. Keri sighed, they had both developed feelings for each other. She didn't quite know how or when it happened, but she knew that's what her friends had been trying to tell her about tonight, she thought.

Lying silently, she tried to ignore the butterflies in her tummy. "God, what have you got yourself into?" she said to the darkened room, throwing her arms over the eyes.

She picked up her phone and texted Kimmy.

'Urgent conf call tomorrow, I have fallen for her? :(x'

'Ohhh babes that's great, isn't it? Ok babes, you want me to call now? X'

'No at Karen's and kids are in bed, tomoz is cool. Love

you x'

'You too sis xx'

* * *

The following day, she made a conscious effort to keep herself busy to try and not overthink last night's conversation and the fact she wouldn't be able to speak to Riley; she'd managed to get her ticket booked for Bodrum. She hope this worked out as well as she was planning, Riley hadn't made any reference to any others going with her yet, which was good. It was all planned. *No going back now*, she thought.

She spoke to Kimmy and spent a long while speaking to her and gaining her opinion on the matter; she was always sensible and logical about everything, that's probably why Keri always went to her. Kimmy's advice was the same as Karen and Dan's, so the decision was basically on her. Was she brave enough to do something? The problem is, she genuinely didn't know the answer to that, she didn't know if she wanted to go through it all again. Revelling in speaking to her nephew, Jason, she felt loads better for that alone.

Riley had managed to text sporadically throughout the day, which she was happy about as she was concerned about the content of the conversation last night and how it would all pan out.

Chapter 31

Riley

Riley felt sick. It was her first welcome meeting and although she was ready there was no doubt about it, she still felt sick. It didn't help that Katie was here to watch it; she was breathing deeply when Katie came and handed her a glass.

"What's this?" Riley asked.

"The only thing that will get you through this morning – drink. I'll be behind the bar, you won't see me at all, ok?" her boss said.

"Ok." She downed the drink. "Fuck, was that straight vodka?" she shouted to her boss who was leaving.

Katie shrugged her shoulders without turning around. "All they had, I'm afraid."

She looked out to the guests; there were only about twenty-five people, she noticed. *This will be fine*, she thought. Quickly running through in her head the start of her meeting, from there she thought the rest she could 'wing it' if needed, then she would get to the sales and was fine with those. In reality it was just talking, more or less talking about them. *Buzz words*, she thought. *Excellent, fantastic, amazing, stunning.*

Having had an amazing time yesterday, the emotions would come through her facial expressions, characteristics, description and demeanour when talking about them and should sell. Well, she hoped for that, as that's what everyone kept telling her.

She breathed in deep. "Here goes," she said. Just as she picked up her homemade map she heard her phone go; recognising the tone, it was a message from Keri.

'Good luck for your first meeting gorgeous; you are awesome and will smash this out of the water. I will look forward to a treat with all your comms :) xxx'

She smiled widely. She felt like she was able to do anything now she'd seen that message, she thought.

* * *

"My god, seriously that was the biggest buzz ever," she said to Katie. "And you're sure, absolutely sure, I did ok, right?" she said again.

"Yes, I wouldn't keep telling you if I wasn't," she laughed. "Are you sure you're definitely ok with your liquidation, the tickets and cash make-up?"

"Yep, perfectly." She grinned happily.

"Well, guess lunch is on you then?" said Katie.

"Charming. Come on then, if I must."

They went back to the Lion, ordering food and drinks. Riley insisted on paying despite Katie telling her she was joking.

"So, did you actually get anyone on Bodrum tomorrow?" Katie asked, eating her lunch.

"No, unfortunately. To be fair, it's a bit soon in

and my sale was kinda rubbish, obviously I haven't been on it so technically blind selling. But I'll be fine, I am looking forward to it and I'm sure there will be a bar close by, worst case." She grinned cheekily.

Her phone started ringing, before she had a chance to acknowledge Katie she had already seen the screen saver and told her to answer it.

"Hey."

"How did it go?"

"Yeah totally awesome Keri, I loved it. I am on such a high and I got a few sales; I'm just at lunch with my boss and she said a lot of them will go away and think about it and then come back too. I'm stoked. You ok?"

"Ermmm yeah, I'm good. Look, if you are out with your boss I'll leave you to it, I just wanted to make sure it went ok."

"Wait, don't go."

"I have to, I have a meeting. Enjoy your lunch Riles and I hope you get more sales this evening."

And she was gone, just like that. Riley sighed.

"Everything ok?" asked Katie.

"Yeah, fine thanks."

"Doesn't seem it," Katie responded.

"No, it's fine honestly." They continued to chit-chat until it was time for Riley to go back to work.

That night everyone went out; she was celebrating and the others were just out because, well, it was the night, which meant apparently you go out. She had tried to call Keri but hadn't reached her; she knew it was the whole Katie being gay thing. But she had never come across that way for a moment; she didn't have any interest in Riley, she could tell. She got her beer and typed a message.

'I'm sorry if I upset you today. I can't not go out with my boss if she asks me; I know it's incredibly difficult when we aren't together, but as I said the other day. I am 99% sure she doesn't want me, but more importantly, she's not you Keri, so… I don't want her. I miss you big time xxxx'

She went back to the crowd, mingling with her team; she did really like everyone, she was so glad of that, as there was so much apprehension after leaving Scott and Sally.

"Hello gorgeous, you been hiding from me?" Ben came up to her, nudging into her.

"Hey you," she said, kissing his cheek. "Sorry, no, been mad busy, but luckily we are good to go now. Well, after boring Bodrum tomorrow," she laughed.

"It is a bit shit to be fair, when you've done Kos Town then it's virtually the same, other than the potion and carpet selling of course, which is just painful. There's a beautiful castle and the beaches are good. Loads of knock offs so you can get some wicked bags and jeans and stuff though, that's about it."

"Oh, amazing. Glad to hear that," she said, checking her phone.

"Got a hot date?" He smirked, downing his beer. "And here's me thinking we might have some time together tonight."

"Oh, how could I take this beautiful face away

from all these admiring women, hanging on your every word?" she said, pinching his cheek.

"Well, we can have some fun alone." He winked.

"You're good thanks, it's erm, the girl's point of the month," she said, squirming for effect.

"Oh, right well maybe another night," he said, laughing.

"You are such a player aren't you?"

"I'm not, I genuinely like you, and I think we could have some fun."

"Well we will, on Saturday if you're up for it?" she said, smiling.

"Yeah? Great, will be made even better with the fact that I will have spent all day looking at your body in a bikini," he said, smiling and raising his eyebrows.

She shook her head. "Right, I'm leaving.

"What, why?" he said to her, shocked.

"I need to be up early, don't I? Don't make too much noise." She smirked. "I'll see you tomorrow night," she said, gently slapping his face.

Riley said her goodbyes and left to go home.

* * *

Riley sat on top of the ferry enjoying the sunshine on her skin; regardless of what the day did or didn't bring, this scenery and part would be an amazing selling point. Ensuring that lots of photos were taken, and getting some amazing scenery ones with the sun sparkling on the turquoise waters, she could imagine putting these photos on the back of her map, where the photos of her excursions were. The reps all had these and said they were better to create yourself and do one side with your map then when you have done your resort and island part you can turn it over as a visual to accompany the sales spiels. Smiling at the thought of the words, 'Making the most of this holiday, why don't you enjoy a taste of another country? Start the day with a smooth sailing coastal ride across the Med, taking in two beautiful countries' scenery, Do this as you glide across the turquoise waters with the sun perfectly reflecting off of them.' Writing down the words in her phone, *Not bad*, she thought. *Not bad at all*.

Her thoughts wandered back to last night again. In the want and craving of having Keri here with her to appreciate all these things, she had text her back last night, putting her at ease and making her aware that she wasn't pissed, she was just a little bit jealous. Riley kind of liked it, she was glad she wasn't the only one that was feeling lonely without the other.

She was brought out of her daydream as the announcement came over that they were just about to dock; finding the details of the guide she received on the bus, the first hour and a half was for them to shop, which she was happy about as it meant she could have a look about before meeting up for lunch and doing the carpet and potion factory. Riley scolded herself for calling it that again, she really should make an effort to correct the terminology on that. If she slipped up in a welcome meeting she'd never get anyone on it.

Riley disembarked the ferry and followed everyone up towards the passport office. She retrieved her passport from her bag and showed the guy in front of her. She walked through; grabbing her phone, she typed a message to Keri, telling her she was now in Bodrum to test the carpets and secret love potions, smirking to herself. Hearing her phone go off immediately, she was surprised at how quickly that had gone through. She lifted her phone, smiling at the message from Keri, but there was no message. Stupidly, she looked to the back of the phone, not really sure why she had done that. But it was their song, it was her ring and text tone that was going off. She turned behind her to the sound and facing her she saw those incredible icy blue eyes, holding her singing phone up to Riley with a smirk on her face.

Chapter 32

Keri

"Keri?" she said, surprised.

"Hey Riley, surprise?" she said softly. Her fear and insecurities were evident now.

"It's you, it's really you. You're here? How? When? Why? My god, I can't believe you did this," she said, stroking Keri's cheek, tears coming down her face.

"Baby, don't cry. This wasn't the reaction I was hoping for," she said sadly.

"Oh my god, you are amazing. Thank you thank you so much for this," she said, hugging her tightly. "But seriously, you choose to surprise me, in a country where we can't even make out," she said, smiling and taking her hand.

"So, how are you, really?" Keri said.

"Honestly?"

"Yes."

Riley sighed. "I've never felt more happy and perfect in my entire life," she said sheepishly.

"Good, I'm glad. So, you told me you were a private person, so I figured a bunch of roses was probably not a wise choice; so discretion is the word. This is for you," Keri said, pulling a carrier out of her bag. She gave it to Riley, watching her open it to see the three packs of Ripple multipacks.

"You said they were your favourite," she said, smiling at the beautiful woman, stroking her hand softly.

Riley was crying again now. "You got me Ripples, oh my god now I know you are a keeper. You really are so perfect," she sighed.

"Oh God, Riles. I'm not perfect, far from it, but I like you a LOT, so I wanted to do something nice, and something a little selfish, because I was missing you so, so, much that I just needed to see you. But, I must confess this wasn't actually my idea, apparently I was pining, so Dan came up with the idea and after a bit of deliberation I decided to do it."

"Why deliberation?" she asked questioningly.

Keri was quiet for a while, deep in thought. She was trying to find the words to say. "Honestly Ri, I'm struggling so much. I have avoided girls, completely, for such a long time, and I was happy with that. I am so close to completing my MDP now and one of the last things I had to do was the course. I saw you and was instantly drawn to you. Glen and I were talking about people we liked and what we liked about them and I just couldn't put my finger on it with you. It wasn't just about your beauty, and believe me that's a big thing, because you're stunning, but… it was more than that, you completely captivated me, that's the only way I can describe it. Then the more I spent time with you, the more I wanted to find out about you.

"You have scared the hell out of me, my friends have commented, my ex is being a bitch again, and I've suddenly lost all enthusiasm for everything I thought I wanted and was working towards. I don't seem to care about anything anymore. I'm with my friends, I think of you; I'm alone, I think of you; my phone vibrates, I hope it's you. I spend every minute of every day thinking of YOU, Riley. And honestly, I don't like it. I know what it, what this means. If I'm honest I didn't want to face it because I couldn't deal with being hurt again. I know we touched on it the other night but you were right, it's now come down to weighing up which hurts less. And that's where the deliberation came in. As I thought back to your family, how you were with them, you just took my breath away, and I if I allow myself to acknowledge what's happening to me, I think it was in that very first moment, seeing you with them something stirred in me. Then, as I saw you with your family in your conservatory," she sighed heavily, "it was then as you sat next to your brother, who there had been this mutual torture the whole time between you both, and in that moment..." She had to stop, to try and control her emotions.

Riley wiped a tear from Keri's face and kissed her cheek where it had landed. Keri took a deep breath. "Sorry. Anyways, you looked so small and afraid, you asked Adam to get your bag because you didn't want to go upstairs to your room again. When I finally became honest with myself, it was at that point I realised I was already in too deep, and I think it was then; it was at that point that something flicked on inside me. I'd be lying if I said I wasn't terrified; but I also know that I would regret it for the rest of my life if

I walked away. From you, from the potential of having you in my life. So I wanted to come and tell you that. I know it's so incredibly cliché, but to me you are so incredibly perfect, you're my perfect, and every moment we spent together, every time we spoke or messaged, when I hear your laugh, or think of your smile, even hearing you sad the other night, then it just reaffirms that from my part I want to fight. I want you Riley. I want everything with you; but for now I'm happy to be the person you say goodnight to, the person you say good morning to, the first person you want to give great news and shit days too; I just want to be the one you want. Ok, I've said enough, I feel completely exposed now, I apologise, and that was not my intention to do any of that, just so you know. I guess I just saw you, and couldn't stop myself. I'm sorry; I didn't mean to ruin this."

Riley turned to her, still crying. "Nobody has ever done or said anything so beautiful in my entire life. You are beautiful on so many levels and you are already my 'first and last girl'. You're my first thought, my last thought, you're the one I want to call when I have something to tell you; hell, if you weren't the one that had just done that, I'd be calling to tell you," she said, laughing behind her tears. "You are already 'my one'. Unlike you, I can't quite put my finger on when I recognised, you being someone I wanted, I needed in my life but, you've done something to me that nobody has ever done to me, and yeah I'm scared shitless, but..." She stopped a moment, sighing. She smiled shyly. "But, I think you're worth it."

"Really?" Keri said, completely dumbfounded.

"Yes, of course. Why wouldn't I? You're beautiful,

funny, intelligent, witty, gorgeous, sexy as fuck and oh my god at some point today you must let me see that tattoo. Actually in fact I need a photo of it. Apologies, digressing. But the point is, you said earlier you're far from perfect, but to me your imperfections are your perfection. And I think you're perfect to me, perfect *for* me. So, as much as I would love to not feel pain or hurt or fear of this fucking up, I want you more than all of that. On a serious note, we have only got a few hours together, I want to go and see this place with you, just us. Do something normal."

* * *

Everything about it was perfect, Keri thought. She couldn't have asked for a better day or surprise. They found a tiny little beach café where they sat hidden away in the corner; there was nobody about so when the waiter disappeared inside, Keri leaned over and kissed Riley's lips softly. "My word you have no idea how long I have waited to do that," she said meaningfully.

"Do you want to go to the beach? We can take a walk, have the water run over our feet?" Keri said enthusiastically.

* * *

As they walked along the beach in silence, it was so beautiful and relaxing. "This is perfect," Riley said. "I wish we had more than one day, or I wish I could at least hold your hand and kiss you in public," she said solemnly.

"Be patient baby, maybe in a couple of weeks when you are settled you can get a ferry over to me? We may have to stay in bed all day though," she said, smiling at Riley.

They spent the next couple of hours relaxed, doing what normal couples do, laughing, chatting, stealing glances, shy smiles, a knowingness buried deep within them both. But it was worth it. They both knew it would be hard, but they were on the same page and that was what mattered.

They spent the day exploring Bodrum, visiting the castle, walking along the beach and doing all the things they could. She felt bad that Riley had missed the afternoon elements that were part of the trip, and was praying she didn't get into trouble. Keri had had an even more amazing time than the sunset day at West Kirby; she loved this day, and was so happy she did it, and that it had worked out this way.

Knowing the day was coming to an end, they began to head back towards the port. "Don't look so sad, we have a plan, baby. We know where we stand, and hopefully where we want to go. I can't wait to be with you again, properly," Keri said with a naughty grin.

They both went through passport control, together this time and spotted a little seating area. "Do you want to get a quick coffee before we go?" she said to Riley, pointing it out.

They sat in silence and drank an espresso each, knowing it was time to say their goodbyes.

Keri sighed. "I'm so glad I came today, you really do mean a lot to me. I hope we can see each other soon," she said. "I need the bathroom quickly before we leave."

"Me too, and we will make sure we speak as often as we can? No worries, I'll go pay and see you in a minute," Riley said to the girl, squeezing her shoulder as she walked past.

Keri returned from the toilet and Riley wasn't back yet. She went inside and she wasn't in there either. Where was she? *Fuck*. She hoped that she wasn't going to miss the ferry and had to rush off. She picked up her phone and saw a message from Riley.

'Don't bother contacting me again Keri. You're not the one for me. Good luck for the future. Riley'

"What the fuck?" she said out loud. "What the fuck has happened?" She couldn't stop the tears falling. What was she going to do? She turned around, looking all around her to see Riley to ask what had happened, why had she spent the day and said all those things if it wasn't the case. She looked on and saw the ferry to Kos closing up and getting ready to disembark. Just like that, she was gone. After the most perfect day, week of her life, she had just gone, like she never meant anything at all to her. Keri wiped the tears from her face and sadly walked over to where her ferry was about to depart.

She didn't recall any of the journey home; she got in, went to bed and played her playlist – the playlist that was supposed to be for her and Riley. She was completely lost and confused but more than anything else she was completely heartbroken all over again. Allowing the tears to fall to entirety, she lay there until she had eventually cried herself to sleep.

Chapter 33

Riley

Riley sighed in contentment; she grabbed her bag and went to the till, giving the table number to the waiter. She remembered Kos town and reached into her bag. She pulled out the small pink and white paper bag, gently removing the tape and lifting out the little leather bracelet she'd brought. She knew it was silly and soppy, but those things didn't seem to matter with her. Riley rarely felt ashamed for being all nerdy and romantic, it wasn't like that with Keri. As she waited for the waiter to calculate the check she rubbed her thumb over the bracelet again, smiling warmly.

"So, you're sure about Keri? She's actually screwing around? I mean she seems so happy."

Riley overhead the name and couldn't help her ears pricking up; she silently laughed, thinking how strange it was that regardless of how many different countries in the world, how many people over the world shared a name, when you hear said name you instantly have to listen. She shook her head, smiling.

"Oh I'm sure; Keri Johnson is, well, making up for lost time. So, get this, she went to the training course, apparently slept with two girls and was bragging about 'shagging the straights'. Then, then she goes and gets with this girl on the last day, blags a lift with her to the airport, and now she reckons she's saying everything she wants to hear and obviously doing what she wants because she's hundreds of miles away."

"Fuck, you're kidding. But why? Why would she do it? What has she got to gain?"

Riley's head was spinning, she couldn't breathe. What was happening? She looked in the mirror behind the waiter who was handing her the check, at the three girls talking.

"I don't know, it doesn't make sense! I mean why would you bother?"

"Game player? Messed up over what happened with Emma? Who knows! Maybe it's part of the MDP? Maybe she wants this chick to write an amazing letter to the UK and hope it moves up her process, I mean she can't want to stay on the island with Emma can she?"

Riley held onto the counter to keep her from falling; she thought she was going to throw up. She threw the money to the waiter. "Thanks, keep the change, thanks," she said, fleeing from the scene and running as fast as she could to the ferry, allowing the tears to fall freely.

PART THREE

Chapter 34

Keri

"So that's it, nothing, you spent the best part of the day in a fairy tale, and then she runs off, with no words or warning like Cinder-fucking-rella? Kel, this ain't right babe, are you sure you ain't missing nothing?" Dan said.

Dan, Karen, and Keri were at Karen's having dinner, that being the operative word on Keri's part. She hadn't eaten all day and now they were attempting to force feed her. She took a small bite of bread, wiping another tear.

"Guys, I get what you're saying, but I'm telling you everything. It's obvious, she saw the sense. Why wouldn't she? She said she didn't want to hurt, she said she didn't know how to deal with it. We spent this amazing day and I know that as there's no way she didn't, I was there, I was part of it! Then facing the prospect of leaving, with nothing but an occasional phone call and the unknowing of when, if, we will see each other again. It's simple, she bolted. It's too much, she's only twenty-four, she's never been in a relationship before and spent her entire life virtually, wanting this job. I am, I would impact on that so of course she bolted; anyone would," she sighed. She started getting upset again, pushing her chair out and shaking her head. "I'm sorry guys I can't do this, I need to go home," and she left, without saying goodbye to her friends, she just walked out.

Keri got into her car and burst into tears again. She had done nothing but cry for twenty-four hours solid and she didn't know how to stop. She got her phone from the bag and looked intently at the screen saver. Examining the photo, she took in the beautiful pink and oranges of the sunset in the background. She studied Riley's long dark hair, sweeping partly over her shoulder, and partly blowing in the wind, she looked at her own mousy blonde hair sitting just below her shoulders. Both of their smiles were wide, full of teeth, she thought. It was an incredible photo, they looked so happy with their heads leaning into each other's; the sparkle was there, in their eyes, in both of their eyes, she thought.

She opened up her messages, saw the last words on her phone from Riley and felt the pain all over again. She began typing. She knew she shouldn't, but she couldn't stop herself.

Chapter 35

Riley

Her phone vibrated on the bed, as she lay in the darkness, swimming in the tissues and damp pillows surrounding her. She scrutinised herself and the situation; why the fuck had she completely lost control over this woman? How had she let herself be so stupid? She picked up the phone and opened the message that had just vibrated.

'I don't know what's happened; I can only assume you can't handle the pain. But I am completely broken hearted, I have never felt pain like this before, and I'm sorry I turned up yesterday. I thought it was right, I thought you wanted the same. I can't blame you, you're young and it's your first season, and you haven't ever had a relationship. There were so many things stacking against us, I'm sorry I rushed you and pressured you into something you weren't ready for. I hope you know, I love you and think I always will. Goodbye Riley, look after you. Keri xxx'

Riley was crying again. "No, NO!" she was shouting in her room. "NO, you are not blaming this on me; this is you, this is YOU. YOU did this, you ruined this, and you ruined me!" she screamed, pounding her fists against the wall. Slowly turning around, she slid down the wall and broke down once more. She put her head in her hands and let the tears run freely once more.

She lifted her head up as she heard a knock on the door; she turned around and saw Katie.

"Oh Riley, what's happened?" she said, sitting down next to her and comforting her.

Riley moved into Katie's arms and just to continue to cry freely. It was a long time until her breathing and the sobs had subsided.

Sitting up, she looked to Katie. "I'm sorry," she said. "What are you doing here?"

"I saw you today, and it wasn't you. I could tell you were upset and something had happened, when you weren't out tonight and Ben said you wanted to be left alone I asked to borrow his keys, to make sure you were ok. What's happened honey?"

"Nothing," she said, trying to curb the tears again.

Katie pulled Riley in to face her. "Riley, your sad face and red and teary eyes are telling me something entirely different. Is everything ok at home? Nobody's hurt, sick, worse?" she said, concerned.

"No, no, nothing like that," she said, wiping her eyes again and looking up at Katie.

Katie eyed her sadly. "So, homesick or woman troubles?" Katie said.

"We've split up. We were together a day." She laughed sadistically. "We were together a fucking day, officially, and she screwed me over. She picked me up and spat me out, like I was nothing, like I was nobody, like I was a nothing more than shag. And you know what? I only wanted to be a shag, I only wanted her to be a shag, when we first kissed that's all I'd envisaged, a quick lay. But, it didn't turn out that way. We kept growing closer, we were drawn and this magnetic pull was doing something; well at least I thought it was but apparently she was just a player. She made me fall for her, all so she can laugh and joke and fuck about behind my back," she said, starting to cry once again.

"Ohhhh babes, I'm so sorry," she said, pulling her close again.

Eventually Katie pulled away. "Why don't you come stay at mine tonight? You shouldn't be here alone, and we can travel down to the port tomorrow for the jolly."

Riley groaned and sighed loudly. "Katie, please don't make me go, I don't wanna, it isn't right."

"Riley, I'm going to have to pull rank on this one, I'm afraid. You need this, you need to meet the whole team from a business point of view, but from a personal, you aren't staying here alone, it isn't good. You will make yourself worse, plus the whole island will be there, you know what they're like, they're all so self-absorbed you won't have time to think about anything else. You can drink your worries away and have a laugh with everyone. You need to do this, Riley, and you need to do this for me. Plus Jayne will be there, I can't cover for you with the island manager when one of my team isn't there," she said seriously.

"Ok." She nodded solemnly.

"Come to mine? I have a spare room, you can crash there. I don't want you to be alone."

"I can't, I'm sorry, I just need to be alone. But first

I need to go out," she said to her boss.

"Right, well, where are you going? Would you like me to come with you?"

"Nope, I'm good; I'm only going to the store."

Katie eyed her suspiciously. "Ok, I'll check in later. I'll drop you a text to check you're ok."

"Don't bother, my number won't be in use. I'll speak to you tomorrow, 8.30 for the catamaran," she said, holding the door open for her boss.

Katie was clearly reluctant to leave, but did as Riley requested.

* * *

Riley went to the store and got a new SIM and a two-litre bottle of wine.

Arriving home, she got a pint of wine and put the remainder of the bottle in the fridge, she switched her SIMs, throwing the old one away. She texted everyone in her phone book with the exception of Keri. She deleted the screen saver and removed the girl's number.

She sat back on her bed, downed half a pint of wine and turned her music up loud, making a conscious effort to purposely avoid any love songs or Gloriana songs.

Chapter 36

Keri

Her heart was pounding. She watched the three little grey dots moving. She was responding. She sat up and waited patiently as they did. Her breathing was so rushed she thought she was about to have a panic attack. She watched and waited; she was praying it would say 'I made a mistake,' and not, 'Leave me alone,' or, 'Thanks, you have a nice life too.' Her heart stopped, the dots disappeared, and she waited for what felt like forever, to see if she was going to respond. That was it. She had gone with no words of why, other than her words in Turkey. That it was Keri, she wasn't the one. Again, somebody else didn't think she was the one. She put her car in reverse and drove home, crying the whole journey home.

It was after 2am, and Keri had done nothing but sobbed for the last four hours in bed. She wondered what Riley was doing, she wondered if she was out enjoying herself with her friends, she wondered if she was even slightly upset. This was all becoming so difficult. She couldn't do it; she needed some closure if that's what it required. She picked up at her phone and dialled her number; she dropped her phone as the tone told her that the line was no longer in use. She sat there, completely stunned. That was all the closure she needed, she thought, as she absorbed the magnitude of what had just happened. Her head was spinning, she thought she was going to be sick, she was sure of it. She didn't know what to do, so she texted Kimmy.

'I need my big sister :(, please call me whenever you wake I don't care what time it is xxx'

Her phone rang immediately.

"What's up hun? Are you ok? Is everything ok?"

Keri sniffed loudly. "What are you doing calling this hour?" she asked sadly.

"You needed me, you told me to call, was I dreaming? Hang on a minute. Yes, you did, you text me. Are you drunk?"

"No, I wish. Yes, I text you, but I meant tomorrow. What are you doing awake?"

"I wasn't, I was in bed. I keep my phone by the bed in case anything happens to anyone, and we have a big family, remember? What's up, kidda? Wait a minute. It's Keri. Yeah, yeah, she's fine. Go back to sleep baby, I'll go downstairs. One moment Kel."

A few moments later she heard a door close and the fridge open.

"I'm back, you are ok aren't you? Do we need to come over?"

"No." She laughed sadly. "Have you just poured a wine?"

"Yes, don't judge. I feel it's gonna be a long night. Talk to me."

She heard Kimmy taking a long gulp. "It's done, she run off, she didn't want me. I put it all on the line and..." She was crying again.

"Calm down babes, go get a drink, something stiff, and blow your nose then start from the beginning, ok?"

"Ok," she sniffled; she could only imagine this was what one of her nephews or nieces sounded like when they thought their worlds were ending.

"You ok?"

"No, I'm really not Kimmy." She took a gulp of her JD and let the liquid slide down her throat and awaken her senses.

"Ok, start from the beginning?"

Keri had told Kimmy every single detail; she'd filled her in already about the course, the airport, but she continued from where she left off and continued to share every morsel of detail.

"So, she was all for it? All day long?"

"Yes, she never let on she was scared. And I don't think it was me imagining it, honestly. Maybe it is, am I going crazy? Oh my god Emma has turned me into a psycho, I'm a fucking psychotic lesbian; she only wanted a shag and then I'm professing my undying love. Oh no, what have I done? My god what if I am her manager next season? Ohhhh, this is so bad." She downed her drink and went to get another.

"Ok babes, you are a bloody good judge of character. You liked me, remember?" she said, laughing. "But seriously Kel, stop running away with yourself, none of this makes sense. It doesn't add up, babe. As I was saying you are a good judge of character, you wouldn't fail so royally. And when you told me about those messages, she is all in, or she was. You would have spotted a player a mile off, Keri. You always have done, even from being a teenager. You knew what you did and didn't want even back then. I don't believe that anyone could have blindsided you that much. She unfortunately may just be scared, but still with a tight family life I can't believe she would just run off, but as you say that could be to do with the fact she hasn't ever done this before and she didn't know how to do it. You think back to your first few relationships, how hard it is, we've all had someone we text or just started ignoring when we want to call it a day. But again, she was invested, you don't put all that shit in messages and calls and your day together, it doesn't add up. What are you going to do? Are you ok? Do you think maybe you should come home?" Kimmy asked, soberly.

"I don't know, I'm considering it. I just can't believe this has happened. I have been with Karen and Dan tonight and I had to leave, they're saying the same as you. I just don't know what to do." She started crying again.

"Babes, fuck. Keri don't cry, I can't get to you, please don't. Do you want me and Mum to come out tomorrow? We can get Glen and your dad to look after the boys?"

"No seriously, I'm fine honestly. It's fine. I'm sorry, thanks for calling."

"Call me tomorrow when you're done with work please."

"Ok."

They said their goodbyes and hung up.

Keri turned over and cried until she eventually fell back to sleep.

Chapter 37

Riley

Riley hadn't slept at all. She felt like shit and her mirror pretty much confirmed she looked like it too. She got changed and picked up her beach towel.

Ben knocked on her door. "Hey gorgeous, you ready?" he said, walking to her and opening his arms.

Riley walked in and hugged him.

"Ok, so I'm not great with all this mushy stuff but I'll hug you as much as you like, ok? I don't know what's wrong, but we'll get through it together, and you know what the best thing in this situation is?" he said.

"Getting laid by you," she said half-heartedly.

"Well that as well. Nope, 'buca."

"Ben, it's like, 7am."

"I don't give a fuck, Riles. You will enjoy today and regardless of time, I feel like this is required." He poured them both a shot and they did it together.

"Thanks mate," she said, leaning into him.

"No worries, gorgeous. I'll be here anytime you need, and I mean that as a friend, nothing else. I've got your back."

"Yeah, yeah, and my front right?" she said.

"Nope, I'm concerned about you; I've got no interest in shagging you any longer. Well, I have, I'm only human, but, there's bets with every girl that lands so don't take it personally, but I needed to bang you before today. I don't care, all bets are off, and I'll tell them all that today, as long as you're ok," he said with sincerity in his eyes.

She started to cry again, and he was there immediately, wrapping his arms around her tightly again.

After a while, he kissed the top of her head and pushed her back, holding onto her shoulders still and looking into her eyes. "Come on, let's get you some booze, beautiful ocean, scenery, and some fun."

They walked out hand in hand, arriving at the hotel to see the bus already there. They ran up and got on, taking in the applause and wit-woos, causing Ben to take a bow. "All bets are off," he said. He took twenty euros out of his pocket and gave it to Katie, who was sat next to Clare, chatting. "Thanks Benjamin. You ok?" she said to Riley.

"Yeah, fine."

"Riley, sit here with us, I saved you a seat." Clare said, moving her bag off the seat in front and handing her a bottle of beer.

"You ok if I go with the guys?" Ben said to her, concerned.

She smiled softly, grabbing his hand and squeezing it. "Thanks."

She heard the coach cheering and leaned up to Katie and Clare, who were looking questioningly at the girl.

"It's fine, I'm gay," she said, smirking.

"FUCK off. Oh my god does he know?" Clare said, smiling like a child.

"Not yet, but I don't think his got any intention of hitting on me. We get on awesome, I think even he thinks that's too big a thing to risk losing."

"No way. This is Ben, he sleeps with anything that moves. Oh, can you imagine if he thinks Riley's the one?" Clare said dramatically to both women.

"Well, I have never seen him call a bet off, and so gracefully pay up; that's concerning," said Katie, laughing.

They arrived at the boat and Riley was feeling a little bit better she was glad she had spent some time with her friends and the drink was going down nicely.

They eventually boarded the boat and it was amazing to think that all these people worked for Hightail. There were at least fifty that all worked for the company. She dumped her flip flops in the crate at the foot of the boat and jumped on board, immediately hit with a young lad. "Beer, wine, vodka, or rum?" he said thrusting drinks in her face. "Oh great, I'll take a beer thanks," she said, taking one and following her colleagues down to the netting area at the front.

The captain went over some health and safety aspects and held his drink up, shouting, "Yamas!" to everyone, getting a replicated response. She guessed it must have meant 'cheers' in Greek and drank her drink, following suit.

There was a tall woman stood talking to the captain, she must have easily been 5 foot 10 or 11. She was in Nike running shorts and a Roxy bikini top; she had an incredibly toned body with long black hair tied back in a ponytail. She was stood with her hands on her hips laughing with the captain and had amazing dimples. She looked about forty, but God did she look good for it. She was getting the mic from the captain and started walking around the side of the boat.

"Hey guys can I have your attention please?" she said into the mic.

Riley thought she must be one of the catamaran staff to go over the agenda of the day or something.

"So, welcome aboard the 'Paradise Sailer'. For the few of you I have not had a chance to meet as yet, welcome on board and welcome to Kos. For those of you that don't know I'm Jayne, the Island Manager of Kos. Before we get too far into it and so those of you whom have already been drinking since five or haven't been to bed yet actually remember what I have to say, here's to the greatest season ever. For those of you that were with me last year I am very grateful that you have returned, well in most part," she said, winking. "We had a great season and I think this one's gonna completely smash it out of the water. For those of you that don't know me, you will see me rarely, but I DO hear everything. It's a difficult gateway to work due to the youth aspect of it but I'm the first to agree with the 'work hard and play hard' mentality, and fuck you guys know I'm a big time party girl, but don't take the piss. I'm lenient and fair and I expect the same back. So, who's up for a blinding summer?" she said, lifting her glass up.

Everyone started screaming and shouting "Yeah!" Riley, oddly felt a thrill in her tummy and a sense of pride. Ben was grabbing her hand, giving her a shot and making her dance on the net with lots of the team.

Riley had been speaking to a number of people from different areas of the island, she'd remembered Clare saying it's difficult because you'll maybe only see them once again at the end of season jolly, but she still made the effort. It was kind of easy too as people didn't know her well enough to know something was up. She sighed, thinking about Keri. She'd not allowed herself to think about it and she knew that wasn't the greatest move, she knew this would happen when she was drunk; she got her phone and went to the photos. She'd removed it from the screensaver but had kept the photo. She looked at the photo of them kissing. Keri wasn't even aware that she had taken it. She swiped across to the next photo. She scanned the scene, and they looked so happy; Keri's eyes sparkled, she looked so happy, those incredible blue eyes. They looked happy, they looked...

"She's very pretty."

Riley quickly shut her phone, shocked, turning around to see the island manager Jayne in front of her.

"Hey, Riley, don't get upset. This is supposed to be a fun day," Jayne said to her, stroking her shoulder.

"Sorry, I'm so sorry," she said, not realising her

eyes had been watering. She rubbed her temples, shaking her head. "I apologise, I'm not normally like this. Ermm, nice to meet you and I'm Riley. But, as you just pointed out, you were already aware of that," she said, smiling half-heartedly.

Jayne leaned over and spoke to the guy behind the 'makeshift' bar and said something in Greek. He gave her two cups. "Here, looks like you need this. Yes, I am aware of who you are. As I said back there, I hear everything," she said. "Cheers."

Was that a threat? Riley thought. She really hoped not, that was all she needed.

"Don't look so worried; I've heard a lot about you, and everything's been excellent. I've got high expectations for you, Riley." She winked and walked off.

Riley sat on one of the inside seats. Was it Keri that had sent positive feedback to the island manager? But why would she do that? If it wasn't for Jayne catching her upset would she have even known that anyone had fed back about her? God she was drunk, and completely driving herself insane over this. She was glad she had changed her number and deleted Keri's because she could feel that she was on the verge of beginning drunken texts.

They stopped at an area for snorkelling; she loved to snorkel but she was aware she was wrecked and didn't feel it was appropriate, so decided she'd much prefer to stay and drink some more. She picked up her phone and opened it to the messages. She pulled up her mum's last message and texted her.

'Miss you lots, Ma. Just out for the day with friends on a

catamaran. Everyone's just gone snorkelling. I miss home a lot; say hi to Pops for me. I will call you soon I promise, I love you both R XXX'

"Is that wise?" She heard a voice, and saw Katie leaning against the doorway, eyeing the phone in Riley's hand suspiciously.

"It's my mum," she said, smiling, "but thanks for the concern."

"Ohhh we've all been there love, such is life and all that, but I am also acutely aware of the fact that alcohol leads to drunken mistaken texts." She smirked.

"Not when you have no number to text." Riley stood up, shaking her phone up to Katie.

She took another drink and walked back to the netting to find Ben and Clare.

* * *

They spent the best part of the afternoon drinking, dancing, socialising, laughing. It was one of the best experiences of Riley's life, and the perfect opportunity to ignore the pain she was feeling, and much needed after the last few days, she thought.

It felt like they were slowly skimming the ocean on the catamaran on the way back home. The water was occasionally smashing off and splashing up over everyone as they were all pissed, laying on the nets, giggling as it did so.

The sun was setting and it was taking everything to stop Riley thinking of Keri. She needed to sort this out – it was over. She had played her, well and truly played her, and it didn't matter now, it was over. *The shortest relationship in history!* she thought. She was now doing her dream job, tomorrow she picked up her first flight; they would be her very own guests and she had a few groups of youngsters so that would mean bar crawls, maybe sexy women to have fun with and more importantly, Cara would be there in just over two weeks. It was good, she could do this, she thought.

They all disembarked the catamaran and Jayne had hired the back of the Lion for them. It was a warm night, as you'd expect of May in Greece, and as they were all still in their swimwear everyone literally dumped their bags and jumped in the pool.

Riley was watching Jane as she interacted with her team; she was still in her running shorts but now had a hoodie over the top of her bikini, and her hair was curly from being in the sea. She was very good looking for an older woman and had an amazing athletic physique. It reminded her of Keri. She sighed again.

"She's hot isn't she?" Katie said, sitting down, startling Riley.

"She's very attractive, yes. She has a body almost identical to Keri's," sighed Riley.

"Ahhhh." She nodded.

"What does that mean?" Riley said accusingly. "Shit, I'm sorry. I should go home." She stood.

"Don't go, Riles. Come on, it happened a day and a half ago. You have such incredible willpower for going and getting the new SIM etc., you will get through this I promise you, and we will all help you. But it won't happen overnight ok? Can I ask you something?"

"Yeah?"

"Do you want her back?"

"She doesn't want me; I was nothing but a quick fuck. End of!"

Katie nodded her head slowly and walked off.

* * *

They finished eating the buffet that Tony had put on and Jayne was standing on a chair in the corner. "Okay, attention please. Ok guys, I just wanted to say a huge, huge thank you for today. You truly are going to be my best team yet."

"You say that every year boss!" someone shouted and everyone laughed.

"And every year you all exceed the last," she said, winking. "Seriously guys, I'd love for us to all stay and party all night long but our distance resorts all need to hit the road now, so it's time to say goodbyes. Anyone hooking up, I don't care, I don't wanna know, but believe me, your managers over there," she said, pointing to the resort managers, "they know who to watch for, and I can assure you, they will be at YOUR properties first thing. So if you wanna pay fifty euros just for a quick shag, then fine, don't let us catch you 'screwing the crew' and don't be late to work tomorrow. Here's to an amazing season. Thanks guys, you are all truly amazing," she said, lifting her drink and downing it in one go. Everyone cheered and started saying their goodbyes to the ones that were leaving.

Chapter 38

Keri

Keri woke from a completely broken sleep, which was basically no sleep at all. She was glad that she spoke to Kimmy, though, albeit in the middle of the night. She was glad all the same though, as it had helped her put certain things into perspective.

Due to the severe lack of sleep she decided to get up and go to the office early. She picked up her phone, checking it, stupidly hoping that because she refused to check it between waking, showering, and getting ready that she might have a message there. She scolded herself for being so stupid, as she wasn't surprised when she saw an empty inbox.

She logged on and got engrossed in what needed to be done, trying to drain everything out of her mind with her work. It was the only thing she could think of doing to stop thinking of everything. Hearing her phone vibrate a while later, she picked it up and read the message.

'Baby, please come home, I have been with Kimmy and she has filled me in. Kerianne, I'm so worried about you, we all are. Kimmy said she has never heard you like this before, I'm worried. :(love mum xxx'

'Hey mum, I'm good. I will get through it, I need to sort my head out, I've worked so hard for my MDP, and I would rather leave having achieved than half way through. Don't worry, wanna phone date this evening? Love you and daddy K xxx'

'Ok baby but you know where we are, Kimmy said about us two coming out so maybe you could consider that option also? We would love a skype with you honey? Let us know when, we'll be home all night. We love you. xxx'

'I'll text you later and tell you when. I love you too. xxx'

"Hey gorgeous," Dan said, and kissed her on the cheek. "How you doing?" he said, concerned.

"I'm fine." She turned away and carried on working.

Keri thought it was like her life was in slow motion. Hours had passed, people were coming and going, but she wasn't really acknowledging or speaking to anyone. She had a lot to do and just wanted to concentrate on that.

"Keri?" She heard her name and looked up at Karen, who looked concerned. Keri looked around and saw Emma in front of her with a cup held out to her. "Do you want a coffee?" she said again.

"Erm, no thanks. I've just had one, actually, but thanks."

"No worries," she said, walking off to the kitchen.

A while later, Keri was feeling the headache starting up. She checked her phone and saw the emptiness once more. She got up and went to the bathroom. She looked in the mirror; she looked peaky, she thought. Sighing heavily and splashing water on her face, she turned to get some handtowels to dry her face when she heard the door open.

"Hey, you ok? Did something happen?" She heard Emma's voice.

She turned around, throwing the dirty towels in the bin.

"I'm fine, thanks," she said, walking off.

"Keri." She looked down at the arm holding hers. "Clearly you're not, what's happened?" Emma said to Keri.

Keri pulled her arm away. "Nothing Emma. I'm fine, okay?" she said, walking out of the bathrooms.

She returned to her desk and Karen was standing there holding her bag. "Here's your bag, were leaving, come on," Karen said to her.

"Karen I can't, I have too much to do."

"Kel, you ain't got a choice babes; I don't want you here. Go with Karen or go home," Dan said from his office.

Keri looked over at Emma, who was watching her with what looked like a slight smirk. She was loving the fact that Keri was falling apart, she thought.

* * *

They arrived at Karen's house and she helped her friend unpack her suitcase into the spare room.

She wasn't happy at all about the intervention, but Dan wasn't messing about and she was going to lose everything if she continued the way she was going, so she surrendered to Karen's words of wisdom about the children taking her mind off of things and packed a case up.

Chapter 39

Riley

"Ohhhhhhh, this isn't good," she said, groaning. "This isn't good at all." As she let the pain sink in, she literally thought her head was going to explode. She reached over to her bedside table to grab some water.

"OW, bollocks," she said, as her bedside table had moved and been replaced with a wall. She opened her eyes and was facing a wall. *Shit, where am I?* she thought. She was terrified of turning around and seeing the bed. Where the hell was she? Why couldn't she remember anything? She felt sick, she felt terrible and hungover to hell but she just wanted to cry. What had she done? She was in love with somebody else, admittedly somebody who didn't want her but all the same it made her feel rotten.

She played back last night. The team left, she was in the pool, they were having shoulder wars; she was on Ben's shoulders. Had she? She wouldn't have, she was gay. My god had she slept with a boy? No, that was actually laughable, although she could have just slept as friends in his bed. He was being really good and brotherly to her, and she may have just needed someone to snuggle with. Turning around slowly, refusing to open her eyes, she peeked open one and breathed a sigh of relief as the bed was empty. *Thank God,* she thought. She leaned over and downed the pint of water on the side; as she was drinking she noticed the window in the room. This wasn't Ben's room, this wasn't his room. Shit, where was she? And the panic set it all over again. Had she slept with someone? Who? She needed to stop drinking so much that she didn't remember things, she thought.

Riley spent the next ten minutes deliberating the different options for her to make a run for it, however, without knowing where she was, how she'd got here, and what had happened, she was struggling to find any positive outcomes. Riley decided she had to do it, she got out of bed. "Oh geez that was a mistake," she said to herself. She was in her t-shirt from last night, one thing, she supposed.

She put on her clothes and opened the door. She was upstairs, wherever she was, and whoever lived here was downstairs – she could hear noises. She slowly made her way down the stairs.

Sighing loudly, she pushed the door that was ajar to where the noise was coming from; she recognised those long legs, she thought. In front of her, in a man's shirt with the sleeves rolled up, her hair tied back high, she recognised the back of the island manager, Jayne.

She pushed the door a little more and walked, in holding her flip flops and bag. "Ermm, hey, good morning," she said quietly.

Jayne turned around, dropping the dishcloth into the sink where she was standing. "Well hello there sleeping beauty," she said, smiling. Leaning back against the side, she crossed her legs at her feet and looked at Riley, smirking.

Riley stepped back, trying to hold herself up. She thought she was going to be sick. Seriously, she wouldn't have been in any fit state to do anything, but who had instigated this? Did Riley try it on with her? She needed to take control of herself. This was getting beyond a joke. She had done the same thing on the course, she thought. Her mind drifted to the course and Keri; she sighed heavily.

"You ok?" said Jayne, handing Riley a pint of water, cup of coffee, and two tablets.

"Ermm, yes fine! I'm fine, seriously, thanks for letting me, um, well, thanks for last night I guess," she said, ashamed.

"Wow, that's what I get. After last night, that's really all I get?" she said to Riley seriously.

She didn't know why she was bothered, Keri was sleeping around all over the place by all accounts, and why should sleeping with a beautiful woman bother her? And she was single. But it did, she was in love with Keri rightly or wrongly, and until she could get past that, she shouldn't be doing anything, with anyone. Least not, the one person who could sack her.

"Erm, I'm sorry. It was… great, fantastic." She heard a door open and looked behind her, confused, from the seat she was now sitting in behind the door.

Katie walked into the kitchen. "Hey beautiful," she said, turning to the side, seeing Riley. "Oh hey you, how's the head? Thought you may need this." She handed her a fresh OJ and some kind of pastry. "What's up? You look like you've seen a ghost," she said, worried.

"She has… the ghost of Christmas fear," said Jayne, laughing, walking over to the table and tearing some of the pastry and eating it.

"Huh? What do you mean?" Katie asked them both. "Jayne, please tell me you didn't."

"Whaaaat? I couldn't help it, she come down looking petrified when she realised it was me, she obviously didn't remember anything. I even got that I was fantastic," she said, smiling widely.

Katie came around and sat on Jayne's lap. "Well that you are, but that's also not very nice. I'm so sorry Riley, she has a very evil sense of humour," said Katie, and stroked Riley's hand. "Are you ok?" She smiled sincerely.

"Wait, so… you two? You guys are sleeping together? And wait, I didn't do nothing, I just crashed here?" she said, taking in this information. "Why did I crash here?" she said.

Katie shifted Jayne onto another chair. "No, we're not sleeping together, we are in a relationship and have been for five years now; yes you crashed here, and no you didn't do anything, and I can assure you even if there was any opportunity for you to do something with anybody, you were in absolutely no fit state."

Riley put her head in her hands, shaking it vigorously.

"Calm down Riley, everyone had pretty much gone. There was only a couple of us; Ben was getting into some holiday maker from the bar and you got upset. I said to Katie I didn't think we should leave you so we brought you back here," said Jayne.

Katie started, "We sat up and gave you some coffee, toast, and water and you filled us in on part of the situation with Keri; you were adamant there were things you couldn't tell us for one reason or another. You got upset again and then when we had managed to calm you down we made you go to bed, and next part is here, now nothing to be worried about."

"I'm so sorry," said Riley, lifting her head up, feeling sad. "I never do things like this, I'm so sorry. Am I going to lose my job?"

"What? What for?" they asked in unison.

"For that," she pointed nowhere, "for being a state, for needing babysitting, for staying in your house?" she said gravely.

"Riley, Jayne and I live together, this is my house. Did I not ask you the night before last to come stay here when I was at yours because I was worried about you?" said Katie.

She nodded slowly.

"Well, we all get pissed and we've all had our heart broken at times, ok? So chill out, ok?" she said, pulling her into a hug. "Drink that and eat some of the pastry. I'm going to grab a quick shower and get ready for work and I'll drop you off home," she said, kissing her girlfriend and leaving the room.

Jayne got up and rustled Riley's hair. "Sorry kiddo, I just couldn't resist," she said, smirking.

"You're evil," Riley said, finally laughing at Jayne.

Chapter 40

Keri

"Shhhhh, you need to be quiet Nikos, you will wake her. Shall we open her eye?" said Eleni seriously.

"Yes, I think she might be dead," said Nikos to his sister.

"I'm not dead, I'm also not sleeping anymore, thanks to you two little runts," she said, laughing and yawning.

"Can we get in, thia?"

"Can you read us a story, thia?" said the kids.

"Are stories not for bedtime?"

"Noooo, silly, stories are for any time," they said, laughing.

The kids were snuggling up to Keri and she was glad that she had listened to her friends. She was already feeling a little better – this is what was important. She hugged them in closer and thought about how much she missed her nieces and nephews.

"There you are. I have told you both already, do not disturb Keri. She is not feeling very good and she needs to have some time to relax," Karen said, looking at her children.

"We know Mama, that's why we came to give her a hug to make her feel better," Eleni said, smiling. The four-year-old was completely adorable and so innocent, with great big brown eyes and Greek features.

"Up, now. You need to get ready for school."

"Mama," Nikos said, standing on the bed, "can Thia Keri take us to school, please?" he said. "Yes, yes please Mama; Thia, Thia will you? I can show you the classroom I am in, and I can too," said Nikos, kneeling next to her and playing with her hair.

"If Mama says ok, then yes."

"Please Mama," they said in unison.

"If you are good and get ready now and eat all of your breakfasts," Karen said, moving out of the way as the whirlwind of the children blew past. "Good luck with that one, you are most definitely going to need it," she said, laughing. "Coffee and toast in ten minutes," Karen said, more as a fact than a question. Keri thought she had better get up and get ready then.

Keri had a shower and was thinking about her parents' words last night; she didn't want to leave midway through her MDP. She had never not completed anything, it wasn't in her; but things had started changing for her in the last twelve months. She assumed she was bored and that was what made her start her MDP for a new challenge, but maybe she was through with it all. She could go home and go back to her business with Kimmy and Drew. They owned an estate agents and basically managed it on her behalf. She could buy a place and do it up and look to settle down once and for all, she thought. It was definitely something to think about, she knew she just needed to get through these early stages, and hopefully a week here would help, she thought.

* * *

Keri arrived at work and felt like she had done a week's worth already by dropping off the kids. She was playing on her iPad whilst she was waiting for her printing to finish.

"Lesbian porn, that will help," said Dan, looking over her shoulder.

"What?" said Karen looking freaked out. "You're a dick; I'm not looking at any porn! I'm looking forward to some me time on my day off tomorrow so I am buying a couple of books to read, and no interest in lesbian porn, I just want an easy read," said Keri.

"Do you fancy coming to mine tonight having a barbecue, opening a bottle or two, pool party, and then if you like you can spend the day at mine with the pool to yourself to read and relax before going back to the little terrors," he said, smirking at Karen.

"Actually, that's not a bad idea you know; how about I say to Yiannis about picking the kids up from school and taking them to the restaurant? I'll drop them off at school and we can have a holiday maker day? We can relax on inflatables, have music playing, drink cocktails and have a day off for a change, unless you would rather be completely alone of course," said Karen.

"No, actually, that sounds great; I think that is just what the doctor ordered," she said. "You sure you don't mind mate?" Keri asked Dan.

"Nah not at all, but you can cook tonight," he said, laughing.

* * *

Keri arrived at Dan's and dumped her bag in the spare room before taking the groceries into the kitchen. She prepped the chicken, marinating it in tandoori and spatchcocked it before putting it on the barbecue.

She threw a couple of jackets on there too and closed the lid, allowing the foods to slow cook. Dan handed her the drink and they went and sat in the shallow end of the pool. It was a nice night and Dan's villa sat in a slightly raised location that allowed a beautiful view of the ocean and sunset. "Oh, I got you a gift," he said. "Lemme get it." He gave her his glass, running into the house and returning with a double lilo. "Wicked, ain't it? Come on, let's get on," he said. He really was like a child. They topped and tailed on the lilo, using the holes in the inflatable to rest their glasses.

"Do you miss this?" she asked him seriously, staring at the sunset.

"What, the sunset? I see it every night." He paddled his arm to turn them around so he was facing the sunset too.

"No, the normality of a relationship? Do you miss not having Nicola here with you every day, to enjoy the simple things like this?"

"To be honest I try not to let myself think about it. I miss her when I've had a shit day and I wanna come home, tell her all about it over dinner, listen to her tell me it'll be ok as we snuggle up on the sofa. I miss that, and I miss having her to cuddle up to every night, that's the worst for me," he said honestly.

"How do you deal with it?" she asked him, still mesmerised by the sunset.

"I think about our future together, of how I'll propose to her, when we'll buy our first house, her glowing as she waddles around in our garden pregnant with our fist kid. I look to all the positives that will come out of it, and concentrate on what we are working so hard for."

They lay on the lilo, silently appreciating the sunset and allowing the words and their meaning settle.

They stayed that way for a long while; the air was becoming a little chillier and Keri knew they needed to get out and she needed to check on the dinner.

"I think I want to go home," she blurted out of nowhere.

"What?" Dan jumped up, not realising the consequence of how such a movement would impact them. Before they could stop it they had both come off and along with their glasses, were both underwater. She came up. "Shit, you dick. What did you do that for?" Keri said, swimming over to the side and lifting herself out.

"Well I didn't do it on purpose. When you drop a bomb on me like that what do you expect?" he said, replicating her movement. They wrapped the towels around them, drying off a bit.

Keri checked over the dinner, turning it over and closing the lid again. She walked back over to the L-shaped outdoor furniture set and lay down on the sofa. "I don't want to leave you in the lurch, and I'm so incredibly happy and thankful for everything you have done, but I don't know Dan, something's telling me it's time," she said seriously.

"Babes, you know I love you more than anything, but I think your heart is talking at the moment. You have had this shit happen to you; you thought something was gonna happen and suddenly it was pulled underneath you and I get at this moment you want to be around your family, but I genuinely don't think you have thought this through properly babes. I don't." He sighed, rubbing his temples. "Can you please not make a decision until a week. The first week is always the hardest and the time with Karen, Yiannis, and the kids I do think will help you, so just see what happens then, for me?"

"It's more than that, Dan. It's not just about Riley, I just don't think I want this anymore."

"That's my point, babe. You were made up with the MDP, you took it as a new challenge and ran with it; you have been doing amazingly well, everyone's said so and you are frontrunner for getting island manager because of the graft you've been putting in. But you said yourself you don't 'think' you want it. Kel, that ain't you, that's the pain talking babe. Please just do it for me?" he said.

"I will, it's the least I can do," she said, kissing her friend.

Chapter 41

Riley

"I can't do it, no more, please," Riley said into her pillow.

"You can. Come on, you're young and we need to go fanny hunting," Ben said. "Come on, we'll have a ball."

"I've been out loads this week, and I don't want fanny, thanks," she said, still whining. She was wrecked. They had been at airport from four that morning taking guests home. They had a delay so didn't even get any time to sleep. Literally got home, collected their bags and went straight to welcome meetings, then liquidated on siesta and straight back to duties. She was fucked, she thought.

"Well if you don't want fanny then anything I can offer?" he said, laughing at himself.

"Piss off, you go out, I need one night. I want movies and pizza, PJs too," she said.

"You're so fucking lame, you're like the lamest rep ever, and you should be like on an OAPs island or something. You'll never get over Keri, unless you meet someone else. Go out, get laid. Come on, we can be each other's wing men. Women. Persons.

Whatever," he said, in his last attempt.

"Seriously, it ain't about her; I'm wrecked. That delay has killed me mate, and then we'll be on it all day tomorrow no doubt. Let me have a little power nap and then I might come out in a bit, yeah?" she said to him.

"You're a fucker, you know that. You best change next week when Cara gets here cause seriously if you don't she'll be left with me every night and you know what that means." He laughed, leaving her room.

"Piss off. I need to call her actually. I tell you what, text me in half hour where you are. I will give her a shout, no doubt that will wake me up a bit and then I might come and meet yous."

"Wicked, see you soon buddy," he said to his friend.

Riley rolled over and picked her phone up – 9.30, so 7.30 at home. *She'll love it, just when her Corrie is starting*, thought Riley. She went to her pictures and opened them up, swiping back until she was faced with the ice blue eyes of Keri. It had been a week since Bodrum; she was still unable to go a day without looking at the photo and thinking about the girl. Riley often woke up in the night thinking it was a bad dream, she'd check her phone only to find there were no contacts for Keri, and remember it wasn't a dream. The girl she wanted to fight for and be with despite the job, had screwed her over. She sighed loudly and came out of the pictures. *Stop it, Riley. You need to stop this*, she thought. She went to Cara's name and pressed call.

* * *

"Yo, yo, yo bitch, how are you?" she answered the phone.

"Have you been watching some shite on MTV again?" she said to Cara, laughing.

"Shut up, I'm packing," she said, pleased.

"You do realise you still have six days, right?"

"Yep, I am away this week so I just want to get everything sorted. How are you anyhow? You ok? Found any new love interests or still too early?" she said earnestly.

"Too early, I don't want that. I will have fun when I am ready, but that's the least of my worries at the moment, ya know? How's all with you, kids keeping you well?" she laughed.

"Nope, still psychotic little shits," she said. "A new guy has moved in down the road, he is fit and apparently no woman, I've been checking."

"So you have been stalking my new neighbour? That's awesome," she said, laughing at her friend.

"No, it's not yours when you are over there, and not stalking, just, hmmmmm, showing an invested interest. Yes, that's what I'm doing. I saw your folks at Asda last night. Your dad was telling me she's insane; she said he keeps telling everyone that will listen to him those words and she thinks it's him that's in fact crazy. Just putting this out there; those crazy arses that are your parents, is where you will end up. No hope for you, although they are so completely in love, they are clearly both mental," she said, laughing.

"Oh I know, you don't need to tell me, so anything else new?"

Riley and Cara spent the best part of an hour chatting about rubbish, family, boys, the impending vacation, Keri; she felt much better when she got off the phone and thought, *Sod it, can't keep moping forever*, so got ready and went and met her friends.

Chapter 42

Keri

"Are you sure? I don't mind. The kids would love it too," Karen said to her friend, helping her put her belongings in the car.

"I'm sure, you have been a star, and you were right, it was exactly what I needed. I am out with my team tonight. I'm going to get settled back into my apartment and try and take control of my life again. I promise you if I feel bad I will call you or Dan. We will ensure we have a weekly dinner as we used to and I will make a point of going out and having fun with my friends and my team. OK?" she said, kissing and hugging Karen.

"Ok, ok. Sorry, you know what I'm like; I was just concerned that's all."

"I know, and that's why you're my honorary momma. It's fine, I can't change what's happened. I will seriously consider this weekend if I want to go home and give it up, but I will not be doing that just moping in my apartment," she said, smiling and hugging the kids goodbye, noticing their tears.

"I know you won't be happy, but children are fickle," she said, smirking, retrieving two bags from her car. "Well, it sure is a shame that I have two crying kiddies in front of me, especially when I got a present for them both."

Eleni reacted first moving part of her head around her mother's leg, still holding it tight and looking up to the bags that Keri was holding up.

Eleni wiped her nose and eyes and walked over to Keri, hugging her tight, sniffling like only a small child does. She took the bags. "Efharisto, Thia Keri," she said, and gave Nikos his bag. Looking into them, she was soon forgotten about as they were removing their toys from their bags and off in a bid to start playing.

"See, told ya?" she said, smiling. Waving once more, she put her car in reverse and left her friend, and the house she'd spent the last week in.

* * *

Keri arrived home; she had about two hours left of her siesta before she needed to head back to see Jack and Tegan on duties. Putting on some music, she started unpacking her suitcase. Putting a wash load into the machine, she threw the remaining clothes into the laundry bin. It was a really hot day today; she missed not having a private pool on days like these. She looked over her balcony to her complex pool; there was only one person there that she didn't recognise. She put her bikini on and grabbed a towel and thought she'd spend an hour swimming. It was far too hot this time of day to go for a run.

Her thoughts were still filled with Riley throughout the day; however, it had become far more sporadic as opposed to being 24/7 any longer. She was aware it was more about the closure, the unknowing, the lack of explanation that caused the thoughts. She had managed to curb the missing, the hurt, the want of the girl now and knew she had to move on, which is what Riley had decided for both of them.

She got closer to the pool and could hear music. She put her towel down on a bed and put her bag down next to it; the girl a few beds down picked up her docking station. "I'm sorry, sorry. I was the only one here, that's why I had the music on," she said, desperately searching the device.

"It's ok, it's fine. It's good, it gives this place a bit of atmosphere," Keri said, smiling.

"Yeah, that's what I thought, but I have only been here a few days and was told off a day later for it." She squirmed.

Keri took her clothes off and went and sat on the side of the pool. "You got told off?" she said, laughing loudly.

"Yes, some old woman was shouting in Greek and pointing to the music. She was NOT happy, I can tell you," she said seriously.

"Ahhhhh, Mrs. Konstantinos. About yea high," Keri said, holding her hand up to reflect that of an approximately four and a half foot woman. "Short grey hair? Possibly holding a sweeping brush?"

"Oh my god, yes, that's her! Is she the owner? I'm terrified she's going to kick me out," she said, concerned. "I've only just moved over here and I don't think it's going to go down too well if I get kicked out of my complex the first week," she said.

"Seriously, do NOT worry. She's fine, she doesn't

like change. She will come round and will still scorn you, sweep you up, or at least try to, and shout at you for not speaking the lingo, but she's harmless, honestly. I lived here last year and she is fine, you'll see," she said.

"Phew, I was about to go tell my manager I needed somewhere else to live as I had a hit on me with the Greek mafia. Do you mind?" she pointed to the edge of the pool next to Keri.

Keri laughed hard, she liked her, she was funny. "Well we best get that hit off you. No, of course not, it's your pool too." She smiled softly. The girl stood up, walking towards her. She had a good body, curves in all the right places, and these were all accentuated by the bikini she was wearing. Keri could feel herself reddening and looked away; she didn't know what to think of what had happened and decided to put it away, making a mental note to assess it later.

"Hey, I'm Steph," she said, holding out her hand to Keri. "Cute tat," she added, pointing to her side.

"Thanks, I'm Keri, nice to meet you Steph," she said. "So you said you were new, and you were working out here. What you doing?"

"Yes, I am Health and Safety Manager for one of the tour ops and cover Greece. I am spending a month in each gateway starting with here. How about you? Worker too?"

"Yes, I am a resort manager."

"So where you been? I haven't seen you at all since I arrived?"

"No, I have been staying with a friend for the last

week," she said matter-of-factly.

"Oh right, so do you flit in between places then?" she asked cautiously.

"No, not at all. I had a bit of shitty time with a break up and my friend insisted I move in with her for a week. She was right her four and six-year-olds certainly kept my mind off things." She smiled. "Anyways, where you off to next?" she said, wanting to change the subject.

"Charming, I just get here and you're already trying to get rid of me." She smirked and splashed into the pool, starting to do some laps.

Keri wiped the water from her legs and leaned back on her arms. She liked this girl, and she seemed fun. Keri could feel the thoughts already starting to creep in of Riley again. Nope, not this time. She prevented them and followed the girl into the pool.

Chapter 43

Riley

Riley looked in the mirror. "You sure I should be doing this? It doesn't feel right," she said, assessing whether the cream V-neck crocheted jumper was too low.

"It's fine, Riles. You look fit. Look you're single, you ain't doing anything wrong. Sit down here a minute," Ben said to her, patting the bed next to him. "What happened between you and Keri wasn't nice, I get that, and I also get it's only been a couple of weeks or just shy of; but babes you can't feel guilty for a date. Jayne and Katie will be there, this is their friend, and there is absolutely no pressure. Go, see what happens. She may be gorgeous and you can have some fun, she may not be your cup of tea, she may turn out to be the girl you end up with. But, nothing ventured, nothing gained mate. Just go, you may turn out to be best mates. As far as lesbians go you're wicked and gorgeous, but you're not really into the whole shag and go, which was what I was really hoping for, so maybe you could do with some lesbian friends," he said, laughing and shoving her. "All joking aside, you are gorgeous, you look stunning this evening, you are an amazing person, you really could quite easily be someone's dream girl, but to do that you need to get back out on the field. I'm not saying go and jump in the first relationship that is put in front of you, but just test the water. You may realise tonight your heart belongs elsewhere, but unless you try you won't know, and if it is the former, then we continue to go out, get fucked up, and drown your sorrows." He put his hands on Riley's face, looking into her eyes.

She could feel that her eyes were teary. "Thank you, I am so glad you are here. You are so not what you portray yourself to be, but thanks, I needed that," she said. She checked herself over once more, sprayed some perfume and left the apartment, kissing Ben one last time.

* * *

Riley arrived at the restaurant and could see the three women sat at the back on the terrace. She took in a deep breath and walked over to the table. "Hey, you guys. I'm sorry, I'm late," she said, looking at her watch as she was never late, seemingly, nor was she this time.

"It's ok, Casey didn't want to sit alone, so we arranged to come a little earlier to meet her; that way there wasn't that awkward sitting alone for either of you," Jayne said.

"Hi, I'm Riley," she said, taking the girl's hand and kissing each cheek.

"Hey, I'm Casey. Nice to you meet you." She smiled shyly.

Riley already knew she was Greek-Australian, and they were right, she was incredibly beautiful; stunning

Greek features and an Aussie accent to match. She couldn't fault Katie and Jayne on their choice of blind date. Riley relaxed, trying to push away the thoughts that kept swimming over her, scolding herself for thinking about someone who didn't want her; seriously, why couldn't she just let it go?

The evening went smoothly; Riley enjoyed the good food, good wine, and good company. Katie had invited them back to their place, however, Casey had asked if Riley would like to go take a walk. She couldn't miss the raised eyebrow that Jayne and Katie gave each other, she thought it was probably a good idea so she could spend some time alone with Casey without the eyes of her boss and her boss's boss.

Chapter 44

Keri

"So what you gonna do then?" said Dan, taking a bite of pizza.

"What do I do? I don't know, I genuinely don't," said Keri.

"Well, you thought she was cute in her bikini, you said. So surely you see if anything comes of it," said Karen, eyeing her suspiciously.

"Well, technically yes, but technically no," she said sadly.

"What does that even mean, Kel?" said Dan again.

"I told you both already; yeah, she's very attractive, funny, and looked great in a bikini, and yeah I was, ummm, I don't know if I would go so far to say I was attracted to her per se. I was definitely impressed, for want of a better word, for a little bit, but in the same respect I felt guilty. I saw the things that weren't Riley. I also felt a huge sense of betrayal on my part, so no, I genuinely don't know what to do," she said to her friends, sighing heavily.

Keri tore off another piece of pizza and took another gulp of her beer before eating it. "I dunno,

I'm not going to lie."

"Well, I think, we should go there after we have eaten; message the team and say we'll try there instead and Dan and I can weigh her up, and then you can see how it pans out. Don't rush yourself, it will only make you feel worse, but you can see if you are ready or not yet," Karen said to her.

"Babes, do you feel ready? In your heart of hearts, if you stopped yourself to think about what's going on, would you still want Riley? Regardless of what happened or not, if she said right now, 'I made a mistake, I was scared, let's try it,' would you do it?" Dan said seriously.

Karen was giving Dan evils, but eyeing Keri suspiciously. "It was..." She stopped and controlled herself, clearing her throat. "It was two weeks ago. Ok granted it was what people may say is 'true lesbian style' as it all was very quick. I don't necessarily think that was 'lesbian style', I think that was 'true love style'. But yes, I'm not going to lie, I would," she said solemnly.

"Well, let's go to the bar and just see what you think from afar. Unfortunately, Riley made her choice and she closed every avenue for one reason or another, so I think this is baby steps which is what we need, plus you also need to remember that," said Karen.

"I agree," said Dan, picking up the last piece of pizza.

* * *

They finished their food and went to the bar, where Steph said she would be with her colleagues;

Keri didn't feel right at all, she wasn't sure if it was Riley or this whole thing of going to check out a girl, it really wasn't her normal style. The reality was Karen was right, Riley didn't want her. Fact. She wanted the single life, go out and have fun, no strings or attachments, so what was the big deal? Keri hadn't told her friends but she was still thinking a lot about going home, so figured seeing how this, whatever it was, went, she would be able to make a decision once and for all.

Dan nudged Keri. "Babes, what's up? If we have forced you into this and you don't feel right we can leave," he said.

Keri smiled, weighing up her response. She noticed Karen looking at her intently.

"Hey, you made it?" Keri heard and turned to the voice.

Steph was stood in front of her. She looked really good, Keri thought – her long dark hair was down and straightened, she was wearing denim short shorts, Keri noticed, sandals and an oversized top which was falling off her shoulder casually, giving a glimpse of her tanned bare shoulder. She looked stunning.

"Alright, I'm Dan and this is Karen, we're Keri's mates and colleagues." Dan leaned in, shaking the girl's hand.

"Alright Dan." She noticed a guy come behind Steph and shake Dan's hand. "I'm Ant, I'm the island manager that's trying everything to keep this one off my back," he said, referring to his health and safety manager. "Long time no see mate, I didn't know if you were back again."

"Yeah, been busy with this one," he said, hugging Keri tightly.

Keri looked up from the hug and looked over at Steph. She smiled slightly. "So, it's my round," she said. "Karen, Dan, same again?" she said.

"I'll come with you," Steph said. Keri turned and looked at Karen, smiling widely and lifting her drink. She loved her friends but she wasn't ready, she had had too much going on. She knew what she had to do, she thought, sighing inwardly.

"So, your friends seem cool," Steph said to Keri.

"Yeah, we have worked together a while, they know me pretty well, warts and all." She smiled, ordering their drinks and another of what Steph was having.

"So they got you through the breakup with your boyfriend too, huh?" she said.

"Ermmm no, actually."

"Oh sorry, I thought maybe that was the friend you were staying with," she said.

"Well, yes it is. It wasn't a boyfriend Steph, I'm gay so it was a split from my gir…" She stopped herself, sighing. "It was a split from the girl I was in love with, yes, and they have been trying to get me through it."

"Still raw then?"

"Pretty much, I'm pretty sure I know what I need to do though," she said seriously.

"Wow, sounds intense; dare I ask?" Steph questioned suspiciously.

"I think it's my time to go back home to be

honest. I've done this job a long time, you know. I think the dream has ended," she said solemnly.

"Shit," Steph said to her. "I'm sorry, I don't know what to say."

"No, me neither," she sighed. "Fancy a shot? I'm all for getting smashed tonight now after all," she asked Steph.

Chapter 45

Riley

Riley and Casey walked down to the beach; it was a warm night and the very slight breeze was blowing her long dark curls a little. Riley shook the thoughts of Keri, creeping back into her mind. She hated the fact that she had a great woman in front of her and she couldn't help but feel guilty about it. Riley was going to call her mum in the morning, she thought. She wanted to speak to her, unless it was too late tonight when she got home.

"Penny for them," Riley heard Casey say.

"Sorry, that was kinda rude; I was actually thinking about my family, my mum mostly, and that I wanted to speak to her. Apologies. It's a beautiful evening isn't it?"

"Yeah, it is. I love it this time of year, not too hot, not too cold, and just right," she said, smiling. "You fancy going and sitting on the beach? We can talk," she said, looking over to Riley.

She was apprehensive, she must be due on, there was no reason for her to feel like this. Smiling, "That would be nice," she said, following Casey over the sand.

They sat down and Casey opened the bottle of wine, taking a swig. "Classy, hey? I wouldn't normally do this, so ya know. But, in reality I wouldn't normally go on a date with someone who was in love with someone else," she said, handing the bottle over to Riley.

"Err..." Riley started to speak.

"Don't worry, it's fine. I'm kinda happy, you have restored my faith in women, and also pretty upset that you seem pretty neat and your heart belongs elsewhere. It's why I wanted to be alone. You are totally cool, and I have really enjoyed spending time with you and the guys tonight, and please don't think you have been anything less than a great date, but I could just see it in your eyes. May I ask what happened?" she said, taking the bottle from Riley. "God, you Poms are greedy with your booze," she said, laughing.

Riley held it close to her chest. "I thought it was mine, to pick my sorry ass up?" she said, laughing and swigging again, before handing it back over.

Riley filled her in on the story of her and Keri. She explained what had happened in Bodrum and the words that frequently replayed in her mind. It was weird, she had only just met this girl and she had told her the whole story, but she guessed it was the least Casey deserved.

"But, well, that don't make no..."

Riley didn't allow her to finish. "Sense, yeah, so everyone keeps telling me," she sighed.

"Sorry, I shouldn't be rude; I get it's not my business, so please tell me to shove off if you feel like..." Casey said.

"No, knock yourself out, it won't be anything I haven't heard already," she said, lifting the bottle out of the sand and taking another swig.

"Well Bodrum isn't particularly close to Rhodes, so she made a real effort to come see you and surprise you," she said.

"No, it's really close, she said once when we were on training," said Riley.

"No. Turkey is close, yeah, but Bodrum isn't. It's like the other side of the island, from Rhodes the daytrips go to Marmaris. I think they only have like maybe one a day, unlike from here where there are hundreds like, every half an hour. So why would you go to all that effort for nothing? Why tell you she's falling in love with you, when you are allegedly screwing everything else that moved? It truly doesn't make sense at all. I'm sorry, this really won't be helping you," she said squarely to Riley.

"I didn't know that about the Bodrum thing. I don't know; I know she was there with me wholly on that day though, I guess that's the person she is! As I said I just don't know. But I just need to get my life back on track, I need to just get over all of it and then I can, well, stop doing myself out of incredible women," she said, smiling.

"So why don't you try to get closure?" she asked.

"Why? And how?"

"Text her or call her and ask why she did it. You'll never move on until you have that closure, because you can't work it out. You'll forever be in wonder."

"That wouldn't be a good idea. I don't think I could talk to her, plus I don't have her number anyhow, I deleted it," said Riley, taking an extra-large gulp this time.

"Dude, you work for the same company. Katie and Jayne would be able to get you that number in, like, seconds. You could even Google it. You would get it, that's not difficult," she said.

Riley sat silent; in reality she was right, she could get it, but she didn't want to know, she didn't want to hear her voice again, and she knew it would upset her too much. On the flip side of that, Casey really was right in what she was saying. Until she found out what she had done so wrong to be treated so badly then she would forever be in wonder, and essentially continue to impede her overseas experience. Riley digested Casey's words.

Chapter 46

Keri

Keri didn't want to do this at all, but she knew it was now or never and she couldn't wait any longer. She had spent a really good night with Steph; she was a nice girl, and incredibly good when it came to giving advice. She didn't agree with Keri's decision, she thought she was giving too much up, but she had come up with a good solution so now she just needed to tell Dan and Karen. It was now or never, she thought.

"Hey, you got a minute?" she said to Dan.

"Yeah, come in," he said, leaning back in his chair.

"So, you into this new bit of stuff? Lemme guess, you had the night of your life and all's good with the world again?" he said, smiling.

"I want to go home, Dan," she said sombrely.

She felt bad for blurting it out, and Dan looked like he had just been punched. "I'm sorry, I will start again. I haven't felt right, this doesn't feel right to me. Interestingly, whilst Riley was never here, everything is reminding me of her and what we could have had. I have thought a great deal about it and if I take you and Karen out of the equation, and the fact I have never not finished something I started, and how hard I have worked for my MDP, then I'm left with nothing. I am unhappy, I'm not me and I'm missing my home, my family, ya know? With that being sa..."

"Stop, I can't do this." He got up, holding his hand up to her and walking towards the door. "Kaz, in here, now," he said.

Karen walked in and looked at them both. "What's going on?" she said.

"She wants to go home." He still was not looking at her.

"What the fuck, Keri? Why the hell do you want to do that?" Karen said. *Shit, Karen never swore*, thought Keri.

"I don't know, I can't explain what's happening. I know you will think it's pathetic, I knew her for two minutes and I'm giving up everything, but I just feel lost and sad all the time. I didn't feel like this with Emma, and I just don't know how to snap out of it. However, I do want to caveat all of that with, Steph raised a good point last night. She thinks I need to get more info, to get closure, which I think may be a valid point. However, she also said when I have such a good circle of friends and all the work I have put into my MDP that I shouldn't give it all up."

"Well, at least someone's speaking some sense," Dan said. He was mad, she could tell, and Karen looked confused and hurt.

"Guys, I don't want to hurt you or throw everything you have both done for me back in your faces, but I genuinely don't feel right with this all. I've never felt a connection with anyone before and I just feel shit, and until I can get some closure, this won't go away."

"So why can't you go over there and see her? Speak to her, get the closure, and come back. I'll ring Jayne, I can do it now," he said, picking up his phone.

"No, Dan, don't. Dan, she made her choice. I don't know why and I need to get to grips with the fact I know I never will. Based on the conversation I had last night, I was wondering, well, if you wouldn't mind, rather than me resigning and leaving the business, how you'd feel if I went home for a week. Summer's still fairly slow and will be for another two weeks, maybe three. I know we don't have time off and I totally get that, but, honestly, it's my last hope. I think a week with my family and friends, get some sense kicked into me, and then hopefully come back to, well, pick myself up, dust myself off and smash the rest of the season," she said idly, unable to look at her friends and just sitting playing with her nails.

Karen leaned over and grabbed her hand. "Yiannis and I knew you'd say about this lesbian thing or it being silly, sometimes people are lucky enough to meet that one true soul mate, life partner, the one, whatever you want to call it. And if your heart was telling you that was her, nothing's silly or pathetic about that. Your heart is talking to you, and it will need time to repair. It was too soon for last night, and I apologise for the part I played in that, I just wanted to stop you from hurting," Karen said.

"On the contrary, I'm glad we did and that I met her and spoke to her, because honestly speaking, this would be an entirely different conversation we'd be having right now; she's made me realise, I should have a little break with people who know me the best and then come back refreshed. Interestingly, for someone who doesn't know me from Adam, I kinda think she has a point," she said, looking over at Dan, who was now looking at her intently.

"What if you decide it's time to go?" he said. "Then what happens?"

"I love you like a brother, I would never leave you in the shit. I will be back in one week, irrespective, and if I decide that I want to go, I will officially resign and give my month's notice and wait until you can get a replacement. That, I will give you my word on," she said.

"Is Tegan, ready to step up? She ain't even started her SDP," he said.

"Probably not, is there anybody else?" she asked.

Dan was quiet for a few moments. "I could ask Emma if she could live without Paula for a week. She's nearly finished her SDP. She'll get team leader I think, next year, so if it's only a week I could give her exposure to be 'acting manager', I suppose," he said.

"I don't want Emma to know anything, in fact I only want you guys to know. I just want them to know I have had to go home for personal reasons, no elaboration needed," she said to them both.

"When do you wanna go?"

"Sooner I'm gone, sooner I'm back, I guess?" she said.

"I sold some seats earlier for the Wednesday flight. I know it's only a couple of days but I could put her on that," Karen said.

"You sure about this?" Dan said seriously.

"I just need me back. If I can't have her and we aren't meant to be, I just need Keri back, ya know?" she said sadly.

"Book it," he said to Karen. "You best go home and start packing. Dinner at mine tomorrow night before you go?" he said.

Chapter 47

Riley

"Hey honey, how are you? How you feeling? What's going on? Are you enjoying it?" her mum said to her in one mouthful.

"Yeah it's good, Ma. How's all going there? It's busy here, we have loads going on and then Cara is coming out next week."

"What's up, love? You aren't yourself, what's happened?" her mum said, concerned.

"I'm fine," she said, trying to hold back the tears.

"No, you aren't, Riley. Talk to me, what's going on?" she said.

Riley sighed heavily and told her mum what had happened with Keri. She silently listened, occasionally throwing in 'hmm hmmms' and 'oh babys' to her.

"I just feel so rubbish, Mum. Like, totally confused as to why she did it. Who treats people this way?" she said, mad.

"I genuinely don't know honey; maybe you got it wrong, I don't know. What I will say is, the words I said to you when you left, you weren't the only one with that look, Riley. She looked the exact same way at you. When we were all in the conservatory and you asked Adam to get your stuff, she was holding back her emotions, and it was written all over her face that she wanted to protect you. This wasn't a one-way thing, darling. I don't know what's happened, whether she does like to keep her options open, but you were most certainly more than an option to her," her mum said softly.

"So what do I do?" she said.

"Riley, none of it makes sense. You are very logical and analytical, that's why you followed in your father's footsteps as an accountant, because he is exactly the same way; but in this scenario, it will eat you alive. Whether you want to or not you are going to have to speak to her and find out why she acted the way she did with you, when she wasn't being entirely truthful and faithful," her mother said, giving Riley a lot to think about.

They continued their conversation, avoiding any words of Keri. It was light-hearted and exactly what Riley needed; eventually they ended their conversation and she lay on her bed, staring at the ceiling, thinking about what her mother had said to her.

She picked up her phone and looked in the pictures. "Why did you do this, Keri? Give me something, please?" she said into the picture, not being able to stop herself from stroking the pretty face. She went to her messages and texted Katie.

'Would you have a directory of the office numbers in other regions?'

'Yes, why?'

'Could you please have a look for Rhodes office specifically

and possibly text me the number when you're next there?'

'Of course, everything ok?'

'Yes thanks, see you soon. Riley'

Riley would at least have the opportunity. If she really thought that was the best option, she would need to sort the fact that she felt physically sick at the prospect of speaking to Keri again, but in reality she could be her manager one day, so they should probably be adults about it. At least that way, Riley could finally move on and get some closure in her life.

* * *

"So, you're really sure about it then?" Ben asked her, passing the bottle of beer over to her lilo.

"What's the alternative? I continue like this and can't move on? I know you think I'm a dick and this is obscene, having never been in a relationship before and being with her for twenty-one seconds…"

"Twenty-one seconds, pah pah pah, I got twenty-one seconds to go," they both sang in unison, laughing and high fiving.

"Anyways, I know it sounds dumb but I'm starting to agree, it doesn't make sense and it's eating me up so I need to just get a response and then I wanna start living this dream. I'm not saying I'm a slag by any means, but I want to have fun too and if I want to hit up some hot girl why the fuck shouldn't I be able to? But until I just hear her say, it was all a joke gone wrong and she's not into settling or whatever, then I'm simply not gonna be able to." She sighed resignedly.

"Ri, I'm not going to judge you babe, I'm not about that. I think it's cool that you're doing that and not just jumping into bed with everyone else, because that's all I'd be doing. I think you're right in what you are doing and I will support you any way I can. Additionally, I'm gutted it didn't work out because although I've not known you that long, I genuinely feel like you were all in with her, and I wish you could have got what you wanted. I mean, to be fair if I can't bang you then you may as well be in a relationship," he said, laughing and handing the drink back again. "Come on, let's go home and get changed. I'll take you out for a curry and we can go and get fucked up and not worry about calling her for tonight," he said to Riley.

Chapter 48

Keri

"I swear to God, you leave me in the shit, I'll never forgive ya," Dan said to her.

"Yeah, yeah, you've said it fourteen times over, Dan. I get it, ok? I genuinely already feel better. I think I'm going to go home and realise what I could have and be back here grinning side to side and ready to be back to my old self; I just need to get to grips that once again, somebody doesn't want me and at this moment in time that don't feel so great," she said solemnly.

"Her loss. You are one in a million, babes, and you will meet Miss Right and she will treat you how you deserve to be treated. I promise you, gorgeous. Go get on the plane," he said, kissing Keri on the cheek and giving her one final hug.

She tried not to think about the last time she was in departures and was boarding a plane. It was different she needed to pull it together; she would do it one way or another, she had to. This was her life. She couldn't stop thinking about what Steph had said and wondered if she should try and get some closure, if maybe that would help at all.

Keri wandered through the airport aimlessly; she picked up a couple of big bags of sweets and chocolates in duty free for the kids and some drink for her folks and Kimmy. Boarding the plane, she took note of the airport looking back at her. She loved it here, she'd remembered leaving last month, unnerved and not really feeling the love for the training course. However, she met Glen and knew it would be a great week. She needed to get back to that, the love of the destination, the job, the lifestyle; she was so incredibly lucky her boss was her best friend and both Dan and Karen had done so much for her, been there for her through thick and thin, regardless. Keri didn't want to let either of them down but just for once she needed to do what was right for her.

* * *

Keri walked through departures and saw Kimmy straight away; her petite frame was the look of a four-year-old trying to get a peek of Santa in amongst the adults. Keri ran over to her and hugged her tightly. "Hey," she said into her big sister's ear. "I'm so glad to see you." She sighed heavily. "Come on, sis. We are gonna get you home, surprise everyone and get wasted. I've missed you so bad," she said to Keri, leaning up and kissing her cheek once more. "How you really doing?"

"I'm ok. Ish, I guess. How's you lot? So, Mum and Dad still don't know yet, huh?"

"Nope; I think your brother might think I'm having an affair though," she said, pulling an awkward face.

"You guys are totally made for each other. You are like my folks, il destino, as they say," she said to her sister.

"You will get that love, I promise." Kimmy squeezed her thigh. "Anyways, this is about happiness and the best week ever to basically make you see, you should, so come back home," she said. "So we have two slight detours before we go home."

"Ok, where to?" Keri asked her.

"It's a surprise," she said like an excitable child.

"Kimmy, please, please do not tell me that you have arranged a surprise party or something. I'll be so pissed."

"Really? Come on, you know I know you better than that. As if I would do that to you, you idiot."

Kimmy was right and Keri knew that. She wouldn't have ever done that to her. Kimmy had known her since she was virtually a kid, she'd come out to her and she truly was the closest person to her in the family, even though she wasn't her relative by blood, only through marriage.

They pulled into Asda and Kimmy grabbed her bag. "Come on, this actually didn't really need to be a surprise in reality, however, we need to grab lots of booze to keep us going for the week," she said. "Plus I thought we'd have a barbie tonight to surprise them all with you."

"Awesome, works for me," Keri said, following her into the store.

They wandered around the aisles, throwing in lots of food for the barbecue to ensure the whole family were fed and stocked up on wine, beer, and spirits. Keri was getting excited about seeing her family; she forgot how much she missed the little things like going grocery shopping.

"So, can I ask the dreaded question?" said Kimmy.

"What?" Keri looked at her, confused.

"Can I see what Riley looks like?" She looked at her carefully.

"Why do you think I have a picture? Why would I keep a picture of a girl I slept with once?" Keri said to her quizzically.

Kimmy grabbed her hand, and nudged her shoulder. "I've known you since you were yea high babes, granted yea high was still taller than I am now," she said, giggling. "But, retrospectively, I know who you are, Keri; I know you, and I know if you are questioning this so massively that it caused you to come home to reflect and assess the situation, then in your phone, stored away, is a photo that is imprinted on your brain. I would go as far to say that you regularly look at it, trying to work out more information from it, and that's what has brought you home," she said matter-of-factly.

"Wow, ok Dr. Phil." she said, shaking her head at Kimmy, helping her put the shopping on the belt. She lifted her phone from her bag and opened her pictures, looking a second before handing it over to her sister.

Kimmy was quiet, taking in the picture on the phone. She nodded slightly and smiled to Keri, handing the phone back. "She's very pretty," she said, and turned around to pay and pack away the last of the shopping.

"That's it, that's all you're gonna give me? Are you kidding me right now?" she said.

"What? I said she was pretty. I can see that you were drawn to her, she has something that would draw anyone to her. But I know you and I know whilst Emma shit on you, you aren't silly. You never have been, Keri. I'm not going to patronise you and talk like you have just let a pretty girl screw you over, because I don't think you would do that. As I said on the phone, you aren't that person, you are so logical. But, I'm confused; I don't want to cause you to think more than you are already so that's why I didn't say anything more. Come on, this has become depressing; we need to get home and start the prepping for this evening and open a bottle of vino. The kids are gonna be all on you, so time's slipping before us," Kimmy said to her, walking back to the car.

* * *

Keri was quiet on the car ride back home. She was examining the words that Kimmy had said in the store. She was right, she wasn't that person. She felt like she had had a major breakthrough when the conversations were had with Riley about their feelings and the fact they were both on the same page. She needed to not think about it this week, it wasn't about that and she needed to focus on her family and friends.

Kimmy pulled up outside the estate agents. "This is the second detour, I thought you'd want to see the place," she said, looking at Keri, grinning.

Keri hadn't been to her business in over a year and

half. Her brother Drew and Kimmy were the ones that basically ran it; it had been going for around seven years now, and they were doing an amazing job on it. She walked into the building and saw a couple of new staff. Kimmy introduced them to the new people that they had needed to recruit to keep up with the growth of the business. They walked upstairs to the director's office; the building was in tip top shape and the pictures of the properties scattered around and the bustling of the office just went to show how well they were managing it. They walked into the office and Drew was on the phone with his back to the door, looking out the window. He turned around, finishing the conversation, as he caught sight of his sister, stopping mid-sentence.

"Sorry, I'll call you back, I'm good with that," he said, finishing the call. "What the hell?" he said, throwing the phone and running over to Keri, picking her up and squeezing her into a tight hug. "Why didn't you tell me you were coming home? How long you home for? And why didn't you tell me? We were here all day together yesterday," he said, looking to Kimmy and finally putting his little sister down.

"You're looking good," she said. Drew had always got her friends' attention at school. He was the tallest of the five, at over six foot, and had always been athletic. He enjoyed playing pretty much every sport. His hair and eyes were identical to Keri's and they were the two things that managed to grab all the attention. They didn't spend much time in the office; the phone was ringing off the hook and as Kimmy had pointed out thirty-seven times they needed to get the food prepped ready for the evening, saying their goodbyes, they left and headed off back to Kimmy and Jason's house.

Chapter 49

Riley

Riley was trying to concentrate on her liquidation, Ben and Clare were messing about, and between those two and the telephone number sitting in her pocket, she was failing miserably.

"What do you think, Riles?" Ben was saying, laughing. She looked up to him and over to Clare who was rolling her eyes.

"Ignore him, he's being filth again. Hey, what's going on?" she whispered to her friend. "You look pissed? Is your licky down?" she asked, looking down to the tickets and cash in front of Riley.

"No, no, it's not that," she repeated. Every week all of the reps had to come into the office to liquidate, which was matching up their tickets to their cash and handing it all over; Riley could understand why her friend was concerned over the tickets and cash not matching up. Every week it would happen to someone and it was up to the rep to pay that money back. More often than not it was the reps dipping into their money, basically working out their commissions and then taking that amount out, but her tickets perfectly matched up, as they did every week.

"So what's going on?" Clare asked again.

"Oh just tired I guess," she said, making a mental note to pick herself up. "So what was he being filthy about this time?" Riley said to her two friends. She felt Ben squeeze her knee and when she looked over to him he winked at his friend; he was so good to her and whilst they were all really close she just didn't want to be telling everyone her life story at this moment.

"All I was saying is, she's a gorgeous girl, who I haven't shagged, I'm a gorgeous guy who she hasn't shagged, and you're another gorgeous girl who I haven't shagged, so I think we should indulge in a little 'ménage a trois' and we can basically fulfil everyone's needs. Riles, you get to shag a ten, Clare gets to shag a ten," he said, pointing to himself, "and also try out a little bit of batting for the other side just for one night only, and well, I get to shag two tens," he said seriously.

"You are off your fucking head, Ben. I'm going to liquidate now and leave you with this very vivid picture in your mind, because actually, that's all it is and ever going to be," Riley said, laughing at him and leaving the table with her licky pouch.

"Still, not a no then babes?" Ben shouted down the office, getting a few stern looks from the managers. Riley put her middle finger up behind her back to him and went and handed over her tickets to the account manager.

Once she'd finished and got her comms, she said her goodbyes to Ben and Clare who were still sat in the reps room, calculating, saying that she'd see them that night. Riley got her bag and put her comms in her purse. She had had a good week, in fact, that would go towards the money she'd left for her and Cara to party away when she arrived in a couple of days. She was walking out the door when she heard Katie calling her. "Hey, money good?" she asked Riley.

"Yes, thanks. Perfect," she smiled.

"As always, ehy? What did you want the number for then?" Katie had asked her.

Riley had not really told Katie the full details, she was sure she knew the reason why she wanted the number. She knew it was someone from the training course, she didn't want to let on it was a manager, as despite what Keri had done to her and why, it wasn't fair in Riley's opinion.

"Of course, top rep me, remember?" she said, smirking. "Oh I just thought maybe I would get in contact with a friend is all," she said seriously.

"Well, if you need anything, you know where we are. Why don't you come to ours for dinner before Cara comes?" she said, holding her hands up. "No dates, we promise," she said, smiling.

"Yeah, maybe, that would be nice," Riley said quietly, making sure nobody could hear. Ben knew she had spent the night at theirs last week after the jolly when she was hammered, and in true Ben style he was convinced that they had a threesome. He really did have the most vivid imagination when it came to sex; some of the stories he was telling her were just... well, wrong on so many levels, she thought, smiling inwardly.

"Oh, hey Riles, did you check your tray? You had a

large brown envelope in there!" Katie shouted after her.

"Really? Nah I didn't, I'll go get it now," she said, running back in and throwing the package in her bag. She left once more, seeing Jason walking over to his car. "J!" she shouted, running up behind him.

"Hey you," he said, "you want a lift back to resort?"

"Yeah, if you don't mind. What time you back to duties? Got time for a beer?" she said to him.

"Why not? I have some time to kill."

* * *

They went to the Lion and had a couple of beers. Having finished licky early, she was still trying to forget about the paper burning a hole in her pocket. She wanted to call it, but she didn't know what she could say or if Keri would even speak to her. To be fair she had got what she wanted and been given that get out of jail free card by breaking all contact with her, so why would she?

"So what's going on?" Jason asked her. "You seem a bit down since that first week. The job treating you ok? Is Ben behaving?" he said, looking concerned and wiping some sweat off of his forehead.

"Yeah I'm good, Ben is Ben. I loathe to love him, but I actually do. He's awesome and been such a good mate, still insistent on the fact he can change me but I think I'd be kinda bummed if he didn't! The job is good too, missing home a little but it's been a month so I kinda figured it would be like that. My bestie is out Saturday so I'm looking forward to that.

Anyways, enough of me, how's you? What's going on with you?" she said, interested.

"Nothing really, you know me, I just plod along," he said, smiling at her.

"Yep." She smiled at him sincerely. "So, hey, I'm taking Cara on the booze cruise on day off. Ben and Clare are going to come and possibly Katie, why don't you come too?" she said to him. Jason looked uncomfortable. She wondered what it was, everyone got on with him, but he never really came and sunbathed with the team. She hoped it wasn't his weight and he didn't feel uncomfortable that she had asked for some negative reason.

"Erm, well, I'm not doing anything, but I wouldn't want to intrude," he said, sounding unsure of himself.

"Come off it, you goon. Of course you wouldn't be intruding. I'd love you to come, I think you'll get on well with Cara, and no, I'm not trying to set you two up or owt I just think it would be a good day for all of us. One more?" She held up the bottle of Corona.

"Why not," he said, grinning wide.

She picked up her phone and dialled the office. "Hey Tony, can we get one more round please?" she shouted to Tony in the little kiosk bar in the hidden employee area.

"Coming up guys," he said back to them.

"Hello? Stamos please. Hey Stamos, it's Riley. You know the booze cruise we are booked onto next week? Yeah, that's it, can we book Jason on it too? Great news. Ok, well he can get on the bus here with us lot anyhow. Thanks, we love you," she said, smiling. "Sorted, you're coming; no backing out now," she said to her friend and lifted up her new beer to him.

They finished their drinks, saying their goodbyes to each other. She had had a couple beers in the sun and she could feel the effects. She was glad she bumped into Jason; the drinks had given her the courage she needed. She walked back to her unit, checking she had enough time before her duties started. "Now or never, Ri," she said to herself, retrieving the piece of paper from her pocket. She got her phone out of her bag and dialled the number; her finger hovered over the call button. She felt sick, but she knew Casey was right; she needed to find out once and for all why she did it, then she could get closure and move on to start enjoying life. She hit call and waited for the Rhodes office to connect.

"Good afternoon, Hightail Holidays Rhodes office. How may I help you?" She heard a woman's voice.

"Hi, I, ummmm, I was wondering if Keri Johnson was available to talk to," she said, sighing heavily, holding on to the rail into her hotel.

There was silence. She was wondering if she had got cut off. "Ermm, hello?" she said.

Emma was quiet. *Is this her?* she thought to herself. "Hi, sorry it's quite a bad line. Who was it you wanted to speak to?" Emma said.

"Oh, I'm sorry, I was looking for Keri Johnson," she said again.

"Oh ok. I'm sorry, no, she isn't here. She's actually left the island and returned home," she said with an evil grin.

Riley dropped down on the step. "Oh, right. Whe… It doesn't matter, thanks. Ummm, thanks for your help," she said, hanging up her phone, unable to breathe. Well that was all the closure she needed and was ever going to get, she thought.

Riley was dazed and confused. She didn't know how to deal with this new piece of information; she was completely puzzled. She could only assume this was part of the reason she was fucking around with her. She got up slowly and walked into her unit, saying hi to the staff, and sat down at her desk area. She opened her bag and got all of her stationary and ticket books. She saw the large brown envelope which she had totally forgotten about. She pulled it out and saw it had a British post mark. It must have come from her mum, and she tore the envelope and pulled out a copy of Diva magazine. Riley looked at it, confused, shaking her head. *She couldn't have*, she thought. Her mum wouldn't have even known how to set up a subscription and Keri had told her about it.

Riley picked her phone up again, and went to her messages and hit respond.

'Hey Mum, hope you and Dad are well? So did you set up a subscription for Diva magazine for me? Xxx'

She prayed her mum had her phone nearby and would respond quickly. She didn't think she could take it if she had to wait. "Yes," she said a little too loudly as she saw the grey spots moving across her phone.

'What's Diva baby, is that the opera boyband? And how can I subscribe to them they're very handsome? X'

'Mum, that's il divo, you loon haha. Don't worry, ignore my message, gotta work speak soon, love you xxx'

Her mum was insane, she thought. She was too funny with some of the things that came out of her mouth. So it wasn't her mum, she knew it couldn't have been but now she had confirmed it. So it was Keri. That's literally the only person that could have done it, but why? Nothing was making sense and it was driving her crazy. She slammed down the magazine. Now that she had left she knew there was no way she was ever going to find out, she didn't know anything more than her name, age, or that she had come from Brighton. "Fuck. Fuck," she said, even more annoyed now.

Chapter 50

Keri

Her mum was still crying, her dad and brothers still rolling their eyes as she kept pulling her daughter in for more hugs. It was a great day for a barbecue and the kids were all shouting and screaming, playing in the sprinkler system. Kimmy had done an amazing job. The whole family were there, all of her brothers, kids, partners, and even her friend Carla and her husband and kids had shown up.

"Mum, seriously, you're gonna scare the kids. Stop crying; you have a week with me. It's only day one, ok?" she said. "I'm gonna go catch up with everyone, but we have booked a spa day for you, Kimmy, Tracy, and me on Monday so we have loads of time together," she said, kissing her mum on the cheek and walking over to the barbecue where Justin was cooking. "Hope you're not messing my food up, buddy?" she said, nudging her younger brother.

"As if. I'm the only one worthy of any culinary genius in this family," he said, leaning over and kissing his sister's cheek. "So what's going on then, sis? What you home for? You haven't been home mid-season ever before. You didn't get back with that bitch did you?" he said to his sister seriously.

"No, dumbass, I'm not stupid."

"Is she still there? Is that why you're home, has something happened?" he said protectively.

"I'm good, we'll go out for a beer when you're off if we can and I'll fill you in. I met a girl and it didn't work out. I'm just a bit bummed as I thought there was something there. You win some, you lose some," she said to Justin. Her brother was only slightly taller than her and the only dark one out of them all, leaving him with years of bad memories from the ridicule and torture from his older siblings of being the 'odd one out'. As he was the youngest, they all used to tell him it was a sure-fire sign he was the milkman's. He had Keri's eyes though and the same dimples she had; they were a lot alike and it wasn't just the fact the siblings were both gay. She loved spending time with him and when they got together with Kimmy, it was always a catastrophe, yet such good fun.

"Her loss, kidda. She clearly isn't worthy of you," he said defensively.

"Well, that strictly isn't true, but thanks for the protection. We'll discuss it properly when you have some time to spare me," she said, smiling at Justin, before running off to play in the sprinkler with the kids. They were screaming and chasing her around, God she could tell she had not run any this last week. Bloody hell, the kids were outrunning her, she thought. She stopped trying to catch her breath and saw the family looking on at her with amusement. She was completely soaking wet and it wasn't long before Kimmy and Justin were joining in and chasing the kids in and out of the sprinklers.

THE LIFE OF RILEY

Her first day was exactly what she needed and wanted; she had had so much fun with her family, the kids were all fighting for her attention. Kimmy, Justin, and her were all acting as young as the kids; as much as her mother was trying to reprimand the adults she was doing so with a huge grin on her face. She loved having all the family together, it was written all over her face.

The night ended early due to the kids' bedtimes and school the following morning. Keri had told her folks she would stay with Kimmy tonight along with Justin and would be back tomorrow. She wanted to have a proper catch up with them both. Everyone had left and Jason had poured the three of them a glass of champagne and let them get on with the gossiping whilst he put his sons to bed and cleaned up the house. It was a pleasant evening so they sat in the garden with the burner on, with Keri filling them in on all the details, and bringing Justin up to speed.

For the first time in ages she did actually feel relaxed; she was able to focus on something other than Riley and what had happened. She felt better for actually talking everything out with her family. Jason had joined them after clearing up and Kimmy was sat in his lap; she wondered if she would ever have that. The complete love that her parents and her eldest brother had with Kimmy; Sean was more manly and private, more like the strong, silent type and whilst he and Tracey seemed very happy they weren't like her folks and eldest brother.

She felt her phone vibrate and saw the message from Dan.

'Hey gorgeous, you get home ok? Missing you already. I

think Paula will do alright though, she seems to be getting on with the guys and she's alright. Hope all's ok, and if you need anything give me a bell. D'

'Hey you, I'm good, good day with the family (not too good don't panic) although Paula is impressing maybe I don't need to worry anymore about not coming back. I miss you guys too; need a night out the day I return with the three of us! Love you pumpkin ;) xxx'

'Fuck off to both parts of that message dumbass – see ya next week x'

She smiled at her parting words to her boss. He was a real boy's boy and when he spoke, that was confirmed even more so. So catching his words to his girlfriend Nicola one night she was there, she never got tired of it and he hated that fact.

"What you smiling about?" Jason said, looking at his little sister.

"Nothing, it was my boss. I'm just winding him up, he's freaking that I won't return." She went into her emails to see what had come in that day; she deleted the majority of them, before noticing the Diva subscription confirmation. She'd forgotten that she had done that, remembering the day at the airport after their time together. She wondered if Riley had received the first copy as yet; she wondered more importantly if she'd worked out it was Keri and if so, what she thought of it. Keri felt deflated once more; she was unsure whether she should reroute them. Realistically, it was being petty by doing so, so she thought better of it and decided to just leave it.

"You ok, sweetie?" Kimmy asked, stroking her leg, noticing the mood change in her.

"Yeah, I'm tired I guess, long day and all that," she said with a slight smile.

"Well, I know I'm not part of the magic crowd, but as an imposter on this occasion and for what it's worth, this my opinion," said Jason, gaining all of their attentions. "You have always been an amazing person, you have always been warm, funny, kind, allegedly sexy; I mean I don't even want to think about shit like that, you're intelligent, you have a business, part ownership of a couple of properties and, well, you're not too bad on the eye either. You're a good catch, Keri," he confirmed. "You are an incredibly good judge of character. Despite the age difference of us all, you always have been, even from a young age, Kel, you were able to point the good and bad apples out. You have guided all of us virtually from one time or another, and I have to agree with your mates, I don't think you would have ever have been so wrong. Yes, you didn't know her for long, however, you were her trainer or teacher, so it's your job to get to know your students on a deeper level, so in effect you would have already established the personality traits she possessed – her behaviours, her characteristics and that. You don't go for assholes, Jesus you're the only one that didn't." He tickled his wife, who slapped his arm from around her, giggling. "The point I'm trying to make is, yes you spent a short period of time with her, but it was intense, it was just you two, it was a bond you clearly both had together. Honestly, from what Kimmy told me about Emma and what she did to you, if all of this had happened days, even a couple weeks after that, then yeah I would have to agree, it was bad judgement on your part. But, you don't dwell, you analyse to hell and then you have a word with yourself and move on. So, I think I would have to agree with the others, I think you need some closure. Personally, I think you have an absolute ball with us lot for a week, see the family, the kids, your friends, then return home and the first day off you get, you go to her. Find out where she'll be and turn up, tell her you are not able to move on until you know exactly what happened, if you did or didn't do something, and explain to her that you have feelings for her and you believed she was worth fighting for. As she clearly didn't agree, the least you deserve is to get some reasoning. No phone calls, texts, emails; she's new at this, prove to her she means something to you and you were in it for the long haul. If she says no, then the least she can do is give you some form of explanation; you can go then go back to your resort and concentrate on getting things straight in life without her in it," he said soberly.

Everyone was in silence and looking at Jason. "My god you are the hottest man alive," Kimmy said, kissing him passionately.

"Really?" Justin and Keri said in unison, pulling their noses up.

Keri was stunned at her brother. He was not the type to say things like that, well at least not to his siblings; he had always been quite reserved and didn't get involved in things like this, so when he had just said all of that he had truly astounded her. She got up and hugged him and Kimmy tightly. "You know what, and I love you guys. Thanks for an awesome day; I'm kinda trashed and wrecked, so if you don't mind I'm gonna head to bed. I have a lot to think about."

She said goodbye to Justin, agreeing to meet up over the weekend and hit a couple of gay bars, and disappeared off to her bed for the night.

Chapter 51

Riley

Riley was on her third shot of the night already. "For someone who doesn't like shots, you're putting 'em back, babe," said Ben, concerned.

"Drowning the pain, you keep telling me I should do this," she said to him, turning around to face the crowd in the bar.

"Do you think that's wise babe? You don't do this and I'm worried. I've never seen you like this before. What's happened? Is everything alright at home?" he said, looking into her eyes.

"I'm fine, honestly. What do you think of her over there? The dark-haired girl dancing in blue? She's hot right, do you think she is gay?" she said to him, ordering another drink.

"From the way that guy's dancing with her, I'm guessing no, Riles," he said. "Hey, you alright?" Ben said to Katie as she walked over.

"Hey Riley, you ok?" Katie asked her.

"Yes, I'm fine." She caught sight of Ben shaking his head to their boss behind her. "Seriously, you moan when I don't go out and stay at home and wallow, when I do come out you are making me feel shit wanting to wallow with booze; what do you want from me! I mean really, what exactly? Because at this rate I'm starting to think Keri had the right idea by leaving the job and going home," she said, getting upset.

"Oh Riley, why didn't you tell me?" Katie said. "Look, I'm not really having much fun. I was just coming over to say bye. I'm going to get a Chinese and go home and watch a movie. Do you want to come with me? I don't mind if you don't want to, but if you do we could go and get a bottle of tequila, get drunk, or I'll catch you up, eat takeout and watch a good old chick flick or, erm, horror if you'd rather steer clear of that?" Katie said, smiling.

Riley contemplated the offer. She wasn't having fun, she wanted to get drunk but that was just making her feel worse, and she was feeling sick. She wanted to come out, get pissed and get laid; she had decided that everything so far hadn't worked so she would try Ben's tactics, but that really wasn't working either. "Yeah, I guess so; I have the next week to get smashed when Cara arrives here tomorrow," she said, waving bye to Ben across the bar.

* * *

"So, you going to tell me what's really going on?" Katie said when they got back to hers and dished up the chow mein and ribs they had bought.

Riley filled a glass each of tequila for them and took the bottle to the room with the glasses. "You know what's going on. I have told you already," she said.

"Well partially, yes, but maybe start at the beginning. Go all the way to the end this time, and we can see what we can do to help you out of it," she said, taking a bite before knocking back the shot.

Riley hadn't wanted to tell her, as she didn't want to make Keri look unprofessional, but now she didn't work for the company anymore, did she really need to worry?

Riley finished the story. She had somehow managed to drink herself sober; she had eaten and they had done half a bottle of tequila. "And then I try to get closure and she's gone, she's left. I mean I could understand it, if I was stalk texting her or something. But she just left, she was so excited about the job and promotion, and then she went and bought me a subscription to Diva. Why? Why would you do all of that if you are shagging twenty other people? Why? I don't get it and I'm sick of how everyone keeps telling me it don't make sense. I'm not stupid, I know that, so why did she do it, Katie?" she said again.

Katie had been supportive and not judged her at all. "Do you want me to get Jayne involved?" she said evenly.

"God no!" she said quickly.

"Look, what I mean is, Jayne could speak to the island manager there, they all know each other well, and he may have an English number for her," she said.

Riley was shaking her head, but as the realisation set in that she still may be able to get an answer, the shakes were getting slower and slower.

"Without asking the obvious here, I guess you've checked social media?" Katie said.

Riley looked at her quizzically; as it sunk in that she hadn't, they both quickly picked up their phones and Katie went and sat next to her. "You check Facebook and I'll check Twitter and Instagram," Katie said. "What's her surname again?"

They looked all over both with Kerianne and Keri and they couldn't find the girl's details. She knew lots of people had settings so they couldn't be found as easily, so she may have been on there but she apparently didn't want to be found.

"Seriously, what the fuck am I doing? I'm stalking the girl now. It was a week for fuck's sake," Riley said, rubbing her temples.

"Riley, Jayne and I were both in relationships with other people. We aren't proud of what we did but we spent five months having an affair. I was the girl that always said no way would I have anything to do with a cheater, no way would I stand for a cheater. I wasn't a cheater, I hadn't ever been that girl; and as I said neither of us liked what we did, we weren't proud of it, but we were just drawn to each other. We couldn't stop it, it took over us and we had no control over it; I guess you would say we were destined to be together and the universe, simply put, was not letting that be forgotten. See, sometimes you can't control it and you just need to go with it; it's not always easy, but if it's meant to be it will be. I'm not saying it's meant to be for you to; it isn't fair to give you false hope. But stop beating yourself up over the time of it all; if you had that connection between you both then you had it, end of! I don't know the girl and unfortunately, it does seem like she has done one on you from what was said in Bodrum, but, I would have to agree there are some missing parts. But if you can't move past this you really are going to have no other option than getting Jayne to see if she can get you contact details. At least that way you can find out why she played you."

Riley knew she had a point but tonight wasn't the night to decide on this; she was glad Cara was coming out tomorrow, she needed that, she thought soberly.

"Ok, thanks. I'll think about it. Please, promise me you won't get Jayne involved? I really want to have a fun week with Cara. She needs fun and so do I, she won't let me sit and feel sorry for myself. She will ensure that I have a ball and we have fun. I'll see how I feel when she's gone and if I still feel that way I will ask you to get Jayne involved. Deal?" she said seriously.

"Yeah, sure." Katie nodded back to the girl.

Chapter 52

Keri

"I don't remember it being like this, the scene's got even bigger," she said to her brother about the gay scene in her hometown; the bar was actually quite nice, which surprised her. Gay bars in her opinion predominantly weren't, but this one had an upper class wine bar feel to it. There was an even mixture of guys and girls too, which she was happy about, finding a seat in the corner where in Justin's words they could 'people watch', knowing full well he meant 'eye up all the talent'. To be fair to him he chose the right place because there was a hell of a lot of talent in there tonight.

They had spent a bit of time in the other bars but were enjoying this one the most and were happily sat drinking, talking, and watching. They had discussed Justin's love life which appeared to be fairly slow as he couldn't find anyone he was really into; he'd met a guy in Newcastle a few weeks back when he'd gone for a few days with work, but he didn't really feel he could pursue it with the distance between them. Keri wanted to help her brother find a guy tonight, she thought.

"I need the loo, I'll be back in a mo, and do you

want another drink when I come back?" she said to Justin.

"Yeah, definitely," he said.

She waited in the line to use the toilets; she took in the fact that even the toilets were loads nicer than what she had ever experienced in gay bars before. "Keri? Keri Johnson?" she heard. She looked over to see Becky, a girl she went to college with. She was also the first girl that Keri had slept with. She looked great, Keri thought to herself. "Hey, Becky. How are you? Long time no see," she said, kissing the girl on the cheek.

"I'm good, how about you? I heard you didn't live here anymore, you lived abroad?" she said questioningly.

"Yes that's correct, I live in Greece now," she said, smiling. "How about you? Still local? Are you married, kids?" she said.

"I moved to London with uni for five years but moved back last year when my girlfriend and I split up. I didn't want to be in a position where I could bump into her. And no kids, not really my thing," she said. "So how long you around for?"

"Just a couple more days. I'm just here catching up with family," she said, smiling at the girl. She still had a gorgeous big smile, thought Keri.

"Shame," she said. "Well, if you get a few hours one night to spare, maybe you can come round and we can, ermmm, catch up." She tiptoed to Keri and kissed her lips softly, holding her waist and gently grazing her thumb over the bare skin below her top. She smiled. "I'm on Facebook if you fancy it," she said, and walked off, smirking.

Keri was speechless. My god, she had always been confident but she just oozed it there and then. She used the bathroom and made her way back to Justin. Filling him in on Becky and what had just happened, he was laughing. "Still got it, sis," he said. "So how did it make you feel?" he said sincerely.

"Kinda good for the first time in ages, like I was worth something," she said sadly.

"Babes you are worth everything. Don't let anyone ever make you doubt that, ok?" he said.

She smiled at Justin. "I felt good. She's cute, I won't deny that. It was nice," she said. She was happy that for the first time in a while, she was finally starting to feel like it wasn't her fault and she couldn't control other people's feelings no matter how much she wanted to; if someone didn't want her, she couldn't do anything about it.

"So you gonna meet up with her?" he said. "Get a bit of action." He winked.

She doubted it, she wasn't really all that desperate to get any action and she only literally had a couple days left here. "Doubt it," she said to her brother.

"Maybe you should try finding her and seeing if you can get a little snog, at least you got something before you leave." He smirked, pinching her cheek.

They finished their drinks and decided to go to a club they used to go to before she left. She downed the last part of her drink and just started to walk away, when Becky appeared in front of her. "You're not going are you?" she said questioningly.

"Ermmm, yeah, we are going to try somewhere else," Keri said to her.

"Ohhhh. Well that's a shame, I have been trying to build the courage to come and ask you if you wanted a drink," she said, looking at Keri.

"Kel, I'm gonna go to the toilets before we leave. I'll meet you outside," Justin said, winking at his big sister.

"Ok cool. Yeah, I'm sorry, I just need to help my brother find someone. There isn't really anyone taking his fancy here, so it's only fair we go elsewhere. After all he's the one that lives here," she said, smiling.

"Well, can I at least get a kiss for old times' sake?" she asked Keri.

Keri wasn't used to people being this forward and didn't really know how to react. The drink was flowing freely in her system now and she liked the brief kiss the girl had given her in the bathroom. *Why not?* she thought. Like Justin said, she may as well get something and this girl clearly wanted to provide that something. "For someone who needed to pluck up the courage to ask me for a drink, you certainly seem to have found that courage now." She smirked.

"Well I may never see you again. You were the first girl I slept with, and god that was a memorable experience, so I can only imagine what you have picked up along the way now; I want to make sure I don't lose out," she said, smiling with a lopsided grin. "Anyways enough of the chit-chat. You haven't said no so I am going to kiss you now," she said, leaning into Keri.

Her lips were soft, and their kiss was slow, gentle.

Becky put her hand on the back of Keri's head and pulled her in a little to deepen the kiss. After a few minutes they pulled away and Becky was smiling. "As I said, I am on Facebook, I'd love to re-hook up; you're not the only one who has learnt a trick or two over the years." She winked and walked off.

Keri walked out to find Justin. "Well?" he said. "One to ten?"

Keri sighed, "Eleven for the kiss, minus eleven for not being the girl I wanted to see when I opened my eyes. Come on, let's get you some hot guy to keep you warm at night," she said as they walked arm in arm down the road.

Chapter 53

Riley

Riley was so hungover again. She was starting to spend more time in this bed than her own, she thought, as she got up from Katie's spare bed. She picked up her belongings and walked down to the kitchen. She noticed Katie out in her pool, swimming.

"Blimey, you are good going with the amount of tequila we had last night!" she said, sitting down and dangling her legs in the pool.

"I'm dying," she said, "but, thanks again. Sorry, I'm not normally like this, I'm starting to make a habit of this shit these days," she said, sighing loudly.

Katie swam over to the edge of the pool next to Riley, resting her head on her hands. "Listen I'm not going to keep going around in circles with this. We spoke about it last night, it is what it is. We will sort it out. We have all been there, you should have seen me when I realised I was in love with Jayne and was still in a relationship. It was horrific and nothing could sort me out. So seriously, it's no big deal, ok? What time will Cara be here?"

"She should be landing in about two hours which is pretty good. I can go back home, spend some time with her at the pool before duties tonight. Thanks again for letting me swap my half day around," Riley said, smiling to her boss.

"No worries at all. I'm staying here all day, do you want to take my car to pick her up, rather than getting a transfer?" she said to Riley.

"That would be awesome, thanks so much." She smiled. "Right, I'm gonna get my sorry ass home, showered, and a big, bright smile painted on my face for a week's worth of boozing, naughtiness and all sorts of other antics." She smiled, getting up.

Katie was smirking with her eyebrow raised in question. "Not like that, you've spent too long with Ben," she said, laughing and leaving her boss's home.

* * *

Riley got a coffee and pastry from the café in the airport; Cara's flight had landed five minutes ago, she would give it twenty minutes and then walk over to the doors and wait for her. She was totally looking forward to seeing her best friend; she didn't even see her before she went on training, so it really had been an age.

She heard her phone go off, notifying her of an incoming message. She opened the messages.

'Hi honey, I'm home... cute boys all around! :) This is lits going to be the best week of my life!! :) This luggage belt is shit, how long does it take, do they not realise they are wasting valuable drinking time ;) xx PS how pissed can you get before work tonight ;)'

"'lits'??? wtf?? Are you turning into one of your students?? I mean "lits"?? Hahaha. I can have a couple beers but can't

get pissed but I will leave you with Ben and Clare when I go back as they will be on half day then. I dunno if I can drink, I'm dying xx'

'You can fuck right off, I'm on my holidays and you will damn well enjoy it whether you like it or not. I HEART "lits" actually; but you're right, one of the kids was texting his mate, when I took the phone to read it out to the class, he'd wrote "I can lits see, misses tits through that shirt", so, I'm liking it? ohhh luggage coming xx'

'PLEASE TELL ME YOU DIDN'T READ THAT TO THE CLASS?? Great news xx'

'Hell yeah I did! The little shit needed to learn a lesson! Xx one case retrieved, yippee'

'You're so evil, OMG you have actually turned into Mrs. Cooper, you wicked cow. Whoa ONE CASE? How many did you bring? You're only here a week aren't you??? xx'

'Shut up, I needed the choice of outfits, you guys work here I don't know if I'm dressing, smart, casual, smart casual; it's all too much! Where are you? You aren't here I can't see you?? xx'

'You could have just asked dumbass! You straights are so painful! I'm here, I see you xx'

"Oh my god, you look amazing, you're so tanned and your hair is a little lighter around the edges," Cara said to her best friend, hugging her tightly. "Here, you need to take this." She shoved her case into Riley's hands.

"Seriously, why the hell have you brought two cases? You are insane," she said, sighing.

"So who's hot then? I have had the term from hell. I only have one week off and then I am back to school, so seriously, you need to get me laid. I have had a shit time, I need to have some fun; and as you so gracefully bowed out of best friend duties and left me I have nobody to go out with or meet people with, so it's the least you can do!" she said as they walked out of the airport. "Holy shit, it's hot. I can't breathe, like literally can't breathe, it's like Cancun all over again," said Cara.

"Have you drunk the whole way over or have you decided to take up class As or something? What the hell is up with you?" she said questioningly.

They arrived at Katie's car and worked together to put the bags in that she had brought. *Jesus it's far too hot for this*, she thought.

"So who's the car belong to?" she asked Riley, playing about with the air con.

"It's my boss's. She is on day off today, and was staying at home in the pool so she said I could use it. I will need to get it back to her at some point," she said, pulling out of the airport.

"Cool, is that the lesbian? So what's the plan tonight then? Well, today I guess. Are there any plans?" she said.

"Yeah she's gay, and with the island manager. They are a cute couple to be fair. Well we will go back now and dump your bags and then we can go to the pool and chill out, sunbathe, have a few beers; the guys will be down in a couple of hours and then I'll go back, get changed and head to duties whilst you stay with them. Then when I get home we can get ready, go for dinner to a dead nice Greek taverna with Ben and Claire, then get on it," she said.

"Sounds excellent," Cara said, smiling widely.

They arrived at the apartment and dumped the bags; Riley was already in her bikini under her clothes so she cleaned the kitchen while Cara sorted some of her things and got changed.

They went to the pool, so she texted Katie about dropping off the car to her again, noticing a message on her phone from Ben. Opening it, she smiled as she could already imagine the content of it,

'You at the lion or ours? Is she ready for me? ;) Bx'

'Fuck off, you sleep with her I swear you will never have sex again, and I swear if I find out you have bet on it, you won't ever want to go to sleep in our apt again? Ours xx'

';) I love you. bets?? I don't know what you mean ;) x'

"I'll fucking kill him," she said to herself.

"What's up?" Cara said, coming out of Riley's room with her towel and bag in hand. "I'm ready. So what's up?" she said as they left the apartment.

"Oh nothing, just Ben being a dick," she said, heading over to the complex pool.

Chapter 54

Keri

Kimmy picked up her mother-in-law and sister-in-law, and the four women drove to the spa. Keri was completely in need of relaxation for the day. They had a couple of treatments booked, and the remainder of the day would be spent sipping champagne, relaxing in the different rooms and steam, saunas, and pool.

They arrived and were issued with their thick robes and slippers for the day. "How many of these do you think get stolen in a week?" Tracey asked seriously. "I mean have you ever found any that are as good?" She smiled.

Kimmy was spurring her on to try and steal one, getting a disapproving glance from their mother-in-law. "Behave, you three. I will buy you all one for Christmas," her mother said, trying to stifle the smile.

"Think that may be a bit warm for me, Mum," Keri said with a raised eyebrow.

The three women stopped and turned to look at Keri. "So you're going back?" Kimmy asked seriously.

"For good?" her mum added.

She sat down on the seat. "I am. I have had a truly

wonderful time, I've loved every minute of it, and it's exactly what I needed, ya know? Mum I won't be there for good, but I have worked my absolute backside off to get my promotion and honestly, I want it, I'm ready for it, and I'm just not ready to give it up yet. I can't do anything about Riley, but this week has made me see things differently. I did develop feelings for her and yes it didn't work out and I'm still hugely upset, but I need to crack down and do what I'd started. Eventually, I know things will get better and I will meet someone that will be happy with me and want me for me. I'll have what all of you guys have, but right now, it's simply not my time. So for now I want to focus on achieving the one thing I have been working towards," she said to them all seriously.

Tracey came over. "It's been wonderful seeing you, hun. If that's what you think is right then you have to do what's best for you," she said, hugging her sister-in-law.

"Thanks T, that means so much," she said, smiling, looking over to Kimmy and her mum.

"I always want you home, you're my kid sister, but I genuinely believe you need to do this. So much so that we have booked a holiday to come and see you at the end of summer," she said, grabbing Keri for a hug.

"You did? When? Oh my god that will be so cool," she said back to Kimmy, before going to her mum and hugging her tightly. "I know you're upset Mum, but it's not time just yet," she said, looking at her mum's sad face.

"I know, baby," she said. "Come on you three, let's enjoy this day together before I have to break up my family once more," she said, trying to put on a brave face.

They had had a wonderful day, and were all feeling completely revitalised and relaxed. Keri had opted for the hour-long full body massage with her mum. She knew she would love to have the joint experience together and she was right. It was exactly what she needed and she felt such a huge amount of the stresses drain away from her body. Even though they chatted a little, she spent the majority of the hour thinking about whether she should try and speak to Riley and get the closure that people kept saying she needed. Although she thought many of them had a point, she had decided after this week that she didn't want to know. She didn't know enough about Riley, she thought she had but in reality it was only a short period of time. She had an amazing time with Riley, and she genuinely thought she was kind, genuine, sweet; in a different time and place maybe it could have worked, but Riley wouldn't have ever been able to keep up a job like this in her first season with a relationship, and more importantly when it was a long-distance relationship too.

Feeling better for her time at home, she did feel somewhat guilty for kissing Becky but it made her realise she wasn't ready to go any deeper yet. The timing wasn't right yet, and she was more than happy to just have some fun with her friends and when the time was right she would know. She smiled inwardly. It was a shame about Steph not staying around, she was good with the advice and she did right on this point; she thought they could have been friends over the summer. Other than Emma there were no other gay women on the Rhodes team, or anywhere else that she knew of that she could have just openly spoke to and hung out with, but she was happy with the friends she had out there.

She couldn't wait to speak to Dan and Karen and tell them, she thought, smiling as she lifted her phone from her bag; she opened up the messages on WhatsApp and went to a group message between the three of them.

'Fancy having a night out the three of us when I arrive Wednesday night, would like a catch up and see you both? miss you guys x x'

She picked up her bag and put her shoes on before they all left and walked around to the Italian down the street. They had decided they would do their hair with the complimentary hairdryer and straighteners and go for a nice meal; Kimmy had been drinking all day and had agreed with Jason that he would come collect them after dinner. They wanted one last night out with the girls before they had to all go back to their normal lives.

Chapter 55

Riley

"Seriously, she likes you and that's fine, I'm good with her having a fling, but don't fuck about with the bets. For me? Please? She's my best mate and you are both adults but don't do that," she said to Ben seriously.

"Riles, I wouldn't do that. I have more respect for you than that; I'm not going to say they aren't betting amongst themselves, but before she even arrived, babes, I said no to them and said I weren't gonna do that to you. Honestly she's fit and funny as, mate. If she weren't I wasn't going to go there, but she is pretty cool, not that I'd expect anything less from your best mate," he said, smiling. "I promise I have tried to keep away but fuck, she's making it so hard for me," he said seriously.

"I know, I know, and she does think you're hot and to be fair she has said she just wants to have a laugh this week. I know full well she isn't about getting loved up and stuff, so you guys are both big enough and ugly enough, but I just don't want bets and shit going on, as I said," she said, ordering a shot surfboard.

"I got it, here, let me take that over there while you

get the beers in. Sure I can't buy this one?" he said.

"No, I'm good," she said, smiling back at him. He walked away whilst she was waiting for the remaining drinks.

"Hey you, how are you?" she heard next to her as she was paying for the drinks. She turned around and saw Cascy.

"Hey, I'm good. How are you? You look, wow, good!" she said, smiling back at the woman.

"Thanks, I have another date." She winked, nodding her head behind her. "Your 7 o'clock," she said. Riley discreetly looked around to her 7 o'clock as requested and saw a leggy redhead talking to Jayne.

"Very nice, she's cute. How's it going?" she asked, interested.

"Awesome, she's super-hot and such good fun. I was unsure about another blind date, but I thought, why not? And I'm glad I did."

"Ouch," Riley said to her.

"Shit, no, sorry. I didn't mean that to be a dig on you, I just meant people keep setting me up on blind dates and I was starting to feel like A) a lost cause, and B) like the island was gonna know me at this rate," she laughed. "How's you anyhow? You made any contact with your girl? Or are you gonna leave it?"

"Honestly, I don't know yet. My best mate's here; I'm just trying to have some fun and then when she's gone I'll make up my mind, ya know?"

"For sure. Anyways, you have a good night and I'll see you around?" Casey said to Riley.

"Yeah, I'm sure I will. Good luck tonight, I hope it goes well," she said, smiling sincerely.

Riley got back to the table and distributed her drinks to her friends; she took a long swig and sat back down next to Clare. She started discussing the barman she'd been seeing, filling Riley in on the fact that she didn't want to get caught up with a worker as they were no different to reps that just slagged it about, in her own words. Apparently he was a great lay and they were 50/50 on the booty calls.

Riley wondered if she hadn't met Keri, if she would have been like this, obsessed with sleeping around. She'd never been like that, she had had one-night stands, not too many but she tended to get to know people on a personal level and then sleep with them. She guessed it was hard overseas though as everyone worked hard and played harder. Plus it was the age-old 'what goes on tour, stays on tour' and all that. She loved her team and she was so looking forward to going on the booze cruise on day off. She'd already done a few things with Cara and she seemed to be enjoying herself, she knew she'd love the booze cruise though and the six of them would have such a laugh together, which is what she wanted and needed, she thought.

She looked over at Cara and Ben getting cosy; she knew she was not going to be able to stop them, but Cara seemed like she was enjoying herself so that's what was important, she figured. Cara looked up and caught her best friend looking at her. "You ok?" she mouthed to Riley.

"Yes, cheers." She smiled widely and lifted her drink to her best friend across the table.

Chapter 56

Keri

Keri walked off the plane, and was so happy this time to be home; she had had an amazing week with her family and even today they were all there to see her off now that the kids were off school. They had a big family meal at her parents' and discussions were held over trying to get the family to add on to Kimmy and Jason's holiday to see her in a couple of months. She had taken a lift from Justin to the airport and he promised he'd come visit as soon as he had got the chance to.

All in all, it was a perfect break, she'd thought, and the flight over was on time and pretty enjoyable even. She felt like she'd turned a corner and she was just praying she didn't get home and start being reminded of everything again. She jumped onto the transfer coach and picked her book up again, whilst she made her hour-long journey home.

Keri got in, dumped her case, and showered quickly. She threw on a pair of short cotton shorts and a bright coral top with an open back; that was the best thing about going home, the shopping, she thought. She buckled up her new sandals and grabbed her bag, leaving her apartment.

THE LIFE OF RILEY

Keri walked down the street to meet her friends in the bar a little disappointed that it wouldn't be just the three of them, due to it being Paula's last night. She needed to remember that she would have to watch what she said; the last thing she wanted was for Paula to go running back to Emma, telling her everything, really hoping that Dan and Karen hadn't said anything to her.

She walked into the bar and spotted them immediately, quickening her pace, desperate to get to her friends. She got to the table and Karen jumped up, hugging and kissing her. "You're back, I'm so glad, you look amazing," she said, pushing Keri back and looking her up and down before pulling her back into another hug.

"Alright sweetheart? Great to have you back," Dan said, hugging her and kissing her cheek. "And this is the little gem that's been looking after your lot whilst you've been swanning about the UK, shopping and spa daying." He winked.

"Hey, nice to meet you," Keri said to Paula, shaking her hand.

"HI," she said, smiling awkwardly.

She sat down and poured some wine. "So fill me in then?" she said to her friends.

The foursome were laughing and chatting, and Keri had missed this so much. She had heard about the delay where the guests were throwing their dirty underwear to the reps, which she was horrified about; a situation where Paula had to break up a fight between two burly men, which appeared to have scared the life out of her.

"God, it sounds like a right nightmare," she said, laughing. "I shouldn't have come back."

"Yes, you fucking should have. No offence, Paula," he said, looking to her sincerely.

"None taken, I've had a ball and your team are ace, but I don't feel ready just yet," she said, smiling. "Here's to you being back, although I must say, I'm not saying anything derogatory towards Emma, she's been a great boss and I've learnt a lot, but I have actually preferred it here, and your guys do rave about you."

"Booooomm," she said, raising her wine glass. "See? Told you I was good." She winked at Dan; she was surprised at how nice Paula was she could see why Dan and Karen had got on well with her. She felt completely relaxed in the environment now, and was enjoying the flowing conversations between them all.

"Yeah, yeah, whatever. So what's the plan tonight then? Unfortunately Paula's gotta go back tomorrow so she's taking a transfer back from resort and then doing an arrival straight back to the top. So what do we reckon, a night of avoiding the reps and getting on it? I might even treat yous to a booth and bottle of champers if you are lucky," he said, smiling at his team.

"Sounds good to me," Keri said. "So anything else happen or was that it?" she said, intrigued to hear everything about the resort whilst she had been away.

"What more do you want, was that not enough?" Karen said. "Poor Paula was ready for running for the hills." They all laughed merrily.

"Ohhh, your pretty lady left the island early; I saw Ant yesterday and there was some health and safety crisis, somewhere else, she said to say bye to you," he said, smirking.

"Piss off, I have no interest. She was cute but, I'm not ready. I've had an amazing time at home and sorted my head out, but I have no interest in jumping into something with anyone else," she said sincerely.

Paula snorted her drink. "Sorry," she said, holding her nose and squeezing her eyes shut. "Jesus that hurt. Sorry, hold up, I'm lost. You're the player of the south are you not? The girl who has a girl in every port?" she said, smiling to Keri.

Karen and Dan were looking confused at Paula, and then looked back to Keri. "What you on about Paula, you had too many vinos?" Dan asked. "Keri has never been around the block, she's only been in relationships. That's why she's been home, because she had a bit of a bad time," he said, looking at her.

"Dan," said Karen, eyeing him. "Look Paula, you are lovely and we have really loved having you here and seriously I'd love to have you down here, but what he's just said can't get back to Emma or Julie, ok?"

"Yeah sure, I wouldn't do that, not at all. I really like you guys," she said soberly.

"So, what made you think Keri was a player? Or whatever you want to call it," said Karen.

"Well, Emma told us. I know you guys used to date for a while, and I assumed that's why you split, but she was saying you'd been 'slagging it about' on the training course and stuff," she said, confused. "As I said, I just assumed that's why you split."

"Slagging it about? Really? Jesus, I met one girl and slept with her rightly or wrongly and fell for her. Hardly shagging everything that moved," Keri said, rolling her eyes at them.

"No, I mean, I am not saying she's wrong and you are lying, please don't think I am; but she definitely told us that, we were having a coffee and she said that you'd been slagging it about, that you had met some girl, and you did your normal thing of playing her. Pretending to be all loved up and was shagging everyone behind her back. She said she was from another island, I can't remember where, but that's how you managed to get away with it. They were discussing why you did it and she said something about you maybe needed to get a good report to the UK for the course," said Paula.

Keri's head was rushing. *What the fuck was she playing at?* she thought.

"Paula, when you say she told 'yous' that, who is 'yous'? Who was she telling this to?" Karen asked her.

"Me and Julie, although, thinking about it, Julie was kind of saying similar things. Like she knew you were like that. I think? Yeah because she was making references about it, like 'Oh that's her all over though,' and stuff, you know?"

They all sat there completely confused. Keri didn't understand. "What purpose could that have possibly served? I don't get it? Was it to try and get Julie there or what? I don't understand," she said, looking between Dan and Karen.

"No it wasn't that, because she was already working there then, she'd already left here," Paula said. "Look I'm really sorry to spoil the night," she said, looking upset.

"Hey, don't worry, it isn't your fault." Keri held the girl's hand. "It's fine. Come on, we can drink more." She poured more drink into their glasses. "Maybe I should text her and ask her why she said it?" she said.

"No, please don't, she'd kill me and I don't want her to cause problems for me. I really want this promotion. When I'm ready," she said, worried.

"It's ok, don't worry, don't panic. I won't say anything," she said to Paula. "When did she say it?" She asked one final question. So much for feeling relaxed and refreshed, she had only been back an hour and was already stressed to the max again. She sighed.

"Oh it was all completely weird, we were in Bodrum. I asked to go with them one day as I hadn't been and I thought it was bizarre they were going there and not Marmaris; anyways I don't think they particularly wanted me to come, but in the end they gave in. So we went there, didn't really do much if I'm honest and then sat in this weird café on the port for hours." She shrugged. "As I said, really weird, and it was there that she had told us and her and Julie were discussing it," she said, looking up.

Keri could feel the heat rising in her face; she looked over to Dan and Karen, who were trying to piece together what they had just heard. Fortunately, it didn't take them long before they got onto the same page as Keri, both of them looking up to her at the same time. "Fuck, Keri," Dan said, looking concerned.

Keri took in a deep breath, and leant over the

table. "I'm going to fucking kill her," she said, getting up from the table and storming out of the restaurant.

"Fuck, I'll go after her," Dan said, throwing sixty euros on the table and running after her.

"Keri, Kel. Stop, wait a minute," he said, running up alongside her and putting his hands on her shoulders to stop her. He looked at his friend and she was crying. "Come here, come here, babe," he said, pulling her into a tight hug and allowing her to cry it out. Eventually her sobs subsided and she pulled back, wiping her eyes. She looked up and was faced with sympathetic looks from Dan and Karen. Paula looked devastated; she felt bad for the girl. She wouldn't have known what was going on, and she would no doubt feel responsible for it all, when in reality it was nothing to do with her.

Chapter 57

Riley

Riley handed the bottle of ouzo to Ben. "Seriously, why did we bring this shit again?" she said, squirming on the seat of the boat. "I was doing fine until we opened this shit. Really, I think I'm going to throw up," she said, putting her head between her legs.

She lifted her head back up again and was faced with Cara and Ben laughing at her. "Seriously Riles, you have never been this much of a lightweight," Cara said, hanging off of Ben, who had his arm lazily around her throat from behind and was resting his chin on her shoulder. He moved Cara's long black from her shoulder and kissed down her neck.

"My god you guys are gross," she said, rolling her eyes.

The DJ on the boat came over the tannoy system, announcing that they were about to start some games. They had been playing lots of different ones throughout the day; she had already had to play a part in the Mr. Kardamena game, where she was being used as a tool for guys to demonstrate without words how they would basically like to bang her. Her friends had all found it highly amusing, especially Katie, who was willing Riley to try it out, finding herself most amusing.

They had announced this time it would be sexual positions. "Oh god," she said, putting her head in her hands again. She could hear the voice on the mic getting louder. "Oh fuck no," she said.

She could hear Cara shouting, "here, here!"

"Piss off, Cara," she said, looking up.

"Come on, it's the end of my vacation, you need to make me enjoy it."

The DJ was there in front of them, pulling her hand up. "And we have another woman."

"No. Nope, no way. She will do it, look them two, together they will do it."

Thank God he turned his attention back to Cara and Ben and was pushing them towards the open space at the front of the deck. "Ok we have couple number two," he said. Shit, he was turning back to her. She saw Katie from the corner of her eye. She was pissing herself. She and Jason were actually very nearly rolling on the floor with laughter, she realised, giving them both an evil look.

"Come on, darling. So we have the last girl and now we need a boy," he said, smiling and facing the crowd again, walking off to the men raising their hands. She stopped and pulled her arm away.

"I'm not doing it. I'm gay, I'll be shit. I know nothing about straight sex," she said, not realising it was into the microphone. "For fuck's sake," she said, sitting down again, ignoring the louder hysterics now coming from Katie and Jason and all the cheers from the boat. "My god, everything is a disaster," she said, mortified, covering her face.

"Come on everyone, what do we reckon? Shall we mix this up a bit, and get two birds up to go against the two straight couples?" he said.

Oh my god, the boat was hysterical. She wasn't ever going to get out of this. *Oh fuck please God, please don't ask for any lesbians.* If she ended up doing sexual positions with her boss, she was well and truly fired and her ass would be on the first flight home. Fuck, why did she always end up in these stupid bloody situations? She was being dragged to the front of the boat by the DJ, and was brought back, with him announcing that they had found the girl who was willing to do lesbian sexual positions with Riley. The girl was clearly lapping up the attention, she would have thought she was by the way she was loving the attention regardless of male or female, although Riley thought she could have just been loving the attention. Suddenly she was there, fondling Riley's boobs. What the fuck? She could hear Katie and Jason still bloody laughing. They needed to stop it, she thought. She faked a smile to the girl and moved her hands from her chest.

The DJ asked everyone to give their names and where they were from; once that was done he went over the rules of the game, which would be shouting the names of three sexual positions and they had to do those each time they were shouted out. He then proceeded to explain to the boat, that as it wasn't all straights today they were going to change the bog standard 'missionary' to 'scissoring'. *Geez, it's getting worse*, she thought. The girl was literally all over Riley and getting as much attention as she could by doing it, this was so bloody awkward.

"Riles, I'm not gonna lie, I didn't expect to be involved in any sexual activity with you when I found out you were gay, but I sure am glad I got a go, once this season." Ben was laughing loudly. She was going to kill them all, she thought.

* * *

"Ok, ok," she said to her team back at the Lion. "Yes, hilarious. Well you've all had a good laugh at my expense," she said, taking a bite of her baguette. "I was mortified, and all I could hear was dumb and dumber over there, laughing at me," she said, pointing to Katie and Jason, who were still laughing uncontrollably.

"I must say though, Ri, I've seriously had the best day of my time overseas. I don't normally get invited to do stuff with the others but thanks for asking me, I've really loved it," Jason said shyly, taking another sip of beer.

"Ahhhh J, you have been my superstar today, we have had a ball with you," said Clare. He seemed happy, Riley thought, and she was glad she'd asked him and he'd gone with them.

Chapter 58

Keri

They were all sat in Dan's lounge; he had opened a bottle of JD for them, which they had consumed in the two hours they had been sat there talking. Keri had finally calmed down a little whilst they were trying to decipher what had gone on and how they could sort it.

Dan had put a call out to the island manager Jayne to get some help off her. She hadn't called him back yet but he had texted her too.

He had also sent an email to HR, explaining the situation and raising that he felt there was a complete breach of trust and confidence and that he wanted assistance in dealing with the situation.

Paula was devastated, she was upset, thinking that she had caused all of this, and had apologised profusely over the last two hours. She had begged Dan and Keri to stay in the south and work with Keri's team, partially because she had formed a great bond and friendship with them all but in the most part because she was totally disgusted that someone who she thought was a good friend and a great leader could be so disgusting. Dan had said he would sort something, one way or another, and would let her know as soon as he could, but in the meantime she needed to keep quiet about everything that had come out tonight, which she was more than happy to agree with.

"I need to get over there, I can't believe all this time she thought I was lying, I was cheating," Keri said, shaking her head and blowing her nose again. "What if she's already met someone? What if she's already moved on? What am I going to do?" she said, sniffling again.

Her mind was constantly racing, she was jumping from why Emma had been so nasty to her, to the 'what ifs' of Riley having moved on. She was desperate to be there, she wanted to see her, hold her, and tell her that none of it was true.

"What if she doesn't think I'm worth the aggro of a psycho ex?" she said to them all.

Karen sat next to her friend and pulled her in close. "Listen, she will be there and no psycho ex is going to stop her if it's meant to be, ok? Stop panicking, let's get you over there first, ok?" she said, squeezing her leg.

Dan's phone rang he looked at it. "Shush, shush, it's Jayne," he said, answering the phone to his colleague.

Chapter 59

Riley

"Nope, nope. I don't want to do it," she said to her manager after her welcome meeting.

"Come on, I promise, the last one? Please, for us. Jayne is really hopeful. Come on Ri; you can take my car and take Cara back to the airport after duties and then drop it off. You can stay at mine and I will drop you off tomorrow," her boss said to her.

"I don't want to, I am just getting myself back together, but I am not quite at that stage yet. It's not fair, it's leading people on. Give it a few weeks and then maybe, but not just yet," she said seriously.

Katie sighed heavily. "Right, ok," she said. "I'll bring the car up later," she said, getting up.

"Don't get the hump with me, I just don't want to do it yet. I feel I'm finally getting my life back together again, and I want to make a decision as to whether we ask Jayne to try and get her contact details so I can get some closure, but this week has been so good and so much fun, I am honestly starting to think maybe I don't actually need to do that anymore. I can only take a step at a time, and I just think it will be just a little bit too much," she said sombrely.

"That's why I thought it. It's been a great week and I really want you to be there and meet her. I know you will love her, but it's fine, I need to go," she said, and left the unit.

"Great," Riley said, feeling annoyed. *Why was she so shitty with me?* she thought.

Katie felt bad that she had been an arse with Riley but she needed to get her to her house tonight. Jayne was right, she shouldn't have gone down the blind date route. There was only one thing left for it, she thought.

* * *

"Sure you got everything?" she checked with Cara one last time.

"Yes, I do." She gave Ben a quick kiss and got in the car, waving goodbye to the guy.

"So you had a good week?" she said to her friend.

"Amazing, I'm so sad to be going. I might need to book another flight for the summer hols; do not say anything about Ben, it's nothing to do with him, I just loved the people, your friends, the place, it was amazing; maybe we should ask Katie if I could stay for two weeks or three?" she said, laughing.

"Bloody hell, I don't think I could manage," she said, laughing. "It's been a blast though."

"Yeah I know, I've loved every minute. I'm gutted I won't be going out tonight with you all and instead be on the plane home," she said, looking out the window at the scenery flying by.

"Oh I doubt I'll be going out, I think I'll just drop the car off and then go home. I need some sleep," she said.

"Lightweight. Ben's right. I forgot you had to drop the car off," she said.

"Yeah, I must do it as well, she's pissed with me."

"Katie? Why? She's ace and loves you, what's happened?" she said, still looking out of the window.

"She has a blind date set for me tonight, and I said no. I said I wasn't ready. But she thought because of the fact that I'd had a good week, I would be up for it, and allegedly she's awesome and I'd love her. Kinda pissed me off, actually," she said, sighing.

"Sorry Ri, I kinda have to agree with her. I think you have definitely turned a corner this week and I think you need to get back on the saddle again. Keri's a bitch, I know you don't want to hear it Ri, but she is. She played you, what are you waiting for? To fall out of love with her? How will you ever do that if you refuse to meet anyone new? You liked that other girl and I get that with her, maybe it was too soon and you recognised that but you were also not having any fun. You were staying in and not socialising by your own admission. Now you have taken a few baby steps, you need to stop being so afraid and take a few more. Keri's not the one and this girl tonight might not be, but for all you know she could be. Or at least someone to have some time with and fun with. You're soon going to run out of lesbians to be with if you keep turning them down. Additionally, If it doesn't work out at least you can tell them both once and for all they aren't no Cillas so need to leave off the matchmaking," she finished.

They arrived at the airport and she checked her friend in and said goodbye to her. She was thinking about what Cara had said; she was partly right. What was she realistically waiting for?

She waved goodbye one last time and hugged her sadly. "I love you, text me when you land and when you get home, ok?" she said.

"Will do. Look after Ben and for what it's worth I genuinely think you should go tonight," Cara said, and walked through the gates to passport control.

Cara picked up her phone and wrote a message.

'It's done; good luck and thanks again C x'

Riley walked back to the car, and got her phone from her pocket, typing a message.

'I'll be there; be about an hour and a half, will need to get a shower. If this doesn't work, no more, I mean it! see you in a bit, Riley xxx'

She pressed send and sighed heavily at the prospect of yet another blind date.

Chapter 60

Keri

"She's coming," Katie said, looking back to Jayne and Keri on the veranda.

"Shit," Keri said, unable to control her breathing. She grabbed hold of the table; she couldn't breathe, she thought. She slowed her breathing down by counting to ten.

"It's ok, take this, it'll be fine, we'll be here," she said, handing Keri a glass of wine.

Keri looked back at the cute couple; she so wanted that with Riley, she thought. She wanted the happiness, the naturalness and normality of being together. She didn't know how tonight was going to work out and if she was honest with herself she wasn't positive in the slightest. It had been too long, she thought. She opened the picture again, she had looked at it every ten minutes since she'd found out what Emma had done; she missed the girl so badly.

Katie and Jayne appeared to think she hadn't moved on and that she hadn't wanted to, which is why she was so reluctant to come tonight, but in reality she had agreed. She had agreed to come meet a girl, to go on another blind date. She felt sick to her stomach. This was going to be impossibly hard, she thought, before downing half of her wine.

"Wow, easy tiger," said Jayne, moving her glass out of her way. She sat down next to Keri. "Calm down, seriously. You need to relax, or you are going to end up messing this up, by not saying what you need to. She has no clue on this, Keri, and whilst we want to assist, were not really in a position to get too involved. Additionally, she will not have any idea on this, Cara has gave you some tips via Katie, but when she sees you, she's going to want to bolt, so you are going to have to ensure you are compos mentis. If you aren't and you don't get what you want to say across, you may have lost your only chance," she said seriously. "Try not to panic, you know this girl, you know what's going to work and what brought you together and bound you both. Calm down!"

Keri sighed heavily. She was having major doubts; she was seriously debating just making a run for it herself.

* * *

The doorbell went and Keri immediately put her hand to her mouth. "You can't be sick now, darling," said Jayne, smiling and squeezing her shoulder as she went to the door.

"You ok?" Katie asked Keri.

"No, I'm really not," she said sadly. Katie held her hand, smiling softly.

"For what it's worth I think you guys are meant to be, and I think you need to not overthink this and just be completely open and honest with her. Just tell her how you feel," she said. "She's here." She smiled softly, looking over Keri's shoulder.

She could hear her voice; she took a large mouthful of her wine and held her phone tightly. "And this is your date for the evening," she heard Jayne say to Riley; Keri looked to Katie, noticing the worried look on her face now. She ignored it and slowly turned around to once again see the beautiful woman she'd fallen in love with.

Chapter 61

Riley

"Hey you," Jayne said, leaning in and kissing her on both cheeks.

"Hi, Katie's keys. Thanks again; how was the UK?" Riley asked.

"Same old, same old. Conferences, piss ups, training, business plans. Beer or wine? You look gorgeous by the way, thanks for coming tonight, it means a lot," she said.

"Wine, red if you have it. Yes, apparently so. The last blind date though! I mean it," she said sternly.

"It will be, come on. And this is your date for the evening," she said, pointing to the blonde-haired girl with her back towards her. She looked at Katie and noticed the look of concern on her boss's face. *Good*, Riley thought, she should feel guilty for making her feel like shit for not wanting to go on a date yet.

The girl turned around to Riley, as Riley smiled to greet the face, before the realisation kicked in and the smile disappeared. She didn't remember what happened next, her mind went blank, and her head was spinning. She heard the smash on the floor of the glass of wine she had dropped as she stepped backwards. She couldn't breathe as she was looking into the face of Keri.

She looked up to Jayne and Katie, shaking her head at them, unable to understand why her friends would have done such a cruel thing to her. She could feel the tears running down her face and turned to run away.

"Riley, please don't leave. It was all lies, it was all Emma, I've only just found out; please," Keri pleaded as Riley continued to walk to the patio door. The words to the Gloriana song 'Kissed You Goodnight' started playing. The song that meant so much to them both, Riley thought.

Riley grabbed hold of the wall; she felt the need to hold herself up, but it didn't work, she just needed to sit. She slipped down the wall and sat on the floor with her head in her hands as the chorus to their song was playing.

"Shit, Riley. You're bleeding," she heard Keri say and felt her hand on her foot. Riley looked down to see the wound from the glass she had smashed. Jayne was there with some wet tissue and handed it to Keri along with some bandages and plasters.

Jayne and Katie disappeared; Riley sat in silence with her head against the wall. She didn't know what to say or how to approach the subject with her; neither of them had said anything since Keri had said about it being lies, but she didn't know whether she wanted to hear more. She was confused and unsure of what to do, she felt like she wanted to call her mum or Cara. Wait, Cara had talked her into this evening, Cara knew about this; she was sensible and she knew

Riley better than anyone, she would have never told her it was a good idea to rush into this. She was a firm believer in not leading people on! Wait, Katie got pissed with her for not wanting to come; they were all in on it together. But why? She closed her eyes, feeling the tears rolling down; Riley felt the finger wipe away her tears, she didn't want to open her eyes again in case Keri wasn't the one touching her face right now. "Would you mind getting me some more wine please? I think I'll need it before we start talking," she said, keeping her eyes firmly shut.

Chapter 62

Keri

"Of course. Ermmm, any preference on colour?" she asked Riley.

"Whatever," she said to Keri, her eyes still shut. Keri sighed heavily, this wasn't how she had wanted it to go, but in reality how did she really think it would go?

She walked into the kitchen and Jayne and Katie were stood talking quietly. "Hardest part is done, sweetie," Jayne said to Keri, handing her the newly opened bottle and two new glasses and smiling sincerely.

Keri walked back out and found Riley sat on a sun lounger, she was looking up to the stars distantly. Keri couldn't help but feel completely overwhelmed at the sight of the girl.

She didn't know how it had all gone so wrong; everything was so right and through no fault of their own, this had all happened because of some nasty cow, and for what achievement? Keri sighed, filling the glass and handing it to Riley; she took her sandals off and went to the edge of the pool, pulling one leg underneath her and dangling the other in the pool;

sitting opposite Riley. She was holding her glass and looking down into it, she didn't know what to do or say, she didn't know if she could make this better anymore.

"Is your foot ok?" she said quietly.

"Yes, thanks for fixing it," she said back.

"Fixing it?" A faint smile appeared. "I was concerned, I only cleaned it up. You should probably pick up some antibiotic cream so it doesn't get infected," she said to Riley.

"Thanks, I will. So why are you here? Why did you come back overseas to see me?" she said.

"What do you mean, come back overseas?"

"Well, I called you last week, the office actually, they told me you had left the business? So why come back, why come to Kos?"

"What? Wait, someone told you I left the business? I was hurting too much, Riles. I thought we were going to have it all; I knew it wouldn't be easy but you seemed to be on the same page. We went to Bodrum and then you just disappeared and told me to leave you alone. I kept trying to do it, to ignore it and not hurt, but I couldn't; I decided to leave and then someone told me I should ask to have a week at home first. Dan was pretty pissed as you can imagine, a manager telling him they want a week off midseason, and so I went home last week. I got back two days ago, I didn't leave; and after the revelations that have recently been unravelled then I can only assume it was Emma that picked up the phone and told you more lies," she said angrily. Taking a large gulp of her wine, she filled it up a little more, in a bid to ignore the silence.

"So you didn't leave?"

"I didn't leave. I'm not going to lie, I very nearly did!"

"But, why?" For the first time she looked at Keri, and it gave her butterflies. Her eyes were so sad and she was desperate to wrap her up in her arms and take the pain away.

"Because, despite the fact that you have never been to mine; everything reminded me of you, and I just… well I just felt pretty crappy that you didn't want me. And without sounding like the whole 'woe is me' bullshit; it was just that someone said they wanted me, but when it came down to me they actually didn't. Obviously that was all based on the fact that you ran off and left me there with nothing but a text saying you couldn't do it," she said sadly.

"But you know why that was now?"

"Not exactly, I had a good week with my family, and realised that I couldn't give it up. I have worked so hard for it. I arrived home and the girl that had been covering me is one of Emma's team and she insinuated I was 'playing around'. My friends have got on well with her, so were confused by where this had come from and, that's basically how it all came out; she said that she didn't really get to do anything but sit in a café and they told her. Sorry, Emma and Julie were talking about me and telling her that I was sleeping about and playing some girl off on another island. That's when Dan, Karen, and I realised what Emma and Julie had done, we just didn't understand how or why."

"I was there, ya know," Riley said, walking over to sit in front of Keri.

"Yeah, I know," she said, confused. "I was with you."

"No, you don't understand. They were in the café, I was waiting to pay and I heard three girls talking. I saw them in the mirror, they said your full name and everything you just said they said, and more," she said to Keri angrily.

"What? So that's why they made Paula sit in the café all day! Bodrum isn't even near us; she went to a hell of a lot of trouble to do that. Why didn't you come find me and ask me?" she said, in what she knew must have sounded like a childlike voice.

"Would you have, Keri? You spent an amazing day with an amazing woman, who allegedly wanted you and wanted to fight for you, and then you hear people talking about said woman, and making it clear it was all a game and she was fucking everyone else. Would you have really? Bearing in mind it was all so quick and intense, would you have come to ask me if it was true?" she said questioningly.

"Probably not, no. And for the record it wasn't 'allegedly', I did want you and was prepared to fight for you, that's why I came over," she said, looking down at her wine glass and running her finger around the rim of the glass, listening to the whistling. "Riley, I'm so very sorry I have got you caught up in this. You didn't need anything like this in your first season; you certainly didn't deserve this nastiness. I am sorry that my psycho ex did this to you; I spent years with her and never saw this side of her. I'm so sorry," Keri said, looking up to Riley, who was looking into the pool.

"Do you regret it?" she asked, finally looking up at Keri. "Do you regret what we did?"

"Riley, I've never lied to you. I had the most amazing night with you on training. I wanted you from the first moment I met you. I will never forget what we had, nor you. So, in answer to your question, no I don't nor will I ever regret it. You're an incredible woman, and I told you I'd fell in love with you, that's no lie; I don't play games, unlike the psychotic ex." She smiled, a lopsided grin.

"Yeah, apparently so." Keri's butterflies reappeared as Riley smiled for the first time. "For what it's worth I don't play games either and I don't think this is your fault and neither will I regret any of it," Riley said, looking at Keri squarely.

Chapter 63

Riley

Riley's tummy was flipping, like there was some form of acrobatics going on inside. She couldn't believe that anyone could be so mental; she could see it was tearing Keri up. "So why are you here? Honestly?" she asked the girl in front of her.

Riley maintained eye contact with Keri, she didn't know what she was thinking but the silence was soul destroying. *Just say it*, she thought. *Just say it!*

"Hold that question, for just a moment," Keri said, leaving and running into the house. She returned with a holdall, and placed it next to them; Riley looked down at the bag, unsure what was happening now.

"I guess there are a number of reasons really. Firstly, I went home and my big brother, out of nowhere," she said smiling distantly, "he gave me this cool speech that I need to come over here, fight for you, make it clear that I was in love with you and that I wanted you, and basically come and declare my undying love. He doesn't normally say stuff like that so it was kind of weird, really, but we all knew he had a point. The point he was trying to make was if I did all that and you still said no, I should have at least got an explanation from you, and then I would finally be able to get some closure. He was right, I need that."

"What else?" Riley said to her.

"Huh? What do you mean?"

"You said there were a number of things?"

Keri was looking at her seriously, and then suddenly a small smile appeared on her lips. God she had missed that smile, it lit up her eyes, her face. Riley didn't know what it was, but in that moment all of the pain appeared to fade away. Keri reached down into her bag, pulling out a large envelope. "Your mum, was another reason," Keri said, still smiling.

"My mum? What do you mean?" Riley asked confused.

Riley noticed Keri looking down at the empty space between them. She looked back up to Riley, unsure. She closed the gap between them and sat with their thighs touching, she could feel the warmth of Keri's skin on her own. She was desperate to touch her and feel her, she thought. She was playing with the edge of the envelope. "So when I got home, there was a package for me." She pulled out a frame and turned it over. It was a picture of them at her home, in her dining room. Keri handed over the folded piece of paper. Opening it, she recognised her mum's writing and read the words.

Keri,

I don't know what's happened between you both, but I saw the looks between you two. Please don't give up on my daughter.

X

Riley looked at the other side; that was it that was all she wrote. She hadn't told Riley she had done that, she hadn't even tried to persuade her to fight, so why had she done this? Riley looked up at Keri, she felt the woman's hand wipe the tear from her face. This time Keri didn't move her hand, she kept it there, softly stroking her cheek. She noticed Keri looking at her lips. *Please kiss me*, she thought. There was a sense of desperation in her, she needed to feel Keri's lips on hers again. She looked up and met Riley's gaze, all the questions being answered in that one moment, as Keri leaned in and met Riley's lips. The kiss was slow and meaningful, and restored all that they had lost. Eventually finishing the kiss, Riley placed her hands either side of Keri's face and rested her forehead against Keri's, sighing heavily. "I've missed you so bad," she said quietly.

"Me too, baby. I…" She stopped, sighing.

"You what?" Riley said pleadingly.

"I love you, Riley," Keri said, leaning back in to kiss her again.

Chapter 64

Keri

"Are you sure you don't want to stay? We have the room," Katie was asking Keri and Riley.

"No, were good. I think we have a lot to discuss," Riley said to them. "Thank you again," she said, hugging her friends.

"Seriously, I can't thank you enough; you have been amazing in all you have done for me, thank you so much," Keri said, kissing both women on each cheek.

"No worries, just get rid of that psycho bitch," Jayne said, smiling.

"Well, that's up to Dan, but she has got a disciplinary tomorrow, so we shall see," she said.

"I'll call him now, and tell him to sack her." She winked.

Leaving the house, they got into the taxi and made their way back to Riley's place. "Stop staring," she said, smirking at Riley, who was watching her. She looked down at their fingers intertwined and brushed her soft skin lightly.

They arrived at Riley's apartment and she'd told her that at this time Ben would already be out and well on his way to finding some girl to spend the night with, smiling. "Do you want anything to drink?" Riley asked her.

"Could I just have some water please? I am not really bothered on having a proper drink," she said.

They went to Riley's bedroom and lay on the bed, looking into each other's eyes in silence. They spent a long time that way, just holding hands and maintaining their eye contact. "Can we put some music on please?" Keri asked her.

Riley looked at her cautiously, nodding slowly. She picked her phone up and was hovering over the screen; she looked up at Keri again before hitting play and placing it on the docking station.

Keri recognised the song straight away and smiled; unable to hold off anymore, she took Riley's hand. She placed her hand behind her head and pulled her gently in to kiss her again. She needed her, but she didn't want to rush this time, wanting to appreciate every moment with Riley; after all the time she had waited and the potential of losing her, she needed to savour every moment.

Keri pulled back as the words of their Gloriana song filled the room. "Are you sure you want to do this?" she said seriously.

Chapter 65

Riley

"Keri, I want you to make love to me," she said, answering her question.

Keri pulled Riley on top of her and slowly lifted her top over her head, she softly glided the tips of her fingers down her bare arms; she was wearing a black lace bra, and from the look in Keri's eyes, she seemed satisfied with the view. Keri pulled her back down to kiss her long and slow. She unclasped Riley's bra and gently removed it, gasping as she felt her breasts against her body. She rolled Riley over, straddling her, staring.

"You're so beautiful, so incredibly beautiful," she said very softly to Riley. Riley could see the truth in her eyes, that she genuinely believed that; it wasn't just words in the moment. Moving down the bed, she undid Riley's shorts; she stopped what she was doing and looked back up to her. Riley knew she was asking for confirmation to continue. She picked up Keri's hand and pulled it to her mouth. Kissing it softly, she placed it on her breast and watched Keri's demeanour change from serious to contented. She sighed lightly and closed her eyes before leaning down and taking Riley's nipple in her mouth, causing Riley to gasp and clench the sheets.

Keri moved back to the shorts and slowly removed them. Riley loved the way she was looking at her and the attention she was paying to her body; she was scanning her from top to bottom now as she lay on the bed in only her black lace knickers. Keri was observing seriously. "God I've missed your body," she said, stroking her torso. Slowly removing Riley's knickers, Keri moved up the bed and kissed Riley softly; she felt Keri's tongue searching for her own, before achieving and dancing together. She very lightly bit Riley's bottom lip, causing her to gasp again. Keri was looking attentively at Riley; she grazed her thumb over her face once more before leaning down to her ear. "You make me feel things that nobody ever has before," she said, so quietly that the slight whisper and breath against her made Riley quiver.

Keri kissed down her neck, stopping at her shoulder where she was gently biting, the whole way through she was unable to remove the eye contact they had. Keri continued kissing down further, stopping at her breast, where she took her nipple in her mouth and softly bit and sucked the area and Riley could feel her body losing control. Keri had such control of her body for some reason. She knew exactly what to do to pleasure her. Riley grabbed Keri's hand and intertwined their fingers, stroking her thumb across the woman's soft skin. She was watching Keri; her dirty blonde hair falling over her midriff as she was making her way further down her body. This was making Riley unable to maintain control; she didn't think she was going to be able to last at this rate. Keri was doing things to her, so many things and she was pretty sure she could tell that, but she was acting slowly, clearly, intent on delaying the process.

After what seemed like an eternity, she finally reached where Riley needed her to be; slowly pushing her tongue deep inside Riley, she groaned into her. Riley was on the verge and luckily Keri didn't feel the need to tease her this time, she looked consumed in Riley as they held hands and kept contact; Riley needed to be on every level with her whilst they were making love, and seemingly Keri felt the same. Pressing her tongue hard to her sensitive area, she cried out slightly. Keri was making small circles with the tip of her tongue and Riley couldn't contain herself, any longer; Keri moved the tip of her tongue slowly down to her opening. She gasped again, raising herself up slightly to allow Keri to go deeper inside her. She felt the build-up, the anticipation inside her, before her body released and the explosion took over, with waves rippling through her body, causing Riley to cry out loudly. She felt so many emotions right now; Keri was still inside her, waiting until her body had settled. Finally she relaxed, and levelled her breathing. Keri moved back up to Riley and laid her head on her chest, tracing tiny circles on her stomach.

Chapter 66

Keri

She had never experienced anything so intense before; she felt emotional and she didn't really know why, causing her to not want to look at Riley. She laid there, listening to a slow song in the background. It sounded like Usher but she wasn't sure. It had been perfect, she couldn't have imagined it being any more perfect, and as much as she wanted to make love to Riley all night long, all she actually wanted in this moment was to lie holding each other and falling asleep in each other's arms.

"Are you ok?" she heard Riley ask.

Keri shook her head into the girl's beautiful body.

"No you aren't," she said, pulling Keri's face to look at hers. She knew she had watery eyes, she could feel it. Riley looked concerned. "Hey, what's up?" she asked her seriously.

"Nothing, seriously Ri, I'm fine, I'm just being silly; ignore me," she said, looking away from Riley again.

"No, I won't ignore you, ever. Please talk to me?" Riley said.

"Honestly, I'm fine, I just got a bit emotional. I guess I never thought I'd be able to do that again," she sighed, leaning in and kissing Riley's lips softly.

"Get undressed; I want to feel your body with mine. Please?" Riley said seriously.

Keri did as she was asked and moved into her open arms, feeling their bodies immerse and become one.

* * *

"So, please tell me you don't normally wake at 4am horny?" she said laughing, playing with Riley's hair.

"Well, I can't make any promises. You shouldn't be so hot, and, you shouldn't have made me wait. I was all up for a night of passion but then you just cuddled me and fell asleep; I mean talk about giving a girl a complex," Riley said, tickling her a little.

"NO! Don't!" Keri said, laughing from the tickles. "And for the record, you should be happy that I am a giver," she said, turning to face her. "I love you, I love your face," she said, stroking it softly. "I love your body, interestingly so much more with the sexy tan you now have. I love your smile... Do... not... dare burst into song right now. Stop it, Riley Laura Sharpe! Stop it." Keri couldn't help laughing along with her, before Riley became serious.

"I feel exactly the same, and I am so glad that you are here and that we found out what she did," she said. "I loved being with you last night, and this morning, and early this morning, and just now." She smiled softly.

"You're so bad." Keri smiled and kissed Riley again.

"Well I don't think Ben would agree, with all that screaming," Riley said laughing.

"Oh my god, I didn't?" she said, worrying, and noticed Riley trying to stifle a laugh.

"You're awful," she said, playfully hitting her. She picked up her phone, noticing the time. "Smile," she said, leaning in and taking a selfie of the two of them. She leaned in and kissed Riley, taking another photo of them. "So what time do you have to leave for work?" she said, looking up to Riley.

Sighing heavily, "Pretty soon, I guess," she announced sombrely.

"Come on, this is ok. If you want to do this, we can do this. And I want to, I want you, we will arrange maybe to spend every other week together. If you want to that is?" she said, smiling, stroking her hair.

"Of course, I do. I want nothing more. I just don't want to be apart," Riley said.

"I'm not losing you again, Ri, so we need to make the best of a bad situation. Ok?" she said, kissing Riley intensely.

Keri moved back and looked up at her, smirking. "Kerianne? Again? Really?" Riley said, pushing her back and getting on top of the girl before pinning her to the bed, kissing her passionately.

Chapter 67

Riley

"No more, I can't do any more," she said, kissing her softly before falling back. "You really gotta go?" she said, making a sad face, causing Keri to laugh at her. "You're a nerd, it's a good job I love you." She winked.

"Yep, I do," Keri said, kissing her.

They heard a knock. "Riles, you up babe?" They stopped and looked at the door, giggling, pulling the sheet around them. "Erm yeah I'm up, I'm just getting ready." She giggled as Keri pinched her nipple, giving her a scolding look.

"Riles, whoever the fuck you got in there, you have till three and then I'm coming in whether yous are decent or not; I'm not missing out on this. One... two... two and a half... three!" he said, knocking again and opening the door. "Well, lookie here then," he said, smirking and leaning against the door frame, sipping his coffee. "Alriiiiight?" he said, looking at Keri.

"Ben, how are you? Nice to meet you," Keri said to him.

"Nice to meet you too darling, and yeah I'm good,

ta. Clearly not as good as you guys, all sex flushed and all," he said, laughing.

"Ben! You can go now; I'll catch up with you on siesta?" she said to her friend.

"Oh you better; see ya later Kel, safe trip home; maybe next time you're over we can all spend some time together?" He winked and jumped out of the way of the teddy bear flying at him. "Laters."

* * *

Keri kissed Riley goodbye one last time. "Ok so next week you're coming to mine, yeah? I'll book the ferry and ask Dan if I can change my days off to match yours and then we can spend maybe every other week or something?" Keri said, kissing her nose softly.

"Yes, that's good. I told you though, you don't have to book the ferry, I'll do it myself," she said, hugging her tightly. "Text me as soon as you get home please? And maybe we'll have a repeat of that phone call," she said to her. "I'll miss you, and can't wait to see you next week," before kissing her one last time, and waving the girl off.

Riley watched the taxi leave. Looking at her phone, "Shit," she said, realising how late she was, and running to work. She prayed that Katie wasn't at her unit. She had a feeling she would be, to find out exactly what had happened with them.

She ran around the corner and saw Katie sat on the step to the hotel; she looked at her watch, smirking at Riley. "I'm sorry, I'm sorry. I have never ever done this before I promise," she said seriously.

"I'm surprised you turned up at all, Jayne bet you wouldn't; here you go, I figured you may, ermmm, need something to keep you awake today," she said, winking.

"You're a star, I'll make the time up this arvo," she said to her boss.

"Forget it. Ok sit, spill?" she said to her, taking a mouthful of her coffee, listening as Riley filled her in on the situation following them leaving her house last night.

"Wow, so that's fantastic," she said to Riley.

"Yeah it kinda is." She couldn't keep the smile off her face. "It'll be hard not being together and expensive and time consuming with the travelling to and from; but we both seem to want the same thing, just wish we could be together. But it is what it is, as they say, absence makes the heart grow fonder and all that rubbish," she said to Katie.

"That it does! We were separated for our first year together. After we got together it was hard, but if it's meant to be you make it work," she said seriously, "and you guys seem to want to. I just can't believe everything that's happened. I mean how much of a bitch is her ex? Who the fuck actually does things like that? When Jane was telling me after she had come off the phone to Dan, I was livid. I hope he sacks her because she's just twisted. I don't know what would possess someone to do something," she said, annoyed.

"Yeah, and we reckon that she was the one on the phone who told me that she had left too. She's a mentalist," she laughed, shaking her head. "I hope she goes too, I don't want to be watching my back for the next knife coming at me, otherwise we might need Jayne to try and do a switch with Amber so she can come and work here," she said, winking. "Anyways, at least it's all sorted now, it was weird last night but then as soon as we got home it just felt so natural again; this morning I felt like we had never been apart, which sounds stupid but… well, as I said, it is what it is. I'm not going to keep analysing everything and just see where it leads us."

"I'll drink to that," Katie said, chinking her paper takeaway coffee cup.

Epilogue

Nine months later...

"Smile," Riley's mum said.

Keri and Riley put their knives and forks down and leaned in again. "Last one, Ma," she said. "Seriously, she's worse than your mum," Riley said, laughing and holding up her glass for Keri to chink.

"Cheers, baby girl," Keri said, leaning over and kissing her girlfriend.

"Put her down," Adam said as he came into the dining room with another bottle of champagne, "you'll put us off our dinner," he said, winking at his big sister.

"So what time's your flight?" he asked them.

"Not until 2.40, so the taxi is booked for midnight. Gonna be a long-ass couple of days," Riley said, feigning sleepiness. "But it'll be worth it," she said, smiling at Keri.

"Yeah, only because she gets a pool now," Keri said, poking her, causing her family to laugh.

"So, are your family coming out then, Keri?" Riley's mum asked her.

"Yeah, they were saying about possibly coming out when the kids break up and get the whole lot over, it will be kinda nice if they can do it; and you guys are booking next week, right?" Keri said to her girlfriend's parents.

"Yes, I don't think we will find a better deal," her dad responded.

"And Ads, you and Lou are coming out in July for two weeks and staying with us?" Keri said.

"Correct." He smiled, piling a large amount of his roast lamb dinner into his mouth. "Don't really fancy staying in any of the hotels there," he said, smirking and causing Riley and Keri to roll their eyes in unison.

"Anyone would think he didn't eat," their mum said to them.

The traditional roast lamb dinner with pink champagne before the airport was ever the success, and Riley loved seeing her mother so happy in those last hours together.

Adam and her dad put the cases into the cab; they said their goodbyes. This time without any words of 'love' wisdom from her mum, she thought.

* * *

They checked in and went to Smiths to buy some magazines and goodies for the plane, before going to the same pub they were in last year and ordering a bottle of prosecco. They sat down and Keri opened her phone to the incoming message she had received from Dan.

'Good luck babes, hope you and Ri have a ball; I'll miss having you here, but go and have a ball and smash it just like I

taught you. If you need anything you call me; otherwise, I look forward to the 200 euros at the end of summer when I smash your ass off the sales and scores leader board ;). Dan x'

She sat smirking at the phone, showing Riley. Reading the message she laughed. "He's a cheeky sod," she said. "But how exciting, I've always had a thing for authority and just think this season I get to go home to the 'big big boss' every night," she said, laughing.

"I know; you'll have to make sure you're a good girl, wouldn't want to discipline you," Keri said, winking at Riley.

"Discipline away, baby. Naked in our pool," she said, laughing and drinking some more of her drink.

She handed Keri an earphone. "For old times' sake," she said, pressing play on the song that had become 'their' song, which they'd listened to in the airport last year. The words began and both women looked at each other, and smiled softly. "I love you with all my heart, beautiful girl, and I can't wait to have you with me every day from now on," Keri said to Riley, before kissing her softly.

The announcement came over the tannoy for their flight. "Ready?" Riley said, holding her hand out to Keri.

"Always. Let's go and see what the delights of Lesbos has for us," she said, smirking at the joke they had been sharing since they found out that they were going to that island.

They boarded their plane and took their seats, putting their ear buds in and listening to the playlist; Keri pulled the cover up over them, stroking her girlfriend's leg. Riley lifted out a gift and handed it to Keri as the plane started to take off. "What's this?" Keri said seriously.

"What does it look like?" she said sarcastically.

"A bloody big diamond." She smirked. "Seriously, what is it? It isn't my birthday," she said.

"Just open it, baby, and you'll see." Keri unwrapped the box and saw a note.

To my beautiful angel, good luck for your new job. Ri xxx

"You shouldn't have done that," Keri said, looking at Riley. She opened the lid and saw a beautiful silver watch. "Wow, it's beautiful, I love it," she said, opening it to put on her wrist.

"Look on the back," Riley said sheepishly.

Keri placed her old watch in the box and turned the new watch over, where she noticed an inscription.

You are the person, they write fairy tales about xxx

Keri read the words and couldn't help the tears falling from her eyes. "Thank you so much. I love it, and I love you more than anything in the world," she whispered to her girlfriend, kissing her hand softly.

THE END

Printed in Great Britain
by Amazon.co.uk, Ltd.,
Marston Gate.